W9-BOB-637

Chenda and the Airship Brofman

Chenda and the Airship Brofman

Emilie P. Bush

EmitoneB Books

Norcross, Georgia - 2009

To Tony, Saralyn and Eleanor.

Table of Contents

Chapter 1
HAIL AND FAREWELL

Chenda Frost sat perfectly still. She balanced, immobile, between a desire to run in panic and the urge to vomit that accompanies the shock of desperate grief. As the short line of cars followed the hearse into the churchyard, Chenda steeled herself for her first, and last, public appearance with her husband. She realized that this was the first time she had been to town with Edison, but she couldn't find the strength to contemplate the irony that this would also be the last time she would travel to Coal City with him. After today, she would never see him again. Forever. She couldn't pull her eyes away from the car carrying his casket, tried not to even blink for fear of losing any part of her last few moments with him. Chenda's driver opened her door, and she stepped out into the misty morning to the sound of flashbulbs and the shout of rabid newspapermen. She raised her dark eyes to focus on the front door of the church, her goal. More flashes sent sparkles across her vision. She ignored what she could of the shouted questions and kept her pale face as placid and unmoving as possible. As quickly as her legs would carry her, she escaped into the cool darkness of the ancient church.

Her eyes anxiously searched the interior of the sanctuary, and she relaxed slightly as she saw Edison's casket arriving through a side door. He was there. She was, at least for a few minutes more, with him again. Even in death, his presence calmed her. Chenda followed the funeral director as he wheeled Edison to the head of the aisle and opened the casket. The assembled visitors hushed for a moment as they gandered at the deceased, then the hurried whispers began again. Chenda found herself cringing away from the stares, positioning herself at the end of Edison's casket, partially hiding herself behind the extravagantly carved lid.

Chenda glanced around at several of the assembled guests. She recognized very few. For the most part, it looked to her just a faceless sea of dark suits and military uniforms. The people to whom she could place names were either dignitaries she had seen in the newspapers, or a smattering of her former teachers or companions – all hand-picked by Edison – none of whom had she seen in years.

Chenda listened as two of her former tutors gossiped about a delicately built blond woman in the second pew, a woman Chenda had never seen before.

"Fancy *her* coming here. I never would have taken Professor Candice Mortimer as a curiosity seeker like these other gawkers," the first said.

"Perhaps she reads the tabloids for fun," the other said. "There's not a front page in the city that doesn't say 'Death of the Recluse Hero' in the headlines. Besides, she's such a serious person. She has to get her kicks somehow. Perhaps funeral crashing is her thing."

The gossiping women wandered away, having quickly lost interest in the professor, who simply sat gazing remorsefully at Edison in his casket.

Candice Mortimer wasn't sure why she had come to Edison's funeral. Truly, sadness filled her as she looked at Edison's scarred face, coldly encircled with pale flowers in the casket. He had changed so drastically from the handsome young officer in her memory. Candice counted the years back to the last time she had seen Edison. Twenty-one years felt like yesterday in some ways. He'd been so dashing then in his Republic Airship Service uniform. *All* the R.A.S. men were dapper to some extent. Strong and brave, each was ready to defend the Republic's coast against Tugrulian attackers. A generation of handsome young men volunteered. Thousands never came back. Too many came home like Edison, broken, disfigured and aged well beyond the intervening 12 years of the war.

Candice cried when Edison's airship, the *Valiant Eagle*, was reported lost. She rejoiced when she heard he had miraculously returned alive. More than once, she tried to see him, but he never accepted visitors and refused all correspondence. Each of her letters returned unopened. Rumors swirled that he was a spy, or had been on a secret mission to corrupt the Tugrulian Empire. Edison never spoke publicly about any of it.

As she waited for the ceremony to start, Candice's sadness turned into disgust. All of those strangers staring stupidly into Edison's casket. How rude! True, she must look as much a voyeur to them as they did to her, but Candice knew who she was, and what Edison had meant to her all those years ago, so she felt no reason to explain herself to anyone. She turned her gaze to the shy woman at the end of Edison's casket, The Widow Frost as all the papers were calling her. Candice's first thought was this girl couldn't possibly be his *wife*. She was young enough be his daughter. Candice bristled and focused on Edison's unmoving form.

Chenda, a receiving line of one, found the assembled crowd respectful and solemn as they filed by, but not particularly grieved. She could feel their eyes on her, judging her, and she heard all the whispered remarks.

"… lucky, I guess. She's the richest widow in the whole Republic."

"… bet it was suicide. Who lives that way? Apart from the world for all those years…."

"… I hear she is a bubble-headed fashion monger, I mean look at her, I've never seen so much expensive silk and satin on *one* dress…."

"… good grief, she's just a child! I guess Frost liked 'em young…."

"… Gee, if he never left his estate, I wonder if *any* of these people ever actually knew him?"

No, Chenda thought, *just me.*

The funeral went on as so many do: prayers to all the

3

gods, kind but generic words from a gray haired priest who laments the death of a man he has never *actually* met, poetry about salvation and songs that move too slowly. Finally, the time came for Edison's casket to be closed for the last time. Chenda stood by herself for one long moment, her hands resting on Edison's casket. She felt fractured and wondered, when she exhaled next, what it would be like never to breathe back in again. She wanted to die, too. The center of her world had vanished, and she now drifted alone, frightened to her core.

Where do I go from here, Edison?

With her emotions momentarily paralyzed, she mindlessly followed the congregants out of the weathered stone church and into a dim, drizzling afternoon. Dozens of flashbulbs again blinded Chenda as she appeared on the church steps. In her turmoil, she had forgotten to prepare herself for the gantlet of reporters in the churchyard. People pressed in on her, trying to sneak a peek at The Widow Frost. The shoving and clamor kept her unsteady. Her field of vision was clogged with a jostling crowd of reporters and spectators, and, losing her footing on the slippery steps, Chenda started to fall. Suddenly, someone caught her by her elbow and she felt another hand reach around her waist, pulling her back to standing but also maneuvering her sideways, out of the heart of the crowd.

Chenda looked up into the plain, young face of her driver, Daniel Frent. He kept pulling her along, using his hip and shoulder to part the throng of people. When they reached the car, he quickly pushed her up and into the raised passenger area, snapping the door closed behind her. Daniel vaulted himself into the driver's compartment. The motor whizzed to life, and the clutch of reporters and onlookers, sensing the show was over, retreated slightly. Daniel pulled away from the churchyard and they were gone in an instant.

Daniel opened the small window between the driver and passenger compartments. "I'm sorry to have placed hands on you so, ma'am. You're not harmed, are you?"

"I'm fine," she said limply. "Thank you for catching me." She turned her face to the gray window and watched the droplets run together and roll down the pane. She sighed.

Daniel coughed politely, and quietly added, "I can see this is a trial for you, ma'am. I'm sorry for that."

"It's kind of you to say," she replied.

Daniel went on, "Did you know, ma'am, that my old man served with Mr. Frost on the *Valiant Eagle*?"

"No," Chenda said. She truly knew very little about Daniel, as he was the most recent edition to the estate staff and had been Chenda's driver for a few scant weeks. "Was he amongst the crew when the *Eagle* was lost?" she asked, unable to think of anything to say.

"Sadly, yes, ma'am" he answered, and then said nothing more.

Chenda bore this new layer of loss in silence. The car traveled quickly through the heart of Coal City, past so many of Chenda's favorite shops and museums. For years, Chenda held out hope that someday Edison would have acquiesced and journeyed into town with her. He never did, and now it was too late. The pattern had developed between them early on that she would go into town and explore, bringing back trinkets and gifts for her husband, and they would spend hours talking about what she had seen and done. As money was no object, the sky was the limit as far as Edison was concerned. Chenda happily brought the world home to him. Now, as the car entered the Frost estate and gently stopped at the grand house's front door, Chenda had nothing to share, and no one to share it with.

Daniel helped Chenda out of the car and opened an umbrella over her, sheltering her from the rain until she stepped into the foyer. Throwing her damp coat into the waiting arm of the housekeeper, she walked into Edison's study, closed the thick paneled doors behind her and collapsed on the floor, weeping. Finally, hidden away from the prying eyes of Coal City and the house staff, she unfurled her grief.

Edison's study seemed the perfect place for her collapse. This room, this intimate space where this unlikely couple shared their stories, was now both a sacred memory and a crime scene. Detectives had long since finished investigating here. They found little evidence besides the unusual knife that was buried deep in Edison's chest, a knife with two points like the forked tongue of a snake. There were no other clues, they said.

"Had Commander Frost been depressed?" they asked.

In the wake of that fruitless investigation, and not knowing what else to do, the staff quietly returned the space to its ordered beauty. Not a drop of Edison's blood remained on the fine mahogany desk, or the Tugrulian carpet beneath. Every soiled paper, every hint of the police, even the smell of the newsmen's flashbulbs had been carefully removed. Clean and proper. Restored.

Shock stopped her tears when she discovered Edison's body, and numbness covered her as she awaited the funeral. Chenda hadn't cried once. She had held her tears in for seven days, and there, in the very room in which Edison had been murdered, it overflowed from her. Chenda kicked her feet violently under her long black satin skirts while she wailed. Her thoughts, barely formed enough to be called thoughts, exploded out of her in rage and sorrow. *Why...Why?* the words bubbled through her mind, rising from her chest finally as a screech, "WHY!!!?!?!?!"

Chenda lay there, frightened and completely lost. She sobbed again and again, fighting against her sorrow, willing herself to pull the pain back in, willing herself to become again the dignified wife of Edison Frost. Chenda allowed herself one final sob as she crawled over to the side of Edison's desk. She rested a moment on her knees there, pressing her face to the smooth desktop, her arms wrapping the dark wood in a weak embrace. She said a small prayer for comfort to any god that could hear her. *Please,* she prayed, *please guide me. What do I do now?*

A thought appeared in her head. *Edison would pull himself together and get off the floor.*

Chenda fought her sorrow and searched her soul for a bit of strength. She wrapped her fingers around the wood beneath her hands and squeezed each side of the desk, pulling herself to her feet. When she let go, she heard a small click. A raised panel on the side of the desk swung open.

What's this?

Chenda's fingers pressed the panel back to discover a

narrow slot, like a small shelf that was covered by the secret door. An envelope made of fine peach-tinted paper fell to the rug. Chenda was printed on the front in Edison's tiny handwriting. She carefully opened the letter.

My dearest Chenda,
    Pretty paper for an ugly message.
    I know that finding this letter means that you are again alone in the world, and for that I am so very sorry. You have been such a blessing to me in my life, and I have loved you always. But, I now have to ask you to forgive me. Your father and I have kept a dangerous secret from you. Chenda, you have a destiny. I wish I could explain here in this letter, but I am not sure you would believe. You will have to find out for yourself.
    Somehow, you need to find a way across the sea to Kotal, and connect with the Tugrulian Resistance. They can take you to a mystic, Pranav Erato. He will help you fulfill your destiny.
    Also, I want you to contact a professor at Kite's Republic University, Dr. Candice Mortimer. Her expertise can help you, and I believe you can trust her.
    Go now, and take the bag with you. Waste no time.
    All my love,
    E

Chenda read the letter again. *Destiny? The Tugrulian Resistance?*

Stunned, Chenda swept her hand into the hidden slot and felt a small velvet bag. With shaking fingers, she loosened the knotted silk cord and tipped the contents into her hand. Out fell a gold necklace with a rather dull, deep-red stone pendent. Two other, larger stones also fell into her hand. One was a pale and uninteresting yellow, and the other, blue, the color of an old robin's egg.

At that moment, Chenda thought she heard someone in the hall outside Edison's study. She quickly scooped the stones back into the bag along with her husband's note and snapped the desk panel shut. She pocketed the velvet bag, patted her hair into place, wiped her eyes and smoothed the wrinkles from her long dress. A moment later, Chenda opened the door to find her housekeeper, Alme, raising her hand to knock.

"Oh, good evening, ma'am, I just wanted to see if you were feeling up to any supper this evening?" Alme's eyes were wide with sympathy.

Chenda frowned. *I probably should eat something,* Chenda thought. *But I just can't sit alone in the dining room tonight, not without Edison. I feel him in every corner of this house now.*

"Yes," Alme sighed, as if she has heard Chenda's thoughts. "Perhaps I could bring you some soup and toast up to your personal study?"

"A very good idea," Chenda agreed as she turned away from Edison's office and climbed the stairs. By the time Chenda reached her suite of rooms, her mind had set on several things:

First, she was sure of Edison's letter. She recognized his writing, and had never known him to lie. Of that she was entirely sure. Edison had cared for her, educated her, and loved her. If he wanted her to follow his instructions, then she would.

Next, she needed to write to Professor Mortimer and arrange a meeting. After a few moments, Chenda had prepared a note inviting Dr. Candice Mortimer to tea the following afternoon and placed it in a silver tray on her desk.

And lastly, Chenda decided she needed to grow up. The time for shopping in town for trinkets and living in her small world was over. Those whispered voices at the funeral may just have been right. Money and fine things were all around her, but what she needed was the ability to take care of herself. To know herself. Chenda looked at her pale, tear-stained face in the mirror. *Who are you now? Can you be more than the Widow Frost? Is there more to you than this?*

Alme politely knocked on the door, breaking Chenda's gaze from her reflection. The housekeeper quietly placed a tray of food onto a side table and retrieved the letter from Chenda's desk tray.

"Please see that letter delivered tonight, Alme. And I believe I will be just fine here for the rest of the evening. I'd rather not be disturbed." Chenda looked again at the mirror as Alme silently swept out the door.

The next morning, a reply from Candice Mortimer was waiting. Chenda's invitation to tea had been accepted. She smiled as she read the letter, and then bit her lip uncertainly. Deciding to follow Edison's instructions was the first major decision of her life, and she wasn't entirely sure she had made the right choice.

Later that day, Chenda stood outside the Terminal Tearoom and considered her options. There weren't but two: go in, or go home. Opening the door meant starting her life anew, but going back to the estate, and forgetting the whole thing, was smarter. Chenda hesitated. The warm and brightly lit tearoom invited, and she could clearly see her intended teatime companion, one Dr. Candice Mortimer, Senior Professor of Geology at Kite's Republic University. There was no need to wait, but Chenda could not seem to find the will to go forward. She let herself become distracted for a few seconds, watching the light spill though the spotless plate glass window and onto her beautiful and, as Edison would have teased, impractical shoes. The rhinestones across her toes caught the falling light and splashed it upward in the form of glittery rainbows that danced across the complicated folds of her long brocade dress.

She felt so strange, standing there in the fog as people jostled past her, rushing from taxis and trolleys to the station's various trains and airships. Chenda listened to the familiar sounds of people on the go: the hard clack of a man's leather shoes on the pavement, the soft swish of several layers of silk skirts brushing over petticoats and the whine of small children, exhausted from being dragged through the streets. Chenda herself stood perfectly still.

She looked up again to see the professor shifting

uncomfortably in the delicate cafe chair. Chenda stopped trying to force her feet to carry her through the elegantly decorated and polished brass doors. She let go of her indecision for a moment, and suddenly, thoughtlessly, effortlessly, she found herself inside the cheery shop. Chenda looked toward the corner table where the tiny woman in a sand colored pantsuit waited, her back turned to the whole of the shop. Chenda's momentum failed her, and she froze again. The Terminal Tearoom bustled around her, the rushing waiters swirling the smells of teas and pastries all around her.

It was safe to say that Professor Mortimer was not accustomed to the afternoon clatter of the tearoom. The fashionable and luxuriant shop was beyond the means of the average university professor, to be sure. Furthermore, the whole facade of the place just wasn't Candice's style.

She preferred the musty stacks of the university's great library and the curling maps and boxes of geological samples scattered all around her small office. Candice often said to herself as she worked late into the night that she had the whole world at her fingertips. Well, at least little scrapings of it.

Candice kept mostly to herself at the university, spending her days teaching in labs and classrooms, and arguing with various committees, jostling to put her research projects closer to the top of the funding lists. Her nights were spent criss-crossing the great library, making connections. Her theories always put forth the notion that, in a very hidden way, all of the world's culture and society was tied to geology. Geology dictated a region's topography, which influences weather, the crops that can be grown, and the animals that appear. That all leads directly to the cultures that develop and everything else that defines a society: language, rituals, philosophy -even art. *It's all rooted in geology*, Candice thought, and she had been single-mindedly unraveling those theories for nearly 20 years.

She was a woman of science, a woman of focus and dignity, but she wasn't entirely sure why she was sitting in a pompous pastry shop waiting for the widow of *her* beloved, Edison Frost.

At that moment, Candice Mortimer, awash in sadness and

annoyance, heard the quiet clack of approaching shoes on the marble behind her.

She turned, glared into the eyes of Chenda Frost and said, "Missy, that funeral was a circus. You should have kept the lid to that casket closed."

Chapter 2
THE STONES THAT SING

Chenda gasped as if she'd been slapped. She wasn't entirely sure what she was expecting from Professor Mortimer, but a dressing down wasn't even on the list. Chenda pulled herself together and said, "Excuse me? Are you *Professor* Candice Mortimer?"

Candice put one elbow on the table and her hand over her eyes. She couldn't believe she had been so rude.

"I'm so sorry!" Candice said, standing up and offering her hand. "It's just the shock of it all, I'm certain. Please, sit," she ordered, waving the girl in to the seat in the far corner, and returning to her own. "Let's start again. I'm Professor Mortimer. You wanted to meet with me?"

"Yes - well, no." Chenda said, feeling like this conversation would be starting again, *again*.

"I'm Chenda Frost, as I gather you already know. My late husband Edison wanted me to contact you."

"Edison wanted? After all these years? Why?"

"I'm not entirely sure. Well, then, you did know my husband. How so?"

Candice looked into her lap as she felt herself blush. Coloring her cheeks from the inside was something she did not realize she could still do. "We were sweethearts many years ago." Candice glanced at Chenda. "I'm guessing it was before you were born."

Chenda shrugged, ignoring the veiled remark about her age. She wasn't foolish enough to think Edison chastely waited for Chenda to become his wife. She conceded there were likely

13

more than a few of his romantic acquaintances out there somewhere. Now, sitting across the table from such a one, Chenda started to resent the solidification of the abstract.

Edison, why have you sent me here?

"Honestly, Professor, I couldn't say. He never *actually* spoke of you. But he's left me a letter-"

Candice cut in, "Letter, what letter?"

Chenda stiffened and paused to delicately clear her throat "I'm getting to that," she said, enunciating each word. She slid the peach envelope out of her coat pocket and onto the small cafe table. Candice reached for it, but Chenda pulled the letter back towards her chest, as if reconsidering.

"Professor, this letter is the world to me right now," she warned. "It's my exclusive desire to follow Edison's instructions. As a woman with an impeccable reputation for seriousness and dedication to study, I ask you hold your mind open." She gently dropped the letter back onto the table and slowly pushed it across. Candice, slightly ashamed of her eagerness, looked past the faint, girlish freckles on Chenda's face and into the brown eyes that were deep with sorrow and resolve.

For the first time in many years, Candice felt regret. Perhaps she was judging this girl too harshly. After all, Edison chose *her* to marry, a decision he would not have made lightly. Candice closed her hand around the envelope, delicately and respectfully. She withdrew the letter and began reading. Her mouth fell open. This letter was an invitation to suicide!

"What! Go with you to... How -- Why? Ridiculous! DO YOU KNOW WHERE KOTAL IS???!!!"

Candice began to reconsider her opinion on Edison's decision making. He must have lost his poor mind! Chenda sat quietly in her corner seat, looking calm and composed.

"Of course I know where it is," she said, staring back into Candice's wide eyes. Breaking the gaze, Chenda started, "I don't really have a good plan for our departure yet, but I think-"

"Hold on a second," Candice cut her off again. "You can't be serious. What Edison suggests is pure insanity. Asking you, and I guess me as well, to go to Tugrulia is impossible. It's just not allowed - by either side. Everyone knows that foreigners are killed on sight over there. Even if you *can* get into the Empire and manage to stay alive for five minutes, what are you going to do then? Hunt some mystic? To what end? What does that have to do with you? or Edison for that matter?"

Softly, but with conviction, Chenda said, "Edison wanted me to go. So, I'll go."

Candice, prepared fully to continue on her rant, stopped short. She evaluated the young woman opposite her. Candice rejected her first instinct, that Edison was being cruel, asking his child bride to blunder into certain death. Her next thought was equally unlikely, that Old Eddie, in the end, simply lost his marbles. Uncertain, Candice read through the letter once more, tisking at the bold folly of it.

"Hmm..." she said. "What's this bit about the bag?"

Ah...she's curious! thought Chenda. She pulled the velvet bag from her pocket and spilled the necklace and stones onto the table.

Candice sucked air in between clenched teeth. "Oh... my." She picked up the blue stone and turned it over in her hands. Her voice rose to a breathy squawk, "Oh, MY!"

"You know what these are?" Chenda asked.

Candice blinked a few times, agog at what lay on the table before her. "Mercy, Matilda! Would you put those things away!" She brushed the stones back toward Chenda and the velvet bag.

"What was Edison doing with THOSE?" Candice whispered as she looked around, checking to see if anyone had noticed what the two women had between them. No one seemed to have taken any note of the pair, so she focused her attention back on Chenda, who calmly slipped the letter and the bag of stones back into her pockets.

Chenda leaned toward the professor and smiled slightly. "I guess you can help me then," she said. "What *do* I have here?"

Candice scooted her chair closer to Chenda and placed the back of her hand up to her lips. "What you have, is trouble," Candice whispered conspiratorially. "Come on. We've got to get out of here."

Candice dropped a few coins on the table, took her companion by the hand and pulled her out of the front doors of the Terminal Tearoom. Chenda, doing her best to keep up, shuffled down the sidewalk behind Candice, waving a hand to her driver Daniel, indicating that he should follow them.

"Where are we going?" she shouted.

"Back to my office at the university," Candice said. "I have something to show you."

Candice burst through the door of her small office, flipping on the lights with one hand and dragging Chenda along with the other. She flapped her arms at the girl, directing her to the empty chair nearest her cluttered desk. "Sit," Candice ordered. "Stay."

Chenda, suddenly feeling a bit like a naughty Pekinese, watched as the professor darted back and forth across her office, collecting books and maps from the shelves, several bits of stone from a specimen cabinet, a small anvil, a hammer and a tiny rubber mallet. All of these, she plopped onto the heavy wood paneled desk in front of Chenda. The professor darted to the window, snapping shut the gauzy, moth-eaten curtains and closing out the last rays of the afternoon sun. Little wisps of dust curled slowly down to the floor. Candice glanced around the room one last time, and stepped to the door again, closing it firmly and sliding the draw bolt. She turned to face Chenda.

"Bring those stones out again," Candice said as she handed Chenda a small felt lined specimen tray. She settled on a corner of her desk while Chenda obliged, placing the tray near the professor.

"These stones," Candice began, running her finger across each one, "are extraordinarily rare." She looked at the stones, not one bigger than the last joint of her thumb. "I'd never imagined I see ones this big." Candice sat for a moment with one hand under her chin, thinking about what to say next. Chenda held perfectly still, anticipating, not wanting to disturb the professor's thoughts.

Suddenly, Candice jumped to her feet and grabbed a jagged purple rock from the pile on her desk.

"Lepidolite," she said, placing the stone on a small anvil. Grabbing the hammer, she smashed the stone into powder with one strike. "That's a plus two on the hardness scale."

"Malachite," she said, smashing a green stone into a

hundred fragments. "Plus four."

"Hematite - plus six" Smash. Slivers of stone slid off the anvil.

"Spinel - plus eight" - Smash.

"Diamond - plus ten" Candice swung the hammer toward the clear stone and stopped at the last second. "Um," she glanced at Chenda, "That one is expensive, but I promise you, it would have shattered."

Puzzled, Chenda asked, "What's your point?"

Without answering, Candice grabbed Chenda's blue stone from the specimen tray, slapped it onto the anvil and brought the hammer down with great gusto.

There was a thunderous crack. Chenda let out a small yelp, and watched as bits of the hammer's broken head fell to the floor. The small blue stone sat on the anvil, unharmed.

Chenda trembled, shocked that the professor would take such liberties with specimens that did not belong to her.

"This is *azul pedradurite*." Candice explained. "It's remarkable stuff. Can't smash it for anything, but watch this."

Dropping the now useless hammer handle, Candice picked up the small anvil in one hand and tilted it sideways. Chenda watched, expecting to see the stone falling to the floor, but nothing happened.

"Magnetic," she said. Scooping the stone off the anvil, Candice reached for the small rubber mallet. Holding the azul pedradurite by the tips of her thumb and forefinger, she gently tapped the stone. The room filled with a rich, clear, musical note, and the stone glowed from within.

Chenda covered her ears. How could a gentle tap create such a loud noise? The professor let the note ring out, pure and strong, for a few seconds more, then closed her fingers around it, choking off the sound.

"The crystalline structure is perfect, you see, and the sound waves simply amplify themselves. It would just about ring forever, if you let it."

Candice opened her hand to reveal the stone, quiet and dull blue once again. She dropped it back into the tray. Picking up the yellow stone, she said, *"Geel pedradurite,"* and with the red necklace, "*Kokivos pedradurite.*" Candice thought a minute and said with a smile, "I'd have those stones sing for you, too, but I'm sure the fillings in my teeth would pop out from the vibration if I did. Tingles a bit, no?"

Chenda, still with her hands over her ears, nodded in stunned agreement.

"These stones are Tugrulian," she said while passing the tray back to Chenda. "Please, I think you may want to put those back in the bag, and keep them there. I'm not sure you'd want anyone to find out you have those."

"What do you mean?" she asked, covering the stones.

Candice turned to her desk and picked up a dog-eared notebook. Leafing through the pages, she began to talk. "Truth be told, I've had an interest in Tugrulian Geology since I began my studies, but with the war and all, that line of inquiry just couldn't be pursued. My interest began when I saw my first pedradurite. One appeared here at the university several years before I became a student, when trade first opened with the Tugrulians. You see, Kotal trade goods were exceptionally desirable here for a time. Fashionably exotic, you could say." Candice sniffed in a disapproving manner, but kept talking.

"A merchant by the name of John Hunkapiller brought a stone here for the professors to examine, a tiny blue one. He said he bought it from a shady priest in the capitol city, Kotal. Let's just say, the amount he *claimed* he spent on that stone could keep me smashing diamonds all day. Anyway, the priest told Hunkapiller these stones were used somehow in a sacred ceremony in the Temple of the Dia Orella. That's the home of the One God of the Tugrulians."

Chenda nodded, willing Candice to go on.

"Hunkapiller left the stone at the University for further examination while he made another trip to the Empire. I guess he was bitten by the geology bug, because he vowed to acquire a full set, that's one red, one blue and one yellow, and he promised to bring them here for more study. Unfortunately, he died soon thereafter in the Kotal Massacre at the start of the War. However, he wasn't the only merchant to pick up a 'Singing Stone', and I saw a few of those stones early in my studies. I haven't seen one recently, though, and Hunkapiller's stone vanished from the University vaults about nine years ago. I assumed it was a faculty member with sticky fingers, but now, I am not so sure."

Candice looked through her notebook again. "I think," she said slowly checking her notes, "everyone who was known to have a Tugrulian Singing Stone is now dead... The question is why?"

Candice glanced at Chenda. "I wonder if anyone knew Edison had these three." She paused, dreading to continue. "I hate to be the one to tell you, Mrs. Frost, but this may be reason your husband was murdered."

The younger woman shook her head, her eyes haunted and confused. Candice went on. "Like I said before, what you have here is trouble." Then, silence lay between the women.

Candice needed to make a decision about the young lady across from her. Chenda's firm decision to go abroad was made in the madness of grief, it seemed. Perhaps it was the first and only life choice the girl had ever made. Even if she died trying, Chenda was committed to fulfilling Edison's instructions. In a small sort of way, the professor appreciated that kind of loyalty.

But what was she to Candice? When Edison left for the War, Candice hid her heart from romantic love, and fed her spirit with the excitement of discovery and knowledge. As a woman capable of great powers of concentration, she focused years ago on science, and never came up for air. For close to 20 years she courted wisdom. Her theories and ideas became like children to her. Was a chance at following these rare stones enough to make her risk her life and follow this mere child to a violent land half a world away? The mystery hung before her. She looked at Edison's widow again. Some unnoticed maternal instinct took over as she assessed this young, confused woman, and she left good sense behind.

"Mrs. Frost," Candice whispered. "I think this quest may just get you killed. You may be in well over your head already, but, for the sake of the discovery of new knowledge, I think I would never forgive myself if I didn't come along."

Chenda leaped from her chair. With eyes full of hope, she grasped the professor's hand and started pumping it vigorously, crying "Oh, thank you, Professor Mortimer. Thank you. This is what Edison wanted."

Slightly embarrassed and already considering with whom she would leave her last will and testament, Candice pulled her hand back from the young woman. "Fine, dear, yes. And enough with the 'Professor Mortimer' business. I guess you can go ahead and call me Candice, as we are now traveling companions."

No longer knowing what to do with her hands, Chenda crossed them over her heart, saying "Thank you, Candice."

A sudden knock on the door made both ladies jump.

"Candice! Candice, dear, open up!" a voice came through the door, followed by a squeaky hiccup. "*Meeep...*"

With a smile, Candice swept her office door open, revealing a short, pleasant-looking woman with a full face set with sparkling eyes. "Ah, Professor Hoppingood, your timing is perfection!" Candice gushed. Sniffing the air, she added, "Have you been drinking with your father again?"

"Never you mind, Professor Mortimer," the woman tisked as she entered. "*Meeep....*"

"I saw your light on from outside as I was heading to diner, and thought..." her voice trailed off as she noticed Chenda for the first time. "I'm sorry. I must be interrupting."

Candice made introductions. "Mrs. Chenda Frost, this is my colleague, Professor Henrietta Hoppingood, instructor of Languages, Literatures and Cultures as well as a researcher into the field of *Esoterica*. She is my most trusted friend."

Henrietta blinked in realization as to who stood before her. "Oh, Mrs. Frost," Henrietta said, holding her head sympathetically to one side. "I'm so sorry for your loss. I read all about your husband in the papers."

Chenda blanched, hating her new fame as The Widow Frost. Candice quickly stepped in saying, "Henrietta, darling, can I have a word with you in the corridor?" She quickly dragged her short friend back through the office door, closing it behind them. Chenda found herself alone amongst the maps and stones.

She tried to focus on the various dusty pictures of Candice displayed around the room. In each photo, the professor squatted over some exotic rock or hole in the ground, clearly pleased by some new discovery. Chenda tried not to listen to the conversation out in the hall, which worked well for a few minutes until Henrietta exclaimed, "Are you DAFT? You'll be killed!" There was some shushing followed by some fast murmuring which turned into a whispered argument. Finally, Candice said loudly and firmly, "*You* owe *me* the favor, and now, I'm cashing it in. Pay up!"

Chenda smiled. It always came down to favors. They were like the secondary currency of the Republic. Everyone seemed to owe a favor to someone else, and it was truly bad form to decline when someone asked for their favor to be repaid. Whatever Candice had asked Henrietta for, she was surely going to get.

The door opened and Candice stepped in. Chenda heard Henrietta's footsteps disappearing down the corridor along with an exasperated voice shouting "As you wish...*Meeep!*"

Candice grinned at Chenda and said, "I believe I've just come up with a plan."

Chenda and the Airship Brofman

Chapter 3
CAPTAIN MAXWELL ENDICOTT

Over the next few hours, Chenda and Candice hatched a plan to undertake what rational people would deem an insane journey. The first step involved developing a plausible reason to put themselves east of the Republic's coastline and over the Kohlian Sea, an action generally forbidden by the government.

"Congratulations," Candice said. "Consider yourself enrolled in Kite's Republic University!"

"I have?" Chenda asked. "How does that help us?"

"Well," she said, "a geology professor, such as myself, often needs an assistant when she takes a sabbatical, and it's usually a student, such as yourself. You see? Your current area of study is the divergent plate boundaries of the Mid-Sea Ridge." Candice sat back with a satisfied look on her face.

Chenda blinked at her.

Then, still receiving no explanation, she blinked at Candice again.

"You know! Sea floor spreading?" Candice said, suddenly frowning. "Studying the volcanic regions of the ocean floor will allow us to acquire the necessary papers. Also, with the amount of seafloor out there to cover, no one will question the time we will be gone, and why we need an airship capable of spending several weeks over the Kohlian Sea. Then all we have to do is find a way to slip over to the Tugrulian Empire and into the capitol city Kotal unnoticed, find a hidden mystic, fulfill your destiny and hopefully make it back to the Republic alive. Simple as that."

Candice isn't one for half measures, Chenda thought.

23

When she steps in, it's with both feet.

"How are we going to get from the middle of Kohlian Sea to the eastern shore?" Chenda asked.

"That's where Henrietta is going to help us," Candice replied. "For a well mannered lady, Henrietta knows some pretty slippery characters and a surprising number of airship captains - most of them shifty. She's going to connect us with the right airship for our ultimate needs." Candice looked everywhere in the room except for where Chenda was sitting. "Hmm," she said scratching her wrist nervously. "This won't be cheap."

Chenda's face broke into a broad smile. "Don't you read the gossip columns? They say I'm the richest widow in the Republic." Her smile faded. "Edison's money will cover just about any expense."

She shifted in her seat, sinking until one elbow rested on Candice's desk. "What I lack is not money." Chenda straightened in her chair and said, "How can I explain? I grew up in the convent school of St Elgin in Wadpole-on-the-River. When the war started, my father left me in the care of the Sisters there. I was two-years old. I have no memories of life before then, and I can't remember my mother at all. The Sisters took care of me, and then Daddy died."

Chenda paused a moment, then carried on. "At Edison's estate, an entire staff waited to take care of my needs - even before I knew what they were. To be honest, I've wanted for nothing my entire life. Now, Edison's money is more than enough to keep me in luxury for the rest of my life – ten lifetimes or more. His wealth, however, won't give me a sense of who I am, and what I'm supposed to do with my life. He says my path is out there, and he's told me where to find it. So, the sky is the limit. If you think we need something, we get it."

"Unlimited funds. Well, thank you, that's one advantage we have." Candice made a dismissing gesture and said, "Look, I see a thousand new students walk into this University each year. Most of them have no clue what they are going to do with their life. It's really unreasonable to ask a teenager to decide what they want to do with the rest of their lives. Maybe one in a hundred have the vaguest sense of direction for themselves. Just like you, they just need a little time and experience to grow up! Don't be so hard on yourself."

Chenda looked away as Candice continued, "At least you've got the means to follow your path, even if it is a dangerous one. You're enrolling in the school of hard knocks, really. And, another thing – stop calling it Edison's money. It's yours now. Own it."

The professor let her words sink in for a moment and then asked, "I've been wondering, and please stop me if I am being rude, but if Edison never left his estate, how did you two meet and marry?"

"Oh, that question is not rude. I was his ward," Chenda replied.

"Ward? Who would give a recluse a child to look after?" Candice realized that her question was a bit unkind, but Chenda just made a sad smile and explained.

"My father, Commander Alexander Bode, did. Daddy was the Commander of the *Valiant Eagle.* They served together for years and were very close. When Edison returned from the war, he came to the convent with letters from my father stating his desire for Edison to be my guardian. On the day Edison was discharged from the Kiter Air Service, he claimed me at the orphanage, then retreated with me to his estate. I had just turned 13, and I was totally alone in the world. Edison came along, and I was grateful. He said he would keep me safe, and I believed him. He kept that promise every day."

Chenda bit her lip, the pain of thinking about her life without Edison weighing heavily on her. "I found him fascinating. He was a stoic, broken man. At first, he remained distant as he healed from his various war wounds, but he carefully arranged tutors, governesses, pets and companions for me. He sent me to town for finishing school, and I learned all the polite mannerisms a young woman of society needed to know – a real blossom of the Republic. As I grew older, he offered a generous allowance and, eventually, a tender ear. I was so lonely sometimes, and he was an anchor of kindness to me.

"When I turned 18, it only seemed reasonable to accept his offer of marriage. I respected him and enjoyed his companionship, and agreed with my tutors and acquaintances that he would, in gentle kindness, care for me for the rest of his life. I never really cared about the extra 23 years he carried. It seemed unimportant then, and I lived happily, without a care in the world. I loved him."

A tear rolled down her face, "That's why I am so committed to following his instructions."

Candice saw once again the bright newness of resolve within Chenda. She found it admirable, even if it was misplaced. Finally, Candice stretched and said, "With a father and a husband in the business of commanding airships, I guess you are an old hand at airship travel."

Chenda shook her head. "Not once. I've never flown before."

"Well, you *are* in for an experience."

Candice frowned slightly as she looked over the young woman's beautiful clothes, fashionable shoes and pampered hair. "It will be required of us to travel quickly and light. Remember, you're my assistant and a student geologist, so look the part. That means ditching the finery. Also, you'll need some aeronaut boots and a flight coat." Candice grabbed a pen and made a detailed list of the things Chenda would need. "I'll take care of getting your various documents, but you'll want to pick up a compass, a pouch-belt, a timepiece, pants, and a variety of small but valuable objects with which we may need to barter. The farther we get from Kite's Republic, the less our paper money will be worth. So bring baubles that are portable and worth a good bit, but nothing dear to you."

"Ah," Chenda said. "Expensive trinkets I have, and the rest I can get tomorrow."

"Good," Candice replied with a yawn. "It's getting late. Let's see what kind of shady captain Henrietta can find for us, and we will meet back here tomorrow, say about three o'clock?"

When she arrived at the Frost estate, Chenda was greeted at door by her housekeeper Alme.

"Evening, ma'am," she said, taking Chenda's overcoat. "Will you be needing anything at present, ma'am? Some tea and biscuits perhaps? Draw you a bath?"

"No, Alme, thank you. I won't be needing anything for the rest of the night, just some peace and quiet until morning."

"Yes Ma'am," Alme said as she waddled away.

Chenda crossed the foyer and stepped into Edison's study. She reached into the folds of her dress and retrieved the velvet bag holding the Tugrulian Singing Stones. She imagined Edison putting the little gems into the tiny sack and tying the drawstrings. Of course, he bequeathed all his wealth to Chenda, but, at that moment, the little bag seemed like the essence of Edison, the one possession that mattered for her to inherit.

If Edison felt they were safe enough here, I guess I'll trust it, too... she thought. Gripping the edge of the desk, she squeezed the dark mahogany until she again found the release for the secret panel. Chenda kissed the letter, and placed it along with the stones into his desk.

She climbed the stairs to her room, where she began to gather the things she would need for her journey. She found a small, simple canvas sack in Edison's wardrobe and sat at her dressing table to sort through her jewelry. She collected her tortoise shell hair combs, a pair of pearl earrings, gold and silver bangles and a cameo broach and dropped them into the bag. Moving to Edison's bureau, she took his pocket watch and fob from the top drawer and slipped it into her bag. She looked through the rest of the drawers, both hers and Edison's, but, aside from a few heavy gold coins, there was little she wished to take with her. She placed her bag of trinkets at the bottom of a small carpet bag and piled some clean clothes, her toothbrush and an embroidered handkerchief on top. She was packed.

She stretched out on the bed she and Edison had shared. She touched his pillow, caressing where his head once rested. She felt her grief rising again.

I've got to get out of here. I can feel that now...

For the eighth night in a row, Chenda cried herself to sleep.

Early the next morning, Chenda awoke with her dreams fresh in her mind. She'd been flying, free in the open air, arms held out low to her side, brushed backward with the speed of her soaring. She wasn't alone. Edison had been there with her. He held her to him, his arm wrapped around her waist, holding her back tightly to his chest as they flew in a brilliant sky. Floating below him as they bobbed along on warm, silky air, Chenda felt happiness – her mood lighter than it had been in days. She looked up at Edison's scarred face, wondering where he was leading her, but she couldn't find the words to ask. Chenda also looked down. Clouds touched with strands of amber and rose sunlight stretched out below her as far as her eyes could see. Every moment of their flight bought them closer to a sound, the clear ringing tone of the azul pedradurite, the blue Singing Stone. Just as the sound's crescendo brought her to where she thought her ears would burst, she awoke.

It was so vivid. Sitting there on the edge of the bed, alone again in the light of day, Chenda felt her heart breaking, yearning for Edison to be there, comforting her loneliness and guiding her.

As Chenda went through the routine of washing the sleep from her eyes and dressing for the day ahead, she tried to fix the details of the dream in her mind. But, as all dreams do, the elements evaporated, leaving her with only the pulpy, raw emotions.

Glancing at Edison's picture on her bedside table, Chenda steeled herself for another day without him. She rejected the intricate braids and curls of her usual up-do and pulled her long, dark hair in a modest bun. The understated look matched her clothing, a colorless blouse and long plain walking skirt in brown silk. She turned away from her mirror and marched down the stairs to find Alme waiting dutifully, at the landing.

"Good Morning, ma'am," she said. "Breakfast? Cup of tea?"

"Yes, and toast please" Chenda said, "I'll take it in Edison's study, thank you." She walked across the foyer, but turned back to Alme.

"Also, I have several things I need from Lilienthal's Aerofitters. Would you send Daniel there with this list and ask him to wait while they fill it? I want these things right away." Out of her pocket, she pulled the short list Candice had drawn up of necessary items for an airship journey, and handed it to Alme. Chenda continued into the study.

She stopped at the first bookcase she passed and started looking for any books that had anything to do with The Tugrulian Empire. There were several tomes on the military struggle between the Empire and the Republic. As she worked her way around the room, her search turned up a variety of books on Tugrulian culture, government and agriculture. Finally, she found a small book entitled *Life under the Dia Orella: the One God of the Tugrulian Empire.*

She flipped through the pages. The dearth of information about the Tugrulians' lone god and the sacred temple, the Dia Orella, surprised Chenda. The book recorded the various tales merchants brought back from the Empire, and the accounts were just a collection of rumors. Some had heard that the Tugrulian sacred writings were kept guarded in the temple at the Kotal, but no westerner, and most of the Tugrulians themselves, had ever read the words of their God or seen the inside of the Dia Orella.

Chenda sighed. The chapter on ceremonies didn't say much either. She found no discussion of *Singing Stones.* None of the other books seemed to mention the word *pedradurite* either. As Chenda continued to read, she began to understand a bit about what life was like in Tugrulia. Their whole society was shaped by nearly unending war. With their agricultural land burned and poisoned, Tugrulians had taken much of their life below ground. There, they propagated a wide variety of fungi, mosses and algae. Much of their protein came from the cave dwelling lizards, bugs and fish raised in underground ponds, or caught in the Kohlian Sea.

Chenda looked up from her book as Alme brought the breakfast tray to Edison's desk.

"Daniel is on his way to town, ma'am," she said. "You will have your things in just a few hours." Alme paused in the doorway, and looked back at her young mistress with a worried and motherly gaze.

"If you don't mind me saying, ma'am," Alme started, "I am surprised you didn't go to shop for yourself. You always seemed to like visiting the shops personally."

"Not anymore," Chenda said, turning back to her reading. "Please let me know when Daniel returns."

Chenda spent the remainder of the morning making a mental list of important facts about the Tugrulians and their Empire. Several sources categorized the men as fierce or warlike, and aggression seemed to be a cultural trait. Tugrulian society isolated women, and most remained uneducated and abused. Women were expected to produce beautiful children for their husbands, and be servile to the needs of all men. In general, the Tugrulians had dusky skin, dark eyes and straight, shiny black hair. For the men, beards and mustaches were very unfashionable, and long hair was acceptable on both men and women, often braided into or twisted around various caps or head wrappings. Tugrulian clothing was loose and layered, meant to be protection from both the hot days and cold nights. Tugrulians favor a variety of acid colors that are produced by the chemicals brought up from deep underground or from various colorful bugs.

Fascinating, thought Chenda, *but, does any of this help me?*

At mid-day, Alme knocked again and slipped into the study.

"Is Daniel back from Lilienthal's?" Chenda asked.

"Yes, ma'am. Just arrived."

Alme followed Chenda into the foyer as Daniel entered, carrying a large, paper-wrapped bundle.

"Excellent," Chenda said. "I'm glad you're back so quickly. I'll need to go out this afternoon for several errands. I'll be ready to go in just a moment, but, first, would you take that package to my room, please?"

Chenda began to turn back toward the study, but stopped when she noticed Daniel standing perfectly still, his eyes wide. Alme stepped forward to explain.

"Daniel's doesn't know where to go, ma'am. He's never been in the house past the foyer, apart from the day that he was hired by Mr. Frost."

"No? I thought all the house staff gathered in the kitchens whey they weren't on duty."

"I keep to the garage, ma'am. It's my place to be there."

Daniel said.

"It's no trouble," Alme interjected. "I'll show him where to go and have him back in a jiff."

Alme led Daniel up the stairs, leaving Chenda to her thoughts. She went into the study and retrieved the small black velvet bag from the secret compartment in Edison's desk and tucked it into the front of her blouse, right over her heart, for safe keeping. She told herself she wanted to keep the stones close at hand in case Candice needed them for some reason, but that was just a lie she chose to believe. The truth was, she felt that, at best, these stones may have been the last thing Edison had touched in this world, and at least, they were the last gift he wanted her to have. Either way, it made them special to her.

She smoothed the front of her blouse and returned to the foyer. Daniel and Alme were already waiting beside the open front door. Daniel dashed down the elegant steps to open the car door for his mistress.

"Where to, ma'am?" he asked.

"The heart of Coal City, Daniel. I'll need to see Edison's attorney and then visit the bank. After that I have an appointment at the University."

Daniel made a quick, acknowledging nod and then closed the door.

Chenda settled into her seat as the car steadily moved toward town. She worried about being swept up in a crush of onlookers as she had been the day before, but, she made all of her errands quickly and, to her relief, unnoticed.

When she arrived at the campus of Kite's Republic University, she felt more at ease with her surroundings. Chenda was eager to hear any new developments the professor had made for their plan to go abroad. She quickly climbed the steps of the university science building, only to find Candice standing in the hallway, staring at her closed office door.

"What are you doing out here?" asked Chenda. Without answering, Candice leaned forward and pushed open her office door. Chenda stepped as if to enter the room, but the professor caught her arm.

"Smell that?" she asked. Chenda sniffed the air. It was

31

subtle, like the smell of a bakery from across the street. There was just a hint of sticky sweetness in the air. Candice pulled the door closed.

"Someone has been in my office, and they weren't snooping for a mid-term. That's the smell of Orellanine. It's a concentrated toxin, one that absorbs though the skin. A powerful poison, but a slow one. It takes about three weeks to kill you. I'm thinking there's nothing I need in my office today, not badly enough to die for it, anyhow. Shall we go?"

Chenda turned her stunned eyes to her companion, "Why would someone poison your office?"

Candice locked her door from the outside. "I think someone is trying to kill me, or maybe you. I'm not sure, but most likely it has something to do with your stones." Candice snorted, "I mean, most of the faculty just leave nasty notes under the door when *they* have a problem, and the students generally don't go through all the effort to boil up an exotic toxin if you flunk 'em."

Chenda looked at her companion with wide eyes and said, "Someone tries to kill you and you tell jokes?"

"They could be trying to kill *you*, don't forget. It's either laugh or cry about it, and I just don't have any tears in me today. We've got too much to do." She turned and walked down the corridor waving for Chenda to follow.

"Speaking of, we've got a meeting in a few minutes with the captain of the airship *Brofman*, Henrietta has found us our ship."

Daniel's eyes widened with surprise when the ladies directed him to their next destination, the seedy area known as Elly's Quay. Quickly remembering himself, and his position, he rearranged his features into dutiful neutrality. With his usual quickness and care, he drove Candice and Chenda to a grimy bar where proper ladies, in his opinion, ought not be.

As he opened Chenda's door, he spoke to her in hushed tones. "With your permission, ma'am, I'd like to linger *inside* the door, rather that out here by the car." It was more of a demand than a request. "It's a rough kind of place that your new friend is bringing you to, and I have my doubts..." his voice trailed off.

Chenda made a tiny nod of her head. As she followed Candice through the door held open by Daniel, she felt ashamed of her own cowardice. Her better judgment warred with her resolve. How could she journey to a land that violently rejected people from her world when she couldn't even find the courage to walk confidently within her own city? Where was her courage? Doubt and fear started to chip away at her resolution to follow Edison's instructions.

Once they were all inside, Daniel lingered at the door, resting his back against one wall while he casually looked around at the nearly empty pub. Shadows obscured most of the tables in the malodorous and dim room. The ambiance promised that one would not be able to see much more than the outline of any other patron. Seclusion was the specialty of the house.

The women crossed a tiny open area in the center of the room and seated themselves at a solid yet filthy table. From her seat, Chenda could just make out the torso of a man leaning against the bar. His face was obscured by shadows, but she could tell he was of average height, but thickly built. He wore heavy, thick soled leather boots and thick canvas pants held up by dark leather braces. His white shirtsleeves were rolled up to his elbow. Every so often, his massive hand lifted a pint from the bar to the shadow surrounding his head. The occasional turn of his torso led Chenda to believe that the man was watching her. After a few moments, he picked up his drink and turned toward Chenda's table. His step into the dim light revealed his clean-shaven face and a head of dark hair touched with gray over his ears. He tipped the glass upward, downing the remains of his drink in one gulp, and walked over to the two ladies. His presence filled the space in front of them, and he asked in a throaty voice, "Are you Henrietta's friend?"

"Yes, I'm Professor Candice Mortimer, and you are...?"

"Endicott," he said, "Maxwell Endicott, Captain of the airship *Brofman*." The man eased himself onto the edge of the empty seat closest to Chenda, but he kept his focus on the professor.

"A pleasure to meet you, Captain Endicott." Candice leaned in slightly. "We are in need of an airship. We'd like to

33

spend several weeks surveying the waters over the Mid-Sea Ridge. Would you be interested?"

"I'm interested," he smiled, "But Henrietta Hoppingood asked me to come here as a favor to her, and she doesn't like to owe people favors if she can help it. From what I gather, you don't need a research airship. You need something that *looks* like a research airship. So, where are we really going?"

Candice glanced at Chenda and then said. "Kotal. Can you get us there?"

Endicott laughed, a great, room-filling bark. "No," he said, still chuckling. "I can't get you to Kotal." Chenda's heart sank, but the captain continued, "I can, however, get you close."

Chenda spoke for the first time since entering the pub. "Define *close.*"

Endicott turned his sparkling gray eyes toward Chenda. "It's not as if I could dock a Republic airship at the front door of the Imperial Palace, doll. I'm just saying that I can get you -- closer than you are right now - for the right price." He turned his attention back to Candice. "Who's she?" he said, jerking a thumb at Chenda.

"My assistant," Candice said, waving her hand as if Chenda ranked just below luggage in importance for the trip. She appreciated that the professor was leaving her name out of the discussion. "It will just be the two of us for this journey," Candice said.

"Two passengers. Fair enough. You call it research, if you want, but I call it bonkers. Then again, who am I to judge. I don't really much care about your reasons or your destination. What I *do* care about is flying, and getting paid."

Candice smiled. "Then I guess what we need to do next is agree on a price."

As the captain and the professor began to work out the details of expectations and payment, Chenda sat back and tried to examine Maxwell Endicott with an assessing eye. She came up with no insights. She sighed quietly as she realized that she had no ability to judge other people's character. To this point in life, she had no need. Edison had been her prime companion for half her life, and she never questioned his motives. As for the Sisters

34

of St. Elgin, well, who needed to spend time assessing the rectitude of Holy Sisters?

She tried again to recognize either virtues or warnings in the behavior of Captain Endicott. She watched carefully as Candice and the captain traded offers and counteroffers, alternating the attitude and position of their bodies. First Candice would lean into the table and whisper a number, then she would retreat back as the captain laughed off her proposal and presented another, himself leaning in to the table. It reminded her of a pair of exotic birds she has once seen living in an ornate cage in a shop on High Road. Sharing a perch, the first bird would step sideways and the second would follow. They would waggle side by side, never touching, calling back and forth to one another, then reversing the steps back up the perch. She had been fascinated then, as she was now, with the complex trade of sounds and movements, the give and take.

Chenda began to look at Maxwell Endicott as if he himself was up for sale in one of her favorite shops. Was this something that she would buy and bring home to Edison? Could this rough man help her to her destiny? How would she know who to trust? Finding no revelations into the captain's character, she waited patiently until Candice and Captain Endicott each sat back in their chairs, grinning.

"Then we are agreed," Candice said. "We'll have the money for you tomorrow afternoon when we depart. I also have the necessary university documents that approve our research. I'm sure you will need those to file your flight plan." Candice handed over a small bundle of papers.

"Terrific." The captain smiled at the two women as he rose to leave. "I'll have my first officer meet you tomorrow at the Coal City Port Terminal - slip 24 - five o'clock. If you ladies will excuse me, I have to make some plans for our departure."

Without waiting for a reply, Captain Endicott turned away and left.

Candice seemed pleased as she turned to Chenda, but the younger woman's expression looked strained, and the professor suddenly looked doubtful.

"I talked him down to four-hundred thousand. Was that

not good enough?" she said, suddenly worried that she had committed too much money of Chenda's money.

"No, I've got more than that on hand," she said. "That's not worrying me." Chenda looked at Candice and slowly found words for her doubts. "But, Captain Endicott. How do you know that he will do what he says he will? I mean, how do you know if you, I mean we, can trust him?"

Candice looked at the woman awash in a sea of self doubt sitting across from her. Her face was an open book.

"For that matter, how do you know you can trust me?" Candice replied, thinking her question rhetorical.

"Edison said I could. That's why I *do* trust you. In full," Chenda answered.

The answer flattered Candice, but still made her cross. "Oh, that's right. Edison's word is gospel. Well, lucky me. Let's just trust that Edison's words are what you believe them to be, and hopefully we won't be killed."

"I'm sure it will be just fine." Chenda said. "But the question is: do you trust Captain Endicott?"

"I only know I can hire him, not that we can trust him. I also know that Henrietta recommended him, and even asked a favor of him to meet us. That means something. We will just have to be cautious and see what happens."

Candice looked at her watch and then placed an envelope on the table. "Now," she said, drawing Chenda out of her contemplation. "We've got less than a day to get things together. I've taken the liberty of getting your papers for you." She spilled the contents of the envelope out on to the table. "Here are your traveling documents, and this one shows you are a student at the University. Keep these with you all the time. She slid the papers back into the envelope and handed it all to Chenda. "We should be going."

Daniel, who had been waiting like a watchdog, stepped from the shadows to lead the women through the door and into the waiting car.

Chapter 4
THE FIRE AND THE FLIGHT

That night, Chenda ate her dinner alone in the dining room. She had been avoiding the room for the last few days. Every time she glanced down at her plate, the outline of her husband appeared opposite her. Each time she looked up to see him more clearly, the vision of Edison vanished. The cruel tricks her eyes played on her were maddening. She finally pushed away her plate, and went upstairs.

She found the package from Lilianthal's Aerofitters lying on the low bench at the foot of her bed. Chenda rolled the neatly trussed brown paper bundle onto the comforter and began to untie the binding strings. She smoothed away the wrappings, spreading the items within across the bed. She examined the first item, a pair of heavy silk pants. She ran her fingers over the tightly woven cream-colored fabric. She stood next to the bed and unfastened the hooks and buttons of her own skirt and petticoat, letting them all fall to the floor. She kicked her clothes aside and pulled on the pants. Chenda looked at the way the heavily quilted britches fit over her hips and thighs.

She looked into the mirror and thought to herself, *If the nuns could see me now. In PANTS! I was just not brought up this way.*

But, these trousers felt pretty good. Unlike so many of the long, tight skirts she wore, these silk pants were roomy in the seat. Nothing was bound up until the knee, where the fabric became thinner and tapered to the ankle, presumably to make the ends of the legs fit easily into the tops of the boots.

Ah, the aeronaut boots. Chenda ran her hands over the deep brown leather and the shining brass buckles. The weight of each boot was intimidating, but, pulling them on, she instantly understood their value lay in their warmth. They seemed to fit her perfectly, and she wiggled her toes into the soft fur linings. She spent several minutes fastening and adjusting the half-dozen buckles on each boot. She walked around her room. The heaviness of the boots changed her gait slightly. She began to lengthen her stride a little, letting the momentum of each heavy shoe swing her leg forward.

Now I know why soldiers swagger: it's the BOOTS!

She picked up the pouch-belt next, and was rather impressed with the cleverness of its design. The crescent of sturdy leather had a buckle on one end and a tongue of holes on the other. In between, a variety of pockets, slots, brass rings and loops hung down for, well, Chenda wasn't exactly sure what all the bits were for, but it seemed a great way to keep everything close at hand. Chenda tightened the buckle over her left hip, and transferred a few trinkets, some money and her papers into the pockets.

Back at the bed, she experimented with a shiny new compass. Chenda watched the needle swirl around as she turned this way and that, but after a moment or two, she tucked it into her pouch-belt as well.

The last item in the package, and the largest, was the flight coat. Chenda pulled the long lambskin coat onto her shoulders. It felt soft and warm over her thin blouse, but she began to wonder if Lilianthal's had made a mistake about the size. Chenda turned again to her mirror and thought the flight coat looked way too big. It swallowed her, and, as she walked around the bedroom, it jingled a bit.

Can this be right?

She tugged at all of the little buckles and straps hidden within tiny flaps throughout the coat, but Chenda couldn't make any sense of them. Not knowing what else to do, she just let them be. Despite its bulk, the coat wasn't particularly heavy, and its warmth brought a slight flush to her cheeks. It would have to do.

Chenda decided to test the outfit in the cool night air. She picked up the carpet bag she had packed the night before, crossed the bedroom, and exited onto the balcony. Making herself comfortable at the small table there, she checked the contents of her luggage one last time. Satisfied that she had everything she needed, she leaned back in the chair and looked up at the pale moonlight and the stars. A cold breeze tickled her exposed neck, so she flipped the fuzzy collar up. She smelled flowers in the air, and the scent mixed with the tangy aroma of new leather. She tried to imagine what tomorrow would be like, but her fears were getting in the way. Dressed so unconventionally in this airship getup, she observed herself as perhaps a stranger would: a poor little rich girl doing something very, very dumb. She pouted. Looking down at her new clothes and boots, she tucked her chin to her chest, the fluffy collar of her flight coat instantly warming the exposed skin of her cheeks.

Perhaps I need to rethink this. I'll speak with Candice tomorrow and call this whole thing off.

She sat there a while longer, trying to think of exactly how she would explain herself to the professor in the morning. "Oops! I'm a coward and hate myself for it" didn't sound like the best thing to say. However, it was comprehensively the truth. Debating the right way to tell Candice about her doubts, Chenda drifted off to sleep.

She awoke with a start and wasn't sure if hours had passed or just minutes. Snuggled within the flight coat and aeronaut boots, she felt no colder than when she first stepped out onto the balcony. As she stood to go back inside, she felt another wave of indecision. Edison wanted her to make this trip, and he'd always looked out for her. She *should* go. Her doubt and resolve wrestled as she stepped back into her bedroom, where she froze in her tracks.

Standing in front of Edison's dresser, Daniel Frent pawed through the drawers.

"What are you doing!?" Chenda demanded.

Daniel whipped around with shock and horror on his face. In a single movement, he leaped at Chenda, pulling her out of the doorway and pushing her roughly facedown onto the bed, crushing her breath from her lungs. Chenda thrashed, trying to pull in more air so she could scream, but Daniel straddled her back, digging the tops of his feet into the back of her knees, pinning her. Daniel looped his left arm under hers, grabbing a handful of her dark hair. He jerked her head back and to the right, covering her mouth with his free hand.

Chenda's wild eyes rolled frantically trying to see Daniel's face, to read there why he was doing this. He brought his face in close, his lips hovering over her ear, and hissed quietly, "Shh... Don't struggle."

The tone of his voice only made Chenda more frightened, and she pulled against Daniel with more fervor. One arm pulled free momentarily, but Daniel reared back and bashed his own forehead into the side of her skull, just behind her ear. For a moment, she thought she might pass out. All fight drained out of her and Daniel's weight settled on her body more completely.

Before she could recover from her daze, Daniel flipped Chenda onto her back. He straddled her hips, pinning one hand with his knee. Leaning forward, he pressed his elbow into her shoulder and his forearm across her throat. She looked up into his crazed face, clawing at his hand as it covered her mouth. He pulled his hand back from her lips suddenly, but as she gulped in a breath, Daniel balled his hand into a fist and struck Chenda hard across the cheek. The pain of it forced the struggle from her limbs again and she tasted blood in her mouth.

"Shut up! Shut. Up! Be still!" Daniel hissed. "So help me, I'll beat you unconscious if you make any more noise." He grabbed her face in one big hand, forcing Chenda's gaze back to his own eyes. Madness looked back at her.

Daniel pulled a knife out of the top of his boot and pressed it to the soft skin under her jaw. "Where are they? Where are the stones?" he demanded through clenched teeth.

Chenda gasped.

"Tell me!" he said in a whisper. "Quietly."

Chenda's mind raced as she tried to decide what to do. The stones were down the front of her shirt where she had carried them all day. If it weren't for the thick flight coat between them, Daniel would surely be able to feel the stones there. She decided to play dumb.

"What stones?" she croaked. Another blow slashed her cheek, this one grazing her eye.

"Don't be stupid," Daniel growled. "Edison's stones. The ones that bastard husband of yours brought back from the war. I need them, and I am betting, since you've been hanging out with the geologist, that you know all about them and where they are. Now give them to me! Or I'll kill you, too."

Understanding began to break through Chenda's terror. "You killed Edison? Over a few bits of rock?"

"No, I killed him because he ruined my life! Your husband made sure that *my* father was blamed for the loss of the *Valiant Eagle*. When Edison returned alive, he testified that during the attack, the Tugrulian incendiaries hit several of the power cells, crippling the *Eagle*. When the chemist remixed the matrix for the cells to re-power the ship, there was a big explosion. Edison Frost pointed the finger at the ship's chemist – my *father*- and he was posthumously court marshaled for negligence. My mother was left with *nothing*. No pension, no husband, NOTHING. The shame of his downfall killed her. Edison killed my mother by throwing my father to the wolves."

Daniel's face ran with tears and sweat. The hand holding the knife to Chenda's throat shook with his fury. "I was 18 and the only one left to pick up the pieces of my family. I should have been on my way in the world, but I had to stop it all to bury my mother, and look after my three younger brothers. Edison stole my future." His eyes rolled back into his head for a second, then refocused on Chenda's terrorized face.

"The stones," he said in a strangled voice, the point of the knife now drawing blood from her chin.

Chenda whimpered, but thought up a quick lie. "There are in a hidden in an inside pocket of my carpet bag. Over by the balcony."

Daniel swung his leg over the bed, standing in a single movement but never loosening his grip on Chenda. He pulled her by one arm, first to her feet, then along the length of the bed. When they reached the footboard, he roughly deposited her on the little bench there. He took a step back, the knife still trained on

41

her.

"Once my brothers were grown," he said, his voice softer, "I came to Coal City to find a way to make my revenge. I found out from one of your maids, a sweet, lonely girl who likes to visit some of the pubs in town, that Edison needed a new driver for his pretty wife. I sent him a letter, explaining who I am and that I was in need of good, honest work." Daniel snarled, "The fool felt sorry for me! He gave me his pity!"

Daniel took a small step back toward the balcony door. "I knew it was just a matter of time until I could make my revenge." Triumph brimmed in his eyes. Daniel shuddered, and then he focused on Chenda again. "As it turns out, I'm not the only person who wanted Edison dead. Since I was going to kill him anyway, it seemed so perfect that I was approached by someone in the city who wanted the same. Why not get paid for what I was going to do anyway?" Daniel frowned and shuddered again, as if his thoughts were wrestling within him and knocking him around from the inside. "Revenge and enough money to start a new life. It sounded like a great deal. Revenge for my father and mother, I have that now, but I only get paid if I can come up with the stones. I knew you would eventually lead me to them."

Chenda sat on the bench in shocked silence. She watched, open mouthed, as he moved backwards another few steps. Never turning away from her, he grabbed the chair from the dressing table and propped it against the bedroom door, ensuring that no one could enter from the hall, and Chenda couldn't run out. He pulled a large bottle out of his pocket, pulled the stopper and started slinging a strong smelling liquid around the room, dousing the dressers, the bed and the floor.

"Chenda," he said, his eyes clearing of his insanity for a moment. "I am sorry."

As quickly as they had cleared, the crazed fury filled his eyes again. Daniel leaped toward Chenda, and she felt the full impact of Daniel's weight into her side as the knife pierced her flight coat. The stabbing blow knocked her backwards, over the bench and onto the floor on the far side of the bed. All of the air left her lungs as the pain in her side shot out in waves. For several seconds, she could not move or breath. Crumpled on the floor, she could not see Daniel, but she heard his animal-like snarl and the sound of a match strike. The whoosh of flames dancing to life came next, and still, Chenda could not make her lungs pull in air. She clawed at the knife handle in her side and discovered that it had come free from her body, but was stuck somehow in the coat. It dawned on her that one of the many hidden buckles had caught the knife, keeping the long blade from fully entering her body. She could feel sticky blood flowing from her side, but the wound didn't feel too deep. The buckle had turned the force of a killing stab into a solid punch that had merely knocked the wind out of her.

After what seemed a choking eternity, she drew in a little air and rolled onto her side. She tugged on the knife again, finally freeing it. She saw Daniel hunched over one knee, rifling through her carpet bag as the flames rose around the room. He picked up Edison's pocket watch, admired it for a moment and moved to put it into his own pocket.

Chenda's mind flared with the rush of her own blood.

He stabbed me!

He's left me to burn!

He killed Edison!

Without another thought, her body started to move. In a single maneuver, she stood, stepped forward and swung the knife in a two handed arc. The blade sank deep into Daniel's neck. His body arched backwards, a hand flailing for the knife. Daniel's spasm knocked Chenda backwards onto the floor. The fire leaped around her as she struggled away from Daniel's thrashing body. She smelled burning hair and realize it was her own. She beat the flames around her face with her bare hands as she crawled toward the open balcony door; it was the only bit of floor left that wasn't burning. She checked herself for a moment, leaning her back against the carpet bag, brushing her burnt hands around her head checking for any more fire. She glanced back at Daniel, lying still on the floor, flames licking his motionless body. During his thrashing, he had dislodged the knife from his neck, and it lay on the floor next to Edison's pocket watch. Chenda reached forward, her hands shaking, and snatched the knife and the watch from the fire. She shuffled back onto the balcony clutching the objects to her, the knife ready to defend against another attack, and the watch suddenly feeling like a protective talisman – a bit of Edison to comfort her panicked mind. The skin across her knuckles had gone pale white, and each drop of Daniel's blood showed clearly across her hands. She could feel the burns on her palms, and the sticky dull ache in her side, but these pains seemed to be borrowed, like they belonged to someone else, and weren't hers to bear.

The flames grew hotter, engulfing everything in the room: the bed she had shared with Edison, her dressers full of fashionable clothes, his picture on the bedside table, the space they lived and loved in. Their life together was burning away. The raw heat pressing against her bloodied face pushed her back, further onto the balcony. She pulled herself to standing and threw the carpet bag over the rail. Tucking the knife into her pouch-belt, Chenda threw her legs over the railing and eased herself down into a squat. She dangled for a few seconds from the edge and then dropped to the walkway below. The aeronaut boots absorbed some of the shock from the fall, but Chenda rocked backwards, and instinctively, she threw her hands back to catch herself. As her burned palms scraped along the rough walkway, she screamed in agony.

She wanted to faint, to lie there and cool her burns and bruises on the chilled paving stones, but a small part of her brain screamed at her: *Get up!*

The voice in her head kept getting louder. *GET UP. Daniel may not be alone. You are not safe. GET UP!!!*

Chenda shook her head to drive away her daze and crawled along on her elbows. Pressing her shoulder to the wall of the house, she pushed up with her legs and then staggered to her feet. As she took in mouthfuls of cold fresh air, her thinking cleared. She had to run away. By his own admission, Daniel was not working alone. She wasn't sure who else was a danger to her.

Ignoring the pain in her hands as the handles bit into her burns along her fingers, she picked up the carpet bag and ran for the tree line just past the south end the house. Several yards into the thick woods, she looked back. Smoke was pouring out of all the windows on the second floor. The belching flames illuminated the house staff as each servant ran out onto the lawn. Alme screamed as she saw the fire sparking out of her mistress's window, and she fainted into the arms of the gardener.

Chenda wanted to run to the plump woman, and tell her not to be frightened, that she was alive and just fine, but her feet didn't move. She was held firm by that part of her brain that sensed the danger in revealing herself. *Hide, and bide your time. You are not safe.* Step by step, Chenda melted backwards into the woods.

An hour before dawn, Chenda arrived at the nearest trolley stop and boarded the first car that stopped there. The pain in her hands made fishing the fare out of her pouch-belt a flaming nightmare. It was all she could do not to scream. She eventually made her way downtown and into the university district. Finally, she reached Candice's apartment.

Chenda knocked weakly on the door frame and waited. Nothing happened. She knocked again, this time with all the strength she had left. She even kicked the drab door for emphasis. She swayed slightly as she stood there, tears of despair and exhaustion building in her eyes. When the door finally opened, Chenda fell through it.

"Gods above!" Candice squawked as she dove toward the floor to grab Chenda's limp body. "What happened to you?!" She reached under Chenda's arms and pulled her toward the small sofa. Candice knew she would never be able to lift the girl onto the couch, so she pulled several pillows and a cushion onto the floor and propped Chenda's back up against them. Chenda moaned and let her head fall backwards to rest on the seat, her arms flopping to the floor. Candice looked down into the young woman's face and gasped! She jumped away from her companion and raced back to the door, pulling the carpet bag in from where Chenda had dropped it and securing the lock. Chenda watched as Candice raced back across the small living room and disappeared into the kitchen.

"Candice..." she whimpered. In what she hoped was a safe place, Chenda finally gave in to the pain. Tears rolled tracks through the soot on Chenda's cheeks. She was sobbing as the professor reappeared with an armload of supplies and a large glass of water.

"I'm coming, deary. Just hold on," Candice said in a motherly tone as she tried to decide where to begin. "Drink," she ordered, pressing the glass to the girl's lips. Between spasms of tears, Chenda sucked in the cool water, and it pushed some of the smoke out of her aching throat. With each swallow, she could feel Daniel's weight on her neck again. She shuddered.

"Let's peel you out of that coat and then you start telling me what happened." Candice slowly unbuckled the flight coat and eased the younger woman's shoulders free. She held Chenda's head as gently as a mother would hold a newborn, and eased her back onto the cushions. As Candice threw the flight coat over her book laden coffee table, she gasped at the dark scorch marks and bloodstains.

"Man alive! What happened to you?"

Through her rears, Chenda recounted the events of the evening. Candice moved her hands over Chenda's body, checking for broken bones and assessing her various other injuries. Listening intently, the professor did her best to disinfect the knife wound over Chenda's ribs and tape it closed. As Chenda recited Daniel's confession and the start of the fire, Candice did her best to gently clean the sand and cinders from Chenda's hands and wrap them in bandages. She wiped the blood from Chenda's mouth and neck as the girl spoke of pulling the knife from her own side and plunging it into the neck of her attacker.

When she finished her story, Chenda leaned her head back against couch. The professor laid a cool, damp cloth over the bruised and swollen side of the young woman's face.

"Wow." Candice said weakly. "I mean...wow."

"I killed him," Chenda whispered. "I killed Daniel."

"No, honey." Candice stroked the side of Chenda's face that wasn't bloodied and swelling. "He died trying to kill you. An important distinction, I must say."

Chenda gave a disbelieving shrug, then winced. "I hurt all over."

"You need some rest," she said. With gentle hands, Candice helped Chenda to her feet and guided her into the bedroom. She pulled off Chenda's boots and covered the young woman with a blanket. Candice turned to tip-toe out as Chenda's eyes started to close.

"This doesn't change anything. We're still going." Chenda mumbled.

"I know," Candice replied, leaning against the bedroom doorframe. "We sure as hell can't stay here."

Chapter 5
THE DEAD WALK AWAY

It took all of one minute for Chenda to fall into a deep sleep. Candice watched her for a few moments more then headed into the living room to have a good think.

Candice long believed that occupying one's hands with menial tasks freed one's brain to pursue practical thoughts. As she sorted through the facts from Chenda's story, she set about putting her living room back together. She stacked the pillows and cushions back on the couch, then she pulled a trash can over to discard the bits of bloody bandage and tape. The smell of smoke that stuck to Chenda's hair and clothes lingered in the air. Candice picked up the flight coat from the coffee table and examined it, running her hand along the scorch marks on the back, and around the bloodstain inside, just under the left armpit. Chenda's blood.

"Someone up there must really be looking out for you, kid, because this could have been so much worse," Candice said to herself as waggled a finger through the knife hole. "We are in so much trouble."

Candice added up the facts – the poison in her office, the attack on Chenda, Edison's murder and the fact that every known holder of a Tugrulian pedradurite in the West was dead – and decided that staying in Coal City, or any part of Kite's Republic for that matter, was cold stupid. Both she and Chenda seemed targeted. It wasn't great, but their only choice was to flee from a rock to a hard place. Perhaps the only way out of this mess, for both of them, was through.

Candice sat on the threadbare couch for several minutes, fuming at Edison. It felt strange to accuse Edison of being both right and wrong to keep such vital information from his young wife. On the one hand, Edison fulfilled his role as a husband, shielding Chenda and protecting her for as long as possible. But, on the other hand, he had in no way prepared her to go forward. Why not equip her with the knowledge that she would need? It was blind luck that the girl hadn't died already.

Candice glanced at the clock. In a few hours, the two women would be boarding an airship, and Candice needed to take care of a few things. She decided to risk a journey out into the city and left a note for Chenda promising she would be right back. Silently, the professor slipped out the door.

As she passed the corner newsstand, Candice saw the headline of the early edition: **Frost Widow Dies in Fire**

She snatched up the pages and threw a coin at the vendor. She stood in the middle of the sidewalk reading the story:

Just two days after the funeral of her husband Edison Frost, the body of Mrs. Chenda Frost has been found in the remains of the couple's estate home just north of Coal City. The Frost mansion burned to the ground before dawn today.

Mrs. Frost's housekeeper Alme Taylor says that the lady of the house was in at the time of the fire, which, according to witnesses, originated in the area of the master bedroom. The remains found in that room are assumed to be hers. Officials believe the blaze may not have been accidental, and are currently investigating the....

Candice quit reading. Dead. Everybody thought Chenda was dead. Well, she thought, *almost* everybody assumed she was dead. Whoever hired Daniel was sure to suspect Chenda Frost was *alive* when he didn't come back with the stones.

Looking cautiously around, Candice tucked her newspaper under her arm and hustled off to gather the last of her supplies for the journey.

Chenda woke up screaming in Candice's bed. As she sat up, she traded the horror of her dream for the horror of her reality. She ached all over, and her hands were on fire. She stank. The odor of sweat, smoke and fear radiated from her. She was altogether disoriented. It took her a moment to recall she was in Candice's apartment. She slipped out of the bed, feeling the protest from all the strained muscles in her arms and back. When she was sure she wasn't too wobbly to walk, Chenda limped out into the small living room.

No Candice.

She worried for a moment until she found the note, and she looked around to see what time it was. Two o'clock. Candice couldn't be much longer if they were going to make it to the airship on time. Her friend would have to be home soon.

Chenda's stomach growled, so she wandered into the kitchen. She helped herself to a slice of bread and cheese, then sat down at Candice's tiny kitchen table. She took a small bite and quickly followed with several bigger ones. Hunger - Chenda couldn't recall the last time she had had an appetite. She went though several more slices, stopping only long enough to liberate some jam from the cabinet.

Despite the pain, Chenda found herself laughing at her situation; it was tricky opening a jam jar with both hands wrapped in bandages. Chenda persisted and her hard work paid off in boysenberries.

As she chewed, Chenda thought about the events of the night before, specifically about Daniel Frent. When she closed her eyes, she saw the scene as if she watched from across from across the room. She saw herself hating him and swinging the knife. His death came from her hands, just as her death was attempted by his. In a very sick way, she felt connected to Daniel through those mutual acts of oblivion. What she didn't feel was regret. There was no remorse, and no doubt. She would always carry the essence of Daniel Frent with her, and strangely that was acceptable, as he was no burden.

Brushing the crumbs off her torn and bloodstained blouse, Chenda noticed her awful smell again. She went down the narrow hall and found a scrupulously clean bathroom across from Candice's bedroom.

As Chenda filled the sink basin with water, she looked up into the mirror but didn't recognize the person who looked back. The entire left side of her face was swollen with patches of blotchy, dark purple. Daniel's final blow to her face must have burst a blood vessel in her eye; the light brown iris now floated in a sea of dark blood. Behind that remarkably unnerving eye and purple cheek, much of her long brown hair had burned away.

Her right side, however, survived the attack unmarked. The familiarity of the right accentuated the anomaly of the left. Chenda stared at herself for a while, closing one eye at a time, making sure the damage to her eye was merely cosmetic. She could still see just fine. She shrugged, picked up a washcloth, struggling to keep her bandaged mitts dry, and started to wash herself. The water felt cool on her fingertips, but the odor of burnt hair just wouldn't rinse away. She decided the only way to rid herself of the smell was to discard the remaining bits of her charred locks. She rummaged around the bathroom looking for scissors, which she found along with a straight razor. She sliced off a giant hank from the right side of her head and let it fall unceremoniously into the trash. She kept cutting all the way around until none of the scortched hair remained, then she worked on the shaping what was left of her hair. The flames hadn't left her much to work with. In the end, she worked her dark hair into a short wispy style that looked, she hoped, vaguely girlish.

It will have to do.

Chenda wandered back to Candice's room searching for something to wear. She kept her own quilted silk pants, but found a simple, clean shirt in the closet. She hoped it wasn't one of

Candice's favorites.

Chenda went back into the bathroom and dropped her torn and bloodstained blouse on top of her hair in the trash can. She took another long look in the mirror. Yesterday, she dressed like a delicate woman, in rhinestone studded shoes and fashionably long silk skirts appropriate for her years and social standing. Today, Chenda looked like an abused pixie, and a boy pixie at that.

Her hand drifted to her chest and she absentmindedly traced a finger over the bag of stones. It comforted her to know they were still there, secured under her shirt.

Candice's pristine bathroom looked like someone had done an autopsy in it. Chenda was doing her best to clean up the fallen hair and dirty towels when Candice returned.

"What do you think?" Chenda asked in greeting. She ran her hand through the sassy haircut.

"Not bad," Candice said, "for a corpse." Candice tossed the newspaper to Chenda, who read for a second and then looked up, shocked.

"I'm dead?"

"Seems so."

"Huh. Imagine that." Chenda dropped the paper into the trash. "Shall we go?"

"Fine by me."

Chenda pulled on her battered flight coat and the two women departed.

The Coal City Terminal Station pulsed with activity around the clock. Not just the tallest building in the city, it was the central point and interchange for all manner of conveyance: trains, trolleys, airships and pedestrian. Chenda and Candice arrived by trolley and dashed past the shops and kiosks to the lines forming before the grand elevators labeled **To the Airship Concourse**. Candice did most of the talking as the twosome passed though the building's layers of petty officials and security. When Candice played the boisterous professor, no one seemed to notice the name on the documents held by her meek assistant. Chenda's badly bruised face, however, garnered a few pitying stares.

After a few minutes ride in the ornate brass elevator, the

women arrived at the very top level and stepped into the center of a large, circular concourse. There were great glass windows in every direction. Down below, the city stretched out like a very detailed map, and a beautiful, cloudless sky surrounded them on all sides. Chenda, who had never had occasion to visit the top level of Terminal Station before, found the view breathtaking.

The docking points for airships – called airslips - formed a circle around the central hub of the elevators. Each slip had its own assembly area, with rows of chairs that faced outward. A set of beveled glass doors separated each waiting area from the narrow platform that ran beside each slip. Chenda and Candice walked quickly to slip 24, where a small slate indicated the next airship to occupy the space would be the *Brofman*. At the moment, however, the slip was empty.

A tall, broad shouldered man in a double breasted canvas vest, thick cotton shirt and black aeronaut boots stood alone in the assembly area, looking out over Coal City. He casually leaned one shoulder against the glass and occasionally glanced over his shoulder. When Chenda and the professor stopped in the assembly area, he took one last longing gaze at the city and then turned his attention away from the view. His face broke into an easy grin as he approached Candice, extending a hand.

"Professor Mortimer, yes?" he asked as they shook hands. "I'm Lieutenant Fenimore Dulal, first officer on the airship *Brofman*. Pleased to meet you."

"Call me Candice," she said with a nod. "This is my assistant, Chen," Candice continued, again sounding almost dismissive in an effort to draw no notice to Chenda.

His gray eyes sparkled under his sandy hair as he turned to Chenda, extending his hand toward her. For a fraction of a second, just as he looked into her face for the first time, his hand stopped moving forward and his eyes hardened with anger, and then softened again.

"A pleasure," Fenimore said as he gingerly took Chenda's bandaged hand, managing the smallest of shakes before releasing it.

"Well, it's almost five o'clock. Will we be departing on time?" Candice asked as she looked around the neighboring slips.

54

"Never fear," he said, "You can set your watch by Captain Endicott. He's never late and he never wastes time. He asked me to welcome you and assure you that all is well and running smoothly."

"Excellent," Candice said as she settled herself into one of the many chairs in the assembly area. Fenimore turned his attention toward Chenda.

"Chen is it?" he asked, politely, his eyes now calm and sparkling. His casual stance conveyed confidence and ease. Chenda nodded.

Fenimore went on, "I don't think you've been on an airship before, am I right?"

Chenda looked surprised. "How could you know that?" she asked.

"Well, you've not adjusted your flight coat to fit yet." He added conspiratorially, "That's the giveaway." He cocked his head to one side, "May I?" He reached a hand toward Chenda, who took a small leap backwards. His movement made her nervous.

"Whoa," he said in a soothing voice, "I'm not going to hurt you." He guessed now that her injuries weren't accidental. Someone had hurt her, deliberately, and very recently, too. He stepped backward as well, not wanting to frighten her further.

"Listen," he said, his voice soft and charming, "you will need to get your flight coat fitting properly before we go. You step on the deck flapping that much loose sail, you'll be blown right off the airship." As he spoke, he held his palms up to her in a gesture of surrender.

Chenda blushed, which brought a fresh wave of pain to the bruised side of her face. She felt foolish to have skittered away from someone offering a kindness. She dug down deep for some courage.

"Sorry," she said, stepping back toward Fenimore. "A little help is always welcome." Using the remainder of her moxie, she looked him in the face and tried to return his smile. It made her face ache. She held her arms out slightly, an invitation for Fenimore to begin.

"This will just take a second," he said as he started to

adjust the various straps and hidden buckles on her flight coat. His hands moved quickly and gently, fitting the coat snugly to her, turning her in a complete circle as he worked. She never caught his slight pause as he noted the bloodstained hole under her arm. It seemed to Chenda that he took special care not to jerk on any of the straps or touch her body in any way. She appreciated that he was being considerate of her injuries, or perhaps he was just being discreet.

"There now. Take a look." He turned her toward a wall covered in shiny chrome, and Chenda took in her reflection.

"Ah. I guess this thing fits after all. I really thought Lilianthal's had made a mistake sending this size." She smiled at him again. "Thank you."

"You look ready to fly," Fenimore said with approval. "Just in time, too. Here comes the *Brofman*."

Chenda turned, eager to see the approaching airship as it glided toward the terminal. The *Brofman* floated majestically through the open air. The hull was sleek and shimmery, like a flying fish. A beautiful wooden railing ran the perimeter of the main deck . Just below it, rows of propellers lined the sides of the *Brofman*, whirling and pivoting, ever making corrections to the airship's course. From the center of the deck rose a glass fronted wheelhouse, where Chenda could just make out the muscular outline of Captain Endicott and another man. The ship was compact, perhaps just twice the length of the city trolley, but the grace of the *Brofman* made Chenda's breath quicken.

Fenimore watched Chenda admire the ship. "I see that you have an eye for a beautiful cruiser. Do you know much about airships?"

"Not really," she said. Despite being the wife and daughter of senior airship officers, she had never seen an airship up close. Edison's stories were mostly about the places he'd been or the people who served with him, not so much about the ships themselves.

"Well, there's much to tell. At this point, it's probably safe to say that the airship is both the pinnacle of the Republic's achievements and it's most fervent disaster," he said.

"I don't think I follow you," Chenda said, watching the

Brofman glide ever closer.

"You know that airships are responsible for the Tugrulian War, don't you?"

"I thought the airships were responsible for *saving* the Republic by defending the coast during the war."

Fenimore nodded. "True, but you have to go back to the beginning of the Republic to totally understand. When Anthony Kite started to research Cyanophyta Saralyndia, a type of blue green algae that creates massive amounts of electricity under certain conditions, he revolutionized energy on the western side of the Kohlian Sea. Kite developed the optimal formula for sustaining the algae and the process for harvesting the energy. His *Aqueous Photovoltaics* enabled people here in the West to generate power where they needed it, or even on the go. You've studied this part of history, right?"

"Sure," Candice said, "who hasn't heard of the founding father of the Republic? I can see why people decided to rally around him. He was the greatest mind of his time. I don't want to sound like my history tutors, but forming a new kind of government may have topped his electric algae discoveries."

Fenimore smiled at Chenda's *electric algae* reference as he continued. "It's a little more complicated than that. See, the research and the ideology go hand in hand. Kite's research subtly affected life in the West. Almost immediately, the availability of nearly unlimited energy led to a dramatic increase in electromechanical inventions. As labor saving devices abounded, new forms of art, architecture, literature and music grew. When Anthony Kite became the first Prime Minister of the Republic of Western States, his new and cultured society began to advance faster than the rest of the world.

"As the West became more interested in self reflection, science and art, contact with the less evolved continents fell away. This strained the already unstable regions of the East. The tribal societies there increased the warring amongst themselves, squabbling over their various resources. The Eastern Kingdoms fought with one another for almost 100 years until finally one society dominated the region: the Tugrulians. "You still with me?" he asked.

She nodded.

"When Kotal Varinian, the leader of Tugrulians, proclaimed himself Emperor, he cut off any visitors from the West. Any explorers or traders who attempted to make contact with the Empire were murdered on sight. Then the Emperor would have the bodies of the dead Kiters packed onto their own ships and set 'em adrift on the Kohlian Sea. People took the hint after a few years and quit going east."

Fenimore stopped abruptly. "How old are you?" he asked.

"Twenty-two," she said."Why?"

"Well, about a dozen years before you were born," he continued, "Prime Minister Mabe Idadell sent a scientific delegation across the sea to establish contact in the Empire. Idadell sent the envoy on one of the Republic's newest inventions, the airship. The flying vessel really captured the imagination of Emperor Varin IV. He began to crave the advanced technology from the Republic, and opened limited trade within the capitol city of Kotal to Kiter merchants.

"It soon became apparent that most Kiters and Tugrulians were never going to see eye to eye. We're just too different ideologically. However, there were a few Tugrulians that began to question the way the Emperor kept such a tight leash on his people, and there was talk of change in the Empire. The Emperor panicked and denounced the Kiters for theological reasons. He mobilized his massive army to slaughter every Citizen of Kite's Republic within the borders of the Tugrulian Empire. The Emperor, still craving the inventions of Kite's Republic, began to send spies and raiding parties across the sea.

"You know the rest of the story from there, I'm sure," he concluded.

"The start of the war," Chenda said sadly. "I was just a baby then, so I can hardly recall."

"Well, I remember it a little," Fenimore reflected. "I was five when the first attacks came. The truce came just before I was old enough to join the R.A.S."

"Can you tell me more about the Tugrulians, Lieutenant?"

"Sure I can, lots. But it will have to be at another time," he said. The *Brofman* floated just a few yards out from the slip now, and Fenimore moved toward the glass doors and out onto the platform.

"Call me Fenimore, by the way," he called over his shoulder.

Chenda followed him onto the platform and looked up at the deck of the *Brofman* where Captain Endicott rested one foot on the railing of his airship. He threw a mooring line to Fenimore, who quickly secured the airship to the pier.

Candice joined Chenda as the captain smiled broadly and waved. He glanced at Chenda and shouted down to her, "Well, *you've* had a rough day haven't you? I hardly recognize you."

His eyes landed on Candice. "Hello, Professor. You two climb on up here and bring my money."

Chapter 6
THE CREW OF THE AIRSHIP *BROFMAN*

Fenimore Dulal took the bags from Chenda and Candice and tossed them onto the deck of the *Brofman*. He backed up two steps, made a running leap, and jumped off the pier. His hands caught the ship's railing, and he flipped himself onto the deck with apparent ease. Fenimore flipped a lever on the railing and a gangway unfolded from the airship and rested at Candice's feet.

"All aboard," the captain said with more than a bit of pride in his voice.

Candice smiled broadly and went aboard with Chenda following close behind.

"Wonderful to see you again, captain, but let's talk again about when *my* money becomes your money, shall we?" The captain took her hand and, with a flourish, placed it on his elbow, leading her along the deck railing toward the wheelhouse.

As the jovial debate between the captain and the professor continued, Fenimore stepped to Chenda's side. He did not make the same overly dramatic gesture of whisking her away, arm in arm. He merely smiled at her, keeping his hands at his sides, and said, "We'll be heading out in a few minutes. Let me show you where you can settle in." He led her to the very center of the deck and down a flight of narrow stairs. At the bottom was a corridor that ran the length of the ship. Fenimore waved his hand toward the bow of the ship. "You'll want to stick to this side of the stairs. The area aft is for cargo and the motor room. Nothing for you there."

He moved forward, pointing to a narrow door on the left. "Captain's quarters," he said, then turned to a matching door to his right. "Guest berth -- for the professor." Fenimore opened the door and placed Candice's bag within; the space looked

61

impossibly small. One tiny bed ran the length of the opposite wall. A tiny porthole above the bed let in some natural light that shined on the rest of the room's simple features: several brass hooks, a small sink basin with a drain, and a little table which folded down, hardly bigger than a shelf. The room definitely was only big enough for one occupant.

Fenimore closed the door and walked farther down the passageway to the next and last pair of openings. These, however, had no doors. Pointing to the left, Fenimore said, "The galley," then the right, "and the crew quarters. You'll be bunking with the crew." He stepped in with her bag. Chenda's eyes grew wide with surprise.

"Don't worry. The fellas don't bite," he said thoughtfully. "Well, not usually."

He looked sheepish for a moment. "I'm sorry if this seems a bit untoward, but we are generally pretty good guys, despite our line of work. We get hired to do a lot of unusual jobs. Mostly, we deal with peculiar cargoes, and we all know how to be discreet. We are good at what we do, and on the rare occasions when we entertain passengers, we try our best to be hospitable." He looked into her much-abused face. "Chen, you'll be safe among us."

Chenda bowed her head, not knowing what to say.

"The captain hasn't told us much about where we will be taking you and the professor..." Fenimore left the thought hanging, looking hopeful that Chenda would fill in the rest.

She didn't.

Chenda looked around at the crew quarters. Eight bunks divided into two stacks covered the whole of the far wall. The inside wall of the cabin held eight lockers. Each door had a name neatly printed on it, save one. Chenda read them to herself: *Dulal, Verdu, Kingston, Germer, Stanley, Spencer* and *Lincoln*.

She ran her fingers over the little door without a name. "Mine?" she asked.

"Yes," Fenimore said as he put her bag down next to it. "And this bunk as well," he said, tuning to point at the bottommost bunk farthest from the door. Chenda squatted down and examined the small space. The mattress was thin but clean, and she noted two small hooks hanging above the pillow, but there was nothing else to note in the coffin-sized berth. She was confident she could fit in that little slot of a bed, but wondered how a man as tall as Fenimore managed.

Standing again, she turned to him. "Looks great," she lied.

Fenimore looked relieved that Chenda accepted her accommodations. Relaxing, he leaned on the post separating the two stacks of bunks.

"Let's see," Fenimore contemplated as he ran his fingers through his sandy hair. "There are several things that you need to know. First of all, it's going to be cold once we shove off and gain some altitude, so you'll want to stay bundled up in your flight coat most of the time – we don't waste power on heat. You're welcome to move about the crew quarters as you like, and the galley, too, but you need an escort for any of the other areas below decks. If you step on the main deck, you will need to *bitter-end*; I'll explain that later."

Fenimore stepped over to his own locker, pulled out a flight coat and shrugged it onto his broad shoulders. He turned back to Chenda, saying, "You have to understand that we move pretty quick up here, and the crew has the right-of-way, so keep an eye out for them and stay out of the way. Understand?"

"For the most part," Chenda replied.

A series of whistles drifted through the ship and Fenimore said, "Time for me to go on deck." He moved toward the door, then paused. "Want to come up as we shove off?"

"Do I ever!" Chenda said excitedly as she followed him back into the corridor and up the stairs.

When they reached the top, Chenda looked around and could see Candice standing beside the captain in the wheelhouse. She took a step toward her companion, but Fenimore grabbed Chenda by the elbow. "Not so fast," he said, and he picked up a small metal box with a clip hook on each side. "This is a *bitter-end*," he said. "It's non-negotiable. You come up onto the deck, you put it on. No exceptions."

He took one of the clips in his large hand and pulled on it, revealing a thin cable. He latched the hook into a stout loop in Chenda's flight coat, then pulled the metal box down and attached the other clip to a ring set into a track imbedded in the deck.

"The box has a spring in it; that keeps the slack out of the safety cable, which slides in this track. You can pretty much walk all over the deck. If someone wants to get past you on the track, one of you will have to pull your cable into a bypass – those are all along the track. Passing etiquette follows rank here: the lower man drifts. In your case, everyone else has the right of way, so you need to step to the side if someone is coming your way and be quick about it."

He tapped on the bitter-end box. "This will keep you safe up here. You'll get used to it pretty quick." Fenimore reached down and attached his own bitter-end to the track.

"I'm really not so clumsy as to just fall over the side," Chenda remarked.

"It's not about clumsy up here," Fenimore gave her a very serious stare. "Between the rolling air current caused by the speed of the ship, and the strong gusts of actual wind from the atmosphere, it's pretty unstable up here. I've seen men twice your size get blown off the deck in a sudden draft. That cable is the only thing that will save you from falling ten-thousand feet to your death."

Looking over the side, Chenda said. "Ah, I see now why you call it the bitter-end." When she looked back up, Fenimore was gone. She saw him amongst the other members of the crew who were taking in mooring lines and preparing the airship to depart. She watched as all the men leaped out of Fenimore's way as he walked near them. The crew moved around each other in an impressive dance. She could see the crew worked like a well-oiled machine.

Another series of highpitched whistles sounded, and the airship shuddered lightly as it began to move away from the airslip. Chenda held her breath. This was it. The point of no return. Panic crept through her as the ship inched forward.

She looked over the side of the *Brofman* and down into Coal City. She'd lived half her young life down there, just outside that bustling and cultured city, and in all that time, she hadn't ventured more than ten miles from there or from Edison. Leaving the city felt like leaving her husband behind. From this point on, everything would be different, a new experience. Chenda's fears grabbed her and she clamped her teeth together to prevent the screaming in her head from coming out of her mouth. She found her hands were gripping the railing so tightly that they were numb, her feet locked to the boards on which she stood.

The *Brofman* moved faster, heading east. Chenda stood there, alone and afraid. No one was there to take care of her. No one could help her cope with her fears. Her knees began to shake, and Chenda started to fight against the quaking, but the struggle seemed only to rattle her bones all the more. As the *Brofman* advanced, the tears in Chenda's eyes spilled out onto her cheeks. Each tear rolled out and was quickly blown away. The wind grabbed at her, pulling her arms, hair and chest.. She wrestled with the pain and fought to control it. The wind pulled at it, too, working against her, trying to drag it all up to the surface.

More tears. More pain. More wind.

When the struggle to contain it became too much, she gave up. Chenda let the wind take what it wanted from her. In letting go of her baser emotions, she found a kernel of strength. Chenda pulled her hands free from the railing, and she leaned into the wind. More regret and anguish for Edison bubbled up, and then blew away. Chenda took a step forward. The airship moved faster. The wind grew stronger. She pulled up worry and dejection, and tossed them toward the greedy air. She took more steps into the gale.

She raced forward to the bow of the airship, her eyes flowing with tears for Edison. Every drop of her grief flew away as she gazed into the open sky ahead of her. She opened her mouth to wail, and the wind reached inside and stole the lament from her. The swirling air pulled at all of her senses then; she tasted it and smelled it until all other memories of scent and flavor left her. The wind bored into her ears, and it was as if no sound had ever been heard before its roar. Most keenly, she felt the constant brush and pressure of the wind on the exposed skin of her face and fingertips, cold and abrasive. On some level, the beating she had taken from Daniel had been gentler.

Soon Chenda felt her eyes stop overflowing with tears. She had run dry of all emotion and felt hollow, but in a hopeful way, anticipatory. Now that she was empty, she knew it was only a matter of time before she started to fill again. The void within was uncomfortable, longing to be filled, but the idea of something, anything, replenishing her soul thrilled her. The empty space felt like a promise. The grief had moved aside, or at least it had started to, and the hole waited there, expectantly, excitedly, for whatever would come next.

In possession of hope, Chenda was content to stand there, looking over the bow of the ship as the miles quickly crept past in the coldness. The *Brofman* would occasionally rock as a sudden surge of wind would nudge it – a feeling Chenda rather liked. She could feel a living presence from the ship and it galloped through the open air.

Into the evening she stood there, watching the rolling countryside east of Coal City slowly flatten. The trees far below became tall and spindly. The horizon ahead faded from bright blue, to silvery gray, to purple as the sun sank behind her.

Chenda heard the captain's voice calling from the wheelhouse. "Dulal! We're passing Musser Point. Go tell Verdu down in the motor room that he's sprung, and then get back here to take over!"

She turned around to see Fenimore walking away from her toward the call of his captain. How long had he been standing behind her, she wondered. She watched him as he lifted a hatch near the rear of the ship and yelled to someone belowdecks. Dropping the hatch again, he trotted back toward the bow and stepped into the narrow wheelhouse. He took the captain's place at the wheel.

Captain Endicott, holding Candice by one elbow, helped her toward the stairs that went below decks. She didn't look so good. Her skin had a green cast to it. Chenda rushed to her friend's side.

"Ugh," Candice said in greeting. "Now I remember why I hate airships."

"Oh, my, Candice, are you going to be okay?" Chenda asked.

"Oh, Chen, I'll be fine in a few hours, I always get this queasy feeling when I fly. Don't worry, I'll just go put my head down in my cabin and whimper till I feel better. Mostly, at times like these, I just need to be alone with my own wretchedness. You seem to be just fine, so enjoy the view for a while."

The captain unhooked Candice's bitter-end and muttered, "OK, Professor, down you go. Just don't go barfing in my ship if you can help it. That's a good girl." He led her down the stairs and toward her cabin.

Chenda turned to the wheelhouse and climbed the few steps to the door. She knocked, and Fenimore pushed the door open. "Do come in," he said.

The wheelhouse was smaller than a broom cupboard. Its main feature, of course, was the large wheel used to steer the airship, but the small space also gleamed with dozens of shiny brass dials, levers, neatly labeled switches and knobs. Fenimore gently leaned against the back of the small space and rested his hands on the helm. He looked through the glass in front of him, watching the light fade in the sky ahead.

"You love it, don't you?" he said.

Chenda, surprised and a little confused, stared blankly at the tall man next to her. She didn't reply.

Fenimore went on, "People have two reactions when they fly on an airship for the first time. Most folks have a variation on the professor's reaction. They hunker down and just get through it as best as they can. Or, as in her case, they puke."

"Oh, no. Poor Candice!"

"It happens, but I can tell you, the captain really hates it when people barf on his ship." He snickered a little. He caught Chenda's disapproving gaze and said, "I only get to laugh because I don't have to clean it up. Rank has its privileges." He smiled again and continued.

"And, rarely, there are people like you who *feel* something." He made a vague yet meaningful gesture over his chest. "Flight is a powerful experience for some lucky few, a changing experience. Do you mind if I ask what just changed for you?"

"Nearly everything," she replied. Fenimore looked at her once again, waiting for her to supply more details, but Chenda felt no compulsion to speak about her emptying sensation. The fact that he saw that *something* was happening to her spirit embarrassed her somehow. She started to feel as if he had intruded into something very personal and private. It annoyed her.

"How long did you stand there staring at me?" she demanded, her voice taking on an uncharacteristic edge.

"Weeelll," Fenimore responded, "I stood behind you for about a half hour or so, but to be fair, you *were* standing in my spot."

Chenda felt suddenly foolish. "I apologize. I never wanted to interfere with anyone's duties. Just tell me to 'shoo' if I am in the way." She bit her lip.

"Eh, it's not that important. I just need to keep an eye out for certain points for navigation so we can head out over open water in the right place. Speaking of, we're nearly to the coast."

Chenda looked out of the wheelhouse and across the bow to see the approaching shore. All her annoyance left her. She'd never seen the ocean before, and she was excited. As she watched, she felt the airship begin to slow. With worried eyes, she turned to Fenimore.

"What's wrong?"

"Nothing," he said, flipping several switches on the instrument panel in front of him and turning several dials. "It's dark, so we're powering down."

"Oh." Chenda still looked very confused.

The door to the wheelhouse opened, and a very young and rather spotty face poked in. "Captain said I should relieve you now."

"Lincoln, meet Chen, Professor Mortimer's assistant. Chen, this is one of our deckhands and sometime engineer's apprentice, Lincoln."

The thin, boyish creature who appeared to be made entirely of knees and elbows stepped into the wheelhouse. "Nice to meet you," he said as he extended a hand to Chenda. She unthinkingly reached back. He gripped her hand and shook it vigorously, which made Chenda yelp. Looking horrified, Lincoln dropped her hand and shuddered backwards.

"Oh, I'm so sorry, miss," Lincoln said.

"It's fine." Chenda said, recovering. She folded her

bandaged hands together over her chest "My fingers got so cold I almost forgot that my hands are burned." She looked down at her bandages, noticing how dirty they'd become, and how the exposed tips of her fingers were chapped and red.

"Oh, burns," Lincoln said sympathetically. "You best go see Kingston. He'll work some of his medical magic on them fingers. Get you better right quick."

Fenimore spoke up, "That's a great idea. I'm getting hungry, too. Kingston is in the galley?"

"Yes, sir."

"Great, well, she's all yours. Just let her drift till she runs out of force. Then just keep us stationary. See you at four bells."

"Yes, sir. Let her drift."

Fenimore motioned for Chenda to step out of the wheelhouse ahead of him, and he followed quickly.

"I don't understand why we aren't flying over the sea tonight." Chenda said, trying to keep her impatience in check.

"We generally don't fly at night. It's not wise," he said. "Walk with me around this way and I'll explain." He changed direction and headed to a raised area of the deck behind the wheelhouse. He reached up and patted one of a dozen or so glass cylinders over his head that were about eight-feet long and a foot wide. Dozens of wires and tubes ran into and out of each cylinder, and a faint yellowish-orange glow seeped from the very center of each tube.

"You've seen these before, right?" he asked.

Chenda nodded. "Aqueous photovoltaic cells."

"Right," he said, "And down here is the battery." He tapped at the raised platform at his feet. "On a nice sunny day we generate about twice as much energy as we need and store the rest of the juice right here to use overnight." His fingers stroked the cell as if it were a pet. "During the day, in any given hour, it takes about 8% of the energy we generate to keep us up in the air. Not moving – just up. During the night, we don't generate much power, so we can't use more than 10% of our battery reserves per hour. We could fly at quarter speed all night or we could make a few short bursts of speed, but by dawn, we would be almost out of energy, and then if we had a heavily cloudy day, or if we lost a cell, well, that could be disastrous. So, the basic protocol is that we reduce our power consumption at night by hovering or docking. Get it?"

"I understand." Chenda said. "You are remarkably patient to explain this to me. Thank you."

"And you're very polite," Fenimore replied. "Now, let's see how well Kingston is using some of that nighttime energy in the galley. Hungry?" he said.

"Starved," Chenda replied.

Fenimore and Chenda walked back to the stairs leading belowdecks and unhooked themselves from the safety lines. The smell of hot food from the galley drifted up as the pair headed down. As Chenda passed Candice's door, she paused and knocked gently. Fenimore continued down the narrow passage.

"Candice, are you all right?"

"Blarrb... go away!" Candice shouted weakly through the door.

"OK. Sorry. I am going to be in the galley getting some dinner. If you need me, just shout or something."

"Ugh, don't mention food. Go away."

Chenda sighed, feeling truly sorry for her friend, and continued on to the galley.

The jovial crew filled the small space almost completely. They laughed and jostled around the narrow table, passing bowls of hot stew and plates of cheese and bread. The atmosphere of fellowship enticed just as much as the heavenly scent of seasoned beef and potatoes.

The captain, sitting at the head of the crowded table, noticed Chenda in the door and waved her in. "One seat left," he said. "You'd best sit down and start grabbing, or you'll be left hungry. These men won't let much come between them and their grub."

"Certainly not table manners or a napkin," said Fenimore, who grabbed a slab of cheese off a plate passing by him.

Chenda took the empty chair in the middle of the table, and gazed into an appetizing bowl of soup. After an awkward minute, she managed to lace a spoon through her stiff fingers and started to eat with gusto. Fenimore allowed her several good bites and then made introductions.

"Chen, this is our engineer, Germer, and his apprentice, Stanley." Fenimore indicated the two men to Chenda's right. The older man, Germer, sat closest to her and smiled through his bushy brown mustache. Stanley, one seat farther down, looked a lot like an orange-haired version of Lincoln: young, gangly, spotted and eager to please. He made a little wave as he stretched a long arm across the table to stab another piece of bread.

"Over here is Kingston, our chemist and, oh-so-valued cook," Fenimore gestured to the man sitting to her left, between her and the captain.

"A pleasure to meet you," Kingston said,."I'm glad you have a good appetite."

"It's delicious," Chenda said as she scooped in more soup. Kingston's round cheeks jiggled as he nodded his approval.

Fenimore's gaze led Chenda's eyes around past the captain to a tiny fellow with mousy hair and pale blue eyes. "This is our other deckhand, Spencer." The young man made a nervous smile at Chenda, then quickly turned his face toward his plate, where he proceeded to push his small pieces of cheese in a circle. Spencer exuded nervousness.

The last person at the table sat next to Fenimore, his dark eyes examining every detail of Chenda. Upon reflection, Chenda decided that *next to* didn't capture the way the chiseled and darkly featured fellow positioned himself beside Fenimore. *Up against* began to capture the attitude of the swarthy man. The two were congruous and complementary in all ways. As Fenimore moved, the man beside him filled the void. As the first breathed out, the other breathed in. The presence of the two together created a bizarre kind of oneness.

Fenimore's voice distracted Chenda from her observations. "This, Chen, is the *second* officer, Kotal Verdu." There was a teasing smirk on Fenimore's lips. The darker man, easily as big as Fenimore, shot a venomous glance at his neighbor.

"As if *second* means much here, Fen. You know that I pilot better than you, and am twice as good in a fight," he growled, his voice revealing a slight, jagged accent. His tone was betrayed by the sparkle in his eye as he elbowed Fenimore in the ribs.

"True, brother," he acquiesced with a smile. Fenimore turned his head once more to Chenda. "First or second, it hardly matters, as Verdu is my very best friend, and we are partners in just about everything."

Chenda felt a blush come to her skin and she was not sure why. She could see a bond between these two men, but she wasn't sure she understood it, and that, strangely, was enough to embarrass her. She bit her lip for a moment, then resorted to a habit she did understand: being polite.

"Nice to meet you, Kotal Verdu."

"Likewise," he said, "but most folks just call me Verdu."

Now curious, she asked, "Kotal, that's an unusual first name, yes? I don't know that I've ever met anyone who shared a first name with the capitol city of the Tugrulian Empire."

Verdu's lips pressed into a sharp line, and Fenimore answered for him, "That's 'cause he was born there. He's Tugrulian."

Chapter 7
A STICK IN THE EYE

Verdu shoved Fenimore slightly with one hip. "You could have lived your whole life and kept that to yourself, Fen. Look at the poor girl; you've frightened her."

The pair moved in tandem again, coming to rest with their elbows on the table, side by side, their arms just touching. "I believe your being a demon spawn of the Empire is what frightens people, not my *saying* it." Fenimore replied.

Chenda sat with her mouth open, her spoon frozen halfway to her lips. Her eyes shifted between the two men, looking for the joke. Finding none, she searched the faces of the other crewmen around the table. Every pair of eyes gazed at her, waiting on her reaction. She had none. Chenda sat motionless.

The captain pushed back his chair. "Thanks for making introductions, Dulal." He said. "Germer, Stanley, Spencer, we've got some work to do in the motor room tonight. No time like the present." He stood up and strode toward the door and disappeared down the passageway. Germer obediently stood and followed the captain while the two younger men made last grabs for the remaining bread and cheese, then trotted out of the galley, chewing noisily.

Chenda returned her spoon to the bowl and closed her gaping maw. She couldn't think of anything to say, so she just watched Verdu. She'd never seen a Tugrulian before, but knew from so many childhood stories that they were supposed to be unpredictable, brutal people. For years, all Tugrulians had been banned from the Republic. But the Empire continually sent spies and saboteurs. Yet here sat the Tugrulian, welcome at the table of this crew and placed in a position of authority on an airship. He was right about her; she was frightened. She was becoming, however, more confused. She wanted the dark man to keep talking, hoping some judgment about him would come to her.

"What's the Empire like?" she asked.

"Vile," he said with a mirthless grin.

Kingston started to clear away the dishes and sang as he worked. His voice rang rich and throaty against the pots and platters hanging in the small galley. The sound of water running into a sink mixed with Kingston's song in a soothing, homey way.

Fenimore and Verdu, moving as one, leaned back against a bulkhead and listened to the cook's melody. At first Chenda tried to convince herself that it was just a coincidence that Fenimore and Verdu were trading breaths again, one inhaling as the other exhaled, but after a moment, they started blinking at the same time, too.

"OK, that's creepy." Chenda said to herself, and then realized in horror that she'd spoken aloud.

Fenimore looked at her curiously. "What's creepy?"

Chenda died a little bit inside because of her own rudeness. "I'm so sorry," she said. "I've never seen any two people share a space the way you do."

Fenimore and Verdu looked at each other and then back at Chenda, who babbled on, "How do you do that? Mirroring and intersecting the way you do?"

"Sorry," Fenimore said. "We don't follow you."

Verdu turned to Fenimore, "Whatever does she mean?"

Chenda bit her lip. "Honestly? You have no idea? I can't be the only one that sees it. Or maybe I don't see it. Yes. I must be mistaken."

Kingston shouted from beside the sink. "For the gods' sakes, would you let the child off the stinkin' hook, you monsters!"

Fenimore and Verdu's faces cracked into matching smiles and they laughed at Chenda's discomfort. They were quite different and yet remarkably similar. Verdu's dark features looked fierce, where Fenimore's tender appearance signaled grace. Dark echoed light. Smoldering brown mirrored bright smoky gray.

Verdu answered for the pair, "Shame on us for teasing you. We know we do it, we just can't figure out *how* we do it. It's been this way since I came on the ship five years ago. Any time we are in the same room, we balance. We sort of operate as if we have one mind. And, yes, it is a little creepy, but we cope."

"Mostly because fighting the tandem turned out to be very messy." Fenimore answered. "We spilled things and fell down a lot."

"Fascinating," Chenda said.

"Ain't it just?" Kingston said as he came back to the table with a damp rag and began to scrub the pale wood clean. "It becomes less fascinating after a bit, and don't play cards with 'em. They cheat."

Fenimore leaned toward Kingston, and Verdu's body followed his friend's.

"If we get the medic kit," Fenimore asked, "do you think you can take a look at Chen's hands? She's got some burns there."

Kingston glanced down at Chenda's dirty bandages and made a disapproving face. "Of course, but you all sit. I'll be right back directly with what I'll be needin'." He slipped out the door.

Verdu assessed Chenda's unease and said, "There were truths and lies in my friend's introduction of me, but there are usually two truths and a lie in most of the words people say. I was born in Kotal, but I am about as Tugrulian as you are. And my name, Kotal, is not for the Imperial City, but for my Great-Great-Great Grandfather, The First Emperor Kotal Verinian. But since I find the whole business of being Tugrulian distasteful, I just call myself Verdu."

"That's -- a lot of truth." Chenda said.

Fenimore added, "He's not a citizen of the Republic either, that's why he's *second* around here. He can't show his face above decks when we dock in the West. But he's twice the airman I am, and that is the truth."

Verdu shrugged a little in agreement, and Chenda saw a slighter, echoing shrug in Fenimore's own frame. The phenomenon started to amuse her and she giggled.

Fenimore looked her over and said thoughtfully, "I think

75

it's time you told us about your truths and your lies, Chen, and start with why we aren't calling you Chenda Frost."

Chenda froze, her eyes wide. Not wanting to answer directly, and hoping to stall until she decided what to say, she asked, "How did you know who I am?"

"I picked your pocket in the wheelhouse and read your travel documents," he said shamelessly, pulling her papers out of his own pocket and holding them in the air. "But I read the papers at the terminal yesterday. They all say the woman named Chenda Frost is dead, died in a fire. Whereas you fit the description of the deceased, and you look *half* dead, I reasoned you must be Chenda Frost. No?"

Chenda nodded.

Verdu narrowed his eyes and looked at Fenimore. "Oh, brother, are we in over our heads again?"

"It's hard to say." Fenimore said again. "I'll wager five that we are."

Verdu observed Chenda. He tilted his head to one side, which tilted Fenimore's as well, and said, "No bet. She's got the look of a votary about her. We're certainly in trouble."

"Oh, Verdu, poor form," Fenimore tsked. "Let the lady tell us herself what she's about."

Two pairs of eyes, gentle but expectant, settled on Chenda. "I don't know what to say," she whispered. "I don't know what I *should* say."

"We're not the law, and we're not confessors set to judge you or absolve you. Our interest is mere curiosity. We just want to know why you've come to the *Brofman*," Verdu replied plainly. "And what level of danger we can expect."

"Let's start with your face," Fenimore offered. "Who roughed you up?"

Chenda pulled her knees up to her chest, trying to take up as little space as possible. She felt exposed, but decided to answer honestly. "Ah, that's an easy question. The man who murdered my husband. Turns out he was a thief as well, and broke into my bedroom, looking to steal something from my husband's things. He attempted to kill me." Chenda looked each man in the eye, "He died trying." Her gaze made it clear that there would be no more conversation on that subject.

Fenimore, and by extension, Verdu, looked surprised. "I see. The body in the fire was his. But why let everyone assume you had died in the house? If what you say is true, why didn't you come forward?"

"Candice and I think that Daniel, the man who attacked me, wasn't working alone. Someone has been trying to kill us for a couple of days now." Chenda rested her chin on her knee. "The newspapers in Coal City may say I'm dead, but it's only a matter of time before someone figures out I'm still breathing. If someone was watching Daniel closely, or my house, they already know."

Now that Chenda was talking, the words flowed out. "It's kind of liberating, having someone try to kill you. Or maybe it's just that my options are now *keep moving* or *die trying*. I was always so scared before. I didn't fit in with the orphans I grew up with. I was always too shy with the holy sisters. I did what I was told and followed all the rules. I don't think it helped me to be a whole person."

Chenda looked at Verdu. "Your guess about me was right – I am fervently devoted to my mission, and may the gods save anyone who tries to stop me."

Kingston's voice drifted in from the corridor. He switched from singing a bawdy song to whistling as he entered the galley and plopped his ample self into the chair next to Chenda. Under his arm, he had a large canvas sack.

"Let's take a look-see, eh?" He plunked the bag on the table and rummaged around it, pulling out a few rolls of bandages, scissors, tweezers and several small, blue medicine bottles. Chenda presented her bandaged hands to the rotund and jolly cook. Whistling again, he began to unwrap the dirty strips, first from her right hand and then from the left. He examined each hand closely, using the tweezers to pull off any stray bits of lint or dirt.

"Hmm..." he mused.

"What?" Fenimore demanded. "That 'hmm' sounded serious. Can you help her?"

"Sure," he said looking at Chenda, "But your fingers are swelling a good bit. I'm worried about permanent damage or infection in that left hand. That ring is gonna have to come off, miss." He pulled a large pair of cutters from the canvas bag. "I'm sorry about this."

All the little bits of Edison are flying away from me...

Chenda considered how much she had lost in the last ten days. The physical things didn't trouble her much. For as much as she liked to shop and bring things home to Edison, the trinkets meant little. Easily bought and easily forgotten. It was the time with her husband that was the real treasure, and that was gone for good.

She wasn't particularly sad that the house had burned, either. The estate and Edison were inseparably linked in her mind. Her life at home was a happy one, but his absence from those intimate spaces perverted the place. Every corner of the house haunted her. Her sole regret was losing her only picture of Edison to the flames. Her memory of him would have to sustain her for the rest of her life.

Finally, it came down to the ring, the last symbol of their union in marriage. It too would go. Chenda said, "Well, I guess you better get on with it then." Her voice broke.

Till death us do part....

Kingston turned Chenda's palm face down and slid the bottom blade of the nippers under the wedding ring. He pressed down hard, and with a small ping, the ring was cut. Kingston reached for a small pair of pliers and widened the gap in the fine gold band enough to let it slide off her finger. The sight of the mangled ring saddened Chenda, but she endured it. Kingston applied a liquid to her hands that stung the raw skin. She sucked air in through her teeth.

"Easy, lass. It will settle in a minute." Kingston reassured her. "Let this dry for a few minutes and then we'll apply a new dressing to your wee paws."

He reached forward and placed one of his big hands on her chin, turning it to better examine her injuries. "Your cheek won't need any salve from me. The bruising will fade in three days at the most, but that eye," he pulled her lower lid down with a rough thumb, looking at the blood trapped around her brown iris, "that will take more than a few weeks to heal on its own. It's going to draw a lot of attention. I could help you with that, if you like."

"That would be nice. I hardly recognize myself."

"For this procedure, I am going to need an assistant. Which of these two yahoos do you want holding you still while I poke you in the eye?" he asked.

Chenda imagined, in the history of the whole world, no one had ever uttered such a string of words. "Either," she answered, but added with a giggle, "which, in their case, probably means both."

Fenimore grinned and said, "I guess I volunteer."

Kingston pulled a chair behind Chenda. "OK, Dulal, sit here. Try your best to listen up and follow along. Put your feet flat on the floor, and then set your elbows on your knees." Fenimore did as he was told and Kingston grunted approval. "Now," he continued, "hold your wrists together and make a U shape with your hands. Good, just like that."

He turned to Chenda. "Just lean back, miss." He placed a big hand on her forehead and guided her head backwards into Fenimore's waiting hands. "This might pinch a bit at some point, but it's important that you stay very still, and leave that peeper open. I'll be dropping some liquid into that eye, every now and again to keep it moist and numb, so don't worry too much."

"Wait," Chenda gulped, "What exactly are we going to be doing?"

Kingston held a syringe over Chenda's eyes. "That bloody mess in there is called a subconjunctival haemorrhage. In here is a micro cell retriever -- basically a tiny machine that will seek out the dead blood cells trapped between the layers of your eye. The retriever shreds the dead cells so that the various proteins and whatnot are washed away. Once we get the little bugger in there, we'll have to keep it working by feeding it with the drops of the aqueous photovoltaic solution. The cell retriever will do its work in about ten minutes or so, and when we stop feeding it, it will quit."

With a note of pride, he added. "I invented it myself."

Chenda rolled her eyes up to Fenimore's face. "Is this gonna work?"

"Kingston is quite talented. When it comes to patching people up, I wouldn't bet against him."

"OK, then."

Kingston pointed at Fenimore. "Don't drop her head." He pointed at Chenda. "Don't move a muscle." He pointed at Verdu. "Give us a story."

"What story do you want?" he asked.

"Chenda's our guest, and our patient, too. Let her advance a topic." Fenimore suggested.

"Hmm... Why not tell me how the great-great-great grandson of the first Tugrulian Emperor found his way to the *Brofman*? Say, does that make you a prince or something?" Chenda said.

Fenimore snorted. "He's no prince."

"Neither are you, so shut up and hold still," Kingston barked.

"A bold request," Verdu sighed. "As you wish."

As Verdu sat quietly for a moment, pulling his thoughts together, Kingston began to delicately drop liquid into her eye, which quickly numbed. After a few seconds, she saw the needle approach her open eye. She flinched, and Fenimore's fingers made tiny, soothing strokes on the side of her head. A moment later, his grip tightened as she felt the pressure of the needle entering her eye.

Verdu started his story. "On the whole of the Eastern Continent there was never such a bastard as ruthlessly cut-throat as Kotal Varinain. He rose to power in a time when all of the Eastern Kingdoms fought with one another. He put his clan, the Tugrulians, at the top of the food chain by starving every other tribe. He poisoned the fields and the water. He snared the men like rabbits while they hunted to feed their families. He burned the villages to the ground. When all other tribes were bled nearly to death, Kotal Varinain proclaimed himself emperor.

"He began to shape all of the continent into his vision. The only morality was his morality. The only songs were songs praising him. The only art was glorification of his image. His motto, carved in stone across his new empire, read *One Law, One Language, One God and One Land.*

"In the first years of his reign, Varinain Varinain forcefully uprooted all the surviving non-Tugrulians from their homes and villages in an action he called *The Great Distribution*. All women of childbearing age were scattered across his empire and forced into group marriages with Emperor Varinain's warlords. The children of those unions were raised in a tight Tugrulian fashion, filling Kotal Varinain's vision of a new, homogeneous society.

"The emperor himself had more than 250 wives, who produced more than 1000 children. So, I'm not so special in that regard. Many, many Tugrulians can claim to be descendants of the first emperor."

He smiled. "And Fen is right; I'm no prince."

"My lineage has little to do with how I arrived here. It has more to do with Kotal Varinain's *least* favorite children. He accepted no imperfections in his offspring. He set the precedent adopted by all of Tugrulian society of killing children with birth defects. He personally ended the lives of 24 of his own children, whose only crimes were to be born blind, without limbs or a finger, club-footed, or ones born like me. When I was born, so they say, my face was cut from the inside of my nose, through my lip and into my mouth."

"Cleft palate," Kingston supplied, dripping more liquid into Chenda's eye.

"Call it what you will, but to me, it was a death sentence. The emperor, so long ago, set the law through his cruel betrayal of his own children. All babies of less than perfect birth are condemned. At the moment of my birth, my mother saw my imperfection. She knew my fate. She also knew that producing such a child would have lowered her meager status amongst my father's other wives, so she did the only thing she could. She bribed the midwife to say I had died, and the woman smuggled me to the coast. There, I was traded to the boat people of the Kohlian Sea, called the Mae-Lyn. They repaired my deformity as best they could, and raised me as one of their own, out on the open ocean. There were many other escaped Tugrulians among the boat people. Several years ago, Captain Endicott encountered the Mae-Lyn family who kept me, and he offered me a place on the *Brofman*. I've been here ever since."

As Verdu's story came to a close, Kingston finished his work on Chenda's eye. He pulled her head back up and asked her to blink a few times.

"Any pain?" he asked.

"It feels okay," Chenda said. "Thanks."

"My pleasure, miss. You'll be right as rain tomorrow." He sat down to re-bandage Chenda's hands.

Chenda turned her head toward Verdu, trying to both look and not look for the mark of a cleft under his nose. "Your story, is that true?"

Fenimore, who was already moving back to the seat next to his friend, answered. "It is. Every word."

Chenda looked at Verdu's face again, searching. "Your face looks fine to me."

"That's Kingston's handiwork again. The Mae-Lyn's repair was crude, but the doc rebuilt this part of my lip and nose." Verdu said, tracing his finger down an almost imperceptible scar. "He used to be one of the best physicians in Kite's Republic."

"But then I got caught with some unlawful experiments, and I was out!" Kingston remarked sourly. "Like so many on Captain Endicott's crew, Verdu and I are good at what we do, but we're outside the laws of the Republic. We are *not to be allowed.*" He grunted. "Misfits all."

Chenda looked at the three men around her. Each had a bit of shame in his eyes. Chenda couldn't understand it. As she looked at them, her most overwhelming thought was gratitude. Her instincts were waking up, and they told her that these men were good people.

"Let me tell you a story," she said. "Two weeks ago, I was a wife, and I lived like I thought a proper wife should live. I appreciated hearth and home. My husband, whom I loved, cared for me and took care of all my needs, and I watched the world go by. Eleven days ago, I saw his body draped across his desk, and my world froze, and me along with it. Three days ago, I watched the lid close on his casket, and my world crumbled. Yesterday, someone I counted on tried to kill me and burned my home. My world has been obliterated, and I am running for my life. I don't know yet what I'm even running toward, but I've made it this far, and I have to keep moving."

Chenda paused for a minute and put her bandaged hand on Kingston's plump cheek. "Today, I placed my trust in this ship and her crew. Meeting you all, and seeing your kindness – well, I don't think I can express what it means to me. Perhaps being here with you, misfits who are outside the laws of Kite's Republic, I can somehow gather the tattered threads of my life. I can begin to rebuild my world again."

She looked into Fenimore's wide eyes. "For that, I will be truly grateful to you all for the rest of my life."

Chapter 8
WHEN MORNING CAME

Candice Mortimer opened her eyes in her dark cabin aboard the *Brofman* and checked her surroundings. Nope, the room was definitely *not* spinning anymore. Progress.

She let her legs fall over the side of the narrow bed and pulled herself into a slouch. Candice felt like a wrung-out sponge. For as many trips and adventures as she had made with airships, she had delusionally hoped to escape her traditional bout of airsickness. After a dozen research trips, she thought she'd earned a gastrointestinal break. She'd have settled for the ability to open a window. Cool air would help a lot. The smell in the air around her wasn't uplifting in the least.

Candice looked at the soft glow of her watch: just past five in the morning. There was no point in going back to sleep, so she snapped on the small berth's main light. She ran a little water in the sink and splashed it on her face. Rummaging around for a hairbrush, she pulled her straight tawny hair down to stroke some life back into it. After a little grooming, she felt more herself, and decided to review her notes. She sat at the head of the bed and unfolded the small writing table from the wall.

She flipped through her notebook on the Tugrulian singing stones. For much of the last two days, she'd been confirming that everyone who had been known to be in possession of the rare stones was indeed dead, and the stones themselves had all disappeared. She could only conclude that someone, or several someones, were making off with them, reclaiming them. Someone was determined to make Chenda's extraordinary set disappear as well, but the girl survived her attacker.

85

Who was pulling Daniel's strings? she wondered. And did that puppet master know where Chenda was going?

She thought on it for a while. Daniel certainly could have been listening when she made the airship arrangements. If he had been, he certainly would have reported what he heard. The chances that someone would be following them were pretty high.

What about Edison? Who could have known he had the stones?

Because Edison never left the estate, it was reasonable to assume that the stones had been with him since his return from abroad. If someone was looking to get the stones away from Edison, they found the perfect opportunity in Daniel, a man with a grudge. Perhaps that other party had waited for years to find a way in.

Candice rubbed her eyes. This was futile; she just didn't have enough information to begin making any assumptions about who was coming after the stones. She just knew that someone would be. Someone wanted the stones badly enough to kill for them. From what she could tell, that person was willing to kill anyone connected with the stones.

Candice pulled her flight coat collar up to her cheeks and headed to the main deck. She snapped her bitter-end into the track and looked out into the predawn twilight. The *Brofman* was perfectly still in the cold morning. She looked over the side of the airship. The moonlight glittered far below, highlighting the coast of Kite's Republic and the small whitecaps lapping against the beach.

She rested her palms against the railing and bent at the waist, pushing her hips back and stretching her spine and her hamstrings. It felt good after a night of retching and lying on a narrow, unfamiliar bed. She looked toward the bow of the airship where the hint of a rising sun teased the horizon. She decided a brisk walk would get her blood moving.

The sound of her tether sliding along the track at her feet pleased her, and the refreshing air washed the last traces of nausea out of her body. She was starting to feel dandy as she reached the bow and circled around to pace down the other side of the deck. She looked up into the wheelhouse and was surprised at what she saw.

Standing at the airship's wheel was Chenda with Fenimore Dulal to one side of her and an equally tall but darkly featured man on the other. Each man had placed one of his hands on top of Chenda's as she gripped the wheel. Candice, who stood unnoticed by any of the occupants of the wheelhouse, looked carefully at each man's face. She had seen enough hormonal teenagers at the university to recognize *smitten* when she saw it.

Suddenly, Candice was annoyed.

"Who-wee! If looks could kill," came a voice on her left. Candice jumped two feet in the air and clutched her chest, turning on her interrupter.

The captain, climbing out of a hatch in the deck, held his hands in mock surrender. "Sorry! Sorry. I didn't mean to catch you so off guard. Glad to see you up and free of vomit."

"Man alive! Do you always sneak up on people like that!? Give me a heart attack!" Candice said, trying to calm herself and rearrange her expression into a look that was neither frightened nor peevish. She failed. Embarrassed, Candice turned and faced the wheelhouse again.

The captain focused his gaze in the same direction and laughed. "Yes, yes. They've all been up all night -- bonding. Those two boys are a little old for crushes, but we don't see many girls around here, and, it's hardly fair. Your *assistant* was too much of a kicked puppy for them to resist. It will be interesting to see how this plays out." He grinned, his eyes twinkling with muted excitement.

Candice noticed the inflection on the word assistant. So, it seemed the cat was out of the bag as far as Chenda's identity. She sniffed in acknowledgment.

"I love a good walk in the morning," the captain said. "Would you mind if I took a few turns with you around my deck?"

Candice nodded. As they walked, the corners of her mouth slipped further into a frown.

The captain glanced at her as they walked. "She's not really interested in either of them, you know."

Candice kept frowning. "It's not about her interest in

them. I just don't understand men, that's all."

"What's your interest in the Widow Frost, anyway? What is she to you?"

Candice shot the captain a surprised look.

"Oh, I knew who she was the first time we met – with her picture all over the newspapers. But when I docked yesterday, I was quite surprised to see her there, still alive. I think maybe she is mixed up in something pretty dangerous." His eyes sparkled. "I mean, it's got to be when going to the Empire looks like the safer option."

"She is. And I guess I'm along for the ride. It's just..." her voice trailed off. Candice and Captain Endicott had reached the stern of the airship. Candice stopped and flopped onto a long, low wooden crate. She leaned her elbow onto the ship's railing and began tapping out her annoyance with her fingernails. The captain sat next to her.

"OK. Tell Ol' Captain Max all about it," he said in a silly, swashbuckling tone.

"Can't I just wallow in my own little puddle for a minute? Honestly, if I say what I'm thinking out loud, I'm just gonna sound petty."

Captain Endicott shrugged. "The world is full of petty. There's a good mix of resentment, shallowness and stupidity out there, too. But you're here on *my* ship, scratching the finish on *my* railing, by the way, so I'm hoping there is at least something interesting to share. So, sate my curiosity. How are you mixed up in this?"

Candice clutched her fingers to her palm. "The easy answer is that Edison Frost asked me to be."

"Interesting," the captain said, "yet not fully satisfying, as far as answer go. When was the last time you talked with him?"

"Twenty-one-years ago," Candice replied.

Captain Endicott barked out a roaring laugh, clutching his sides. "Oh, you've lost me!" Candice realized that she actually did want to talk about what she was thinking and was making a mess of it. She laughed in spite of herself.

"Let me back up a little-" she started, but another laugh cut her off.

"Back further than 21-years? How long is this story?"

"Surprisingly short," Candice chided, "assuming you let me finish. Short and old. Do you want to listen or just have giggle fits?"

Captain Endicott clamped both hands over his mouth, but his eyes continued to laugh. It seemed that mirth was his constant state. To a serious woman like Candice, the condition was unsettling, but not wholly unappealing.

"I met Edison Frost 25 years ago, or there about, when I entered the Republic School for the Sciences."

"Go! ATOMS!" the captain cheered. Candice slapped him on the shoulder and he put his hands over his mouth again.

"Anyway, I was young, and like most teenagers, I was in over my head hormone-wise. Edison happened to be the first boy I saw and I went bonkers for him. He was handsome, smart, kind and willing to give me the time of day.

"As a student, I was pretty average. There was a distraction for me around every corner, and usually it was Edison. We dated casually for the first year or so, but as the months came and went, we grew steadily closer. Eventually the war started, and Edison chose to join the Republic Air Service."

Candice paused, as if trying to pick the best way to explain. "When he left, he said that I shouldn't wait for him. By all indications, the war was going to be a long one. It soon became obvious that it was going to be a bloody one as well. I never *decided* that I would wait for him, I just did. It wasn't like there was anyone else there to tempt me. The city was empty of men my age. I remembered the joy I had with Edison, and I guess that each time I recalled him, I perfected him. I erased any faults he had. I forgot any defect between us. No one could live up to the *idea* of him. I threw myself into my study. As the war dragged on, my love turned to fear. I saw many of my college friends who were crippled by the loss of their husbands in the war. I vowed that would never happen to me. So I bottled up my feelings for Edison and decided to never look at them until I saw him again.

"But I never did see him. Well, not alive anyway. What it comes down to is this: I have some degree of envy for Chenda. Edison picked *her* and forgot about me. That hurts. But before

89

you think me so shallow as to be jealous of the newly widowed, I also have great sympathy for the girl. I yearned to marry Edison, but the possibility of losing him stopped me from loving, not just him, but everyone. I *feared* losing him, but it actually *happened* to her, and in such a brutal way. I have my work, which I love, and good friends, too. She only had him.

"So, in a strange way, I love her, because he loved her. And I envy her for the same reasons. However, in the last few days, I have come to see that she is made of some pretty strong stuff. She is going to follow Edison's directives if it kills her. He sent her to me as part of this insane journey, and he promised that I could help her. So I guess I will."

Captain Endicott made a show of pulling his hands off of his mouth and said, "I guess, in the end, it's pretty clear that your old flame *hadn't* forgotten about you at all." He thought for a moment and continued. "In fact, I would say he knew you pretty well. He must have known enough about you, your work and your character to feel like he could entrust his wife to your guidance."

"Well, when you put it that way..." she blushed.

"Let me give you a piece of advice," he said. "And keep in mind, I'm just a stupid fly-boy. If I were you..."

Candice looked over to see why the captain had stopped talking. Captain Endicott reached toward Candice and cupped one hand behind her head. In one smooth motion, he pulled her toward him, dipped her across his lap and brought his lips down hard over hers. Captain Endicott released a kiss so powerful and passionate that Candice's eyelids fluttered and her spine got loose. Before she could think, he pitched her back upright, and let her go.

"... I'd throw overboard your bottle-o'-love for the dead man. There's plenty of love in the world, and plenty of ways to find it. Chasing after a feeling that's 20 years old, well, that way lies madness." He patted Candice's knee and gestured to the wheelhouse. "And those lads' fawning over her doesn't negate any of Edison's love for her, or hers for him, but I think you knew that."

He stood up and offered his hand to Candice. "Shall we

finish our walk?" he said. Candice looked agog at the captain as the first rays of the morning sun glowed on his gleeful face.

She stood up and looked over the side of the ship. She put her hand over her heart and pulled it away, imagining she was holding her bottled up emotions. She kissed it and pitched it over the side. As they walked toward the bow, Candice placed her hand on the captain's arm and said to him, "You have some pretty persuasive advice."

"Any time you need a little more counsel, you just come see me. I'm just full of it."

"I bet you are," Candice replied, and the twosome laughed as they walked under the early morning sun.

Chenda and the Airship Brofman

Chapter 9
ATOLL BELLES

Chenda waited in the wheelhouse for the first rays of a new day's sun to come over the horizon. She, Verdu and Fenimore had spent the whole night talking. Kingston, less inclined than the others to sacrifice a night's sleep for good conversation, stalked off to bed well before midnight. Fenimore and Verdu spent the remainder of the night regaling Chenda with stories of their adventures aboard the *Brofman*.

To hear them tell it, there was little Captain Endicott wouldn't do -- especially if the price was right. He smuggled a wide variety of cargoes, from stolen art to brides with cold feet. He traded in a variety of contraband, and, as he had done with Verdu, he'd brought foreign illegals into the Republic.

Fenimore said, "He does what he does to thumb his nose at the Republic. The money is just a way of keeping score."

"He doesn't sound particularly patriotic, and some of his exploits sound as if they border on treason" Chenda said.

"No," Verdu said. "He loves the Republic -- for many reasons. He even served during the war, medals and everything, but there are certain... injustices... that he feels he needs to correct."

"Injustices?"

"Take all of us for example," Fenimore said. "Most of the crew is made of members who the Republic as a whole would condemn: Verdu is Tugrulian, Kingston practices medicine without a license, Stanley, Spencer and Lincoln were troublemakers, each on his way to a life of crime. Germer was a junkie. The point is, Captain Endicott believes in second chances.

93

He believes in the goodness of people. He gives people the freedom to learn from their mistakes and make amends in their own way and time."

"Captain Endicott is no saint, but he is a good man. He tries to keep us from making deals with the devil," Verdu said, shooting a glance at Fenimore. "Sometimes he can't."

Chenda, unsure if she should let that cryptic remark go by, turned to Fenimore. "I notice you left your crimes off the list."

"That I did." Fenimore said in a tone that indicated he would discuss it no more.

"Fen has a temper." Verdu whispered.

"Oh, when you say it like that you make me sound scary!" Fenimore snapped. "It's like this: I got into a brawl when I was 19. It was just a good night out at the pub with friends, until it wasn't. I have no idea what the fight was about, but when the dust settled, I'd beaten an old school buddy of mine into a coma, which is where he is today. I went to jail for a year. And when I got out, I fell in with Captain Endicott. I've been here for five years, and every penny I earn or swindle or salvage, I send along to help pay for his care. I'll do that for as long as he or I live."

He tucked his chin to his chest, his face awash in shame. Chenda could only feel compassion for him. "Making amends. I see," she said.

The trio stood silently in the wheelhouse as the sun, glorious and bright, breached the horizon. In that sparkling instant, Fenimore and Verdu dropped their hands from Chenda's and started working in tandem, flipping switches and moving dials. The signal whistle blew through the airship as the *Brofman* came alive for another day of flight.

It was a thrill to watch her new friends work the controls, their hands quick and sure. She was glad those same hands had brought her to helm of the *Brofman* when she asked what it was like to pilot an airship. They placed her shaking fingers on the wheel, their own hands covering hers, reassuring her. It wasn't like she was actually flying the ship; after all, it was nighttime, and they were just hovering. It also didn't bother her that they never let go of her hands, and that they both stood so close.

There was something about this airship that negated the

boundaries of personal space. Until she encountered the constant nudge, bump and jostle of life aboard ship, she never knew how starved she was for physical contact. Only one set of hands ever possessed her in her old life. She realized that his touch had been all touch to her for most of her life. The nuns at the orphanage never were much for hugging, and her companions there were not the intimate sort. She searched her memory, and she couldn't recall a time when Alme or any other member of the house staff had ever touched her. Well, except for Daniel Frent. Other than the day of the funeral when he caught her mid-fall, Chenda didn't consider him to be full of *good touch*. Her last week of human contact was the worst. Cold handshakes at the funeral. The emptiness of the house. The absence of Edison's rough hands on her face, kissing her goodnight. She still missed Edison's physical presence, but her yearning for him was no longer the soul sucking ache it had been yesterday.

Chenda realized a new truth about herself; she *liked* the close physical presence of other people and wanted more of it. The vitality present on this airship made her realize that she had been blissfully unaware of the sensual variety in the larger world beyond the walls of her pampered life. There were thousands of hands offering a million sensations in the world, and that thought overwhelmed her. The possibility distracted her.

Chenda's concentration broke as another series of whistles twittered though the ship. The three deck hands rushed up the stairs, snapped their bitter-ends into the track and trotted to the power cells behind the wheelhouse. They moved efficiently, tugging on pulleys to angle the cylinders upwards to catch the first rays of the sun. The boys meticulously polished the tubes to make sure that every ray of sunshine entered unreflected.

In the wheelhouse, Fenimore lifted one more lever and Chenda could feel the *Brofman* make a small shudder. The airship was ready to leap forward and fly into the rising sun. "Verdu," he said, "Sadly, I am still on duty. Would you please be so kind as to escort Mrs. Frost to the galley, where she will find both the captain and a hot breakfast?"

"It would be my fondest delight," Verdu said as he offered an elbow to Chenda and opened the wheelhouse door. Chenda accepted his arm, but took no step to leave. "Fenimore, Verdu, please call me Chenda. I want to thank you for spending some time with me tonight, and for showing me around. I really did have a wonderful time." The men did a matched, bashful shuffle, neither immediately coming up with anything to say.

As Chenda and Verdu stepped out, Fenimore said, "Come back anytime, and call me Fen, like he does, if you want."

"I'll see you later, Fen," Chenda called over her shoulder.

In the galley, Kingston fussed over his special oatmeal. He believed that every meal deserved his best, even simple breakfasts like this one. So few people grasped the power of oatmeal. He considered it a personal challenge to make every member of the crew *ooh* and *ahh* over this most basic dish. He loved a good culinary trial.

Candice and the captain were the first to arrive for the morning meal, and he served up two heaping bowls. He'd had the professor, and more specifically her rocky tummy, in mind when he picked oatmeal for this morning's chow. Easy to keep down. He worried that the ample portion he'd served would drub her, but was pleased when she heartily started in on her dish.

"Wow! What you do with oatmeal is remarkable!" she praised, and Kingston knew it was going to be a great day for his ego. He lived to feed.

As the captain finished eating, Chenda and Verdu entered.

"Good morning!" Chenda greeted the room. "Oh, oatmeal! I'm famished." Kingston looked pleased as he spun another pair of steaming bowls onto the table as the newcomers sat down.

"Captain," Verdu said, "Dulal has readied the airship and is awaiting your orders. Would you like me to convey them, sir?"

"No, no. You stay and eat your breakfast. I'm not having Kingston give me the stink-eye because your food got cold." He winked. "I'm going to check the weather again and make a decision about where we will end up tonight. I'll be back."

Chenda watched the captain leave and turned her attention to Candice. "You look so much better, not nearly so green around the gills. Is the worst over?"

"I am pretty sure that I have found my airlegs again. You look better yourself. Your eye looks almost healed."

"Really? I haven't had a chance to look since Kingston worked on it last night. He put some salve on my hands, too. It took just about all of the sting out of the burns."

Kingston appeared at Chenda's side with a shiny kettle in one hand. "Yes, yes. I'm a genius. Take a look," he said, holding the makeshift mirror up at eye level.

Chenda was amazed at the improvement. "I just can't thank you enough," she said. Kingston blushed and shuffled happily back to his stove. Chenda enjoyed a few more bites, and called after him, "What's the secret to this oatmeal anyway? It's remarkable!"

Verdu tsked at her, "He'll never tell. He likes his *secret ingredients* too much." His voice dropped to a whisper. "But I think he boils some peeled apples into a pulp and then adds the oats. I suspect a hint of vanilla in there, too."

The pleasant eating and conversation went on for a few minutes more. Another series of whistles piped through the ship, and Verdu said, "Hold on!"

Candice and Chenda gripped the edge of the small table, and a second later the airship shot forward. "And we're off on another fine day in the air," Verdu noted. Stanley and Lincoln ambled in from the passage and sat down. Stanley looked into the bowl Kingston presented. "Woo-hoo! Oatmeal," he said, feeding Kingston's pride. The young men started inhaling their food. As the cocky cook served up seconds all around, the captain returned.

"What's our course, Captain?" Verdu asked.

"We're going to hit some weather a bit later today," he replied. "It won't be too rough, but it's going to sap our power a bit. I think it's best for us to play it safe and dock tonight. Our heading is for Atoll Belles."

Hearing this, the two deck hands hooted loudly and bumped fists. There was also much snickering between them.

The captain gave the pair a hard look. "Don't be too convinced that I will give either of you leave to go ashore tonight. Not after what happened last time." The boys' joyful looks suddenly sank. They glanced at each other, then stared sadly at their bowls. The captain said, "Prove to me that you are worth your wages today, and I may reconsider." The boys jumped up and nearly fell over each other trying to clean up their breakfast dishes and find something useful to do. The whole way out of the galley, Lincoln promised complete satisfaction for the captain, "Yes, sir, you won't regret this, sir, we've learned from our last time, sir, it will never happen again..." and the pair was out the door.

"Oh, I'm sure I'm going to regret it," the captain muttered to himself, "probably in a new and interesting way." He sighed. "Those boys..." he started afresh into a rant, but he let the thought drop with a resigned sigh and another mouthful of oatmeal.

"So, what's Atoll Belles?" Chenda asked Captain Endicott.

"It's an independent airship dock almost a day's flight off the coastline. As it hoists neither a flag for the Republic nor for the Tugrulians, it's a pretty popular destination for folks who are avoiding one or the other of those two entities. Mostly, it's Mae-Lyn traders who frequent the place. But some others, much like us, come to conduct business and pleasure."

Verdu rolled his eyes. "Those boys will be wanting the pleasure of a visit to McNees's Opera House, and that will not end well."

"They don't seem the opera type," Chenda noted.

The captain released a sharp, barking laugh, "Let's just say that the boys are interested in the *under*-study of a few chorus girls."

Chenda missed the joke. The captain tried again, "The boys are hoping to get their instruments tuned." He laughed again.

Chenda blinked at him.

Captain Endicott's smile faded, clearly annoyed that his best jokes were lost on this demure girl. He looked at Verdu, "Dear gods, help me out, man!" he pleaded to his second officer.

Verdu made a half grin. "Chenda, McNees's is a whorehouse with a musical theme."

Chenda gasped and then laughed out loud. "There is so much in the world that I just don't understand. I honestly didn't

98

see that coming!"

The captain regained his usual mirth. "They have more than just the girls of negotiable affection, mind you. You can separate yourself from your money at the card tables, and they've got a decent liquor selection, too."

Candice eyed, with slight disapproval, her companions around the table. The thoughts of the recent attempts on her and Chenda's lives were still fresh in her mind. "Is it safe?" she asked.

"The Atoll is safe enough, and the trouble one finds as McNees's is of the usual variety: drunkards, swindlers and card sharks," the captain said. "But enough about me. We'll keep our guard up, nonetheless. Besides, I plan to find you a connection to your final destination there."

He looked over at Candice's doubting face. "Relax, professor" the captain said. "We do this kind of thing every day. We'll get you where you are going, no problem."

Chenda stifled a yawn. She was full of delicious oatmeal, and it had been a long, exciting night. She turned to Candice. "Do we need to be doing anything at the moment?"

"I don't think so. Until we cover considerably more ocean, we are obliged to hurry up and wait. Are you finally going to get some rest?"

"Mmm-hmm" Chenda said as she dragged herself out of the galley and into the crew quarters. She sat down on the floor next to her bunk, and squeezed herself onto the tiny slot of a bed. She was snugly warm in her boots and flight coat, and she fell asleep in less than a minute.

Sometime during her slumber, she went from toasty to broiled. Chenda woke up drenched in sweat. She rolled out of her bunk and onto the cool floor, splaying her arms and legs wide trying to throw off the heat. She pulled her flight coat open trying to catch her breath. It wasn't her imagination. The room was hot. Too soggy to sit up, she wiggled out of her coat as she lay there, and peeled her clinging shirtfront away from her skin.

Ewww... I'm sticky. This is going to lead to smelly...

Chenda looked up from her supine misery to see Stanley and Lincoln crowding each other at the mirror over the small sink, each primping like mad.

"Are we there yet?" she croaked in a dry voice.

Lincoln turned around to look at Chenda sprawled on the floor. "We dock in half an hour."

"And a half hour after that, the captain said we could have *four* hours of shore leave." Stanley added. "That reminds me. We need to wake Dulal. He'll need to get up to the crow's nest soon."

Chenda looked back toward the bunks. Just above her empty bed was Fenimore, stripped to the waist and fast asleep. One muscled arm was draped over his eyes and forehead, shielding him from the dim light in the crew quarters. His large frame looked squashed into the too-small space, like a doll shoved into a shoebox. Chenda realized she was staring at his smooth, peachy skin stretched over his muscular torso. She watched his ribs slide under his skin with each breath. Abashed, she blushed.

A balled up, sopping wet washcloth smacked into Fenimore's side with a splat. Chenda was surprised that he didn't smack his head as he flinched awake. Fenimore reached an arm down to grasp the wet projectile that was dripping water onto the edge of his mattress. He rolled onto his stomach and looked down at Chenda.

"You throw this?" he asked sleepily.

"Nope," Chenda whispered in a raspy voice. She pointed over her head. Fenimore's eyes followed the line of her finger to Lincoln standing at the sink, still working over his looks. "If you will be so kind as to excuse me," Fenimore said as he quietly stood up and stepped over Chenda, stalking up to Lincoln and Stanley. He raised his giant hand over Lincoln's head and squeezed every last drop out of the washcloth onto the boys' locks.

"HEY!" Lincoln shouted. For a bit of extra emphasis, Fenimore rubbed the boy's whole hairdo flat, ruining what appeared to be several minutes of thoughtful coiffing.

"Love the hair," Fenimore smirked as he pushed the two younger men to the side and elbowed his way to the sink. "I'm sure that will do the trick tonight with the ladies." He splashed some water on his face. Lincoln, now separated from his mirror, sulked and sat on his bunk adjacent to Chenda's.

Fenimore looked into the mirror and said to Stanley and Lincoln, "Remember boys, it ain't love if you have to pay 'em. Save your money and court some nicer girls."

Stanley snorted. Fenimore's advice had fallen on deaf ears.

"What time is it?" Chenda asked Lincoln.

"It's near the end of the First Dog," he grumped.

"Dog-what?" Chenda asked.

"Oh, um, you'd say close to six o'clock, I guess," Lincoln said distractedly. "Hey, Dulal, the captain says you need to be up-the-nest real soon. We're about to Atoll Belles."

"Right, sure." Fenimore mumbled as he walked over to his cupboard. Opening it, he turned and looked down at Chenda still lying on the floor. "You okay?"

"Just hot. Not ready to exert myself to stand yet. Why is it so warm? I thought you said it would be cold the whole time," she said. He leaned over and propped her on her feet.

"We've dropped altitude, and we've moved significantly south into a tropical zone. You'll feel cooler when you head out on deck where the air is moving." He opened his cupboard and tossed her a wide belt with several rings on it. "Leave the flight coat. You can clip the bitter-end to that belt. Buckle it tight."

Chenda hitched up the belt and walked out into the passageway. She saw Kingston toiling in the kitchen and he called out to her, "Too hot for dinner down here. I'm bringing sandwiches up to the deck in a second!"

"Oh, great," Chenda replied as she made her way toward the steps. She knocked on Candice's door as she passed, but there was no answer. She opened the door and slipped inside, grateful to find a little privacy. She pulled off her shirt and tried to wash off some of the sweat at the tiny sink. Chenda felt a little cleaner and cooler, but dreaded donning her stink-shirt again. Sadly, there was no help for it. She didn't have anything else to put on at the moment. She checked to make sure Edison's singing stones were still secure in their hiding place in her bra as she re-buttoned. A second later, she left the tiny room and climbed the stairs into the cooler, breezy air above deck.

She could see Candice at the far end of the ship, sitting on a long crate shaded by the glowing photovoltaic tubes. She waved. Candice waved back, stood and walked toward Chenda.

"You've missed a boring and increasingly cloudy afternoon at sea," Candice said. "In fact the clouds have just now broken up and left us." Candice pointed behind her to a brilliant sunset that highlighted the retreating line of thunderheads. "And look what's ahead!" She turned Chenda toward the bow and a bump on the horizon.

"Is that an island?" Chenda asked.

"No, It's Atoll Belles. It's a wonder of geology, an atoll. Thirty million years in the making. Part blossoming Mother Nature, part decaying Father Earth. Fascinating."

Chenda smiled at the professor. "You really love your work, don't you?"

"Of course," Candice said with pride. "Geology can give you quite a bit of perspective on life. Take the atoll, for example. Basically, an island is a mountain sticking up out of the surface of the sea. An island can appear in a day. All it takes is one volcanic eruption, and poof, there it is. An atoll starts out as an island. But slowly, as a reef builds up around that island, millions of years of wind and surf and rain break the land apart until all that remains is a reef with a shallow lagoon in the middle. In all of our human life, we'd never see a change in this atoll, but change it must, very slowly, and by degrees. Forever evolving and becoming new again in its degeneration."

"That's kind of romantic," Chenda said.

"Ick. Please, child, it's geology. That's so much better than love."

Kingston appeared on the deck with a tray full of sandwiches and drinks. The ladies settled once again on the crate in the stern, enjoying the breeze. Chenda couldn't get enough of Kingston's refreshing beverage. It was slightly minty and honey sweet, but had a mild vinegar taste as well.

"What is this?" she finally asked.

"Oxymel. Refreshing, ain't it? Nothing beats the heat like that does. It's good for preventing dehydration. Since some of our boys will be drinkin' tonight.... Well, cheers." He poured another glass for each of the ladies, then took his tray of sandwiches around to the other crewmen. He tossed a pair of sandwiches tied in a napkin up to Fenimore, who sat high above the deck in the crowsnest.

As the minutes rolled by, the airship sank lower as it approached the atoll,.Chenda could now see the bright blue of the shallow lagoon, and the airship terminal piers radiating high from a central tower on the far side of the narrow ring of land.

Fenimore began madly waving a pair of small flags at the spire. He would stop every now and again, watching for a response. After several exchanges, he dropped the flags into the nest and hopped over the side, sliding down a thin cable and landing gracefully at the door to the wheelhouse. He opened the door and said, "We're all set, Captain. They want us to come about and take slip number seven. Their prices are officially outrageous these days."

The captain's barking laugh came through the open doorway. "It doesn't matter. I'll meet Jason Belles for a few hands of cards later and it will all come out even."

"Whatever you say, sir. Who do you want on first watch?"

"Germer is staying aboard, along with Spencer. Too much temptation there for those two. Please remind the two idiot boys that they are to be back here at midnight, or they will be cleaning the chemical tanks with their tongues tomorrow!"

"Yes, sir."

"And we'll be departing well before dawn tomorrow, so the rest of you be back well before four bells. Dismissed."

Fenimore closed the door and smiled as he headed toward the bow and his usual post. As the airship approached the tower, it made a wide arc and eased toward slip seven. Fenimore unclipped his bitter-end and, taking a coil of rope in one arm, he climbed up onto the railing and jumped over the side. He landed on the last few inches of the pier and ran along the side of the gliding ship as it inched into the slip. He looped the mooring line around a solid, shiny cleat and, as the airship pulled the line taut, Fenimore ran up it like a tightrope walker. He leaped the last five feet up and over the side, landing gracefully on the deck.

Several whistles sounded through the *Brofman*, and the crew raced onto the deck. They lined up along the rail and turned their attention to Fenimore.

"Germer, Spencer, you two have drawn the short straws. You're on watch while we dock. Stanley and Lincoln, get us hooked up for water, and check the quality of their desalinization. I don't fancy using our own power tomorrow to have to clean it again. Once the two of you have done that, accompany the captain to pick up supplies. Then the evening is yours until midnight. May the gods spare you from my wrath if you aren't here by the first bell of the middle watch. Am I clear?"

"Yes, sir!" the young men nodded with excitement.

"We'll be departing the atoll by four bells," Fenimore informed the rest of the crew. "I'd hate to leave anyone behind." He grinned. "That is all."

The crew fell out of formation, all except for Spencer, who stood there looking annoyed.

"Sorry, lad," Germer said to the small young man. "Your turn will come around. Let's get some cards." Germer led Spencer belowdecks.

Fenimore and Verdu talked as they leaned on the ship's rail for a few minutes and then made their way to where Chenda and Candice sat.

"Good evening, ladies," Fenimore said with a grin, "and welcome to Atoll Belles. I'm Fen and would be happy to give you a guided tour. This is my assistant tour guide, Verdu. Our fees are modest and negotiable. What's your pleasure?"

Candice laughed out loud at the bogus sales pitch, but stood and said, "What the heck! If someone is on the atoll already looking to kill us, I doubt we will be any safer up here than we would be down there. Show us the town!"

Fenimore flipped the lever that lowered the gangway to the pier. Verdu led the way, followed by Candice and Chenda, with Fenimore bringing up the rear. The group stepped toward the central point of the tower, a bank of elevators. As they boarded the next available car, Verdu suggested, "The market might be a nice place to start our tour. It's down by the lagoon, and there are dozens of traders there. Lots of people to watch."

Chenda smiled, "I happen to know a bit about shopping. This could be fun."

As the elevator doors opened and the four stepped out, Chenda realized how far from home she really was. The platform where she stood was surrounded by an iron barrier several yards out from the elevators. Inside this fence, a few dock officials milled around, checking documents and posting schedules. But outside, beggars of every size and color pressed against the bars, their hands reaching in. Chenda froze as she looked at the pleading faces. Their anguish overwhelmed her.

Fenimore put his hand gently on her back and started pushing her toward the exit. Chenda's eyes settled on a small woman. Her dark purple gown hung loosely on her thin body, and she gestured to Chenda. With her fingers pinched together and her palm upturned, she tapped on her own lips, then turned slightly and touched the lips of the small baby tied to her back. Her hand stretched out to Chenda weakly, beseeching. The woman's eyes were dead as she repeated the motion again and again, begging for food for herself and her child.

"Chenda, keep walking," Fenimore said as she turned her eyes to him.

"Can't we help them?"

"No, not now." Fenimore's eyes were resolved. She could see he was struggling not to look at the starving woman, as if focusing on her would cause his resolve to break. "We can help them when we come back. We'll be mobbed when we step out among them if they think we have anything to give. Step lively now, and follow my lead. We'll be taking a rickshaw to the market, so be ready to jump into the first one you see."

Chenda took one last look at the tiny woman as she cleared the exit barrier, and in a few more steps, Fenimore pushed her into a waiting bicycle cart. As they began to move, Chenda spied Candice and Verdu stepping into their own rickshaw.

"The marketplace," Fenimore commanded the driver.

"Who are they?" Chenda asked Fenimore solemnly.

"People call them the Wanderers – an ironic name, since they don't *wander* anywhere. They are stuck here because they've been left behind for one reason or another. Some were abandoned, some ran away, many are sick or insane. Some are refugees. They live entirely off the kindness of strangers. They have no home or boat or airship."

"There were so many. What a horrible existence," Chenda whispered.

"I know," Fenimore said softly. "It could be worse, though. Jason Belles allows them to beg at the foot of his tower, which is more than what a lot of private docks allow. Some places throw the Wanderers into the sea to drown or feed the sharks." Fenimore's eyes took on a hard, angry cast. "I can't decide which fate is worse."

"Being left behind is bad enough." Chenda said.

The rickshaw rattled along the narrow path to the atoll's market on the boat docks. When it stopped, Fenimore paid the driver and the pair waited in sad silence for Candice and Verdu to catch up.

Verdu unfolded himself from the rickshaw and tossed the driver a coin. Candice looked happy to be walking on solid ground again, and eager to stretch her legs.

Chenda's mood lightened as the small party entered the long line of stalls in the marketplace. The first stall boasted a hand-painted sign over the door that read *My God is Able, Industries*.

"Hmm," Chenda turned to Fenimore. "The name gives me no clue what they sell."

"No, indeed, but they have faith that their god will help -- whatever they do."

Inside the boxy stall sat a small boy who dragged a stick across the dusty floor. When Chenda entered, he jumped up and started chattering to her in a language she didn't understand. He grabbed little packets of soap and snack foods and pushed them into her hands. The boy tried to show her all the goods he had all at once: cracker tins, jugs of water, a few beat-up old books and spools of thread. He chittered ceaselessly.

Verdu watched Chenda become more overwhelmed with the goods the boy foisted on her until she looked as if she might collapse. He stepped forward, brows scrunched together, wagging one finger and growling at the boy in the same guttural language. The boy leaped forward and collected back all the goods from Chenda's arms and then dropped to one knee, his eyes downcast.

Verdu barked again at the boy and drew his hand back as if to strike the child. He glanced at Chenda and said, "Do step out of here, please."

"Don't," she pleaded.

"Oh, I won't. It's just that he expects me to. I'm going to let him think I will for just a few seconds more. He'll be fine." Chenda paused for a moment and then backed out of the stall.

Unaware of the scene inside, Candice stood with Fenimore, happily looking atsome of the items hanging on hooks outside.

"What just happened?" Chenda asked as Verdu appeared by her side. "Was that boy speaking Tugrulian? What did you say to him? Why were you so mean?"

"These shop boys get overly aggressive sometimes," Verdu said calmly. "It's understandable, as his father likely beats him if he doesn't maintain a certain level of sales. He's a dyed-in-the-wool Tugrulian, however, and knew he had no business touching the hand of a woman who was not of his family. He saw me and assumed I was your husband. He knew I saw him brush your hand and that he was in big trouble. You seemed overwhelmed, so I let him think I would beat him to death for his indiscretion. Then all he wanted was to get us out of his stall."

He smiled a vicious smile at Chenda. "I could go back in again. Was there anything in there you wanted?"

Chenda gave a nervous chuckle. "No, thank you." She thought for a second more. "Why did he think that I was your wife?"

"Ah, well, it's your face. When he saw me follow you in, he assumed that I am just the average Tugrulian man and put those bruises on you. It's a common hobby among husbands in the empire. They beat their women. A lot." Verdu's voice dripped with disgust. "But worst of all, they make the women think they deserve it. Eventually they start believe it, too."

Chenda's heart felt tight as she imagined a continent of abused women. She turned her eyes to Verdu's and saw he felt the shame of it dearly.

"Let's be moving on," he said. "Keep your arms folded across your chest and stare down any hawker who gets too pushy.

Most of them are quite harmless. Besides, Fen and I are right behind you. There is a lot more to see."

The group moved from stall to stall, looking at goods from across the globe: repair parts for airships and boats, books and maps, exotic animals, chemicals, spices, fabrics and weapons. Chenda heard languages she didn't recognize and saw many people conducting business entirely in gestures.

Chenda quickly began to understand the basic rhythm of the market, the push and pull between buyers and sellers. It wasn't like the fancy shops she visited in Coal City, where every object had a price, and you either could afford it or you left. Here the peddlers watched to see what a buyer was interested in, then guessed the highest price they could get from that particular shopper. The first asking price would be absurdly high. Then the dance would begin. Haggle. Swagger. Feigned loss of interest. Give and take. Finally, a bargain would be struck.

She even tried her hand at the negotiations herself when she found a few clean shirts at a Mae-Lyn merchant's stall. Chenda dickered well enough to get the trader to come down by half, but Verdu was horrified when he realized how much she paid in the end. "For what you plunked down on two shirts, I could have had ten, Chenda!"

"Maybe," Chenda said with pride, "But you are not the one that smells like last week's garbage. I needed something fresh and clean." She pulled one of the new shirts on over her stinky one, and wiggled around until she could pull off the soiled layer below. "How do I look?"

Fenimore looked at Chenda's new, heavily embroidered blouse. "It suits you. Very colorful." Verdu mirrored Fenimore's nod, but Chenda wasn't sure if it was Verdu showing agreement or just moving in uncontrollable tandem again.

Chenda looked at the dirty shirt in her hand. "I have half a mind to throw this one into the lagoon, but it's not my shirt."

Candice laughed and said, "Don't feel like you need to rush to get it back to me. I can wait until it's doesn't smell like my sophomore class on a hot day."

The four continued to browse, but soon reached the end of the market. Lingering there, they looked out over the shallow lagoon. Several rough buildings led away from where they stood, but farther down the arc of the atoll were a few larger buildings. These had lights and music flowing out their doors and onto decks that stretched out over the water.

"The night is still young," Fenimore said, noticing where Chenda and Candice were gazing. "What's your pleasure?"

Candice pointed ahead to the largest building. "What's that?"

"McNees's Opera House," Fenimore answered, "But you ladies wouldn't want to go there."

Candice and Chenda looked at one another, and their eyes registered their mutual curiosity. Chenda could also see a glint from Candice that said she wasn't about to let a man tell here where she didn't want to go.

"Yes. We do," Candice said as Chenda nodded vigorously.

Verdu looked meaningfully at Fenimore. "I suppose it would be fine if we just take a second and see if Lincoln and Stanley are keeping out of trouble. Perhaps seeing us inside will remind them of the time, and that they have a strict deadline tonight. It would be very wrong of us to leave our companions outside while we went in to check on our young shipmates, don't you think?"

"You make a fine point, my brother. I'm sure we will only be a moment there."

Fenimore shrugged in tandem with Verdu, and the pair turned as one to escort Chenda and Candice to a house of ill repute.

Inside the Opera House, and already several hands deep into a game of cards, Captain Endicott took a moment to watch the fat man across the table from him start to sweat. Try as he might to bluff, Endicott knew the fellow just didn't have the cards. The man dabbed his balding head with his handkerchief and then folded. "Take it, Max," he said, and he threw his losing hand onto the pile of cards and money at the center of the table.

"I love taking your money, Jason." Captain Endicott said, his eyes twinkling.

Jason Belles eyed him pleasantly. "I know I'll get it all

109

back when you pay your docking fee. It usually works out that way between us. How long will you be darkening my door this time?"

"Just for tonight, I'll be heading east before sun-up." The captain shuffled the cards and offered them to Jason to cut.

Casually, Captain Endicott said, "Maybe you can make an introduction for me. I have a cargo bound for Kotal. I need to hook up with a boat that can take it the rest of the way in. Do you know anyone who is still making runs into the Empire?"

Endicott dealt the cards, and then sat back, listening as the throbbing music picked up speed again in the bar below. It looked like another profitable night for Jason Belles: lots of sweaty guys with money to burn, lots of women ready to sell drinks, dances and whatever else the men could afford. Jason picked up his cards and frowned. "I have a few ideas. Let me think on it a minute."

"Take your time. I've got all night. Shall we play while you ruminate?"

Jason grunted and threw the first card. Captain Endicott threw a better one and swept up the pair and the anted coins. He threw another coin and another card. Jason frowned and dropped his answering card and another coin. He lost again. The captain pulled another card from his hand and Jason held his finger up, stopping the game. "I'm stinking up the joint tonight. Better to quit before you own my place. I can tell you who you need. There's a Mae-Lyn schooner called the *Tjalk* that makes a run into an inlet about 35 miles northwest of Kotal. I can tell you where it will be two days from now, and that will be just enough time for you to catch up with it. The *Tjalk's* captain is a Tugrulian by the name of Taboda. He and I go way back. I could make an introduction for you, for the right price."

Endicott smiled. "Or I could just call in my favor. We could be even."

Shock registered on Jason Belles's face. "You'd let me off the hook for *that*? Just one little introduction? What's the catch?"

"You guarantee your contact. It's paramount you make sure in that introduction letter that you express all seriousness. Tell him that *my* cargo gets where it's going, or *you* will be personally put out with him. I know how much weight you carry

110

around these waters. You can get what you need out of people. What I need is to get my cargo to the shore, safely."

Jason sat back and rubbed his goatee. "I'm guessing human cargo."

The captain made a curt nod and waited.

"I'll do it. But you will need to pay Taboda his fee. It will run you 20-thousand or so. I'll put that in the letter as well." He smiled broadly. "If you'll excuse me, I'll draft that letter right now. I hate to be under your thumb for another minute. I'll send it along to your airship, along with some coordinates."

"Thank you, Jason. It's always a pleasure to see you."

Both men stood and shook hands. Jason said, "Don't be a stranger, my friend."

"We'll be back here in a few weeks, I'm sure," Endicott promised as Jason Belles walked away.

Chenda stood in the foyer of McNees's Opera House with wide eyes. She had to admit, the place had a unique style. If one wasn't overwhelmed by the thumping music flowing out the door, then the aroma of exotic perfumes and potent liquors surely would finish the job. She hadn't really known what to expect, but the fact that she wasn't completely repulsed surprised her more than a little. There was a strange harmony about the place. The colors, mostly reds and golds, and the textures of all the furnishings enhanced the sounds and smells floating through the air. This place hadn't just happened; she could tell. Considerable thought had gone into every detail. It was warm, embracing, and layered with stimuli. This place existed to make one *feel*.

The small group hadn't been through the door for more than a minute when a pair of outrageously costumed girls in theatrical makeup wiggled under the arms of Fenimore and Verdu. Neither of the men seemed to be surprised or mind. Candice and Chenda looked at each other and closed ranks. Shoulder to shoulder, they followed Fenimore and Verdu, and their sudden companions, to a burgundy banquette upholstered in a rich velvet. The first girl pushed Fenimore into the seat and then sat down next to him, wrapping one of his arms around her shoulders and nuzzling his ear. The other guided Verdu to a free

111

seat down the row. When Verdu sat, she boldly straddled his thighs, pressing her body against his chest.

Candice stopped dead in her tracks and clutched her hand to her chest. "Oh, my!" she said, her voice rising several octaves higher than usual. The ladies realized they were suddenly way out of their comfort zones.

Chenda said, "This may be too much for me. If I blush any more I may catch fire. I think I need a drink."

"First round's on me, and the quicker the better," Candice trilled.

The ladies backed away from the young airshipmen as fast as casually possible and sat at a nearby booth, just far enough away that they could still see the men but not have to pay much attention to what the entertainers were doing with them.

"Awkward, yes?" Chenda asked Candice.

"Indeed."

They flagged down a barmaid and ordered doubles of the house whiskey. Chenda hazarded a peek over to Fenimore and Verdu. The girls were dancing now, and the men watched with matching grins, and nearly vacant eyes.

"Men. So easily distracted. I guess we are on our own now." Chenda commented.

The drinks arrived. Candice raised her glass to Chenda and said, "We've made it this far!" The professor downed her drink in one fiery gulp. She signaled to the barmaid and said, "Keep 'em coming."

Chenda took her drink a little more slowly, sorting out her thoughts about her surroundings. "It's coarse, but now that I've had a minute to soak in it, I don't mind. Does that sound strange?"

"I've never been so uncomfortable in all my life!" Candice downed another drink. "Mercy Matilda! If my mother could see me now she'd roll in her grave. Gods get me out of here!"

"I'm sorry, Candice. Let me see if we can get the fellows to take us back to the airship." She stood to look over at the men, but Candice shushed her and waved her back into her seat.

"Do you think I'm just being a ninny? Those lads don't get to have much of a good time and I just don't think it's fair of me to drag them out of here because I am embarrassed. I'm a grown woman. I can cope. If not, I can drink. I thought I told that barmaid to keep 'em coming!"

Another round came to the table, and a few minutes after that, Candice relaxed a little. "Nice drinks," she said, smiling.

"How do they do it, do you suppose?" Candice asked Chenda. "These girls here -- who just slink up to the next guy who walks in the door -- how do you suppose they make love to them?"

"I supposed in the usual way?" Chenda said more as a question than an answer.

"No, no, no. That's not what I meant. How do they separate the feeling of love from the act? How does one put passion into... you know... when one doesn't know the other partner?"

Chenda sighed. "When it comes to relations, I only know what I know, and that was Edison. Our love was not a burning desire, but a steady one." Chenda bit her lip and then grasped Candice's hand from across the table. "I have to confess something. I've been a bit envious of you. Can you tell me, what was he like when he was young? Was he passionate, lustful? I know I embarrass you with this, but Edison, when we married, was a broken man. When we made love, it was cautiously, a delicate act. Please." Sadness crept into Chenda's voice. "Tell me what he once was."

Candice thought carefully about how to respond. She put her free hand on top of Chenda's and stroked it soothingly.

"I think the Edison I knew all those years ago was not so different from yours." Candice said in little more than a whisper. "He was a vigorous man, and full of energy, as well as kindness and restraint. But let me be clear, I was never his wife. He could plant a kiss that would make your skirts fly up, but he was never such a cad as to go diving under them when he did. He was a gentleman, and respected my virtue." Candice smiled. "Not that I didn't pull him close to vice more than once."

Candice looked into Chenda's surprised eyes and confessed, "It probably would have been easier for me if Edison *had* loved me and left me. I might have gotten over him before this morning."

113

"What happened this morning?"

Candice giggled and downed another whiskey, "Captain Endicott made my skirt fly up."

"WHAT! How did I miss that!"

"Ah, you were in the wheelhouse with Monkey-see and Monkey-do, holding hands." She giggled again, obviously getting drunker by the minute. "So, wish-y one of them do you fancy?"

Chenda rolled her eyes, suddenly regretting opening this line of discussion.

"Shpeek of the devil," Candice said. Chenda turned her head to see Captain Endicott walking toward them.

"Good evening, ladies. I hope you are enjoying yourselves." The captain looked all around as he greeted them. He waved at Fenimore and Verdu, who saluted back at him. For as much as they were enjoying the attentions of McNees's ladies, they had been subtly keeping watch over Chenda and Candice as well.

"Mind if I join you? Next round on me?" the captain asked.

"Shirtanly," Candice answered as she patted the bench next to her thigh. Captain Endicott sat down.

"So, what's our topic of conversation tonight?" he asked.

"Skirts," Chenda said slyly. The drinks made her propriety lax.

"I am fond of the garment myself," Endicott said with a laugh. "Funny that I've never bothered to own one."

"Chenie-chen-chen here was just about to tell us which of your crewmen will turn her head."

"Oh, that's easy," Endicott said. "Neither."

Chenda gave a relieved look to the captain as he continued. "Not any time soon."

He looked appraisingly at the professor. "Now, Candice, I believe we need to take you out into the fresh air, and walk you around a while before you head back to my airship, because, my dear lady, if you barf up there again, I'm pitching you over the side."

"Shtinker," Candice said with a pout.

He hooked his arm around Candice's waist and hauled her

to standing. Candice sagged a bit toward the captain. Fenimore and Verdu, now prostitute-free, appeared at Captain Endicott's side. "Shall we help you, sir?" Fenimore asked.

"No, no. Candice and I were just going for a bit of a walk. I'll get her back to the *Brofman*. Please look after the young lady, won't you? Enjoy yourselves." He turned to leave, dragging Candice along.

"Yes, sir," Verdu said to the retreating pair. The men sat down across from Chenda, who gave the men a cross look. "What? Done so soon?" she said tartly. "Those girls seemed to move pretty fast, but I thought the two of you would take longer."

They shrugged in unison. "They only let you sample so much for free. The rest you have to pay for," Verdu said.

"And we make it a point never to pay for it," Fenimore said. "But the samples *are* really a treat. Don't you agree?"

"Oh, I don't know," Verdu said. "They smell nice, but it stings a little that they lose all interest when they realize you won't be paying. They just drop you like a dead fish."

Chenda frowned at the pair. "Disgusting," she said.

"Probably," the two men said as one.

Chenda finished her drink and dug a few coins out of her pouchbelt. "I've experienced this as much as I care to."

"Off we go," Fenimore said.

Chenda made a beeline toward the exit before Fenimore and Verdu could even stand. She realized halfway to the door just how much she misjudged her own alcohol consumption. She sagged sideways, brushing into a burly redheaded fellow sitting in an overstuffed arm chair. Before she knew what was happening, the man reached his arm around her waist and pulled her down, laying her backwards across his lap and the arm of the chair.

"Oh, yes," he said in the most salacious way possible. "You'll do." He slid his hand from her ribs up to her breast, giving it a playful slap.

In the next second, Chenda felt herself being scooped out of the man's lap. She watched as a big, dark fist made sudden and meaningful contact with the burly man's nose. Verdu. She looked up at who was carrying her toward the door. Fenimore. They were quite a team.

Fenimore kept trotting along with Chenda in his arms until they were out of McNees's and several hundred yards down the narrow street. As her feet touched the ground, she looked back and saw Verdu laughing as he caught up.

"I can't take you anywhere, Fen. You steal the best girl in the room every time."

Fenimore smiled back at Verdu and then looked at Chenda. "He didn't hurt you did he? Just say the word and I'll go back in there and clean up what Verdu left behind."

Chenda felt shocked more than anything else. "I'm fine. I think he mistook me for one of the working girls." She frowned. "What do you suppose that says about me?"

Verdu and Fenimore laughed out loud. They stepped to either side of Chenda and each took an arm to steady her. "Let's just walk back to the airship tower. It's about a mile this way – the stroll should clear your head. But only if you feel up to it." Fenimore said.

"Let's give it a try." Chenda replied.

They walked while Fenimore whistled a bouncy tune. The night was cool and the breeze off the ocean smelled clean and fresh. The narrow path beneath their feet soon became all that separated the atoll's waters. To the left was the deep, dark water of the sea, and to the right, the shallow water of the lagoon shone pale blue in the moonlight. It was a glorious night.

Suddenly, the sound of quick and heavy footstep came from behind them. Chenda dropped Fenimore's arm and turned to look behind her, thinking she might have to scoot out of someone's way. That's when she saw the burly man from McNees's racing up to Verdu, fists flying.

Verdu, turning his attention too late to defend himself, shoved Chenda backwards as he took a blow to the side of his head. Chenda stumbled, lost her footing on the narrow path, and fell to the water to her left. She hit the sea and it felt as pleasant as sinking into a warm bath. She rolled backwards and down, her back scraping against the rough coral fingers of the atoll. She held her breath and calmly believed that by the time she floated back up, Fenimore and Verdu would likely have ended the dust-up with Mr. Burly-man. He was big, yes, but it was two against one.

116

But she didn't float back up.

After a few seconds, she realized she was stuck, peering up to the surface, in deep water. She panicked. She started to kick her legs wildly. She couldn't find what was holding her down. Her feet were free. Her hands weren't caught. It started to feel like the middle of her back was glued to the rock behind her.

Her lungs burned. She needed to breathe. She struggled again, willing her lips to stay together. She could only hold on for a few seconds more before she sucked in the dark water. It filled her nose, her mouth, her throat. She gagged, sucking more water down into her lungs.

A hand gripped her leg. She reached for it with her own, frantic for contact, desperate to not die alone. The rough hand smacked her clutching fingers away and grabbed her under her arms. It pushed her deeper into the water then away from the rocks. She was free and floating upward, but her vision was darkening.

Breaking the surface, she tried to breathe in the cool air, but there was too much water inside her already. Verdu reached down from the path and pulled her out by one arm. He dropped to one knee and wrapped both arms around Chenda's waist. He curled his torso around hers as he tipped her forward, bringing her head down, pressing her torso from all sides with his own body. The sea water burst out of her. Out it flowed, more than she thought possible.

Verdu released his crushing grip and Chenda gasped and coughed. Verdu rolled her onto the ground, holding her on her side as she brought up even more water. She pulled her knees up to her aching chest. Verdu wiped the seawater and dirt from her face and looked into her panicked eyes.

Fenimore appeared in her line of vision, just over Verdu's shoulder, dripping wet with a look of horror on his face. "Oh, gods, Verdu, is she going to be all right?"

"Fen, it's okay. She's coughed most of it up already," Verdu said, but he still looked worried. "I squeezed her pretty hard, though. We'd better get her back to the *Brofman* so Kingston can take a look at her."

Chenda coughed and gasped once more as Verdu hauled

her up and slung her over his shoulder. He started trotting up the path and Chenda saw the burly man sprawled several yards back down the way, out cold.

"I knew you would have him taken care of before I floated back up," she mumbled, and then she passed out.

Chapter 10
EASTWARD

Chenda found herself in a wide open space, surrounded by blue sky. Soft clouds floated past her. The air around her felt good, neither too cold nor too warm, and as still as the grave. This she found odd because little white puffs of cloud scooted by her in a quite a hurry. Sunlight warmed her back and it soothed her aches almost completely. She looked down at her feet and noticed they were bare. That surprised her only slightly less than the fact she was standing on nothing. She was floating.

Oh, my. I'm dead, she thought.

"No. Not yet," said a voice behind her that Chenda would have known anywhere. She willed herself to turn around and it was done, without movement – instantly. Out of the sunshine walked Edison. He moved toward her down a path of cloud.

She sprang forward, half running and half swimming through the air to his open arms. Chenda wrapped her arms around his neck, burying her face into his cheek, and he gripped her firmly around the waist, holding her close to him. They held each other for a long time, slowly turning in the air.

Finally Edison released one arm from around her, and he brushed his hand up her back to the short spiky hair on her head. "This is new," he said, brushing his hands through her hair, stroking his fingertips all around her, tracing around her ear and down the edge of her jaw to her neck. Edison cupped his hand under her chin, tilting her face up, eye to eye with him.

"You, darling, are a mess. I'm sorry you have had such a rough time of it since I had to leave. You have to know I didn't want to," he said.

Tears spilled from Chenda's eyes as she looked up into his face. His scars had softened and faded. His eyes, ever so haunted by the past, stared clearly back at her, now full of hope and joy. There was no pain. There was no sorrow. He seemed younger somehow, more vital than she had ever known him.

"Daniel killed you," she said.

"I know."

"He tried to kill me."

"That I also know. And then you took him." He brushed the tears from her face. "I forgave him, and he me, for all my sins against him and his family."

"I'm not sure I forgive him. He took too much from me. He took you."

"Don't hate him for causing my death. I consider that my punishment for my sins against you."

"You never sinned against me. You were ideal as --"

"NO." He cut her off. "No, I held you away from the world, selfishly. I needed to be where I was, apart from people. I needed the solitude. The mystic Pranav Erato can tell you about that, because I'm running out of time. The pouch of pedradurite stones has allowed me to stay with you until now, but I had to leave the limbo of the stones to reach you. My soul will drift free now, to go wherever souls go when they are not bound. I'll have to go soon, and you need to wake up. You're really scaring your friends."

Chenda's body tensed in Edison's arms. "No, I want to stay here."

"Impossible," he said looking around at the clouds as they darkened. "I can't even hold myself here much longer."

Talking quickly, he said, "Chenda, you are doing very well in the task I set for you." He placed a hand over her chest, and turned his head slightly as if listening to her body through his hand. "I'm glad you have poured out most of your sorrow over me. It wasn't fair of a broken old man to take a bride so young and turn her into some matron of solitude. I want you to try to be young again. You need to feel the power of your youth before it's too late. Promise me that," he demanded.

"You ask it of me, so I'll... promise I'll try." Chenda

whispered.

"You don't know it yet, but fate, in the last few days, has given you most of the elements you need to follow your destiny. Erato will help you put it together. Now listen carefully, as we only have seconds left. You need to take Verdu and Fenimore with you when you leave for the *Tjalk*. They are now tied to your destiny. You need them, and what they know. Keep talking to them, they are half bound to you already. They MUST come along."

"*Tjalk?*"

"The captain has found a boat that will take you the rest of the way into Tugrulia. You'll find out about it when you wake up."

He paused, and looked at her with complete love. "I am dead. I won't be able to come to you again -- ever. You must live your life, and love again." He let out a long breath that Chenda couldn't feel. "You were the love of my life, but I was not the love of yours."

"That's not true."

"From this side of death, one can see things so clearly. Love is still out there for you, and someday you'll find it. I can give you a clue. You will know the love that is meant to be yours forever when you feel it, and it will feel something like this..."

Edison pulled her face toward his, and kissed her like he never had in life. His lips met hers with hunger and desire, and waves of tingling energy rolled over her. Flames radiated down her spine and blew away all sensation except for her need to return the kiss. Her body responded fiercely. An animalistic groan escaped her as she pulled her legs up and around Edison's hips. His hands moved to embrace every part of her, sliding down from the small of her back, fingers raking delicate skin. They rolled together through the air, tumbling and falling though bliss. It rained over them. No breathing, no thinking, no sound or sight. She could only feel and taste an unbridled passion that was being channeled through Edison. She knew at that moment she would search for this feeling, even if it took the rest of her life, because she couldn't – no, wouldn't – live without it. Her heart became a bigger place. Alive.

Edison untangled his wife from his body, and cradled her to his chest in the complete darkness that surrounded them now. "I wish I could have done that for you in life," he whispered. "Know that your every touch made me feel that way." He kissed her on the top of her head, a kiss like so many that Chenda remembered from their marriage, and she floated free. Edison's last kiss was also the final message he needed to deliver.

Goodbye...

She knew he was gone forever.

Her arms grasped outward, flailing and reaching out of the darkness. Her eyes burst open and flooded with light. The weightless sky was gone and all of her pain flooded back to her; the burning from her lungs, throat and sinuses, the scrapes down her back, and the aching of her ribs charged forward. She groaned her agony.

A large pair of hands grasped her flailing arms, restraining her. The light burning her eyes settled and her irises adjusted. Two faces came into focus: Fenimore holding her hands together, firmly but gently, and Verdu, who cradled her to his chest.

"Take it easy!" Fenimore demanded.

The strain on Verdu's face showed that he was doing his best not to drop the flailing woman. Chenda froze. She looked around to discover they were all in an elevator car. Wide eyed, she asked "To the airship?" Her own voice sounded strange to her, rough and raw. It was painful to talk.

Fenimore sighed his relief as he dropped Chenda's still hands. "Yes. Thank the gods you are finally making sense! We thought you'd dashed your head on the reef. And then you were thrashing around. Then you made some, um, yummy noises... and then more trashing. I'm just glad you opened your eyes and – "

"Shut up, Fen," Verdu said. "Let her breathe." He bounced Chenda upward to get a better grip on her. She turned her head toward the big man's chest and pressed her forehead into his shoulder. She tried to remember all the details of her dream, not wanting them to slip away from her. Edison. *Tjalk*. Fen and Verdu. Erato. Passion.

She mouthed the words *Edison. Tjalk. Fen and Verdu. Erato. Passion.*

The words tumbled out of her mouth, "Edison. *Tjalk.* Fen and Verdu. Erato. Passion."

Fenimore and Verdu looked at her, their mouths agape. "What?" Fenimore said.

"I'm trying to remember my dream, the message," she said quietly. "How long was I out?"

The elevator doors slid open. Verdu carried her off and said, "Just a few minutes. When you passed out, I started to run back to the ship. We figured that if you were really bad off, Kingston would be the man we needed. I hope he's made it back to the *Brofman* already."

Verdu moved quickly down to slip seven and up the ramp onto the airship, passing a very surprised Germer on the deck. He was about to carry Chenda down the steps to find Kingston, when Chenda tapped him on the arm. "Stop," she said. "I'm okay. Just hold on. Let me catch my breath."

Verdu stood there holding Chenda, one foot on the deck and the other on the stairs. Fenimore stood right behind them. "What's wrong?" he asked. "Why are you standing there?"

"She said stop."

"She's half drowned and perhaps has a blow to the head. Not to mention a few strong drinks. You're listening to her?"

"Shush," Chenda said. "I want to stay up here, in the open air."

Verdu frowned slightly, and turned to Fenimore. "She's heavy after a bit," he warned as he stuffed Chenda into Fenimore's arms and tromped below deck. Chenda looked up at Fenimore and gave a halfhearted grin.

"I guess he's been carrying me for a while?" Chenda said.

"About a mile and a half, counting the elevator. Shall I put you down? Can you stand?"

"Won't know till we try."

Fenimore lowered her legs to the deck, but held her around the shoulders to make sure she didn't collapse. Although she felt an ache in her body from the balls of her feet on up, every part of her seemed to still be working. "I think I'll live," she said at last.

"That's a relief. I wasn't looking forward to pitching your

dead body over the side." He laughed, and attached a bitter-end to his belt. He reached over and handed a line to Chenda as well."

"Up here, these belts and lines are supposed to save us, but tonight, yours almost did you in," he said as they slowly walked toward the stern of the airship.

"What do you mean?"

"Your bitter-end belt. One of the rings got hooked on some debris in the reef when you got knocked in. That's how you got stuck. I guess you didn't realize it. Getting you un-stuck was simple: all I had to do was push you down a little and up you floated."

Chenda realized then that she hadn't thought to thank either man for helping her. The dream about Edison distracted her totally.

"I'm sorry." She turned to Fenimore. "You really saved my life, you and Verdu both, and I don't know how to say thank you. My thoughts are just so overwhelming." She sat with Fenimore on a long crate for a while and chewed on her fingernail.

"What's wrong?" Fenimore said, wrapping one arm around Chenda again.

"I'm going to Kotal in Tugrulia," she said. "That's my destination."

"Ah, I see now. You're insane."

Chenda snorted, which really made the inside of her face hurt. "No, I'm just being honest with you. See, after all that's happened tonight, I know now that I can trust you. You and Verdu both, because you could have let me drown, and you didn't. I know that *you* aren't trying to kill me."

"Reasonable assumption given the evidence," Fenimore said. "But since I went through all that trouble to keep you alive, why let the Tugrulians kill you? What can you possibly be thinking?"

"I started this journey because Edison told me to. I keep going because I need to find out who I am, what I'm made of. I can feel myself changing. I thought I needed to grow up and take care of my own life, learn about my own character. But in light of what's happening to me lately, I think that I need to draw on my strengths and my youth. These are the gifts the gods have given me. I need to use them, and be grateful."

"Get over yourself. Go take a class. Learn to paint. Traveling to Kotal is not finding yourself. It's getting yourself killed. The captain is never going to take you there. That's for sure."

"He's going to get us close. That's our agreement. I think tonight he's found us a way to get me and Candice the rest of the way there. Be open minded about this for a second, okay? I think maybe I had a vision tonight. I think after I drowned a little, I got a message." Chenda looked up, searching the stars shining above them for some sign to keep talking. She focused on the dark outline of a few small clouds drifting along and, feeling the need for real contact, reached out for Fenimore's hand.

"I saw my husband, Edison. He told me that I am doing well, and I need to get on a ship called the *Tjalk*. And I need to take you. He was very firm on that." She searched his eyes to see if he was hearing her.

Fenimore's expression spoke for him. His eyes said Chenda had lost her mind. When he finally spoke, it was in a tone one would use to coax a frightened puppy out from under the porch. "OK... come on... let's just go see our old buddy Kingston. He'll take a little look-see. We'll just make sure we haven't hit our wee heads. OK?"

Chenda rolled her eyes. "You go. I'm fine. I'm just happy to sit right here until it's time to go." She let go of his hand. "I am serious. I want you to go with me." She judged what she knew about him and went out on a limb. "You know who I am and how much money I have. Name your price."

He scoffed at her. "Can't pay me if you're dead," he said with a shrug. "And I can't spend it if I'm dead. An offer of dead plus dead is not a compelling payoff."

He stood up and walked away, then turned back to her. "Chenda, you're putting faith into a fantasy here. You were unconscious. You had a dream. I can't begin to imagine how much you miss your husband. Your grief must have dragged this 'vision' out of you."

"I've already purged my grief. It was too heavy to carry around with me. He let me go tonight. He showed me something to live for, and I am ready to search for it. I know that my path leads me to Kotal, and back out again. You need to take the path with me. Don't say 'no' yet. Think it through."

Fenimore saw clearly; the woman before him would not be moved.

It was then that Lincoln and Stanley stumbled up the ramp onto the airship. Stanley walked shakily across the deck and, making two attempts at it, found the stairs leading belowdecks. He sat down on the top step and slowly started making his way down, pulling himself forward and letting his rump fall to the next lower step, giggling like a maniac, high as a kite.

Lincoln seemed slightly less drunk, but Fenimore guessed that whoever had given the boy a black eye also acted as a sobering agent. Lincoln saluted crudely. "Dulal! We have returned within our pripper, um popper, er, proper curfew. No problems."

"It won't be a problem if you all are ready to work in four hours when we depart. Sober up, son, and I will see you at four bells."

"Yes, shir." Lincoln said as he stumbled below deck.

Fenimore pinched the bridge of his nose and sighed. "The world's gone mad." he said.

"Ahoy, *Brofman*," a reedy voice floated up from the pier.

"Ahoy," Fenimore replied. Germer appeared from the bow of the airship.

"How can we help you?" Germer asked the small man standing at the end of the ramp.

"Letters for Captain Maxwell Endicott from Mr. Jason Belles. Permission to come aboard?"

"Please do." Germer said. The messenger brought the letters to Fenimore, who stood with his hand out. His job now done, the boy dashed back off the ship and away.

Fenimore looked at the first envelope; it was addressed to Captain Maxwell Endicott. He flipped to the second letter, of which the envelope read:

Letter of introduction
for Airship Captain Maxwell Endicott
to Captain Taboda
of the Sailing Ship Tjalk

He stared at the envelopes for several seconds and then handed them to Germer. "The captain will want these the moment he returns. If you will excuse me." He turned without waiting for a reply.

Fenimore strode to where Chenda sat in the stern and knelt down in front of her.

"I think there is a lot more we need to talk about. I'm starting to believe your Edison may really have spoken, because it looks like the *Brofman* will be making a rendezvous with the *Tjalk*."

Chapter 11
KEEP TALKING TILL THEY HEAR YOU

Chenda smiled at Fenimore. She put one of her wet bandaged hands on the side of his face. "Edison told me I just needed to talk to you, to tell you more, and you would understand."

Fenimore's face contorted with unease and confusion. "I'm unnerved right now, it's too bizarre for me, and I don't think I understand any of this. People talking to you from beyond the veil of death? How does that happen?"

"I don't really know. But I fully believe Edison did; he knew how to make this happen. But I don't think it will happen again." Chenda dropped her hand and patted the space on the crate next to her, signaling that he should sit beside her again.

"Start at the beginning," he said. "I want to hear everything Edison said to you, everything that you saw and felt."

"I'll try, but some of it was so... intimate..." She blushed. "Maybe I should just stick to what's relevant. At least to you, that is."

"Fair enough." he replied. "Talk."

Chenda took a deep breath. "He said his soul was holding on to this world so he could tell me that you and Verdu need to come with me aboard the *Tjalk*, and then onward to the Tugrulian Empire. He said that what you know is necessary to my journey. He insisted I'll need you -- both of you. He said that Pranav Erato will be able to help me understand what happened, and why Edison had the stones. He's the key to what I am supposed to be or do, I think. The rest of his message was... um, mostly

129

personal."

Fenimore gave her a sly look. "I guess that explains the yummy noises."

Chenda blushed.

"Mostly, he was letting me go, and saying goodbye." Chenda wrapped her arms around herself. "I felt him leave. He gave me a wonderful gift, being there one last time. He was different, weightless and light. Free from all that agony that he carried through life. And yet he was my Edison. He said he put himself into the stones to stay here, with me, and he had to come out to give me his message. When his soul wasn't bound anymore, he just faded away..."

Fenimore wrapped his arms around Chenda and rubbed his hands on her back soothingly. "I'm sorry," he said. "It must be so difficult to lose someone you loved so very much."

They sat in silence, each mulling over his or her own thoughts.

Fenimore spoke first. "You lost me on the part about him putting himself in the stones." Fenimore looked at Chenda "What stones?"

Chenda shifted, wiggling free from Fenimore's comforting arms. She reached down the front of her shirt and pulled out the black velvet bag. She opened it carefully and poured the contents onto her lap. Edison's letter, now wet from Chenda's spill into the sea, lay limply under the three stones. Chenda handed the stones to Fenimore.

He held each up to the dim light that shone out of the center of the dock tower. Fenimore looked unimpressed, handing them back. "These dim pebbles?" he said doubtfully.

Chenda held the two loose stones between her thumb and forefinger on each hand. She clacked them together, and they began to sing out two beautiful, harmonizing notes. Fenimore's eyes opened wide with shock at the loud rich sound. Chenda let them ring for almost a minute then muffled them with her hands.

"Edison left these stones for me, along with this letter. I found them on the day of his funeral. Candice explained to me that these pedradurite stones, called Singing Stones, come from Tugrulia, and every stone of this kind that appeared in the West

130

has gone missing, and the owners have ended up dead. Edison was murdered because he had these stones. The night Daniel burned my house, these are what he was looking for. He was prepared to kill me to get them. I think that someone tried to kill Candice, too, because she knows all about the stones."

Chenda frowned and looked at the heavens. "Edison said that if I keep talking, you would come with me. I'm listening to my own story and I think maybe you are better off keeping far from me and these stones. They attract death, it seems. In the few days I've been holding them close, I've been stabbed, choked, beaten, burned and nearly drowned. A smarter woman than me would throw these over the side and go home. But..."

"...you can't." Fenimore finished. "It doesn't make sense, and yet you keep going. I know that feeling. We all have our demons that drive us. I guess I shouldn't be one to judge the motivations of another. If you need to follow your vision, your path that Edison has challenged you to follow, then maybe you should."

Chenda brightened slightly. "Come with me, Fen." She looked into his face, a face shaped by doubt. "I feel like my life is finally begun, and you are a big part of that. You, and this airship and Verdu, Candice. It's remarkable that I've only known you all for a short time, but I can't remember my life very well before you. Besides Edison, there wasn't much to my life worth committing to memory. I could try to go back to my life in Coal City, but I would *not* be fine. Not when I know that there is a bigger world out there. Not when I know there is something calling me."

Chenda slid off her seat and onto her knees in front of Fenimore. "Come."

"You ask too much," he whispered. The silence lay between them. Chenda leaned her head forward and rested it on Fenimore's knee. Fenimore closed his eyes, and turned his face away from her.

"Fen, come with me." She said again. "Tell yourself whatever you need to, but come. I promise it's the right path. Please, come with-"

"Enough," he whispered. "Let me sleep on it." He stood

131

and pulled Chenda up, too. "You're sopping wet, and so am I. Let's go below and get cleaned up." He leaned over and picked up the velvet bag and letter. He handed them back to Chenda, who tucked the stones back inside her shirt.

As they went down the steps to the narrow passage, Fenimore spoke. "So, I'll let you go ahead into the crew quarters and get changed first, so you can have at least a little privacy. The other lads in there should be dead asleep, and I'll make sure nobody's awake or walks in on you. OK?"

Chenda closed her eyes and said something she had never said before in her life. "Crap!" She slapped both of her hands over her mouth in surprise. Her outburst cracked a smile on Fenimore's face.

"What's wrong?"

"I just realized that every shirt I own, including the two I bought tonight, are soaked in seawater. I just can't win with my clothes these days."

They entered the crew quarters, and Fenimore whispered, "I'll lend you one of mine." He rummaged in his cupboard for a moment and tossed her a clean shirt. "I guess it will be more of a dress than a shirt for you, but at least we can rinse out the rest of your clothes and hopefully they will be dry by morning. Give me your boots, I'll clean yours while I do mine."

"Thank you," she whispered as she sat on the floor pulling her boots off. "You're a nice guy." A small puddle of seawater trickled onto the floor." Fenimore took the sodden boots and walked to the door. "I'll give you that privacy, then. Take your time," he said and walked out.

Chenda looked over at the wall of bunks, and realized she was hardly alone. Lincoln and Stanley were already hard asleep in their small bunks, and Kingston was muttering in his sleep as well, one beefy arm draped over his eyes and the other dangling out over the side. The idea of stripping off her clothes with these men in the room, asleep or otherwise, grated against her upbringing. The nuns would faint! Chenda bit her lip. She reasoned that the two younger men had just visited the ladies at McNees's Opera House, and likely had seen all manner of girl parts there. Kingston was a doctor, also in the know about female anatomy. She decided that she was being pretty foolish.

It is what it is, and here I am. Let's get on with this...

She stripped to her bare essentials and draped Fenimore's shirt over her shoulders. It hung almost to the backs of her knees. She walked over to the small sink, making wet footprints as she went, and looked at herself in the mirror. Chenda examined her abused eye, and it looked well healed. However, the bruises all around it on her face were still a dark greenish-purple. Most of the blood trapped in her battered skin had risen to just under the surface, to the point where bruises always look their worst. It would get better tomorrow, she decided. She twisted herself to check the new scrapes from the reef on her back, letting the top of Fenimore's shirt slide down to her elbows. *Minor*, she thought to herself. She felt the bandage over the place Daniel had stabbed her. It, like the bandages on her hands, were soaked with brackish water. Chenda tore off all the soiled bandages. Her side had scabbed over and was healing. As for her palms, Kingston's ointment had worked wonders. Her hands seemed mostly mended, but still slightly swollen. The repaired skin looked in the dim light to have a slightly silver tint. She flexed her hands, feeling the tightness in the skin. Her nerves seemed exceptionally sensitive, like they were very close to the surface now.

She turned on the tap and, tying Fenimore's shirt around her waist, she leaned her head over the small basin. Scooping handfuls of water over her head, she rubbed a bit of coarse soap into her hair, scrubbing gently. As she rinsed, she watched the bubbles and bits of seaweed and sand swirl down the drain. She worked her way down her neck and arms using a corner of her soiled shirt as a washcloth. With each cleansing rub, she scoured away a part of herself that she no longer felt: her small doubts, her fear of what lay ahead, the sensation that perhaps she wasn't strong enough to lead her own life. As she finished washing her feet and ankles, she straightened up and looked into the mirror. For the first, time she accepted what she saw.

This is what I have to work with today: me.

She shrugged the shirt back up onto her shoulders and rolled the sleeves up. She worked her way back to her bunk, using the soiled shirt like a mop, cleaning up the mess from her wet pants and aeronaut boots. She glanced up at the bunks behind her and noticed Lincoln quickly closing an eye. She stretched up on her tip toes and looked at his closed eyes, squeezed a little too tightly to be truly lodged in slumber.

"Enjoying me bathing?" she asked.

Lincoln winced but didn't give up his charade. "Very much," he whispered.

She flicked his ear. "Shame on you!" she hissed. He blushed.

"I'll thank you to be a better gentleman in the future," she chided.

"Yes, ma'am," he said, still holding his eyes closed. "I'm sorry."

Chenda turned with her armload of wet clothes and left. She found Fenimore in the passageway beyond, hanging their aeronaut boots upside down on the hooks there. They dripped quietly into narrow pans below.

Fenimore smiled at her. "You look fresh as a daisy. Still feeling okay?"

"As good as can be expected," she replied. "Got my soggy clothes here. Where should I wash them?"

"Ah, I have a bucket set out in the galley. You go ahead in and I am going to get cleaned up myself." He stalked into the crew quarters.

She stepped into the galley, and she found Verdu there, singing quietly to himself. He smiled at her and kept on singing. Chenda looked into the sudsy bucket on the table, then tipped in her clothes. She swished them around and listened to Verdu's song.

The language was a mystery to her, but the meaning of the song was clear enough. The melody spoke of tenderness, devotion and loss. After several minutes, Verdu's song drifted to an end, and he sat silently, motionless, a dark shadow in the corner.

"That was really lovely," Chenda said, wringing out her shirts. "You sing very well. What was the song?"

Verdu breathed in slowly. "It's a forbidden Tugrulian lullaby, loosely translated it's called 'I love you more'."

"Forbidden?"

"Yes. The song is sung by a mother, sitting at her window late one evening. She cradles her young son in the moonlight and tells him that she loves him, the child of her lover, more than the children she has borne her husband." He made a sour grin. "The song is deemed *culturally perverse* by the Dia Orella Heirarchy. The Tugrulian leadership fears that it will lead women astray. It's not sung in the Empire under pain of death."

"Not a forgiving place," Chenda said as she finished wringing out her clothes. She piled the wet lumps on the table and crossed the galley to pour the dirty water into the sink. "You and I have something in common," she noted as she refilled the bucket.

"Oh, what's that?"

"We were both essentially orphans, but not exactly. My father left me with nuns while he went away to the war, but he was alive yet absent for most of my youth. From what you said before, I'm guessing that your parents were alive during your childhood as well but they were nowhere near you."

"True enough," he said. "Growing up among the Mae-Lyn, I found that some of the best people I know are orphans. The gods seem to be close to them. Do you mind if I ask what happened to your mother?"

"I wish I knew," Chenda said. "My father never told the nuns, and he died before I could ask him. There was never any other family to ask either. I imagine that she died in childbirth or something like that."

"Not knowing is the hardest part. I doubt that my mother is still living," Verdu said. "Tugrulian women don't live much past their fertility. The men don't much care to have unproductive mouths to feed."

Chenda was shocked. "How barbaric!"

"How Tugrulian," he replied flatly. "Can you tell me about your father?"

Chenda shrugged. "Sort of. The last time I saw him, I was two-years old, when he left me at the convent in Wadpole-on-the-River. I mostly know him from his letters and gifts. For ten years, Daddy sent wonderful gifts for my birthday. There would always be something special for me, from some far-off place, but he also sent gifts for me to share with the other children living with the

Sisters of St. Elgin, the real orphans. For my sixth birthday, he sent a beautiful, hand drawn map showing delicate illustrations of the four continents and the locations of all the great cities of the world."

Chenda giggled as she swished her clothes in the rinse bucket. "It's a little silly, but I would mark the map with little X's each time my father sent a letter or gift. I imagined that I was there too, in some exotic place. After just a few years, I had marked the map into a dark mishmash of ink. All except for the continent labeled *The Tugrulian Empire.*"

Sheepishly, she looked up at Verdu. "All children in the Republic, even the ones cloistered deep in the countryside, knew stories about of the savage Tugrulians, and how they murdered foreigners on sight. The Tugrulians shaped the fate of many of the children living with the Sisters. Several of the orphans had lost both parents in one of the many Tugrulian attacks on the Republic's eastern coast. A few of my playmates had barely survived the attacks themselves, and their disfigured bodies spoke for them about the brutality of the foreign invaders..."

Verdu frowned and said, "I know. I wish I could apologize for my people, but I can't. Go on with your story. What happened to your father?"

Chenda swallowed hard and went on. "When I was 12-years old, the Mother Superior called me to her office and offered me this limp hug and some sticky toffee. Like candy was going to make what she was going to tell me any less devastating. Anyway, I hadn't received any letters in the previous weeks, so I already knew the old sister would tell me my father was dead. It seemed ironic that, after ten years, I finally was an equal to my peers, alone in the world, an orphan. The nun shared all she knew; my father's ship, the *Valiant Eagle*, had been lost over the Kohlian Sea. There were no known survivors.

"You know, Verdu, for a little while, my life went on just as it had before. Aside from not getting any letters, everything was just the same. I went to class and to worship. I made my bed and ate my meals. When my birthday came, the truth sank in. No more letters. No packages. No father. The pattern of my life broke that day, and I finally understood then that my father really wasn't

136

going to come back."

Chenda stood in silence for a minute and said, "The next day, Edison appeared at the convent and claimed me as his ward. I never doubted that I should leave with him. It just seemed like there was nothing left to wait for in Wadpole-on-the-River."

Verdu looked at Chenda with sympathetic eyes. "There is a lot of gravity in your life, I think. You get pulled along by some very strong fates."

Chenda smiled again. "That sounds about right. The less I fight it, the better off I am. Kind of like that unique connection between you and Fenimore"

"Ah, Fenimore," Verdu said. "He says you're going to Kotal, and you've asked him to go."

"That's right."

"He told me about your vision, and said you are going to ask me, too."

"True again."

"Show me the stones," he suggested.

Chenda sat down beside Verdu and pulled the bag of stones out. She poured them into Verdu's waiting palm. He closed his fingers around them and kissed his hands.

"Oh," he said quietly. "Oh, Chenda. I... Yes. I'll go with you." He looked up into her eyes, looking deeply as if he were searching for something important within her.

Chenda smiled and put her hand on top of his. "I'm happy that you will come, but I would be lying if I said I understood why."

"I'll be lying if I try to explain. Let's just say that, for now, I'll follow you anywhere."

Chenda put her arms around Verdu as he clutched the stones to his chest. "Thank you," she said. "Thank you for saying you will come with me. Thank you for pulling me out of the sea. Thank you for wringing me out. You saved my life, and I won't forget it."

"Anytime," he said.

Chapter 12
FINDING THE *TJALK*

Chenda sat in the galley amongst her drip drying clothes and listened to Verdu's beautiful voice. His songs were lilting and joyful. Chenda settled behind the small table and stretched her bare legs across the next chair. For the first time in recent memory, she felt relaxed and safe.

As she lounged, enjoying her own private concert, Captain Endicott and Candice entered the galley. Candice slid into the seat opposite Chenda as Verdu finished his song. The ladies clapped joyfully, and Captain Endicott slapped his young officer on the back.

"If you are quite done with your show biz auditions," the captain remarked, "we've got work to do. I'd like to shove off in just over an hour, so let's do the pre-flight inspection. Start by counting noses and make sure we have a full complement. If everyone is accounted for, you tell Germer to pull up the plank and put him off duty."

"Yes, sir," Verdu said. He looked at Chenda with searching eyes as he left the galley.

Captain Endicott turned his attention to Candice. "My dear, I hate to leave you to finish sobering up alone, but duty calls. We've got appointments to keep!" He stepped to the doorway. "Get some rest if you can, ladies," he said as he stalked out the door.

Candice and Chenda, alone once again, looked across the table at each other.

"So, what happened after Max and I left?" Candice asked.

"Looks like you fell in the sea."

"Indeed I did, and it's Max now is it?" Chenda said with a smile. "That seems a little personal."

"I'm starting to *feel* a little personal about him. But that's not important. What happened amongst the three of you? Verdu is looking at you like a landed fish looks at water."

"Ah, well, I nearly drowned, he and Fenimore saved me, I had a vision, I talked with Edison - who gave me more instructions - and I've convinced Verdu to come along with us into the heart of the Tugrulian Empire. What's new with you?"

"I've fallen in love with the captain, but somehow that seems irrelevant at the moment." She sighed. "Really? I missed that much? We were only apart for an hour or so."

Chenda laughed and said, "Let me catch you up."

She started at the beginning, and left out no details. Candice sat quietly, nodding at various facts and gasping only occasionally. When Chenda finally finished recapping her last two hours, Chenda said with excitement, "Well, Verdu obviously knows about singing stones! I can't wait to pick his brain about this."

"*That's* the detail of my night's experience about which you are most excited? Really? The bits about Edison and fate and passion and 'bring Verdu and Fenimore along,' nothing?"

"Yes. All very important details. But there is much more to be learned here. Edison even said so in your vision. I can see why Verdu will be an asset; he speaks the language, and knows the culture. I wonder why Fenimore is 'necessary' in Edison's opinion. Hmm...." Candice tapped an index finger on her chin as she thought.

"I'm glad Edison sent me to you," Chenda said. "I've never had a friend like you before."

"It seems to me that, apart from Edison, you never had a friend at all. But I thank you just the same, I think. I am fond of you, too."

Chenda pulled a sly grin. "So, falling for the Captain, huh? What happened on that walk? Was it romantic?"

"HA! The walk was meant to sober me up, so romance was not called for from the start." Candice slurred only slightly,

Emilie P. Bush

proving that the sobering was not quite finished.

"Did you vomit?"

"Oh, worse. I barfed like a sick pig," Candice said. "However, Max was pleased that at least I did the deed *off* his airship."

Chenda giggled as Candice reached over to the water pitcher, pouring herself a glass.

"I got about 20 feet outside the whore house and let fly – gracelessly – into the lagoon. Of course, I felt much better after that, but it was so embarrassing. Max just seemed amused. He kept saying that it was fine, and it's happened to better men than me," she said.

"We walked and talked, my head got clearer, we kept going. We stopped by the marketplace and got some tea, nice minty stuff that really clears away the cobwebs of whatever we drank. Max is quite an interesting fellow. Very bright. Great conversationalist..." Candice trailed.

"Go on!" Chenda said.

"We walked the whole way back to the tower, the long way, and we had an elevator car to ourselves, and..." Candice smiled. "He planted a kiss on me I may just never forget! My arms tingled and I think I even kicked one foot out behind me. He's really good, I must say."

"A little passion is a good thing," Chenda said remembering her own kiss with Edison.

Captain Endicott strolled back into the galley, smiling as ever. He glanced at the two ladies, hunched together in conspiring conversation and said, "Oh, I see you are in the middle of something, don't let me interrupt." He turned to walk out again, but Chenda jumped up and waved Captain Endicott back toward the newly emptied seat near Candice.

"I'm just exhausted," she announced. "I think, ah, I'll just trot off to bed." She practically ran past the captain. At the door she turned and winked at Candice. "Good night, Candice, dear." She flitted across the passageway and into the crew cabin on silent feet. All of the bunks were filled except for her own and Verdu's. The rest of the sleeping men would all be hard at work again in a few short hours. She crept to her floor level bunk and knelt down beside it, her face level to a sleeping Fenimore. She could just make out his profile in the dimness. She moved close enough to smell the fresh scent of soap on his back and hear his soft, slumbering breath.

"Come with me, Fenimore," she said in the barest of whispers as she slid into her own bunk below his. She held her breath, expecting him to wake, but he didn't stir. *Good*, she thought. As she waited for sleep to overtake her, she thought of Candice and the captain. She felt sympathetic joy for her friend, glad that she found something to spark her long silent heart. At the same time, she worried about the dangers yet to come. Chenda realized that perhaps her friend may change her mind about accompanying her to Kotal. The captain may tempt her to stay with him. Her joy and her fears rattled around in her head until she drifted off into a deep sleep.

Chenda awoke with bitter coldness biting into her bare legs. Her eyes fluttered open and the room was bright with natural light. She'd missed their take off from Atoll Belles. Judging by the gentle sway of the ship and the cold temperature, they were pretty high in the air. Stiffly, she rolled on her side and tucked her legs up into Fenimore's loose shirt in an attempt to hold in a bit of heat, but the thin fabric was outdone by the chill. She saw on the floor next to her bunk that someone had placed her flight coat, one of her own shirts and her quilted pants, all dry and neatly folded. Her aeronaut boots stood next to the clothes.

She pulled on her coat first, telling herself that it was just too cold right then to take off Fenimore's shirt to change back into her own. With relief, she pulled on her quilted pants, cutting the air's icy touch to her thighs and calves. As she pushed her foot down into her boot, her toe poked something warm and a slightly squishy. She turned the boot over and out fell a baked potato, still warm. Chenda smiled. *Boot warmers! How sweet.*

She buckled on her toasty boots, gathered up the edible heaters and crossed over to the galley where she found Kingston cleaning up. Chenda guessed she had missed breakfast, but the plump man pulled a heaping plate from of a warming drawer in the stove.

"Good morning, sleepyhead. Here's one o' the house specialties." He placed the plate before her with a flourish. "Curried eggs with pan fried toast." Chenda stared at the overflowing plate of speckled yellows and golden browns. The smell was heavenly.

"Thank you!" Chenda salivated. "And thanks for the boot warmers, too." She dove into the plate of savory eggs.

"Boot what?" Kingston asked.

Chenda mumbled through a mouthful of toast "I found these in my boots this morning when I got up. It made my feet nice and warm. I thought the idea was yours." She handed the potatoes to Kingston while she scooped in more eggs.

"Ah," Kingston muttered, mostly to himself. "I wondered why Verdu wanted baked potatoes for breakfast - 'hold the salt,' he says to me. I see now." He shuffled back to the stove and threw the potatoes into the warming drawer as he hummed a zippy tune.

Chenda mulled over how she would thank her dark friend as she joyfully worked through her breakfast. Between mouthfuls, she quizzed Kingston.

"Did the captain tell you where we are going?"

"More or less," he said, his tone suddenly grumpy. "I can't say that I am happy that we are heading so far east. You'll be wanting to keep those boots tight to your feet now, my missy. The further east we go, the higher we will be. We'll be wanting ourselves out of sight and out of range from any Tugrulians in the waters off the coast."

Chenda downed her last bite of toast and chewed slowly. "So, what happens if we are spotted by Tugrulians?"

Kingston pulled a chair up beside Chenda and leaned in toward the table. "You're young, but I'm sure you've seen veterans of the war, right? Scarred and broken. The Tugrulian venom bombs are the maker of that misery. From the decks of their sailing ships, the Tugrulians could launch these flaming bombs. A lucky hit from one of those fireballs could burn airships out of the sky, but even a graze could cripple near every man aboard. All sorts of nasty bits in some of those bombs. Sometimes it would be acid that would eat through parts of the airships and their crews;

other bombs, when they exploded, would spray a venom around the ship. Horrible, gasping deaths went along with them buggers. Tugrulian weapons are spiteful and unpredictable - always horrible. That's why our best option to protect the *Brofman* is to stay very high, above the clouds if we can. They can't hit what they can't see." Kingston patted Chenda on the back reassuringly. "We can be hard to hit if need be."

"How long will it take us to get where we are going?" Chenda asked.

"Oh," Kingston thought a moment, scratching absently at the silver stubble on his ample cheek. "We'll likely be where we're heading by tomorrow evening."

"That's sooner than I thought." Chenda said, pleased but suddenly anxious.

"Captain said you and Candice would be leaving us then. I don't like it, missy, not at all. It's too close to a very dangerous part of the world. I worry the gods won't look after you there." His lips pressed into a disapproving line and he shook his head. "No good ever came out of that place."

"Verdu came out of that place," she said. "He seems better than good."

"An exception that proves the rule," Kingston snorted. "But if he hadn't made it out as a baby, I wonder if you'd be singing a different tune about him. The point is- you ladies won't be safe. No, sir."

"Well, safe or not, that's where we are going," she said firmly. She patted his hand and spoke in a softer tone as she stood up to leave, "The eggs were divine. Thanks for keeping me so well fed."

"You're welcome. I aim to feed." He said, glowing in her praise.

Chenda secured her bitter-end and stepped on deck where the cold wind sliced past her and thready clouds scratched across the sky in every direction. She saw Verdu in the wheelhouse and Fenimore in his usual position in the bow, looking out toward the horizon.

Verdu tapped on the glass and waved at Chenda; she grinned back at him and pulled her knee up to rub her boot as if warming it, then hugged herself. Verdu acknowledged her thanks with a small bow and turned back to the helm. Chenda giggled as she left the windbreak of the wheelhouse and walked toward Fenimore in the bow. She wondered if she should press him for an answer or if she should wait a little longer. As she approached she decided to let Fenimore speak first.

She stood by his side and leaned on the railing opposite him. He broke his gaze from the horizon to glance her way, but his serious expression made no change. Refocusing again on the sky to the east, he said nothing. She waited silently. The minutes ticked by and Chenda began to sense that no amount of talk would help Fenimore make his decision. She put her hand on his elbow and let it travel down his arm, pulling his hand into hers. Fenimore resisted her at first but quickly relented. She laced her fingers into his and gave a reassuring squeeze.

She didn't want to speak and break the moment. *Whatever you decide is fine*, she thought, *but I want you to come with me.*

Fenimore glanced at her again, his eyebrows drawn quizzically together. She met his eyes, released his hand and backed away. He blinked, his features returning to neutral contemplation as maintained his vigil at the bow.

Chenda spent the remainder of the day learning what she could about the Tugrulian Empire from Verdu. His manner of educating her was a bit exotic, but fairly entertaining. They stood side by side in the wheelhouse as Verdu sang Tugrulian songs to her. After each performance, he translated. Verdu's people seemed to have a song for everything. Some songs were political, and touted the strength of Tugrulian men and how they could best serve the Empire. Other songs illustrated the basics of Tugrulian religion and how to live one's life in a way pleasing to the One True God. Some strains were practical, describing how to find water in the desert, make poisons and medicines from various mushrooms and how to make a type of pancake bread from moss and algae. Verdu even sang a few children's songs, including one that listed a variety of animals and the sounds they made. As the most plentiful Tugrulian creatures are lizards and deep cave fish – silent creatures for the most part – it was a highly ridiculous song.

145

Verdu, who had always been friendly and jovial toward Chenda, seemed more formal with her now, and he expanded the physical distance between them. She felt like he was holding a bubble of space between them, like a cushion. He touched her as little as possible in the wheelhouse's confined space. What he held back in physical contact, he replaced with other attentions. He continually asked after her comfort: was she tired, or could he bring her something to eat or drink, perhaps another song? Chenda didn't know what to make of the subtle change.

At seven bells, Lincoln came to the wheelhouse. "Captain sent me to relieve you, Verdu. He asked if you would be so kind as to drop by his quarters for a word."

"Of course," Verdu replied. He turned to Chenda, "Forgive me, great lady, duty calls."

As he hopped down onto the deck, Chenda also left the wheelhouse, but she decided not to head below. She saw that Fenimore had not moved from his position at the bow.

Not knowing what else to do, Chenda stepped to the front of the wheelhouse and squatted on her heels. She sat behind a coil of mooring lines and watched Fenimore's unending vigil over the horizon. Her eyes flicked from the distant sea to his silhouette. She wondered where his thoughts were leading and pushed down her urge to run to his side to beg him to come with her.

The minutes moved glacially. *I hate waiting,* she thought, but forced herself to give Fenimore the time he asked for, the space he deserved to sort things out.

Chenda heard Captain Endicott roaring at Fenimore before she saw him charging past the wheelhouse toward the bow.

"Did you know about this?" Captain Endicott barked.

Fenimore never took his eyes off the horizon. "If you mean Verdu ditching us, then yes, I knew that was coming."

"Stop him," He ordered. Captain Endicott no longer shouted, but the wind blew his words back to where Chenda squatted. She felt like this conversation was one she wasn't invited to hear, but she couldn't seem to make her feet carry her elsewhere.

Fenimore scoffed. "I don't know if I could if I wanted to. Verdu's a big boy. He listened to what Chenda and Candice had to say, and he's made *his* choice. It's pretty tempting, I suppose, the chance to change one's circumstances."

The captain roared again. "Are you thinking about jumping ship, too? What about that vegetable you've been taking responsibility for? Who's going to see to his care if you go off and get lost in the far side of the world? After all I've done for you both, you're going to leave me high and dry!?!"

Fenimore kept his voice calm and said, "Captain, I love you like a father. I know *exactly* what you've done for me, and I live in a world of gratitude for that. But I have a choice to make, and I haven't decided yet what I am going to do. I don't really understand what Chenda is looking for, and I shudder to imagine what may happen to those women once they get into the Empire, but go they will – no matter what I say or do. It's beyond reason, but Chenda believes wholeheartedly that Verdu and I must go as well. He will. I may. When I decide, I will be sure to let you know in short order, sir."

"Fine. FINE!" Endicott turned and stomped away from the bow. As he passed the wheelhouse, he spied Chenda squatting behind the mooring coil.

"YOU!" he barked, pointing his finger. Chenda cringed as Captain Endicott turned his anger toward her. "I called in some very expensive favors to get you what you needed. I felt sorry for you, and you repay me by taking the best part of my crew? I *never* should have taken this job!"

He stormed off and down the stairs before Chenda could stir up a response, his curses and growls floating up the stairs for the wind to whip away. She sat stunned. It was never Chenda's intention to cause this kind of strife. She ran down the stairs to Candice's cabin and pounded on the door. The Captain's furious ranting spilled out of the galley interspersed with Kingston's calm and soothing voice, the exact words of which Chenda couldn't quite make out.

As soon as Candice opened her door, Chenda shoved her way inside. There was barely enough room for the two women to stand together. "Oh, Candice, I think I've made a mess of things." Chenda teetered on the verge of tears. Candice cleared the various notebooks and maps off of her narrow bed and guided Chenda to sit down on the thin mattress.

"What's happened? I can hear Max barking from here."

"Verdu's told him that he's leaving with us, and that perhaps Fenimore is, too. He's pretty angry with me for breaking up his well oiled machine. Honestly, I don't blame him. My quest is pulling away his most seasoned crew."

Candice harrumphed. "Oh, no you don't, missy! Don't you feel guilty for the choices of those two men, or the tantrum from their captain. He can fly this ship all by himself if he has to. He just likes having his boys around him!" She threw her various papers into a satchel on the small folding table, gathered herself up to her full yet meager height and marched out the door into the passageway.

A moment later, Chenda heard the captain halt in mid tirade. His rant was replaced by the sizzle of Candice's annoyed voice. Chenda was honestly afraid to follow Candice, not knowing whose bark was worse, the captain's or the professor's. She waited.

After a few minutes the captain knocked on Candice's open door. He looked at Chenda cowering on the bed. "It has come to my attention that I have been rather rude to you just recently. Please forgive me." He coughed nervously then said, "I think I will retire to my quarters."

With that, he crossed the passage to his own cabin and slammed the door.

Candice appeared in the doorway, her face showing annoyance and her voice muttering chastisements. "...as if he was some king or father over those boys, indeed!" She looked up at Chenda and said, "Quit cowering in my bed, missy. I have work to do - as do you. Scat!" She flapped her hands at Chenda as the young woman escaped into the corridor. The professor snorted in Chenda's direction and then slammed the door.

"Thank you," Chenda said into the sudden silence around her. She turned and continued down the passageway to the galley. The smell of hot food and the sound of Verdu's soothing song met her as she stepped into the room.

He sat with his back to the world, joyfully singing a Tugrulian song. Without saying a word, Kingston handed Chenda a steaming bowl of chicken with dumplings and pointed to the table. Chenda pulled out the chair next to Verdu and he suddenly stopped.

"Oh! Don't stop, that was lovely!" she chimed. "I could use a beautiful song right now."

Verdu looked slightly embarrassed, "No, maybe another time – that song was just about finished anyway."

"OK, then, continue my education. What was that song about?" She held the soup bowl under her chin, letting it warm her cold hands and face. She blew on the stew, waiting for the next stories from Verdu, but none came. "What is it?" she said. Verdu scooted his spoon around his own empty bowl, wishing he had something to put in his mouth so he could delay.

Chenda plunked her bowl on the table and gave Verdu's elbow a playful shove. "So, you're willing to belt out your song with great bliss, but aren't willing to tell me what it means?" she said.

Verdu hid his eyes. "Yes. It's just that this is another of those forbidden songs."

"Well, now I just have to know," she said. "Please?"

Verdu caved. "The song is about the Pramuc, the one who comes to free the people. Loosely translated, it says something like, 'We are who we were, we will be ourselves again. The false god and the king are no match, for we wait for the Pramuc, the one who comes to save us. The holy one, raised by holy ones, commands the world and all its parts. The ones who follow will lead the way. The land will jolt and we will throw off the yoke. We will rise from the emptiness of the caves and reclaim the lands, the daughters will flow in the water, sons will fly in the air. Mothers will harvest from the land and fathers will tame the fire. And the Empire will be no more. We will be ourselves again when the Pramuc comes.' "

Verdu looked timidly at Chenda, fearing her response. But Chenda only looked puzzled. She couldn't understand why he had seemed reluctant to tell her about this song. The lyrics didn't seem particularly revealing or embarrassing to her. In fact, they hardly made sense. Chenda knit her eyebrows in concentration.

"So, I don't get it. What does that mean?"

The answer came from behind her. "It means not everyone in the Empire is a good Tugrulian." Fenimore snapped. "It's superstitious nonsense."

"It's prophecy." Verdu corrected in a soft tone. Sitting between them, Chenda could feel the tension between the two men.

"It's why he's going with you," Fenimore growled, answering more to Verdu than to Chenda. "Isn't it? He thinks you are going to fulfill the prophecy and free his people." He leaned forward and pointed an accusing finger at Verdu. "She's just a girl. Don't get yourself killed over this mumbo-jumbo. Since when are you a believer, anyway?!?"

"Wait a second," Chenda cut in, her eyes focused on Verdu. "You think I fulfill some kind of prophecy? You think I am this... Pramuc?"

Verdu looked timid. "It's possible," he whispered. "I'm not saying I believe; I'm just saying it *could* be. You possess the stones, and that's a start."

Chenda sat with her mouth open. Shock didn't even begin to describe what she felt. It would have been less bizarre if Verdu had accused her of being a rutabaga. "I think you are rather mistaken," Chenda whispered.

Verdu stood, his body mirroring Fenimore's, and he look sweetly down at Chenda. "Don't close yourself to it, dear lady." He stepped around the table and positioned himself between Chenda and Fenimore, his posture suddenly defensive.

Fenimore roared. "You're going to get her killed with this talk. She's in enough trouble already; you don't need to weigh her down with this, too. It's insanity and you know it!"

The two men moved as one, the space between them disappeared and they crashed into one another in the center of the room. Each grabbed the other by the shirtfront. Fenimore gave Verdu a single, violent shake. "Don't twist her destiny to suit yourself."

Verdu arched his back in rage. "If you weren't such a coward, *you* would ply your fate to *ours*." He thrust his head forward, and with a mighty crack, impacted Fenimore's forehead with his own. Fenimore staggered back, releasing Verdu.

Chenda jumped between the two of them, a hand to each of their chests. "Stop!" she shouted. Verdu took half a step back like a dog called to heel, separating himself from her touch. Fenimore grabbed Chenda by the wrist and pulled her closer to himself. Verdu snarled, "Take your hands off her!"

Fenimore looked into Chenda's eyes and said, "Don't let *him* get you killed." He let her go, half shoving her back toward Verdu as he retreated out the door and down the passageway.

Verdu chased after him, anger clear in his eyes. Chenda reached toward his retreating back, but was too late. The shock of what had happened left her speechless. She turned to face an equally shocked Kingston, who stood motionless with a dripping ladle in his hand.

"Better let those two work it out on their own, Chenda." Kingston said. "There's more between them than you can guess, and you don't want any part of it. Certainly, you won't want to get stuck in the middle."

"I think perhaps I already am," she said sadly and she slumped down in her chair. "Captain Endicott is mad at me, the professor thinks I'm a marshmallow for not standing up to the captain, and those two are fighting over me because I want them both to come along on my witless expedition. I'm some kind of curse, Kingston."

The stout cook wiped his hands on his apron and put a comforting arm around her shoulder. "I don't know about that," he said. "So there's a wee bit of struggle rounding the ship tonight. It will pass. Other than that, Mrs. Frost, how did you like the stew?"

Chenda laughed at Kingston's culinary vanity until she snorted. Then she put her head down on the table and cried. He patted her back and cleared the dishes from the table while Chenda sobbed. "They won't be mad long, you will see," he assured her. "They'll be thick as thieves again by morning. You will see. There, there, sweet baby."

She retreated to the crew quarters and her bed. She felt like every life she touched recently had fallen into upheaval. She slouched onto the floor, resting her back against the beam that separated the two columns of bunks. She stretched her left arm out onto Fenimore's bunk, and her right onto Verdu's, sadly feeling the emptiness of each. She let her hands fall to her sides.

Kingston said that the men would work out their differences, but he wasn't standing between them in that tense moment. He didn't see the hateful glint in Fenimore's eye, or the resolve in Verdu. Chenda felt crushed in their impasse, paralyzed by the gravity it created.

Tomorrow, the day they would rendezvous with the *Tjalk*, the day she, Verdu and Candice would part company with the *Brofman*, raced toward her. She despaired. Chenda had never felt as safe as she did here, even through the barking and bickering. This company of rough men, kind in spirit, were the fathers she had never known and the brothers she never had. Is this what it meant to have a family? The thought of leaving made her shudder. The *Brofman*, more than any other place, felt like home.

She slumped onto the floor, her tears already flowing. Chenda rolled into the narrow slot that was her bunk, her own little, borrowed slice of the *Brofman*, her home. The tight space embraced her. There, in the grasp of the airship she loved deeply, she cried herself into a deep and dreamless sleep.

When she opened her eyes, she was in darkness. How long had she slept, she wondered. She rolled onto her back, bringing her shoulders off the mattress and out onto the floor slightly. Chenda looked up at the other bunks. Almost all were full, and Fenimore was in his place just above her. By Chenda's reckoning, it must be some time before four o'clock. She scooted her torso back onto her mattress and tried to go back to sleep. She failed.

She thought about how unwilling she was to leave things so spoiled between herself and Fenimore. She brushed her palm along the smooth boards of the bunk above her.

Oh, how I need to talk with you, Fenimore, she thought. *We must work this through, because I can't leave this kind of pain in my wake.*

She sighed as she finished one last stroke. Fenimore's left hand fell over the edge of his bed and reached over to grasp Chenda's. His rough fingers captured her right hand before she could drop it back to her side. His hand was warm, and he laced his fingers into hers, just holding her hand in the air for a minute, his thumb making small strokes in her palm. She heard the brush of his face on the pillow as he pulled his head to the edge of the bunk and whispered down to her "I'm glad you're awake. Let's talk somewhere."

He slid his legs over the side and knelt beside Chenda's bunk, never releasing her hand. Chenda slid out as well and he helped pull her to standing. Together they left the bunks behind and Fenimore pulled her down the passageway. Rather than going up to the deck and the cold night above, he pulled her around the stairs and further down the passageway, deeper into the airship where she had never been before. They passed several doors but took none until they reached the end of the passage. Fenimore pushed open a door marked **Engine Room** and stepped in, pulling Chenda in behind him.

As the door swung shut, Chenda's feet, so willing to follow Fenimore to this point, resisted more steps. Her eyes marveled at the great, beating heart of the *Brofman*. It glowed. Great silvery wheels flew past one another, flashing in the dim light. The quiet whirring sound of this great engine, to Chenda's ears, was the most pleasant sound ever made. The look of its graceful yet powerful motion soothed her like nothing ever had.

Fenimore looked back at her, seeing the wonder in her eyes. "Ah," he said. "I knew you were one of us. You have airships in your blood, I think."

Chenda nodded, not taking her eyes off the engine for a long time, soaking in the hum. Fenimore waited patiently, letting Chenda soak in her marvel, then said, "Come this way..."

Reluctantly, her legs started moving again, and she followed her guide to the far end of the engine room. Fenimore released her hand, stood on a small crate propped against the stern bulkhead, and pushed on a light fixture until Chenda heard a little pop. A crack appeared in the wooden paneling next to Fenimore. He slid his fingertips into the fissure and pulled it toward himself, revealing an entryway to a very narrow space.

"What is this?" Chenda asked.

"Cargo storage," Fenimore said. "Undeclared." He stepped in and said, "We can talk here and not be disturbed."

153

Chenda stepped in and looked around. The hold, just three feet wide, ran the entire width of the *Brofman's* stern. The scratches and scuff marks in the space hinted of many years of quickly hidden cargoes and other hasty seclusions. At the moment, the hold was almost empty – only a bedroll and an empty crate remained. Fenimore took Chenda by the hand again and guided her to take a seat on the crate. Still holding her hand, Fenimore rested himself on the bedroll.

They said nothing for a long time, but then blurted out together. "I'm sorry."

Chenda giggled, "This is what it must be like between you and Verdu."

Fenimore shook his head, "Naw, that was just a coincidence of mutual regret. What I share with Verdu is something else. Which brings us to what we need to talk about: Verdu."

"I was hoping we would talk about you, Fen."

"Later, I promise, but I need you to understand that Verdu believes *you* are the savior of his people, and he is a man of great tenacity. Right or wrong, he'll drive you to fill that role. He'll make it be so, even if he kills you in the process. With your eyes open, you must see that he's not following you, but the stones you carry. Not. You. Do you understand that?"

"Yes, but it doesn't matter. He's coming, and that's all I want. His reason is his own." Chenda looked down at her hands in her lap, one still entwined with Fenimore's. "Not that I am saying you should, but why don't you let go of me?" She ran a finger down the back of his hand.

"I honestly don't know," he said. "And I don't want to think too much about why, either. Much like with Verdu, I just can't fight the feeling when you are near." He chuckled to himself. "OK. It's not the same as it is with him, but it rhymes." He looked doubtful for a moment and said, "You really don't mind?"

Chenda smiled. "It's nice. I like having people so close here on the airship. It's one of the many things I'm really going to miss. I hate the idea of leaving it tomorrow, but I must." She paused. "So, did you work things out with him?"

"More or less," he said, rubbing his forehead. "We have agreed to disagree, for now."

Chenda's heart sank. Surely this meant he would not be joining her. "I really am sorry that you two fought. I never wanted to have my task come between you. I'm like some kind of disease."

Fenimore laughed. "More like you are the cure to our regular routine. Don't be so hard on yourself. We're all grown-ups here."

"I guess I am just a selfish grown-up, then. I don't care much at all *why* Verdu is coming with me; I am just pleased that he is. Edison said it needed to be so, and there it is. I've made my leap of faith, with Edison's letter and the vision. I know that I have to follow where it leads."

"I understand. Really. But I worry. I really don't think you will mange well in Tugrulia without someone like Verdu to help you along. He will help you find the man you seek. The problem is getting back out again. I'm worried that Verdu will keep you there too long, or try to get you to be something you aren't. I know him, and he may just try to do something noble that will get him killed, leaving you and Candice unprotected and trapped by a world you don't fully understand.

"But there's more to it than that. Verdu is like a brother to me. You've seen the way we are tied to one another. It's beyond friendship, beyond brotherhood. I'm not sure that if we separated for very long, part of me wouldn't just die. I'm truly afraid of that. Even though I have not known you very long, I feel a similar pull toward you as well."

Fenimore shook his head. "So, as you have asked me to do, I have thought it over and I'm going to go with you. Not because Edison told you I needed to go, and not because Verdu needs someone to keep him from taking on the Emperor personally. I'm going because I can't be left behind. Verdu follows you because he thinks you are the Pramuc, and I follow you both because I want to be where you are."

Chenda dropped her hand from his and wrapped her arms around his neck. He sat very still as she pulled him close and whispered in his ear, "Thank you." After a long moment, she held him at arm's length. "I know this was a difficult choice for you, but I am happy you've chosen to join us... me. This is right, I can feel it."

She embraced him again, and this time she felt his arms wrap around her. She sighed and sank into his chest, feeling like some key had just fit into a lock within her, freeing her to go on to the next part of her life.

Fenimore and Chenda held each other until they heard the bells chime the hour. "It's time I head up on deck. I need to take over in the wheelhouse." He released her from his warm embrace. "Say, would you like to watch the sun rise again?"

Captain Endicott stood outside Candice's door. He hated to apologize, but as much as he hated to admit it, he was squarely in the wrong. However, he was also thoroughly a scoundrel when he needed to be. He wanted to keep his crew together, and perhaps Candice would help those lads see reason if he was persuasive enough.

He knocked.

Candice swung the door open wide and scowled at Captain Endicott. "Max," she said in an unfriendly greeting.

"Candice," he said in a singsong voice. "May I come in, darling?"

"It's your airship, but keep your 'darling'," she said stepping back. He entered the small space and sat on her bed, stretching his legs out in front of him and crossing his forearms behind his head. He drew up his most charming smile and let his eyes sparkle at Candice.

"Oh, here we go. I've seen that tack before. You look like a delinquent freshman who wants a second crack at a failed term paper." She crossed her arms in front of her chest, defiant.

"I'm just here to say I'm sorry," he said. "You are right. Those boys *can* choose to leave my ship at any time. But what kind of captain would I be if I didn't try to keep my crew safe and out of trouble?" He dropped one arm and gestured Candice to come sit beside him. Candice frowned slightly, but she sat anyway.

His voice dropped to a sultry whisper and he put his arm

around Candice's shoulder, "I want to keep *you* safe, too. There is something about you – it suits me." He started to pull her towards his chest, but Candice resisted.

"I see what you are doing here! NO!" She slapped at his pulling arm. "Fiddlesticks!" She slapped again. Twice.

The captain laughed out loud at her mock resistance and swept her into a bear hug, tipping her backwards across his lap. She gasped, but didn't struggle.

"You're gonna forgive me," he said smiling.

Candice sniffed her denial, but her eyes smiled at him. "Max, I'm not going to help you talk Verdu and Fenimore into staying on this ship."

He frowned slightly, and tapped Candice on the end of her nose. "It was worth a try," he said. "Now, about you and me," he whispered. He kicked his foot off the bed, knocking the door to Candice's cabin closed. He pulled her close to him and he kissed her, hard. All of Candice's professorial dignity melted and years of pent up longing were released as she wrapped her arms around the captain, her captain, and she let her long dormant passion take over.

For Chenda, the day passed quickly. She spent the first part standing beside Fenimore in the wheelhouse. She loved watching the crew bring the *Brofman* out of her slumber and power up for the day. Fenimore lived to pilot the airship. His hand flew over the controls as the first rays of the sun released energy through the photovoltaic tubes. Chenda thrilled at the flurry of activity and the airship's leap forward. Fenimore checked their heading and relaxed at the helm, pleased at the feeling of gentle vibration that ran through the wheel into his hands. He and Chenda stood there, standing hip to hip, talking the morning away. They spoke of a hundred unimportant things: about growing up, about going to school, people they had met along the way, books, songs, food and dreams, one story leading into the next.

Verdu arrived at midday to relieve Fenimore. Chenda eyed each man curiously as Verdu entered the wheelhouse.

"I'll take her from here." Verdu said quietly.

"The girl or the ship?" Fenimore asked slyly.

"Both, if you let me, brother."

The exchange seemed friendly, but there was still a thread of tension as the men passed each other in the small space. Chenda could tell the worst of the conflict had passed, but there was still something that needed resolving between them.

Verdu turned to Chenda, "Your companionship is welcome here if you wish to stay."

Her eyes flicked from Verdu to Fenimore. "Sure," she said. "I love being here in the wheelhouse. I'll stay a bit. I'll see you later, Fen."

Fenimore nodded and backed out the door. Chenda focused her attention on Verdu. "How are you today?"

"I'm excited," he replied. "It's always exciting for me to sneak into the Empire. The trick is sneaking back out again. That's where the danger is."

"So, you are going to help me get back out again?" Chenda said timidly.

"Of course I will. Why wouldn't I?"

"Well, Fen seems to think that you might not want me to leave, that you might keep me there to fulfill the prophecy or something...." She trailed off, not wanting to look up at Verdu's expression.

"He doesn't know where your destiny leads, and I won't keep you where you don't want to be." He took one of his hands off the wheel and rested it on the back of Chenda's neck. He stroked the skin under her jaw with his thumb. "I promise, I will be your guide and protector as best I can, but your will is your own. I won't pilot your fate."

Chenda sighed and wrapped an arm around the big man's waist. "Thank you," she said. They stood there in silence for a time; then Verdu started to sing. Chenda recognized it as the song of the Pramuc. She started to hum along, and he hugged her closer. The bubble Verdu had held between them seemed to have burst, and Chenda was pleased to share his contact again.

The captain and Candice emerged from her cabin in the middle of the afternoon. Endicott kissed the top of her head and released her from strong arms. She handed him his flight coat, which he pulled on as he walked up the stairs. She sighed and returned to her room to pack.

Up on deck, the captain finished buckling his coat as he walked toward the bow, where Fenimore stood watching the horizon. The young officer took one look at the captain's placid smile and said, "You didn't?"

"I did," he said, his grin widening.

"You dog!"

"Woof!" The captain said with a laughing bark. After a moment his frivolity evaporated. "You. You're leaving me, too, I guess."

"I am. But I will do whatever I can to get each of them back safely. I think I am even going to ask you for a favor."

"HA! After what you two are trying to pull on my ship. I ought to throw you overboard." He snorted with indignation. "You're lucky that you've caught me at a very happy and relaxed moment. Let's hear it, then."

"I don't know how long this little adventure is going to take, but I think if we can get in and out fast, we have a better chance of living through it. As soon as Chenda meets up with her... whatever he is... I'm going to beat a hasty retreat. I know it's out of your way, but if you could see your way clear to dock at Crider Island sometime soon, I will try to meet you there. That island is the closest free port to the Tugrulian Coast. I'll owe you."

"You already do, but I will let you owe me again." Endicott smiled. "Here's what I can do. I'll make it my business to do a little trading there in ten days time. I'll dock one night, then I will need to deliver some cargo back to Atoll Belles. I'll see if I can get a bit more to trade there and come back. Let's call that another ten days. If you can't make it back to Crider Island in 20 days..."

"... Rest assured we're dead," Fenimore finished the thought. "Feel free to hold our memorial service."

"It's a deal, and thank you." The two men grasped each other by the wrist in a meaningful handshake.

"I really - REALLY - want you to bring Candice back to me." He smiled.

"Captain Endicott in love. That's something," Fenimore

159

replied.

"I've never met a woman with that much personality. I want to fight with her again! Now, I'm going to keep watch for the *Tjalk*. You get Germer to prep two monowings and a parachute. We're too close to the Tugrulian patrol routes for me to risk dropping down to sea level. I want the *Brofman* out of range. That means we need to drop sans ship. Understand?" Captain Endicott turned his attention forward as he searched the water below for the *Tjalk*

"Yes, sir," Fenimore said, already in motion.

As he passed the wheelhouse, Fenimore tapped on the glass, and Verdu poked his head out the small side window, looking down on his friend with questioning eyes.

"When we find the *Tjalk*, we're flying down by monowing. Tell Chenda what to expect, and that she needs to get ready to go."

"Right." Verdu slid the window closed and relayed the message to Chenda, who asked, "What's a monowing?"

"Germer invented it. It's like a personal, powered glider. With it, we can fly a man down to the deck of a sailing ship and land. Then we can fly back up again to the airship. It's quite clever, really. We have two monowings on the *Brofman*, and they are strong enough to ferry two of us at a time down to the *Tjalk*. But they are only powerful enough to fly one person back up to the airship. Since we are planning on staying on the *Tjalk*, it works out perfectly. We've delivered cargo that way more than once."

Verdu looked at the wary expression on Chenda's face and said "Don't worry, I'll carry you down myself. I won't let anything happen to you."

"I'm sure it will be fine," she lied, unconvincingly.

"You need to get ready to go. We'll be moving fast and light from here on out. Take only what you really need."

Chenda hurried to the crew quarters and filled her pouch-belt with the contents of her trinket bag, and all the gold coins. She filled one pouch with a fist full of cash, but left most of the Kite's Republic paper money in her carpet bag, which she closed back into her cupboard. She stripped off her flight coat and

160

Fenimore's shirt, which she laid across his bunk. She put on her two clean shirts, one over the other, and decided that was all she needed for now. She put her coat back on and left the crew quarters, willing herself to not look back.

Slipping down the passageway, she knocked on Candice's door. When the professor opened it up, her expression was wistful. "Is it time?" she asked.

"Soon." Chenda said. "Will you be ready to travel fast and light? It seems we will be flying to the *Tjalk* by monowing. Do you know what that means?"

"Ick! I can guess." Candice suddenly looked a little green. "I guess it can't be helped. I've got most of what I need in this shoulder bag. I'm glad I took the time to condense my notes into one book. You've got the stones secure on your person?" Chenda nodded. "Good. And we are all set with items to trade?" Chenda patted her bulging pouch-belt. "Excellent. I guess that you are ready for the next leg. I'll be set in a bit. I'll meet you on deck."

Candice closed the door to her cabin. Chenda was about to head back up the stairs when she heard Kingston call after her.

"Chenda! I have something for you! Wait!" Kingston was waddling down the passageway waving what looked to be several kitchen towels knotted together. "Here," he said. "It's a variation on hard tack." He flung the lumpy cloth over her head and shoulder like a bandoleer. "Each of these six knots contains a high nutrition bread. It's enough to keep all four of you going for about a week, if you are careful, and you can get at some water. Oh, that reminds me." He reached behind him and pulled out a canteen, which he clipped to Chenda's pouch-belt. "There," he said with fatherly satisfaction. "May the gods' love be with you and bring you home safe." He grabbed her in his beefy arms and squeezed.

"Thank you for all that you've done for me," she said. Then she kissed his cheek and climbed the stairs. She tried to ignore her tears.

Up on deck, she felt the slowing of the airship and saw Captain Endicott strapping a parachute to his back. He called to her, pointing over the side. "There she is!" He waved Chenda over. "The *Tjalk*." Far below, she saw what looked to her like a tiny white speck on the surface of the sea.

Captain Endicott turned to Verdu. "Give me about 20 minutes to present my letter of introduction and make the arrangements. Then you can come on down with the ladies. Germer! You're in charge till I get back." He hopped backwards and landed in a seated position on the wide railing of the airship. Checking the straps crossing his body one last time, and scooting further back on the rail, heclipped a thin line onto the *Brofman*, then gave a glorious smile to Chenda and Verdu.

"GODS! I love what I do!" He pitched backward over the side of the ship. Chenda ran to the railing and watched the captain tumble away from the ship, his bright parachute already popping open and filling with air. He swirled ever downward, guiding himself toward the tiny sailing ship far below. Chenda's heart raced. After what seemed like an eternity, the tiny dot that was the captain landed on the speck that was the *Tjalk*.

That. Is insane.

Verdu glanced at his watch and said, "We'd better get you ready to go now." Chenda, still staring over the side, whimpered. Verdu patted her back reassuringly. "It will be fine, I promise. Here," he said, handing her a complicated harness. "We need to get this on you, and Candice, too. Come quickly," he called to Candice, who had just appeared above deck.

"Where's the captain?" Candice asked.

Chenda pointed over the side. "Down there."

Candice looked over. "Oh, my!"

"We're next."

"OH, MY!"

"Ladies," Verdu said with acres of patience, "harnesses, please?"

He helped Candice and Chenda step into the straps and tugged and tightened until he was satisfied the women were secure. "We're ready. Now all we need is Fen with the monowings."

As if on cue, Fenimore rose from the stairs with his arms filled with gossamer fabric and a big pack over each shoulder. Verdu took the shimmering cloth from Fenimore, dropped half of it to the deck and gave the rest of it a good shake. It snapped into a rigid, shimmering V about 15 feet across. Verdu dropped his

162

flight coat onto the deck, and reached for one of Fenimore's packs, which he strapped securely to his own back. Then he picked up the gossamer monowing and slid it down over the backpack where it clicked into place. Verdu looked like a beautiful silver winged bird.

He took Chenda by the hand and pushed her gently to the railing of the *Brofman*. "First things first," he said in soothing tones, "I'll be with you the whole time. You won't be falling, you will be flying, so don't panic." He lifted her up and set her on the railing facing outward. "No thrashing of arms and legs, please; you'll just be kicking me. Now stand on the railing." Chenda, her mind not fully controlling her body, did as she was told. She felt Verdu's hands release her bitter-end clip, cutting her last tether to the *Brofman*. A tear rolled down her cheek. "Hold very still." Verdu stepped up onto the railing next to her. He moved closer to her side, then stepped behind her, his feet apart, straddling her. He attached her harness to his with two quick snaps at her shoulders and at her waist, and he leaned forward. Chenda, cantilevered over the side of the ship, looked down into empty air. Verdu continued with little instructions about how they would land and when she should bring her knees to her chest, but Chenda could only grasp the thought of all the open air before her, so cold, so... empty.

He wrapped both of his arms around Chenda, pressing her hands to her chest. "Arms in, and hold on. Ready?"

"In a hundred ways, no. But let's go anyway."

Verdu grasped the handles of the monowing and fell forward off the airship.

The glider bit into the icy air and Chenda's terror quickly gave way to joy as the wind blew through her and around her. She dropped her arms from her chest, the force of the wind blowing her hands out and back. She felt free and alive, more than she ever had. Through her watering eyes she looked off toward the horizon, the thready clouds there kissed violet and amber in the early sunset. She wished to fly off toward them, never wanting to land again. She turned her head to look over her shoulder and caught a glimpse of Verdu, his face scrunched in concentration as he wrestled the monowing. She half expected to see Edison behind her and realized she had been here before, flying. Just days ago in a vivid dream, it was another little gift from Edison.

A warm feeling crept over her, a sense of deep satisfaction. Floating and circling in the air with Verdu at her back, it felt like a confirmation she was on the right path. Her heart raced as she shouted over the wind, "Verdu! I love flying! Don't be in a hurry to land, if you can help it!"

"Anything for you, dear lady," he replied, his lips brushing her ear. The monowing swooped upward, and Verdu eased into a nearly flat arc high over the *Tjalk*. Chenda giggled out of sheer delight. She tried to etch every sight and feeling to her memory. She never wanted to forget how wonderful this was. She felt whole as they slowly spiraled down.

Verdu fought gravity for as long as he could, but the *Tjalk* loomed ever closer. "Tuck up," Verdu whispered as they made one last spiral around the ship's main mast. Chenda lifted her legs as Verdu kicked forward, planting one foot onto the rail of the *Tjalk*, and then jumping down at a full run to the deck. He dropped his hands from their hold on the monowing and wrapped his arms around Chenda, cradling her as he skidded to a stop at middeck.

He quickly released her, and her feet found the smooth deck beneath her. Through the sun-bleached boards, she could feel the roll of the sea below, so solid and heavy – nothing like the lightness that cushioned the *Brofman*.

Verdu disconnected Chenda's harness as Captain Endicott stepped forward with another small man. Her legs wobbled with all the excitement of soaring through the open air, and she reached out to steady herself, placing her hand on the mast. Chenda already missed the throbbing heartbeat of the *Brofman's* engine.

"Welcome aboard the *Tjalk*," the stranger said.

Chapter 13
TUGRUL AQUABA

Chenda breathed in the warm, moist ocean air. Her cheeks and hands, blown cold by the rush of flight, stung like they had been plunged into a hot sink. She loosened her flight coat as Verdu helped her escape the monowing harness.

"I think dis one enjoyed de descent more so dan de other one," the stranger said pointing to the bow of the ship. There sat Candice with her head between her knees. Fenimore stood next to her with a slightly annoyed expression on his face.

Chenda turned her attention back to Captain Endicott. "Chenda, Verdu, please allow me to introduce you to the skipper of this fine ship, Captain Taboda." She met the captain's eyes and extended a hand to him. His reciprocating grasp was surprisingly soft. His look and coloring was much like Verdu's, but in diminutive proportions.

"Thank you for accommodating us. I am truly grateful," she said.

"Vell, when one receives a letter of introduction from Jason Belles, one adheres to de rules of etiquette," Taboda said. "I drop what I am doing and serve you as best I can. Shall ve discuss business, you and I?"

"Yes, of course." Chenda, flanked by Verdu, stepped away from Endicott and closer to Taboda.

"De airship captain says he needs to deliver you to the Tugrulian Resistance, and de sooner de better, no?"

"That's correct. Can you do it?"

"Of course, I can have you der by morning, no problem. You can pay?" The small man's eyes twinkled.

165

"Yes. In Republic currency."

Taboda rolled his eyes. "Dat's not so useful out here."

"But it is a fine currency when you are dealing with Jason Belles, yes?"

Taboda sniffed. "Indeed. I say 40-dousand."

"Done," Chenda said. Both Verdu and Taboda stared at her, their eyes bulging.

"What?" Chenda asked as she pulled a large wad of cash out of her pouch-belt and quickly counted out 40 bills.

"You... didn't want to negotiate?" Verdu asked, almost in a squeak.

"No." Chenda said with a smile. "I want to get moving. Captain Taboda, may we begin?"

He blinked at her a few times and then seemed to regain his senses. "Yes, yes, yes! Off ve go." He half scurried away, then trotted back. "Please, make yourselves at ease. Der is a comfortable sitting area aft." He waved his hand to an area behind Chenda. "I'll be back to discuss other details vith you straight avay." He scurried off again.

"Fen! Bring Candice this way," Verdu called. Candice looked moderately better now that she had been stripped of her harness and flight coat. Fenimore and Endicott, each taking a side of the slightly greenish professor, guided her to the cushioned sitting area at the rear of the ship. Candice leaned her head back and pinched the bridge of her nose. Chenda flung off her flight coat and sat beside her, putting an arm behind her head.

"I think I love flying," Chenda said.

Candice opened one eye and glared at the younger woman. "I have long suspected you were insane," she quipped. "At least we are done flying without an airship now."

Verdu collapsed his monowing and packed the shimmering wad of fabric into a mesh bag, which he attached to the flight back pack. Fenimore was helping to fit his flight pack on to Captain Endicott's back. He was about to snap in the wing when the captain held up his hand. "Just a moment," he said. He strode over to Candice's side and knelt down.

"Candice, darling, please be careful." He kissed her on the forehead and she placed a hand on his cheek. He picked up her flight coat and said, "I'll keep this safe for you until you come back, okay?"

"Yes, thank you. I'll do my best," she replied. "Until we meet again."

"Until we meet again, hopefully very soon."

Endicott turned to Verdu and Fenimore. He put a hand on each man's shoulder and said, "Take care of each other, my boys. And take care of them."

He dropped his hands and signaled for Fenimore to set the wing in place. There was a soft whirring sound as the pack hummed to life. Endicott grasped the coat and collapsed monowing in one hand and hopped up onto the rail. Captain Endicott looked back once at Candice, then leaped into the air. He was up and swirling away in an instant.

Chenda dashed to the railing and watched as the captain circled upward to the *Brofman*. The *Tjalk* was picking up speed, and in just a few minutes, Chenda lost the airship to the clouds. The sun, nearly set, distorted on the horizon and threw long shadows across the deck. Chenda settled onto the cushions with a sigh.

"I want to fly back up some day," she said wistfully to Verdu. "That looks like such fun."

"Bleck!" Candice groaned from the floor. "I'd rather eat dirt!"

Verdu smiled at Chenda, "I will happily arrange such a flight, dear lady."

"I can't remember the last time I was a passenger on an actual sailing vessel," Fenimore said. "I have no idea what to do with myself now that I'm not a part of the crew. This is very strange."

"Welcome to my everyday," Chenda replied, slapping the cushion next to her. "Sit. Be useless like me."

The crew of the *Tjalk* was busily resetting the sails and the rigging. They seemed indifferent to the new people on their ship. Pointedly uninterested was more the case. Chenda began to wonder if Captain Taboda instructed his crew to be aloof. She whispered her thoughts to Verdu, who sat nearby.

"It's likely," he said. "I suspect that the *Tjalk* has some run-ins with Tugrulian patrols from time to time. The crew can't talk about what they don't see. These sailors have been conditioned to ignore a lot, I suspect."

Chenda thought on that for a while, as she watched the final brilliance of the sunset over the stern. She lounged with her three companions in the steamy evening. A few early stars shone overhead as the moon slowly started to rise. Verdu began to sing, softly, and mostly to himself. Candice's natural coloring returned quickly in the relaxed atmosphere.

"Shouldn't I be tense right now?" Chenda asked Candice. "I mean, we have reached another no-turning-back point, I think. Tomorrow promises a certain amount of danger, and I have no clue what I am supposed to be doing once I get into the Empire. Why am I so calm?"

Candice looked thoughtfully at her young friend. "You passed the point of no return ages ago. Probably before we met. Likely, it was the moment you opened Edison's letter. I've never met anyone as single minded as you. But strangely, your mind is also vastly open – perhaps not open so much as accepting. You let fate pull you along. I think your peace tonight comes from your faith in fate. Look around you. Your faith is strong enough to pull us all along with you. Besides, worry is something that can keep you busy all day, but in the end, it won't move you one inch closer to your goal. I think your head and your heart are just fine were they are."

Captain Taboda arrived among Chenda's little group with a platter of food and several mugs which he laid out before them. "Eat, and I vill tell you vhat is to come."

"Thank you," Chenda said as everyone gathered around the sampling of unusual foods. Chenda watched as Verdu smiled slightly at the dishes before him. She followed his lead and ate with one hand.

"Ve sail tonight - due east. By da morning ve will be sailing up de Xaa-Jair. De mouth of dat stinking river is about 30 miles north of Kotal. About one mile into de Xaa-Jair River vill be a dock. Ve von't be stopping, but you can jump off as ve sail past. Dat should be just as de sun begin to rise. Be ready. I have a few gahment for you vomen. Dees - dey will need to disguise der fair skin. Da dock vill be empty, or almost, so der shouldn't be any trouble for you. You vill need to go due south very quickly. Sight onto a mountain dat looks like a lizard head, vant to bite da sky. Der is cave entrance at de base of de mountain. Inside you vill find a group of vomen. Say dat you have been sent by me, and ask for Ahy-Me. Once you are alone vith her, vere no one vill overhear you, tell her 'de river is rising and stars are bright.' She vill know dat I send you for sure, and she vill help you."

"The river is rising and the stars are bright." Verdu said. "I've got it. Thank you."

"I vill leave you now to enjoy your evening. My crew, apart from the vatch, vill remain below tonight, for der safety. I know you understand. You can not say vat you have not seen, no?"

"Of course," Chenda replied. "We all understand."

He turned without further delay and went below.

"At least it's a beautiful night." Fenimore conceded. He looked at Verdu. "But I can't say I trust Taboda at all. First watch you?"

"Second watch you," he replied.

Fenimore finished eating and reclined even further onto the cushions and settled down to get ready to sleep. "After tonight, we may be unable to get any good rest for some time," he said to Chenda and Candice. "I think you should try to get some sleep."

Chenda leaned back and turned onto her side, facing Candice. "Tomorrow," she said.

"Tomorrow," Candice murmured as she closed her eyes.

The air temperature dropped during the night, and Chenda found herself in a Verdu and Candice sandwich when she woke up. While they slept, each had instinctively scooted closer to the next warmest thing around and huddled against it. She lifted her head and saw Fenimore leaning against the mast, his back to her.

"Psst! Fen!" she whispered. "Help a girl up?"

Fenimore turned and looked at Chenda's predicament, grinning. "Gee, I don't know. You look all warm and comfy there," he whispered.

169

Chenda pouted, and Fenimore extended a hand to her. She grabbed his wrist and he easily pulled her up from between her slumbering neighbors. She stood up next to him for a moment then shivered in the cold. Fenimore found her discarded flight coat and wrapped it around her.

"Thanks. How much longer?" she asked.

"The sky is lightening, and I can see some details of the coastline. The *Tjalk's* crew are up in the rigging already, so I am guessing that they are going to trim some sail here as we enter the mouth of the Xaa-Jair. So, not long at all."

"Should we wake the others?"

"Oh, we can wait a minute or two." Fenimore took the platter that Taboda had brought them the night before, offering the leftovers to Chenda. "Breakfast?"

"Mmm..." she said. "I really liked the... what was that green stuff?"

"No clue. But I hate to waste it when I have no idea what the next meal will be, or when." He took a few morsels and popped them in his mouth, and Chenda followed. The taste was alien to her, but not disagreeable. After a few minutes, the two had cleared the platter.

The sky continued to lighten, and soon, the Tugrulian Coast was clearly visible in the distance. The only word that Chenda could think of to describe the land was *bony*. It was as if some giant sea creature had died, and its chalky white bones lay in the water, limbs twisted in odd angles and poking up through the surf. The sun and waves had bleached and eroded the rock into millions of giant ivory ribs. Landing a small ship in the Tugrulian Empire along this stretch of coast would be impossible. Having to beach a vessel here would mean certain death, dashed against the columns of rocks.

Chenda reached down and patted Verdu on his calf. "Wake up and tell me what I'm looking at."

Verdu stretched and was on his knees quickly, turning his eyes to where Chenda was gazing. He groaned. "It's the Tugrulian Empire. It looks like the region called Reforcho Sahil. We are very close now." He leaned over and tapped Candice on the shoulder "Wake up. We're almost there."

Candice rolled onto her back and sighed. "OK," she said in muted tones.

Taboda came up onto the deck with several colorful garments in his arms. "Good day!" the little man greeted. "I trust you are vell? Good! It's about time you get off my ship!" He handed the clothes to Verdu. "Dress dem! Quickly. Quickly!"

He scurried off, shouting commands to his men in the sails. The speed and direction of the *Tjalk* changed, and the ship began to dash toward the coastline.

"Chenda," Verdu said handing various clothes to her. "Candice," he said, giving the rest of the clothes to the professor. Turning back to Chenda, he helped her pull on a shapeless dress tinted bright orchid. He grabbed the next article, a heavy veil with a gauzy eye slit, and covered her head with it, wrapping it intricately around her neck and shoulders. Lastly he took a wide scarf and bound it around Chenda's waist, again tying it with great complexity. Verdu moved on to adjust Candice's gown. Chenda turned to face Fenimore.

"Well, how do I look?"

"Tugrulian. Unrecognizable. Frumpy." He thought a moment more. "That's pretty good, I guess. Best we could hope for."

Fenimore took a small tin out of his pocket and opened it up. He scooped out a waxy reddish-brown paste and rubbed it between his hands, then smeared it all over his face, neck and forearms. In moment's time, he went from the fair poster boy of Kite's Republic to a candidate for Verdu's identical twin. Other than his sand colored hair, Fenimore looked rather Tugrulian. Fenimore pulled a long strip of cloth out of his pocket and started to cover his head, finishing by looping several long wraps down his back.

Verdu finished helping Candice into her clothes, then checked Fenimore's appearance. "Not bad," he said, smoothing some of the dye on Fenimore's face with his own hands. "How long did Kingston say this stain would last?"

"A few days, but I have plenty more to do touch-ups if I need to." Fenimore grinned. Verdu grinned in response. It was like watching a man smile into a mirror.

171

Taboda whistled from the bow of the ship and pointed into the distance. The *Tjalk* was entering a narrow river mouth, and in the distance, Chenda could see a few spindly docks jutting out into the river.

Verdu pushed the women toward the railing. "Let's get ready to jump. Fen, you first, then Candice and Chenda. I will go last. Hit the dock running and make room for the person behind you. The last thing we want is to hit the water. Nasty what's in there." Verdu shuddered.

Taboda gave a series of shrill whistles to his crew. High up in the rigging, several sails lost their tension and flapped uselessly. The *Tjalk* quickly lost speed.

"UP! Up on the rail. Hurry now!" Verdu instructed. Everyone hopped up. "Spread out, and we'll have a better chance of it." Fenimore danced up the narrow ship's rail like a tightrope walker, and Chenda scooted along toward the bow as well. Although the *Tjalk* had slowed considerably, the narrow dock was coming up impossibly fast.

"Fen! Be ready!" Verdu shouted. The dock was just a few hundred feet from the bow of the ship now. Chenda could smell a foul, brackish aroma growing around her. The river stank of dead fish and marshy stagnant water.

"And.... GO!" Verdu roared.

Fenimore jumped high and far, landing squarely in the middle of the bleached boards. He let his momentum carry him several feet down the dock at a quick run.

"Chenda!" Verdu yelled, and she sprang away from the *Tjalk*. When she hit the dock, her legs tangled in her bulky dress and she sprawled across the planking, the wind knocked out of her.

"Candice!" The professor jumped and tried to step over her young friend, but was hobbled by her skirts as well. Verdu looked at the tangle of arms and legs on the dock and waited for the last possible second to jump. He landed hard on one foot and slid off the side of the dock. As he fell, he caught a rough board with one hand and dangled helplessly. Fenimore appeared in an instant, grasping Verdu's wrist and lifting him back onto the dock.

Captain Taboda, now waving from the ship's rail,

bellowed at the party on the dock. "Tugrul Aquaba! Joide du carda Va!" He laughed heartily, then whistled to his crew. The *Tjalk's* sails snapped taut and once again filled with the bright morning's gusty wind. The small ship drifted away from the shore and charged up the Xaa-Jair River.

Verdu picked himself up from the weathered dock, and snorted. He shook his head in the direction of the fleeing *Tjalk*.

"What did that little weasel shout?" Fenimore asked.

"He said, 'Welcome to the Tugrulian Empire. Enjoy your stay.'"

Chapter 14
RESISTANCE

With Verdu back on the dock, Fenimore helped untangle Candice and Chenda and hauled them to their feet. "Come on," he said. "We're too exposed out here." The small group walked quickly off the dock and angled due south, just as Taboda instructed. Like the coast, the landscape here featured weathered and windsanded stone. Occasionally, Chenda could see small, scraggly plants nestled into the crags and pits of some of the rocks. The little brownish-green tendrils looked as if they clung to their toeholds for dear life, as if at any minute they would be swept away by a gust of wind.

While the foursome briskly strode along, Verdu arranged them. "I'll take the lead," he said. "If we come across anyone, I'll do all the talking. As women, you two will walk one behind the other, with Fenimore at the end to see that you don't run off." He smirked. "Sorry to say, no talking, ladies. A Tugrulian woman would never speak in front of a man who is not her family, and then only when spoken to."

Candice snorted her disgust.

"I'm not saying it's a right and proper thing, I'm just saying it is. You are in Tugrulia now. Blend in or we're all dead." He turned his head toward Candice and she made a curt nod.

For miles, all they passed were rocks and scrub vegetation. Chenda could see a few low mountains in the distance, but they never seemed to get any closer. The cool morning faded quickly into a stifling midday. Chenda wiggled around within her baggy gown to strip off her heavy flight coat. Fenimore called quietly from behind her, "Let it drop, and I will carry it for you." Once she was free of the bulky coat, she found that the Tugrulian clothing was well suited to the heat. With each step, air circulated around her body, whisking away the sweat. She felt more comfortable, but found she was getting very thirsty.

Chenda took the canteen from her belt and unscrewed the cap. She started to take her veil off, but Fenimore hissed loudly in her direction. She stopped to look at him.

"There are people watching us from the top of the rocks far to the east," he whispered. Chenda looked to the left casually and saw a few men lounging across several giant boulders. Each man was dressed just the same as the others, in red and orange uniforms, and all carried shiny short swords at their hips. They were far enough away that she was sure they could not hear her, but she whispered nonetheless.

"Soldiers?" she asked.

"I think so," he answered quietly. "They've been keeping an eye on us for a mile or so." He closed the gap between them a bit more. "Drink through your veil, it will be just fine." Chenda took several swallows, then trotted ahead to Candice, tapping her on the shoulder. Candice took the canteen and drank through her veil as well.

As they continued, the Tugrulian soldiers seemed to lose interest. Their expression showed that it was too hot to bother with checking up on the small group. Chenda soon understood the full extent of that notion. The heat became crippling as the hours passed. Soon after Candice and Chenda finished the last of the water in the canteen, Chenda found it hard to continue walking in a straight line. All she could focus on were the small trickles that ran down her back. She could tell she was walking slower with every passing mile, and she tried to recall if Taboda had mentioned how long the journey should take. Another mile passed beneath her feet, and she couldn't remember where she was going or why, just that she needed to follow the vague, person shaped shimmer in front of her.

Finally, she stopped. She swayed for moment and watched darkness creep into the edges of her vision, then she crumpled to the dusty ground.

Chenda lay there and took several breaths. Then tried to

get back to her feet. Several pairs of hands found her and helped her back up. She couldn't get her eyes to open properly. They felt so sticky and dry. She could hear Fenimore's voice by her ear, and in the quietest of whispers, he said. "Don't. Speak." The tone of his words frightened her. She sensed she and her companions now found themselves in some kind of danger, and her adrenaline started to flow. She perked up slightly, and focused on trying to see and think clearly.

Fenimore's hand shoved her forward a bit, but didn't let her go. He was guiding her as she stumbled along. She trusted that there was a good reason why he wasn't letting her stop and rest for a moment, but she couldn't put the pieces together. A moment later, the blazing heat and blinding sun suddenly dissipated. Fenimore's hands pushed Chenda fast now. She could hear the sound of trickling, bubbling water and Verdu's voice, talking very fast in Tugrulian. As they caught up to his voice, Fenimore stopped and pulled Chenda close to his side.

There was another voice, that of a woman. She sounded surprised as she spoke to Verdu. As the two continued speaking, Chenda heard splashes of water very near to her. She ached all over at the sound of it. She clawed at her veil, desperate to see and hear, to clear her nose and mouth of the muffling fabric. Fenimore's heavy hands reached around her body from behind and pulled her arms to her sides, pinning them there.

She groaned, but he hissed in here ear. "Shh!" If she could have summoned the energy to cry, she would have. She knew water flowed just inches from her, she could feel it, hear it and smell it. Why wouldn't Fenimore let her have it?

Verdu prattled on with the unknown woman, back and forth, and Chenda started to tremble. Finally. The talking stopped, and Chenda heard several pairs of footsteps walking away. Chenda tried to move her hands again, but Fenimore held her fast. Another terse whisper, "Wait." The seconds ticked by and felt to Chenda that the whole span of her life was passing again. Her body started to quake.

Finally, she heard Verdu's voice. "Now, be quick!"

Fenimore dropped her hands and pulled her veil off. Chenda could see again, and her eyes searched wildly for the water she knew was near. Fenimore's hands pulled her down to her knees and guided her shaking hands to a small pool of water collecting in a shallow depression in the rocks before her. With reckless abandon, she scooped and threw water into her dry, cracked mouth, gulping it in. Fenimore's hands were beside hers, gathering water for himself. The inefficient scooping irritated Chenda, so she lowered her face to the pool and quickly sucked in the water, only stopping when she ran out of air to breath. Fenimore took her empty canteen and filled it and then pulled Chenda away from the stone basin, making a space for Candice and Verdu, who likewise flung themselves at the opportunity to relieve their thirst.

Chenda leaned against a low rock looking up at Fenimore, who gulped more water from the canteen and poured some down the front of his shirt. He offered more to Chenda, who grasped the canteen and drank deeply. She looked around as she swallowed. They had entered the shadow of a mountain. She could see the direction from which they had come, and the waves of heat snaking up from the bleached stony ground. Although she could see for a great distance in all directions, she saw no sign of the person to whom Verdu had been speaking.

"What just happened?" Chenda asked no one in particular.

"We found our mountain," Verdu said between gulps. "And I think we may have found the women of the cave that Taboda spoke of." Verdu started splashing water over his head and neck, soaking his long black hair. The water trickled down, making dark splotches on his shoulders and chest. He sagged against the rocks nearest the basin. He turned to Candice, "Well spotted, Professor."

"Thank you," Candice said, her voice raw with dehydration.

"I'm so lost, someone catch me up," Chenda croaked.

Verdu picked up Chenda's discarded veil and dunked it into the water. Wringing it out over his own head, he said, "A few hours ago, we saw the mountain shaped like the head of a lizard, our key landmark, and we angled toward it. About two miles back, Candice recognized a few formations in the rock that would most likely lead us to a cave entrance. She was spot on." He turned to Candice with a smile, "Of course, the fact that you said you were sure there would be water here made me want to marry you."

"HA!" Candice said. "Keep your flattery. It's simple geological observation. I just knew what to look for."

Verdu stood and cautiously looked around, "Let's take one more round of water each and then get you ladies covered up again. I'm not sure yet if we've found safe company, and I want to be sure you all stay under veils until we are resting in the bosom of the resistance."

"That sounds very sensible," Chenda said as she knelt to drink. "So where is this cave?"

Candice pointed to a shadowy crag about 100 yards to the west of them.

"Sorry, I don't see a cave," Chenda said.

"The entrance is low and tiny," Candice said between gulps. "I bet when we get over there, it will drop almost straight down, and it will look from the top like a dry well. Most people wouldn't see it at all. You really just have to know it's there."

"You know it's there," Chenda said.

"Well, Taboda told us it would be there, so we knew to look and there you have it."

"Ladies, veils, please, I think I hear someone coming. Hush," Verdu said.

Chenda covered her head again, the wet fabric cool and soothing on her skin. She arranged the eye-slit properly and turned to the sound of approaching feet. Three veiled women appeared from the shadowy crag and walked toward them. When they were ten yards away, Verdu started talking quickly, gesturing to Candice and Chenda. He clasped his hands together pleading. The lead woman spoke a few subdued words, and motioned for the group to follow her. The other two women stayed at the small pool, looking cautiously out into the heat away from the mountain's shadow.

Candice had been correct about the shape and angle of the cave entrance. The veiled woman gave instructions to Verdu, and then jumped down the hole.

"I'll go first," he whispered. "I'll help you at the bottom."

179

Verdu jumped in.

Chenda looked into the hole and could see Verdu's dark outline below. He made two quick hisses, indicating he was ready to catch, and she jumped. Chenda tried to relax as she raced toward Verdu, but all she could think of were his words as they left the *Brofman* - "This is flying, not falling." Now she was falling, into a deep hole no less. She hated it. She fought against the panic. Before it could overtake her, Verdu scooped her out of the air and set her down on the sand at his feet.

She shivered from the fear that still gripped her, and he started to soothe her in a language she didn't understand. She couldn't understand his words, but his intention was clear. It was enough to help Chenda pull herself together. There was danger here, and she needed to keep her emotions in check. She nodded to Verdu and pressed her back to the wall of the cave, trying to take up as little space as possible.

Verdu hissed again and Candice appeared. Then Fenimore. The group turned and followed the mystery woman through a small gap in the stone. This path led sharply downward into the cool darkness. The woman carried a small, glowing lantern, but its light only helped a little. Chenda stumbled along on the uneven ground. Deeper into the mountain they went. Chenda and her companions walked for ages. She wondered how they would ever find their way out of the dark maze should something happen to the woman leading them. Eventually, the path became more level and wider, then emptied out into a great cavern, where they stopped.

Verdu asked what sounded like a question to the leading woman. She replied, gesturing for them to sit on the low rocks; she turned away and disappeared down another dark passageway with her lantern. Chenda expected to be left in total darkness, but the vast chamber had a subdued glow to it.

"Candice, why can I still see? Where's this light coming from?" she asked quietly.

"This mountain is only a bit of a thin shell in places. When it formed, this chamber was a bubble in the molten rock, and a rather dirty one at that. As magma bubbled up and formed the mountain here, ribbons of sand got mixed in and melted into

180

columns of glass. Some of that glass leads from the outside of the mountain to this cave. Millions of threads of glass that just kiss the surface, and swallow a bit of daylight. It's a rare phenomenon, but not unheard of."

Verdu chuckled, "I'd always wondered why the glowing caves glowed."

"What little light that makes it down here bounces around and gets reflected off those gemstones," she added.

Fenimore perked up. "Gemstones?"

"I've seen several types since entering this cave structure." She pointed around the chamber. "Ruby, sapphire, tourmaline, aquamarine, chrysoberyl, andalusite, apatite, citrine, iolite and kyanite. Oh, and rhodolite and tsavorite garnet."

Fenimore tried to look around himself with nonchalance, but he failed. "So, um, which of the stones are worth the most?"

"The rubies and sapphires, probably. But the iolites are plentiful," she eyed him meaningfully, "if you are looking to grab some low hanging fruit."

Fenimore picked up a few stones, eyed them critically and frowned. "I can't tell which stones are what."

Candice sighed and said, "Come here, I'll show you what you need to look for." They went to the far side of the cave where Candice started to point at various stones. Fenimore listened intently.

Verdu rested with his head in his hands. Chenda asked, "No prospecting for you today?"

He shook his head, exhausted. "I'm sorry I pushed you so hard. I knew we needed to get across the open ground as fast as possible, and get to fresh water. If we had stopped to rest, we would have all baked to death in the sun. Here in the caves we should be able to find water with less trouble."

Chenda shook her canteen and took another deep drink. "I understand," she said, handing Verdu the water. "I'm glad to be out of the scorching heat. Nice and cool down here. I hate that I got all weak and wilty."

"I'm just hoping that we haven't jumped from the frying pan to the fire. The elements above may not be our worst obstacle. The woman who has been leading us says she is a member of the Tugrulian Resistance, but I don't know if we can trust anyone here. Spies are everywhere, to be sure. I am trying to get to Taboda's contact so we can find your mystic and get you out again. We can't hide from the spies for long. All areas of Tugrulian society have various agents; the heirarchy spies on the Resistance. The Resistance keeps tabs amongst the soldiers. The Emperor has men everywhere. Never forget it. That's why I'm keeping you ladies covered and silent. I can pass for just another Tugrulian, but you will have a harder time."

Chenda scooted closer to Verdu and put a hand on his arm. "I appreciate what you are doing for me. Thank you."

"No, thank you. You-" his voice broke off. "I hear someone walking this way." He made a quick double hiss to Fenimore, who grabbed Candice by the hand and pulled her quickly back to where Verdu sat. He looked relaxed but positioned himself between the approaching footsteps and his friends.

The veiled woman reappeared and spoke in Tugrulian to Verdu, who looked pleased. The woman turned and went back the way she had come. Verdu signaled for the group to follow, and they plunged into another dark passageway.

After several minutes, they entered a chamber where water trickled down the rocks, plinking and plopping from stalactite to stalagmite. Sitting against the far wall next to a dim oil lamp was another woman. Unlike all Tugrulian women they had seen so far, this one wore no veil. She was short with a round, pleasant face, dark hair and eyes, and skin much fairer than the average Tugrulian. The woman leading Verdu started speaking in a manner indicated introductions were being made between him and the seated woman, then she made a small bow to each and hurried away down a nearby tunnel.

Verdu spoke again and Chenda only recognized a few words, "..... Ahy-Me.... Taboda.... Tjalk...." Finally, he gestured to Chenda and said, "Pramuc."

The woman turned her head skeptically to examine Chenda. She spoke to her in a tone that sounded like an order, but Chenda didn't understand. She glanced at Verdu for assistance. Verdu spoke again to the woman, who nodded.

"Ah," she said, "I see. I vill try to speak du words of de Republic." She struggled onward. "Take de cloth away from da face, voman."

Again, Chenda turned to Verdu for guidance. He reached out and helped her remove the veil. Chenda imagined how she looked after a day in the maddening heat, sweat and dust. The round-faced woman stepped closer to Chenda and put a hand on either side of Chenda's face. She looked deeply into her eyes and a distrustful expression crept into her face.Then she nodded.

"She thinks she is Pramuc, not!" the woman accused Verdu.

"Yes, I know, Ahy-Me. But it doesn't matter what *she* thinks she is, it only matters what Pranav Erato thinks. She also has the Great Singing Stones." The woman dropped Chenda's face and made a small hop backward. "Show her, please," Verdu said with an encouraging head bob.

Chenda dug around amongst her many layers of clothing and pulled out the velvet bag. She wasn't sure why, but her fingers were trembling as she opened it and pulled out the two loose stones and the gold necklace with its stone pendant. She extended her hand and the stones to Ahy-Me, who slowly started to back away, her eyes wide.

She suddenly turned to Verdu and started chittering wildly in Tugrulian, waving her hands and pointing. She turned to Chenda and started pushing the hand holding the velvet bag toward the hand with the stones. "Avay! Avay!" she begged, looking around to be sure no one had entered the dripping chamber.

Verdu said something in a soothing voice to Ahy-Me. He said the same words to her over and over, and the small woman began to calm down.

"Yes," she said. "Yes, I can live dis part of my life vell, and vill take you to du Pranav Erato. You make rest now. I do go, and come soon."

"We will wait in peace here, Ahy-Me." Verdu said in his most soothing voice.

Ahy-Me scurried away from them and then suddenly turned back and raced up to Chenda. She placed her hands on the sides of Chenda's face again and pressed her forehead to Chenda's. A second later, she dropped her hands and ran off down a dark tunnel.

Fenimore said, "Well, well. I think that went smoothly. I think your 'she's the prophetic liberator' bluff worked."

"Who's bluffing?" Verdu said and both men shrugged in unison.

Candice, sensing an impending philosophical argument, changed the subject by asking, "What was that forehead touching business about?"

"That is how Tugrulians greet their holy men," Verdu said. "You may need to get used to that, Chenda, and respond appropriately."

Chenda bit her lip. "Greeted as a holy woman? I don't know... it seems so dishonest. I don't want to go around pretending to be something I am not. Especially to people who have faith. I... just don't know."

Verdu took Chenda by the shoulders and turned her to fully face him. "You need to go along with this, and do so convincingly. Otherwise we are not going to find Pranav Erato. Ahy-Me is a gatekeeper, for lack of a better term. It is only through her that we will find your mystic. I want her to think that you are the Pramuc. It helps your cause."

He placed his hands on Chenda's face just as Ahy-Me had. "So, here's what you do..." he brought his forehead to hers. "Look in the eyes, always. Look deeply - never away. They will be looking for answers in your eyes, so be relaxed. They will see what they want to see there. Put your hands behind my ears and brush your hands down my shoulders to my elbows." Chenda followed his instructions, but felt foolish. "Now," he said, "push me back slightly by my elbows." She obeyed, and then Verdu dropped his hands. "It's the most formal of greetings," he said, "and a blessing to boot."

Chenda, who had grown accustomed to very close proximity with Verdu, felt like this was too intimate, too unnatural. "It rather makes me uncomfortable," she told him.

"Perhaps you should practice a bit," Candice offered. "Here, let me help you." Chenda turned her body to Candice and

184

repeated the greeting several times. Verdu commented on each attempt, "No, you never lean in," he instructed. "Always keep your gaze focused on the eyes."

Finally, he was satisfied. "That looks great. Keep it in your mind, I think you will be needing to do it a lot before we are done here." He looked around but heard nothing but dripping water. "We should rest a bit."

They sat together, and Chenda passed out some of Kingston's traveling bread. The dense, chewy food was surprisingly filling, but not especially tasty. Chenda, sitting on the ground in front of Fenimore, leaned back against the tall man's knee. "I need a nap," she said.

"So take one," he replied, tossing her flight coat onto the ground next to her. "You all should, I'll keep watch for a while." Chenda's flight coat, soft and fluffy as it was, couldn't ease all of the lumps out of the rock beneath her, but it hardly mattered. She dropped into a deep sleep after just a few moments.

She dreamed of caverns filled with people, all dark haired and olive skinned. Each reached for her, wanting to be blessed by her touch and her gaze. They crowded in on her, pressing her back to the wall of the huge cave, one after the next, touching her face and wanting her sanctification. She was pinned there, and still the crowd pushed forward. Chenda felt herself melting into the rock behind her, first her head and then her torso and arms, on down to her feet, until the crowd finally pushed her into nothingness. She was trapped inside the stone.

She awoke then with a yelp and sat straight up. Verdu rushed to her side. "What's wrong!" he demanded.

"Nightmare," she said. She looked around. Nothing in the cavern had changed, except that now Verdu kept watch as Fenimore slept. She returned to the warm cocoon of her flight coat and tried to close her eyes to sleep again, but couldn't seem to shake her dream. Verdu paced around the cavern, occasionally looking at Chenda's restless repose. He started to quietly sing the forbidden lullaby. As Chenda focused on the song, she began to relax again, and eventually returned to a dreamless rest.

The passing of time in the dark, dripping cave was unknowable.

When she awoke, Chenda couldn't begin to guess how long she slept. The others were already quietly talking. Chenda yawned and rolled from her side onto her back. She ached from sleeping on the hard stone, and her tongue felt huge in her mouth. She craved water and, strangely, pickles. She crawled over to the pool of water that collected around the stalagmites, and started to drink. It was cool and refreshing, but tasted strongly of minerals. She drank until she could drink no more, trying to drive off the last of the feelings of dehydration. She refilled her canteen as well, and then looked into the dark pool.

Between drips, she could see her reflection in the dim lamplight. She looked so different. Her short hair was tussled and dirty, and her cheeks had lost some of their youthful fullness. Her eyes held the most striking change; they *looked* now instead of just being open in sight. She smiled at her rippling reflection, and thought, *So this is what I am today...*

Candice's face appeared next to hers in the puddle. "Lose something down there?" she asked.

"Nope, just thinking of dunking my head," Chenda said.

"Sorry, my dear. We are out of time. Verdu says he hears someone coming."

Chenda stood and returned to Verdu's side as Ahy-Me arrived. She was loaded down with a heavy pack, but greeted the group warmly. "I come, you see! We go now, or yes?"

"Yes!" Verdu said. "Please lead us."

Chenda had many questions for Ahy-Me as they walked. "Where are we going?"

"Ve go to Pranav Erato. Under Kotal. Many miles," she answered.

"Will we travel underground the whole way?"

"No. Ve rise one night walk. Den down under again."

Chenda thought for a minute, then asked. "What is he like, Pranav Erato?"

"Very small and very beeg," she said. "You like heem, I know."

"How is it that you speak the language of Kite's Republic?"

Ahy-Me smiled a wicked smile, "Vhat? You dink de

186

Republic is du only to send spies? No, Tugrul make spies, yes. Only girl spy get school. I learn to spy, but no go to Republic. Me..." she frowned, struggling for the right word. She spoke to Verdu for a moment.

"Ah," he said, "You washed out of the program."

"Vash out!" she said. "Yes. Send me back home. But I see too much in school. I can no stay vith du old ways. I hear dat girls come to certain caves and make resistance. I come. Pranav Erato see me and say 'you know vhat you see vhen you see. I use you.' He teach me all de..." another word questioned to Verdu.

"Prophecy," he supplied.

"Yes. He show me. I listen. I help very much." She smiled, pleased with herself. "Ve climb now."

The tunnel ended in a large chamber. At the far side of the chamber, the small group stopped beside the rubble of a rock slide, hundreds of feet high. "You follow. Ve all be fine." Nimbly, she started to scale the rocks, and the others followed in her footsteps. They climbed for hours, until at last they reached an opening that led to a tunnel that sloped gently upwards. Chenda's limbs ached from the climbing, but she could do nothing about it. On they marched, until, finally, light could be seen in the distance up the passageway.

Ahy-Me turned to the others. "Ve come to the end of dis tunnel system. Ve must pass over land next. Dark ve vait for - dree hours. Rest, yes?"

Wordlessly, everyone hunkered down where they stood.

Chenda wadded her flight coat and propped it behind her head, closing her eyes. It only seemed like a few heartbeats later that Fenimore gently shook her awake. "It's dark now. We need to move on."

"So soon?" Chenda hauled herself up and started walking again; the light at the end of the tunnel was gone. A few minutes later, they were under the stars. Chenda filled her lungs with fresh air. The rocks around her were releasing the heat collected from a long day of blazing sunlight. A cool wind blew from above, swirling together with pockets of hot air rising of the stone. The countering sensations sent shivers up her spine.

"Ve must go faster here," Ahy-Me said. "Patrols are strong

here by du Capitol. Make dis slow run." She started to trot away across the dusty rocks. The others followed, they continued on with a mixture of trotting and walking for several hours. Ahy-Me called them to a stop.

"Ve rest here, few minutes," she said.

"Where are we?" Candice asked.

"Ve half vay to next tunnel," she answered. "Dis vas one time greatest farmland in all vorld. Den de wars come. Dees land - poison. No grow now. No grow ever." She spit on the ground.

Candice looked at the ground around her, a loose mix of rock, soil and dust. She picked up a handful of dirt and rubbed it between her fingers. She brought it to her nose and inhaled deeply. "Hmm...," she said thoughtfully. "Chenda, may I have the canteen?"

"Sure," Chenda replied. "What's with the soil sniffing, Candice?"

Candice poured some water onto the dirt in her hand and then slurped up some of the muddy water. "Interesting."

"Why are you drinking muddy water?" Chenda asked.

"Tasting, not drinking," Candice muttered. "Here, you try it." She held her cupped hand to Chenda. "Seriously!" she added.

Chenda shrugged and put her lips to her friend's palm and sipped. She felt the grit in her mouth, sliding against her teeth and her tongue. She tried to clear it from her lips, but the more she tried, the more the dirt seemed to saturate every part of her mouth and throat. She could smell the soil in her nose, and as she breathed, the sensation of earth expanded in her body.

She let out a moan. "Ick,"she said. "Why did I do that?"

"Can't you taste it?" Candice said. "It's sweet soil. Fertile. There's no bitterness to this earth, no overwhelming saltiness either." She sniffed another sample of dry soil. "Other than the dryness of the soil, there's no poison left in this field. Don't you see? This whole business about toxic Tugrulian land seems to be a lie. All they need to grow food here is a bit of irrigation, some fertilizer and a sack of seed."

Candice turned to Ahy-Me. "When was the last time anyone *tried* to grow crops here?"

The Tugrulian woman looked stunned. "Not for 100 years,

maybe more. De law forbids. No one dare."

"This land," Candice said with conviction, "could grow anything."

Ahy-Me pressed her lips together and committed Candice's words to memory. Fury played across her face. Ahy-Me's round face said it all; she would spread the word to everyone she knew - *we need not starve, the Empire lies to us, we can grow crops again in the valley.*

"Dank you, great teacher," Ahy-Me said as she placed her hands on each side of Candice's face. Candice returned the embrace of respect with the appropriate caress.

Ahy-Me jumped up. "Ve must go now. Yes!" On they went, jogging under the star-filled sky.

As the morning twilight sparked in the eastern sky, the party reached a rocky hillside. Ahy-Me led them to a deep crack in the stones, an unremarkable fracture in the mountainside that opened into a smooth tunnel. In minutes, they were deep inside another cave system.

Chenda could plainly see Ahy-Me relax as they moved further into the hillside. Being above ground was not her usual habitat. She scurried through the caves with ease and grace.

"Dees way." Ahy-Me would call back to her followers. "Not long. Soon." She moved faster. This cave system seemed dramatically more complex than the first. Every few hundred yards, Ahy-Me would turn off into a new cavern or passageway. The tunnels changed direction often, and Chenda had no clue how far they had come, or if they were above or below the level at which they entered the hillside. After an hour of this frantic, twisting journey, the companions entered into yet another small cavern. This space however, had no other passage out. They had reached a dead end.

"Vait here," she said, leaving her companions at the tunnel entrance. Ahy-Me walked across the small chamber and pulled a dirty square of cloth down from a lumpy rock, exposing what Chenda thought was a skeleton. But the skeleton stirred to life, and sat up to look at Ahy-Me. He place one frail hand in hers and smiled.

She alternately nodded and shook her head several times,

as if answering silent questions from the extraordinarily emaciated man. Without taking her eyes from his wizened face, she pointed at Chenda. He turned his attention to her.

Chenda was shocked to see the brilliant, sparkling blue eyes. They were the eyes of a child, clear and wondering, set into the face of a leathery, old man. The fellow gathered his spindly legs beneath him and practically danced toward Chenda. His delicate arms floated out beside him as he approached, bobbing as if he were at the direction of a puppeteer. It was a peculiar kind of grace, both delicate and unstoppable. His body halted before Chenda, but his limbs seemed to keep floating, as if each arm and leg were doing a happy little dance all on its own. One hand drifted to Chenda's face, a single finger brushing her chin, and she felt his greeting wash over her, his message arriving in her head without actually escaping his lips.

Welcome, Chenda, my dear one. I am Pranav Erato. Alexander and Edison did well in protecting you, and to them I am most grateful today. I have been waiting for you to return here for more than 20 years. Let me be the first to welcome you home...

Chapter 15
PRANAV ERATO

Fenimore's voice intruded on Chenda's now wildly swirling thoughts. "Are we there yet? Is *this* the man we have been looking for?"

Pranav Erato looked at Fenimore, then made a wild series of joyful nods. He approached Verdu, who placed his hands on each side of the mystic's face. Chenda watched in wonder at the deep holiness Pranav Erato conveyed through the returning caress. *His* touch was a blessing. She felt the grace that the tiny old man bestowed on Verdu, it filled the cavern. As Pranav Erato released Verdu, he made quick, floating bows to Fenimore and Candice, emanating gratitude. He returned to Chenda's side and clamped one hand around Chenda's wrist. He looked to Ahy-Me. *My blessed angel, will you please take these others to a place where they can rest? Let them know that I will be with the Pramuc for a-time.*

"But I'm not the Pramuc," Chenda interrupted, speaking out loud.

The mystic turned his sparkling eyes to her. *I know you are not, but you may yet be.* He tilted his head to one side and with much sympathy thought to her, *I can see the suggestion burdens you. We will think on it no more for the time being. There are so many more things to tell you first.* His attention drifted back to Ahy-Me. *Let the others know that I will be with Chenda for some time. I will call for you to return soon. Until then, Chenda and I will require solitude.*

"Ve go now! All but Chenda. Come! You come to food and rest. Pranav Erato vill speak only vith Chenda." She waved

191

them toward the tunnel leading out of the chamber like she was shooing chickens.

Fenimore protested. "No. We've brought her this far, we are not going to leave her unprotected now." He stepped quickly around Ahy-Me and reached a hand out to take hold of Chenda's free arm. As his fingers closed around her elbow, Chenda felt a tingle shoot through her and a blue spark jumped from her fingertips to Fenimore's chest with a loud snap. Fenimore rocked back on his heels, and the shock would have landed him on his backside if Verdu hadn't been right behind him, breaking the fall. Pranav Erato giggled silently, holding one withered hand in front of his thin lips. The sparkle in his eyes conveyed mischief. *Let your soldier know I can protect you, too. I am no threat to them, and never to you.*

Chenda turned to Fenimore, "It's okay. I will be fine here. Pranav Erato has much to tell me, and I am curious to hear. After all, his answers are the reason I came. I will be back with you soon." She gave a thankful smile to her friends as Ahy-Me hustled them out of the chamber and down the tunnel.

You must have a thousand questions for me, my darling girl. I have all the time in the world to answer them. But first I need to ask you some things. I know that Edison, gods rest his soul, instructed you to seek me out, that I would be able to tell you what you need to hear, but why would you risk so much, everything, for simple answers? You could have lived your whole life in comfort where you were.

"I know. But I felt... compelled. At first I thought it was because I loved him, and I wanted to fulfill his last wish. I know now that reason was as naive as I was. I also wanted to know who I am. I began on the day of Edison's funeral to wonder of what am I capable. It seemed that the answers lay to the East, here, with you. I needed to know that you existed, and discover what you meant to Edison. How did you know he had died?"

The mystic's eyes sparkled. *I know a lot of things. And, yes, compelled is right. As are we all in this world. Edison was compelled to love you, and Alexander was compelled to be a father to you. I am compelled as well. Your companions and I are also at the mercy of our fates, as you will see. It's not inescapable*

– fate – just compelling. It's hard to break a path once you are on it, but you can if you choose. Let us sit a moment and I will tell you who I am, and who you are.

He pulled Chenda over to a dim lamp resting on a low boulder and pushed her toward a stool sized rock beside to it. He squatted down before her, his bony knees resting under his chin. His long arms reached out and cupped her hands. *Let us begin...*

You are not Chenda Frost, the wife of Edison, or Chenda Bode the daughter of Alexander. You are not the orphan left behind or the widow left alone. I tell you what you are not only to open you up to the past you need to throw away. You are more than the life you have been leading. You are more than you know about yourself. You were born here, in this cave system, could you have guessed that? His eyes sparkled.

"No," she said, "I don't believe it," she whispered.

It's true; I witnessed your birth myself. Hold very still and I will show you.

He screwed up his face in a comical pucker and a sudden flash burst before Chenda's eyes. Instinctively, she closed her eyes, and, once she no longer saw the chamber before her, a vision appeared inside her mind. She saw a young woman supported by several others, struggling to give birth. The supporters were all dark skinned, Tugrulian women, but the laboring woman, moaning through the pain, had creamy skin, exactly like Chenda's. Her hair covered much of her face, tendrils sticking to her moist skin. With a loud groan, the woman bore the baby forth, and a midwife joyfully shouted as she cut the umbilical cord and loosely wrapped the tiny newborn girl in rough cloth. She handed the squirming bundle to the mother, who clutched the child to her chest. She kissed it three times on the forehead, and with each kiss, Chenda felt the light pressure of lips on her own head, the perfect memory of her mother's kiss. The woman lifted the child and Pranav Erato's spindly hands reached forward. Chenda realized this was his memory; she was seeing though his eyes. His hands lifted the squalling infant, and the babe was all that could be seen from the mystic's point of view. The child's eyes opened and Chenda recognized herself in their shape and color. She also saw deep into herself, as Pranav Erato

193

did on the day of her birth. She felt the stir of a deep chime ringing through her. The infant her, as well as the grown body she had become. She felt the overwhelming joy and hope he felt on the day of her birth. She sensed also the horror of what the mystic was about to do, or more truthfully, had already done.

Chenda's eyes burst open, "You took me and ran!" she accused.

Pranav Erato nodded sadly. *I did. Your mother never forgave me, even though she came to understand the necessity of it in time. You needed to be far away from here. The priests of the Empire knew you were coming - there had been so many omens. When you were born, there was a great earthquake beneath the Temple of the Dia Orella. It blew the doors right off the hinges!* He silently shook with laughter. *There was no doubt that the Pramuc had been born. I had to get you far from here. The priests went wild looking for you. That's when I found Alexander Bode and convinced him to take you as his own child.*

Chenda held up her hand. "Wait, my mother didn't look Tugrulian. Was she? And if Alexander Bode wasn't my father, then who is?"

Pranav Erato sighed. *Yes, your mother was born in the Empire, but she was born with "undesirable coloring." Her parents knew she would be a burden to the family – unmarriageable. They sold her into servitude. Eventually, your mother, Abhya by name, served as a maidservant to Bhagnee, a third daughter to the 14th wife of the Emperor. A nobody as far as Imperial Princesses go. Traditionally – the Emperor will give away these lower princesses as gifts – it seems to these men that's what daughters are best used for. One day, word came to Bhagnee that she was to be presented as wife to a wealthy Mae-Lyn trader who had impressed the Emperor. Bhagnee was terrified of the obligation laid before her and hid in the palace. Her mother, certain that the Emperor would be furious with her and her child if his decree was not met, dressed Abhya head to toe in Bhagnee's wedding clothes, darkened her skin with dye and passed her off as a little princess. The Mae-Lyn trader took his new bride, got drunk and did with Abhya what all newlyweds do. By the end of the night, Bhagnee's mother found her. She tracked down Abhya*

194

in the honeymoon suite. With the groom fast asleep, Bhagnee's mother made the girls switch back again. The bridegroom awoke in his marriage bed later and was none the wiser. Bhagnee sailed away with her arranged husband, and Abhya was tossed away like stale bread. Exiled by Bhagnee's mother, alone and, as she soon learned - pregnant, she eventually found her way to me.

   The man you knew as your father, Alexander Bode, I freed from a Tugrulian prison. He was scheduled to be executed – convicted of spying. He really was one you know – a spy. As I hid him, I came to know him well, and trust him. When you were born, I saw an opportunity and arranged to have him return to the West with you. I placed you in his arms, and he loved you as if he had fathered you himself. He also recognized the vast potential for power that was born within you. He knew, if the legends were true, that in the hands of the Emperor, you could be turned into a weapon that would destroy the West. So, he took you away and made you his own. However, his love for you clouded his judgment. Once he brought you to his home, he never intended to bring you back here or tell you about your destiny. But Fate has a way of making itself heard.

   The war started, and your father was obliged by the government of the Republic to become involved once again. When your father's ship came too close to the Empire, it was shot down. Most of the crew died in the accident, but Alexander and Edison survived. They found themselves adrift on the Kohlian Sea. Luckily, a ship sympathetic to the Resistance picked them up. Alexander spoke enough Tugrulian to ask to be brought to me. Your father was dying, and he begged Edison to collect you and care for you when he returned home. Edison, gravely injured himself, rested here as he recovered. I taught him all about the prophecies and he saw the value of the Resistance to the Republic. He shared a good bit of his military strategy with them. He discovered that the Emperor was using the rare Singing Stones as a way to control several Tugrulian generals. The Emperor found that he could harness the power of the stones to listen to the thoughts of various people, and even command them, from great distances. Edison knew that he could cripple the Empire if he could capture the stones. Without the stones to help

195

them, all of the coordinated attacks would fall apart.

Edison's plan to steal the stones was brilliant, but as he entered the chamber where the stones were harnessed, something went wrong. When Edison stepped into the place reserved for the true Pramuc, he touched the stones, and they somehow infused him with a special sensitivity. From that day on, his mind was bombarded by the presence of others. He couldn't make sense of it and it pained him greatly. I believe it has to do with the vibration created by the sounds and motions of people. Somehow they were amplified within him, just as sound is amplified in the Singing Stones. That is why he held himself apart from the world once he returned to the Republic. He spent much of his time looking for a way to make his nightmare stop. The closest thing he could find to relief was separation.

As the prophecies detailed, the stones were the birthright of the Pramuc. Before your father died, Edison made a vow to unite you with the stones, and help you find a way back to fulfill your destiny. The Resistance agreed to help him get home, and helped him to communicate with me over the years. I had much concern, however, about his fondness for you. You see, he considered it a curse, what the stones imbued in him, but I think that your stillness enhanced his preference for your companionship. It soothed and pleased him, and he fell in love with you as the years passed. Fate had a hand there as well you see. As you said, your love compelled you to come home.

Edison saw his death approaching; he heard Daniel's torment. He also knew that he had waited too long to bring you to your birthright. The spies from the Empire found a tool in that boy, Daniel Frent. These spies controlled him just as the Emperor controlled his generals. It was not in Daniel's nature to murder, but by grouping the Lesser Singing Stones, the ones that surfaced and disappeared in the West, the Tugrulian spies were able to manipulate him – just as the Emperor had done with his generals. In his last minutes of life, Edison did what he could to help you. He wrote you that letter and hid his soul among the stones to help you get onto your fated path.

Pranav Erato's eyes bubbled with excitement. *And here you are.*

196

"It's too much," Chenda said. *"You've shown me too much. What you've told me, it helps me to understand who Edison and my father were, but I feel like it has all been built on a grand misunderstanding. I am not the Pramuc. It's just not me."*

I'm sure you're right. Pranav Erato bounced to his feet, his arms and legs waggling like a marionette's again. *The pull you felt to return here is inexplicable.* His sparkling eyes charmed her. *Let's take a walk and I will tell you another story.*

Pranav Erato's bouncy gait led Chenda out of the chamber and down several twisting and turning tunnels. She followed him in silence, her mind working through the avalanche of information she now possessed. The text of Edison's final letter tugged at her memory. She had focused on the passages instructing her to find Pranav Erato almost exclusively, but she had glossed over the other task he had set before her: *to believe.*

What is it that I need to believe...? she thought to herself.

Pranav Erato's thoughts sounded in her head. *Now you are asking the right question!*

They entered a long gallery with very high ceilings and very straight walls. This chamber had been carved from the solid rock. The mystic lowered his lamp to a channel in the floor that ran the length of the room. It caught fire, and the space filled with light. Chenda could now see deep, intricate carvings covering the high walls of the gallery.

Stories are so much better with pictures! Pranav Erato danced with excitement. He pulled Chenda to stand before the first stone image. He waved his arms theatrically. *BEHOLD!* his voice boomed in Chenda's head. The sound of snickering followed as she staggered under the weight of Pranav Erato's shout.

Ah, I love doing that.... He started again, with less drama.

Behold! the prophecy of the First Pramuc of the East. One-hundred and thirty years ago, or there about, these images were committed to the rock by him at the time of the Great Distribution. The gods of the various people were being pushed out, set aside by the One God of the Tugrulians.

He turned his crystal eyes to Chenda.

The gods are powerful, but only when there are people to

worship them, to believe. It's the biggest flaw that gods have. See, even the gods have problems! He turned his face to the carved wall again.

The gods, as they were dying, for lack of a better term, pulled together as one and shot what remained of their power into the future. They set in motion a series of events that would result in the eventual coming of a great liberator, one who would help the people of this land free themselves to discover their gods again. They gave this vision of the future to a man, dubbed him Pranav, and bid him to keep the spark of their existence alive until the Pramuc arrived.

Here is what each of us Pranavs have been tasked to look for in the Pramuc:

He pointed to the first image, a woman straddling the world with each foot on a continent and a hand resting on the sea. *The Pramuc will be one with the three great peoples of this world.*

He dragged Chenda to the second image, a child held aloft by a circle of women wearing long robes and halos. *The Pramuc, the Holy One, will be a held apart and raised by Holy Ones.*

He stepped to the third tableau, a woman flanked by three others: a man clenching a fist, another with a halo and a third with a book. *The Pramuc will be companioned by the Soldier, the Saint and the Scholar.*

The fourth carving showed a woman burying three stones in the dirt. *The Pramuc will hold the Great Singing Stones and return them to their home.*

The last image showed a woman circled by waves, clouds, swirling sand and fire, all of which seemed to be spiraling toward her. *The Pramuc will hold the Four Elements within her, to command as she will.*

Pranav Erato vibrated with excitement, dancing in a small circle. *It's uncanny, no? You see yourself there as if you gazed into a mirror.*

"Um, I don't see it. None of that describes me," Chenda said with relief.

Are you so sure? Wasn't your mother Tugrulian and your father Mae-Lyn, yet you were raised amongst the people of Kite's Republic? Three worlds can claim you.

Chenda shrugged and said with a voice full of doubt, "Maybe..."

Pranav Erato plowed ahead. *Your whole childhood was spent with the nuns of St Elgin... women of a holy order.*

"That doesn't make me a holy one, though."

Your companions: Fenimore is your most fierce protector, your own personal Soldier. Verdu works to bring you to what he believes, as all Saints do, and Professor Candice Mortimer...

"A Scholar of the first order," Chenda finished.

You have the stones, yes?

"Yes," she said, her hand clutching her chest where the velvet bag lay hidden. Chenda's head snapped up and she looked defiantly into Pranav Erato's gleeful eyes. "But I don't know anything about controlling any elements."

Don't be so sure. Pranav Erato said as he took both of her hands again. A blazing blue spark flashed before her eyes again. A series of memories flashed before her eyes: Falling into the fire while struggling with Daniel Frent, the pain of the fire entering her hands as she beat the flames out of her hair. Standing near Fenimore in the bow of the Brofman, the wind filling her and carving her sorrow away, her tears blowing and splashing against Fenimore. The sting of the salt water as Verdu squeezed the sea from her lungs. The grit of the wet soil mixed with mineral water sipped from Candice's hand, an earthiness that permeated her whole body.

From the first moment you touched the stones, the elements have been assembling within you. When you are ready, you will be able to command them. You will have power beyond imagining.

Chenda pulled her hands away from the willowy man, shaking her head in denial. "No, not me." She sank to her knees, her minds so occupied with rejecting these new ideas that she could hardly remember to breathe.

Pranav Erato laid one finger on Chenda's shoulder. *Peace, my child. Take your time and think things through.* He folded his legs beneath him and sat next to her. He waited beside her for a long time, listening to her disjointed thoughts. On the one hand, Chenda felt the original impetus of her journey had been

199

resolved. She had found the man she had been sent to find, and he had the answers she sought. By all rights, her most pressing goal achieved, she was free to choose what she wanted to pursue next in her life. She felt whole in that respect, resolved. However, this fulfilling information, these answers she understood deep within her to be the truth, also cut her off from the free will to choose her next path. If she chose to believe the answers for which she traveled so far, she would have to believe that destiny ruled her life. She could not accept the truth in slices. She had to accept it all, or none of it.

"I can't decide what to think," she said at last.

I can see that.

"It's a lot to take in," she said. "And even if I accept it, that I am the Pramuc, what am I supposed to do with that? Where's the carved stone wall that tells me what I'm supposed to do with all the great power of the Pramuc?"

Oh, that's written on the wall behind you.

Chapter 16
DECISIONS

Chenda leaped from the ground and ran to the wall at her back. It was perfectly smooth. She scuttled the length of the wall, brushing her hands along it, looking for any kind of carving or writing. There was nothing. Chenda felt the panic start to rise in her. She wanted to find an answer.

"Where is it?!" She stumbled back toward Pranav Erato. looking with wild eyes at the blank wall.

The mystic, his face serious, drifted toward Chenda with his hand outstretched. She clasped it, hungry to hear his thoughts.

What do you see? His voice asked kindly in her head.

"Nothing. It's just a blank wall. You said the answers would be written in stone there, and there's nothing. Why would you lie?"

Lie? Who lied? I am offering you one last fact, perhaps the most important fact that will help you decide whether to embrace your destiny or turn from it. He turned her to face the long, empty wall. He stood behind her, lifting her hands and stretching his thin arms out wide. *That is your future.*

Chenda stood stunned.

"My future is blank?" She turned and faced Pranav Erato.

Yes! Isn't that wonderful?

Chenda stood there, blinking.

Only your potential is set in stone. What you do with it, your future, is yours to decide. Accept your destined gift, and you will still be able to choose for yourself what you do. Prophecy only gets you so far, the rest – you make up as you go along – as you encounter the destinies of others. You can choose to liberate

Verdu's people, and we all know that's what he wants, or you can choose to return to Kite's Republic and pick up life where you left off. Live among the boat people if you choose. You fear that accepting destiny means that you will be devoid of choice, and that is not entirely true. To put it another way, I was destined to become Pranav, but once I did, I made the most of it, through my choices.

My advice is that you claim the gifts the gods have left for you, then do what you feel, or do as you please. He smiled at her. *I doubt you will be able to consider yourself complete until you do.*

"You make it sound so simple."

I think it is, but then again, I talk without moving my lips and I live in a cave, so perhaps my reasoning is unconventional.

Chenda snorted.

Think about all I've said. When you want to claim your place as the Pramuc, you can.

"Tell me about controlling the elements. How would the Pramuc do that?"

The complete set of Singing Stones, held in the right place by the right person, will unlock the Pramuc's elemental power. The four elements, earth, air, fire and water, rule most aspects of the world. Of course, you have seen the four elements, and how they can behave both destructively and constructively. Shifting earth can bury a whole village, or reveal valuable resources. Swirling air blows away all the seeds from a field or can be harnessed to ease the burdens of man. Fire can destroy or cleanse a wound. Water can erode or refresh. When one controls the elements with only one's will, what could not be done? You could crush the world, or heal it.

She whispered. "The thought of one person holding so much power frightens me."

If it did not, you would frighten me. My visions have shown me the power's potential, which will be formidable, but I cannot see clearly how the Pramuc will wield it. Should you chose to undergo the process of claiming the power, you will need to discover how to use it on your own. My visions can give you some guidance, but once you accept the power, well, I'll be just as

202

surprised as you are about what happens.

He turned his head to the side, as if listening to something. *Your companions are anxious to see you again, especially your soldier. He fears for your safety. I will meet with all of you tomorrow. I believe they will be most necessary to you then.*

Pranav Erato dropped Chenda's hands and floated backwards from her. Chenda's arms fell to her sides. She turned to face his retreating figure as Ahy-Me appeared at the far end of the gallery.

"Thank you. You've given me much to consider," she called after him.

He bobbed his head in reply and his wispy limbs danced away with him out of the gallery and into the darkness.

Ahy-Me cleared her throat politely, "You vill come and join your friends, yes?"

"Yes," Chenda said, striding toward the small woman. "I very much need my companions right now."

As Chenda followed Ahy-Me in silence down the dark passageways, she realized that she thought best while walking. The cadence of her feet, rhythmically ticking off the yards, distracted her slightly from the overwhelming weight of her own potential and the choice that she needed to make. She reflected on the stone carvings the Pranav showed her. She could now see herself in the words of the prophecy, as he had said. But that wasn't what troubled her. Accepting that she was the Pramuc would mean agreeing to control and wisely use the power of the elements. She doubted her self control, she questioned her wisdom and she despaired that her character would not be up to the task of finding what was right.

Suddenly, more than anything, she wanted to go home, but she wasn't sure where that was anymore.

Ahy-Me led Chenda into a tiny round cave with a small but very bright fire in the center of it. The room was a living chamber with four tidy beds and a narrow table already laid out with platters of food. A small fountain bubbled and slopped sparkles of water into a carved basin.

"I vill return vid you friends very soon. Please, sit. Eat." Ahy-Me pulled a heavy curtain across the doorway as she left

Chenda alone in the warm chamber.

Chenda felt exhausted and hungry. As she passed the fire, she noticed the flames gave off a sweet, pungent aroma. She sat down at the table and started to nibble on some of the food. She could identify the tangy meat as a preserved fish, and there were some very tasty pickled mushrooms as well. As her hunger abated, the smell of fire and the tinkle of the water on the rocks relaxed her. Her chest, seized in tight anxiety since meeting the Pranav, loosened with every incense-laced breath. She pulled off her aeronaut boots for the first time since slipping into them the morning after the *Brofman* left Atoll Belles. Chenda turned sideways in her chair, propping her bare feet up on the seat beside her and pointing her toes toward the bright flames. She rested one elbow on the table and cupped her palm under her chin. Her mind emptied as she watched the unusually white flames until her eyes closed.

She had no idea how long she sat there dozing at the table, but she awoke to Candice's voice, piercing her nap. "Chenda! My gods! Are you all right?"

Candice was dashing across the small room to Chenda's side. She knelt down as Chenda slowly opened her eyes and smiled.

"Oh, there you are, my scholar," Chenda said. She saw Verdu and Fenimore looking at her over Candice's shoulders, matched expressions of worry on their faces. "Hello, my soldier and saint," she giggled.

Candice frowned. "She's as high as a moon beam!"

"Oh, I'm fine. The sweet smell from the fire just made me all rappy and helaxed, er, happy and relaxed." She looked toward the flames again and noticed that they had dimmed from bright white to an orange-yellow. "Awww... the fire got all dim," she said with her voice heavy with disappointment.

The other three looked from Chenda to the flames and back. Candice stepped to the firepit, examining the area around it. Verdu and Fenimore each took Chenda by an arm and hauled her up to standing. Without a word, they half-walked and half-dragged her to the water basin and splashed her face with water. Chenda gasped as the cold water shocked her back to alertness.

"Eek! Stop it!" She stood up straight, swaying only slightly, and pushed the men back from her. "That," she said, "was uncalled for." She turned on her heel and headed back to the table, almost managing to walk in a straight line. She flopped into her seat again, and returned her feet to the neighboring chair. She folded her arms over her chest and assembled her face into a slightly sulky look.

Candice, who had been kneeling by the fire, tossed a few orange, chalky looking chips into the flames, which burned bright for a few seconds, puffing forward a tendril of sweet smelling smoke. "Interesting," she said, waving her hand to dissipate the vapors. "Verdu, do you have any idea what that is?"

"Sure, it's called the Chalk of Contentment. It's mostly harmless, a cake of herbs and minerals that act somewhat like a soporific. I think our hosts wanted to make sure Chenda wasn't stressed. No harm was meant by it. One could even say that whoever put this in the fire was just trying to be polite."

Fenimore's expression turned furious. "How can you say that? We come back to find her passed out! A thousand horrible things could have happened to her that way! Polite, my ass!"

Chenda waved a limp hand at both of them. "Shh.... Stop it. I have to say, after all I've had to take in today, I honestly don't mind." She smacked her lips together. "I am a bit thirsty, however."

Fenimore took an empty cup from the table and filled it at the basin while Verdu and Candice took the empty seats across from Chenda. Fenimore brought back the drink and handed it to Chenda, who started to pull her feet back to allow him the last chair. Fenimore scooped her legs up and slid into the seat, dropping her feet into his lap. "I don't mind," he said with a smile, "Be comfortable."

Chenda sipped, "Well, thank you."

She looked at the faces around her, highlighted by the soft flickering light. They stared at her patiently, until Candice barked, "Well? Spit it out!"

"Oh, sorry. My mind is a little empty now." She shook her head trying to clear it. "I love sitting with my feet up and I hate shoes," she said, apropos of nothing.

Verdu's lips twisted into a half-smile. "The side effect of the smoke is a general loosening of the tongue. She's likely to say anything she's thinking at this point."

"I see that," Candice frowned. She snapped her fingers twice. "Focus! What did Pranav Erato tell you?"

"Hmm... where to start? Well, much to my surprise, it turns out I *am* about as Tugrulian as you are, Verdu." Chenda told her companions the whole of what Pranav Erato revealed about her parentage, her husband's role in the Resistance after his airship crash, and the carved gallery of the First Pranav. She babbled on about how the Singing Stones had drawn the four elements to her body, and how each of them was part of the prophecy. Chenda lamented about her fears over being infused with power. Finally, she ended her long telling by blurting out, "And I really don't know what I should do, but I have an overwhelming desire to just run away, and I really love the way you are stroking my ankle, Fen, it's really quite comforting at the moment."

Chenda slapped both hands over her mouth, embarrassed over that last bit.

She peeled three fingers back and said, "Somebody please find a way to shut me up."

Fenimore raised his hands in surrender. "Wow."

"Wow is right," Candice said, "What are you going to do?"

Chenda looked deeply into the faces of her companions, her closest friends in the world. "What would you do if you were me?"

She turned to Fenimore first. He regarded her soberly. "If *my* instincts were telling me to run, I think I might just do that. If you want to go home, I'll take you there. I've already got a plan, sort of, to-"

"Go home?" Candice interrupted. "What's left for her there? She's not even *alive* as far as anyone is concerned. Her life has been irreparably altered. There is no going back." She turned to Chenda and reached for her hand across the table. "I'm not saying you need to embrace Pranav Erato's prophecy, but you'd be foolish to think you can ever go back to the life you once knew. If

206

you try to be Chenda Frost again, there will be too many questions about where you've been, and who the charred dead guy was in your room. I don't know if I would want to explain that. And don't forget the people who are trying to kill you. There is no reason to go back to the Republic and wear a name tag that says, 'I'm Chenda Frost. Please line up here to bump me off!'"

Chenda looked to Verdu, who said, "I think you already know what I would do." He looked at her with sad eyes. "I can only guess what will lie ahead of you if you chose to take on the role and the power of the Pramuc. It won't be easy. I don't think that anyone has ever had that kind of potency before. It may not even work, or it could kill us all for the trying. There has just never been a Pramuc before. Uncharted territory, this. But I would do it if I were you. There are just too many people in this world that could use the help. If I had a way to act, to try, and I didn't do anything, it would feel like a lie – a big one – and it would last for the rest of my life."

She sighed and closed her eyes. "So, you, collectively are telling me 'Yes, no and maybe.'" Chenda closed her eyes for a moment. "Well, your perspectives give me food for thought. Thank you all for helping me get this far. I never would have made it without your help and guidance. I just need to think a little longer."

Verdu spoke, "If it helps, I will stand by you no matter what you choose to do."

Fenimore chimed in, "Whatever you need from me, just ask. I only want to make sure you stay safe. I'm here as long as you are." He stroked her ankle again, hoping to be a comfort once more.

"And I'm sure my office will still be poisonous for another week or two, so I've got some time to stick with you, as well," Candice added, and they all laughed.

"I wonder, can we get any more of that Chalk of Contentment?" Candice asked.

The next morning, lying in the darkness of the small chamber, Chenda decided that all three of her friends were right. Chenda knew that there was no returning to her old life, and starting life over in the Republic would leave her always wondering *What if....* Verdu's sentiment about turning her back on a gift, a unique one from the gods no less, made her heart heavy. Regret would plague her if she didn't try. Clearly, Chenda had made her choice. When she met with Pranav Erato, she would accept the role of Pramuc.

She listened to the gentle breathing of the others, each still sleeping. She rolled out of her bed and crawled over to where Fenimore slumbered. Chenda leaned close and asked the stupidest question one can ask a sleeping person, "Fen, are you awake?"

"Hmm, narf," he answered. He breathed in deeply. "Chenda? What's wrong?"

"Oh, nothing's wrong," she answered. "I've just decided what I am going to do. I'm going to try and embrace being the Pramuc. I will, but I am really frightened. I don't want to talk with the others about how much of a coward I am."

"There's nothing wrong with being frightened when you are about to plunge headlong into the unknown. Don't be so hard on yourself."

"Thank you for that. I only mention it because I want you to help me with one thing."

"Sure, whatever you want."

"I want you to keep that retreat plan in mind. If I can't control this thing... I mean, I don't want to hurt anyone, and, if it turns out that the vast power of the elements is more than I can control or endure, you've got to find a way to get me out of harm's way, someplace I can't devastate the landscape or something. If it's really making me suffer, or I become some kind of monster, I need you to help me end it. Can you do that for me?"

"End it? Or end you?" Fenimore asked.

"I think you know what I'm asking," Chenda said.

"We can just go now and skip all the terror, if you want."

"I don't think I can," Chenda replied taking Fenimore by the hand. "Will you protect the world from me if this all falls apart?"

"I will try. I promise you that," he vowed. They sat there in silence. Chenda found that Fenimore, more than any other person, put her at ease. Eventually, the others began to stir. Fenimore dropped Chenda's hand and tousled her short spiky hair.

208

"Look at that," he said. "We begin again in a new day. Let's see what happens to us next."

A small, hunched woman tottered quietly into the chamber carrying a bundle of fuel for the fire in one hand and balancing a tray of food in the other. She tossed a few briquettes onto the low flames as she passed and the room brightened considerably. She placed her platter on the table and backed away, bowing.

The serving woman faced Verdu, and patiently waited for him to address her first. He made a greeting, and then the woman quietly delivered her message.

"Ah," Verdu said turning to Chenda and Candice, who had already begun an examination the breakfast selections. "She says that Pranav Erato will see us in just over an hour's time, and if you ladies wish it, she will be happy to escort you to a hot pool to bathe."

"Whoopie!" Candice said. "I offend even myself. Let's go!"

"Dear gods, yes," Chenda replied. "All my fortune for a cake of soap, please."

The two ladies started to follow the little woman out of the room, but Candice turned and trotted back to the table to snag a few tidbits from the breakfast tray. "No point skipping breakfast," she winked at Verdu. Fenimore also grabbed a handful and stood to follow the ladies.

Candice held a hand up to him. "No, no, no. You are not going to follow us to the baths," she said firmly.

"I won't follow you in, I just want to be close by, in case you need me."

"Don't be absurd." She flapped her hands at him, "Go. Sit." She narrowed one eye at him and said slowly, "Stay." She turned on her heel and marched out.

Fenimore glanced at Verdu, who said, "I'd listen to her, brother, or you may not live to regret it. I've never heard a command so serious."

Fenimore gave another withering glance at the curtains, still gently swaying from the women's exit, and he sat. "I've been cowed by a woman half my size," he said shamedly.

A moment later, Chenda burst back through the curtains

and ran to Verdu's side. "I'm trusting you to keep these safe for me," she said, pressing the black velvet bag into his hands and running back out again.

Verdu grinned at Fenimore. "That's surprising. I guess she finally trusts me."

"Don't be too sure. I would bet you five that she's hoping you steal the little buggers so she won't have to go through with this."

Chenda, stripped naked and resting in a pool of very hot water, scrubbed at the dirt which had collected in the crook of her elbow. The rough cloth did a fairly good job of scraping off the gunk, but she wished for some bubbles.

"Why don't we have any soap, do you think?" she asked Candice, soaking in another pool across the steamy and low ceilinged cave.

"Well, I guess they don't have any lye, and you need lye to make soap. No hardwoods to use for fires means no wood ash. No wood ash means no lye."

Chenda considered her missing clothes. The serving woman had gathered them up as they entered the steaming pools, pantomiming a scrubbing motion with them. Chenda assumed that meant her things were destined for a laundering. She was surprised how attached she had become to her warm silk pants and her flight coat. "So, how do you think they will get our clothes clean without soap?"

"Easy," Candice said as she dunked her head under the water and resurfaced, splashing and blowing bubbles. "Fuller's earth. It's kind of like clay, and it absorbs odors and grease. Useful stuff." She dunked again, and came up speaking. "Or maybe they use alkaline water. I don't know if there are enough people in the Resistance to collect that much urine, though."

"Ew. I'm hoping for the fuller's earth now." Chenda examined the small bowls of various pungent pastes that a serving girl placed at the edge of her bathing pool. She glanced at the young woman in the corner. She watched Chenda intently, waiting to spring forward should the bathing woman required any assistance. Chenda pointed at the first bowl and shrugged her shoulders, hoping to convey that she had no clue what to do with the contents. The girl, with beautiful, richly dark skin and deep brown eyes, dropped to her knees and scooted over to Chenda.

She picked up the bowl and sniffed at it, then offered it to Chenda, placing it before her nose. Chenda inhaled the bright, almost minty smell. "Mmm..." She opened her mouth and pointed in, her eyes asking, *do I eat this?*

The girl laughed, a sweet bubbly sound, and she scooped out a walnut sized blob and began to rub it into Chenda's hair. As she massaged it down to her scalp, the girl eased Chenda's back against the wall of the hot spring, settling her onto a smooth bench. It felt so nice. The girl's fingers massaged the paste through her hair, down her neck and into the shallow divots behind her ears and jaw. The smell of mint and the vapor of the water relaxed her almost as much as the young woman's touch.

The girl picked up another cup from the side of the pool. She tipped Chenda's head back until it rested on the girl's lap. Dipping her delicate fingers into the cup, she transferred an oily liquid to Chenda's face. It smelled spicy and felt warm on her skin as the girl slowly smoothed it across her cheeks and down her nose. Chenda looked up into the girl's sweet face for a time, seeing the concentration there; she wanted to do her job exceptionally well. The girl's eyes flicked to Chenda's and she smiled pleasantly. Chenda could tell that the girl was slightly uncomfortable under her stare, so she closed her eyes, enjoying the sensation of the girl's fingers on her forehead, her jawline and neck. After a few minutes, the girl finished Chenda's massage, and blotted her face with a soft cloth.

The girl patted Chenda on the shoulder and she opened her eyes. The girl pointed to her head and then the water. She wanted Chenda to dunk her head, it seemed, so Chenda did. She could feel the minty paste dissolve as she went under. She swished her fingers through her short hair, and was surprised to feel how silky it had become. She rose from the water again, and looked over to where the girl had been, but she was gone. In her place was an older woman, with much fairer skin, holding a large square of gray, fluffy cloth.

"I guess I'm done then," she said to the woman holding the

towel.

She knelt down and offered a hand to Chenda to help her out of the water. As Chenda stepped up onto the stone bench, she took the woman's hand. The older woman's expression changed to one of long felt pain. "Chenda!" she said, her voice hardly more than a whisper.

Chenda focused on the woman's face as she pulled a towel around her shoulders. "Yes?" she asked, fairly sure the woman didn't understand her language. Once she looked closely, she noticed that there was something familiar about this woman.

The woman patted Chenda on the chest. "Chenda," she stated. Then the woman touched her own chest. "Abhya," she said.

All the pieces fell into place for Chenda in an instant. This was Abhya, the fair skinned one. Sold into service. Swapped for a princess too scared to be a bride. Exiled to the Resistance. Robbed of her child.

"Mother?" Chenda gasped. "MOTHER!"

Chenda leaped from the water, throwing her arms around her mother squatting by the side of the warm pool. She pressed her face into the woman's neck, and she, in turn, wrapped her arms around her daughter. She started to rock Chenda back and forth, as one would rock an infant child. The two women sat there for a long time crying tears of joy, which mingled with the drips of water falling from Chenda's body. Naked as the day she was born, she sat there, holding her mother and being held in return. No thoughts came to Chenda other than the fierce joy of reunion.

Candice, who had heard Chenda exclaim, quickly realized what was going on, and who the older woman with Chenda must be. As she wrapped herself in a thick towel, she felt like an eavesdropper or some kind of emotional peeping Tom. Candice retreated into a shadow toward the back of the chamber and tried to be unobtrusive as the mother and daughter reunited.

Abhya pulled the towel up around Chenda's naked shoulders, and then held her at arm's length. She traced her daughter's features with her fingertips, crying and laughing at the same time. Abhya started talking excitedly to Chenda, and it hardly mattered that she couldn't understand. The rhythm and tone of her mother's voice filled Chenda's heart with gladness.

It occurred to Chenda that she and her mother needed to go back to Verdu. He could help them to talk to one another. She pulled Abhya to her feet and pulled her toward the exit. The woman followed her for a moment and then grunted, pulling her hand back. She pulled up the corner of Chenda's towel and giggled.

"Oops, I'm naked. I might just give those boys a scare if I walk in like this!" Chenda said.

Her mother whistled toward the corner where Candice skulked, waving the woman to come forward. Abhya then turned to a basket on the floor, where she pulled out a few articles of bright Tugrulian clothing. These garments were significantly nicer than the old and plain ones Captain Taboda had given them aboard the *Tjalk*. The gown Abhya pressed into Candice's arms shimmered an iridescent blue, and it practically dripped in intricate embroidery and faceted gemstones. Chenda's gown, equally adorned with expensive needlework, was the palest purple. Hundreds of small and medium sized amethyst beads accented the wrists and neckline. Chenda pulled the exquisite dress over her head and her mother reached out to help her settle it around her shoulders.

A thrill of joy shook through Chenda at her mother's touch. She turned to Candice." She's my mother! Can you believe it?"

Candice accepted a pair of soft, embroidered shoes from Abhya, nodding a thank you. "I can see the resemblance, dear. I'm very happy for you." Candice smoothed the front of her gown and looked herself over. "Well, we are dressed as smartly as one can imagine. I guess we have a big day ahead of us. We should get back to the fellows, as we have an appointment soon."

"Indeed," Chenda replied, a little sadness in her voice. She slipped on a pair of beautiful shoes offered by her mother, and tucked her pouch-belt up under her dress, buckling it tight around her hips. Chenda then grabbed her mother by the hand, intending to never let go again. Abhya patted the girl's hand, understanding, then gestured toward the door. "Verdu," she said. Chenda nodded and walked toward the opening to the dark passageway.

The young girl who had helped Chenda with the bath ointments burst through the curtains covering the door, shouting at Abhya in panicked tones. The older woman listened for a moment to the flood of words from the serving girl, then Abhya gasped, covering her mouth with her free hand and clutching Chenda's wrist tightly with the other. A moment of decision flickered across Abhya's face, as she glanced at her daughter. A moment later she grabbed the small lantern by the door, and ran, pulling Chenda along. Candice raced after her, nearly knocking down the young serving girl on the way out.

Abhya and the two women raced down the passageway, darting down twisting tunnels like rats in a maze. Chenda never let go of her mother, but checked often to see if Candice still followed. The further they ran, the more rough and unused the passageways began to look.

Chenda gathered that they were running away from something, but she couldn't imagine what. She was afraid. There was panic in her mother's eyes, and Chenda could do nothing to relieve it. On they ran, until the passage deadended into a small cavern. Chenda saw the slightly plump figure of Ahy-Me standing next to a rock slide at the back of the cavern, her face twisted in concern. She brightened considerably when she saw Chenda and Candice.

She blurted several words of relief in her own language, then said, "Vorry not. You safe for now. Pranav Erato send me to help you. Hide you. Come. Ve climb."

She started up the steep rock slide, leading the way. Abhya pushed the lantern into Candice's hands and then grabbed her daughter, wrapping both hands around her neck. She shook with fear and tears. She brought her forehead to Chenda's and placed her hands on each side of Chenda's face. Automatically, Chenda returned the gesture as she and Candice has practiced. When Chenda reached her mother's elbows and made the gentle push, Abhya stepped back slightly, and with a great sob, turned and ran headlong back into the dark passage. Chenda stepped to follow, but Candice restrained her.

"No," Chenda said, swatting at Candice. "No, NO, NO!"

She turned and shouted up to Ahy-Me. "What's going

214

on?!"

Halfway up the wall now, Ahy-Me looked down at Chenda. "Soldiers come. They follow the spies that seek you from across the sea, followed you here. They bring the boat man you know. The caves safe no more, we run. Maybe we find friends again. Hurry. Come!" she begged.

"But where has my mother gone?" Chenda pleaded.

"Abhya makes to lead the soldiers away from this path." Ahy-Me said, climbing once again. "Give us time to run."

"NO! I just found her. I won't let her go!" Chenda pulled against Candice's restraining hand, trying to race after her mother.

"No, honey," Candice said softly. "I know you want to follow, I understand. But you'll never catch up to her now, not in the dark. We'll find her again when we can. Count on it."

She pulled Chenda back toward the rock wall, and pushed her up onto the first rock. Chenda's tears clouded her vision and frustration hung on her limbs, making her move slowly. Eventually she made it to the top of the tumble of rocks. Hidden in the shadows at the top was a narrow crack. Ahy-Me's hand reached through and caught Chenda, pulling her in. Chenda crawled further into the small space to make room for Candice, who climbed through as well.

"Go!" Ahy-Me ordered, pointing up the tiny tunnel. As the other women crawled as best they could through the narrow passage, Ahy-Me used her short, powerful legs to shove loose stones over the opening they had just crawled through, blocking it. They crawled for a short while and the passageway opened up into another tunnel. Chenda and Candice could stand up there, and they waited for Ahy-Me.

When she arrived, the effort of shifting the heavy stones was apparent on her sweaty face. "Whew," she said as she leaned against the wall. "Forgive. I rest," she panted.

"Tell us," Candice said. "What do we do now? Where are Verdu and Fenimore?"

"Du boys defend Pranav Erato," Pant, pant. "He find dem and run. He see de spies and soldier come." She tapped the side of her head. "Pranav Erato call in my head to come here. He see your mudder bring. Yes,"Ahy-Me said. "Ve go. Up." She pointed along the passageway, and started along it, holding the lantern high. They trotted along, moving slowly upwards for several minutes. Up ahead, Chenda saw dim light.

"Are we coming to the surface?" Chenda asked.

"Shh..." Ahy-Me waved her hands at Chenda. She crept along now on tiptoe. Leaning her chest against the wall, she looked through a series of tiny holes. Curious, Chenda did the same. Through the gap, she could see down into the same glowing cave where Ahy-Me had left them to rest the day before. Soldiers filled the cavern below now. They formed a circle around a small man laying face down on the rocks. Three officers circled around the little fellow, and Chenda could hear them taunting him as they circled.

"What's going on? What are they saying?" Candice asked. She too had pressed her eye to one of the peep holes.

"Dees soldier says You say de Republic girl come to this place? Why she no here?'" Ahy-Me gasped, "De man is Taboda!" Ahy-Me hissed a Tugrulian curse. Chenda closed her eyes, feeling again that all of the lives she had touched recently had suffered, and it was all her fault. Ahy-Me listened some more and relayed what she heard. "Now day say de spies follow you from de Vest. But dey lost you ven you entered de caves, but some in de Resistance cough out. Say Pramuc comes, very soon." She made a little growl at that information, clearly annoyed to hear that there were spies among the Resistance, the people she trusted.

A scuffle started on the far side of the chamber and the crush of soldiers parted to let another group pass to the center of the ring. The newcomers dragged a small person along with them. Chenda held her breath as she recognized her own flight coat and aeronaut boots on the limp ragdoll of a person. With a tone of gloating pride, the soldiers tossed the person in Chenda's clothes down next to Taboda, who turned his head to examine his new neighbor.

Ahy-Me spoke again. "De new soldier say dat he got you. He boasting."

Taboda wheezed out a little laugh, which grew until one of the soldiers dragged him up by the hair.

"'Vhat so funny vile one?' des soldier say. Taboda say, 'dat not du Pramuc, dat nobody he see on de *Tjalk*. Not even Kiter nohow.'"

The soldier below holding Taboda by the hair threw the captain against the rock floor, where he giggled weakly. The soldier grabbed the impostor Chenda by the back of the coat and flipped her over, straddling her limp body. Chenda needed no translation to understand the demand the soldier was making of the pretty serving girl from the bathing pools.

"'Vere is she?'" Ahy-Me said. "De girl say, 'I know not, and I never say.'"

The boasting soldier flew into a rage and grabbed the girl by each side of her head and began smashing it on the rock floor, again and again. Chenda saw it as a sacrilegious perversion of the holy greeting. Chenda watched in horror as the girls arms whipped around, violently spasmodic, until her delicate hands fell limply to the floor. She watched as the blood puddled around the girl's head like an expanding halo.

Chenda's knees began to shake. She was unprepared to deal with the brutality she witnessed. She crumpled against the wall behind her, pinching her eyes closed trying to stop seeing the quivering fingertips, the cracking bones, the blood. Even behind her closed eyes she could see it. She felt powerless and weak, responsible for yet another life snuffed out.

Candice grabbed Chenda under the arm and hauled her up, giving her a quick slap on the cheek. "No time to wither now," she said in a whisper. "Run."

The word moved through Chenda and started her feet without actually passing through her brain. Mindlessly she followed Ahy-Me as she trotted silently up the passage. They moved steadily upwards for several minutes, until they reached another small chamber.

"Oh, thank the gods!" It was Fenimore's voice. Chenda's heart leaped with hope. Waiting there, were Fenimore, Verdu and Pranav Erato. Chenda threw her arms around Fenimore and Verdu's necks, tears of relief flowing down her cheeks. They both patted her on the back at the same moment, in the same way, then kissed her on the top of the head. Even now, they worked as one.

"I was so scared for you!" she said. She stepped back from them and noticed the bloodstain on Fenimore's shirtfront, hands and sleeves. "What happened? Are you hurt?"

"The blood is not mine," he whispered, "mostly. We just had to knuckle our way through a tight spot, but we're all going to live."

"Looks like whoever followed us finally caught up," Candice said. "They had Taboda, but I can honestly say what he told them about us was not given up willingly. I don't think he is going to survive this."

Everyone stood silently, fearing Taboda's fate. Ahy-Me broke the strained silence, "Pranav Erato asks ve all join hand." The group turned to look at the wispy man and grasped the hand of the closest person. His voice appeared in each of their heads.

I am sad that we have been discovered so soon. I must ask, Chenda, have you made your decision?

"Yes," she said, new resolve in her voice, "I will accept the power of the Pramuc, I will do it."

Very well. We have a ways to go, and we will need to move quickly. We will run now to a chamber that rests below the Dia Orella. From there we will all have a role to play. Focus on your tasks alone. Chenda felt a sensation like a cue ball slamming into a rack of billiards. Several complex thoughts shot out of Pranav Erato and scattered into the various people around the circle. The thoughts bounced around and fell into each man and woman as if they were pockets on the table. Everyone staggered back except Chenda. Pranav Erato held her hand solidly and pulled her toward a tunnel. The others, shaking their heads and blinking, followed.

As they ran along, Pranav Erato spoke with Chenda.

I've had twenty years to work out my theories on how the power will fill you. I hope that what I learned about the stones from Edison's curse will help. I believe it will be necessary for those people who helped you, stood nearest to you as you absorbed the four elements, to stand with you as you achieve your power. I think that when Edison stole the stones from the chamber above, when he stood there alone, the stones overloaded him. He absorbed only a fraction of their power, but it was all wrong within him. He was never meant to stand in the place of the

218

Pramuc – and no one was ever meant to stand there alone. Of course, I am not totally sure, but I think it will be better if your companions are there to buffer the experience.

"But Daniel was the person closest to me when I absorbed the fire, and he's dead. Am I one man short?"

No. His body is gone, but you still carry part of him with you, do you not?

Chenda thought about it for a minute and recalled the feeling she had in Chenda's apartment, the feeling that she would always be entwined with Daniel Frent. "Will that be enough?"

We shall see.

They ran for several more minutes, until they stepped out into open air. They were on a hillside overlooking Kotal. The heat of the sun hit them like a hammer, and the city shimmered and danced as they looked through the rising waves.

Pranav Erato pointed to the largest building in the city – an imposing facade of carved marble towers topped with golden spires. *The Dia Orella.* The glittering stone spoke of the building's age and stability. Its hugeness reminded everyone in the city that there truly is only One God, and don't you forget it.

Quickly, we need to cross over to another tunnel system. Once inside, we will run directly to the tunnel below the Chamber of Singing Stones. From there, we are all but done. GO.

He ran across several hundred yards of scrub plants and boulders, dragging Chenda along behind him. It still mystified her that, even at this rushed speed, he looked as if his arms and legs all worked independently, as if taking orders from very separate controllers.

They plunged down a tunnel and into darkness again – the blazing heat traded for the chill of deep earth. Chenda looked over her shoulder and saw her companions racing behind her. They all rushed onward, steeply downward again.

"How much longer?"

Not far now. Are you ready?

"Not one bit," she said.

Oh, well, I hope you can cope with the surprise of it all.

The tunnel narrowed and the sides were now rougher, looking like they had been recently excavated. The tunnel came to a sudden end. Pranav Erato looked gleeful. The culmination of a lifetime of waiting, Chenda's lifetime, was about to resolve; the Pranav was about to fulfill his purpose.

Wanna see why I don't talk? Well, not in confined spaces anyway...

"Huh?" Chenda asked.

Pranav Erato dropped Chenda's hand and pushed her back several feet. He cupped his hands around his mouth as he turned his hear toward the ceiling of the carved tunnel.

"Boo!" he shouted upwards. There was a resounding crack and a shower of sand and pebbles rained down into the cave. The hole above Pranav Erato was straight and smooth. He smiled at his handiwork, and took Chenda by the hand again, sending his thoughts through to her brain.

Up you go. This is where all the magic is going to happen.

Chapter 17
INVESTITURE

Pranav Erato laced his fingers together and cupped his hands to give Chenda a leg-up. It surprised her that the willowy mystic was strong enough to launch her straight up and through the hole. She landed face down on a cold, marble floor that was smooth as glass. She sat up smartly, frightened that there could be more vicious Tugrulian soldiers waiting for her, but quickly assessed that she sat alone in silence in the most beautiful room she had ever seen.

Apart from the ragged hole beside her, the floor stretched away in all directions in slick, bright marble perfection. Every few yards, a stout column of intricately carved stone rose into the air. Every inch of the 40 or so pillars around her contained row upon row of human figures, lizards, plants, fish and birds. Some columns featured giant statues of what Chenda guessed to be past Emperors. All of the images around her on the massive columns held up an intricately carved ceiling, dripping with delicately carved willow plants, flowing waterfalls and flying birds.

Gemstones accented all of the carved columns and the walls. She followed the glittering images, taking in the beauty of this chilly hall until she came to an area of the floor that opened up under a domed ceiling. In the carvings above her, perfectly formed and shimmering white, she saw tiny flakes of color: dull reds, yellows and blues. She could see they were tiny bits of pedradurite, chips of Singing Stones.

This must be the place, she thought.

She sighed, and the sound amplified to a near roar under the dome of the Singing Stones. A bony hand pulled her away from the rotunda.

Ah, ah, ah! No starting early. Not until we are all here. Pranav Erato smiled benignly at Chenda. Candice, Verdu and Fenimore stood behind him.

"Where's Ahy-Me?"

She stays below, in the tunnel, ready to warn us if soldiers discover our passageway. But let us not worry about what is below. Focus only on what lies ahead of us here. Pramuc, your companions know what they are to do, you now need to make ready. Have you the Great Singing Stones?

She turned to Verdu, who held the velvet bag out to her. "Yes," she said, taking the bag and clutching it to her chest, as if it were her long lost child.

Marvelous. Put the necklace on so the stone touches your skin, then hold each of the other stones in your hands. Chenda opened the bag and followed Pranav Erato's directions.

Take care not to speak as you assemble your companions under the dome. You will know exactly what to do as you begin. No worries.

He touched her cheek with his free hand. *Be calm, my child. You are right where you are supposed to be. You will not be alone, for those you love are near. Quickly, go.*

With a small push toward the dome area, he let her go. She took a hesitant step forward, and then another. She saw Verdu reach his hand out toward her, and she took it, instinctively. He pulled her to the very center of the dome, where Candice and Fenimore waited. The three joined hands around Chenda facing away from her. They circled around her, adjusting slightly so Chenda and Candice stood back-to-back. Fenimore and Verdu settled at her left and right, their hands holding the wrist of the other. She could feel them all, so close to her, shielding her from the whole of the world, leaving her free to focus on the matter at hand.

Her instincts showed her the way. Now that she had started, she had the feeling there was no way she could stop even if she wanted to. She had no desire to turn back. Something big and miraculous was on its way – she was sure of that. She held her arms up, wide above her head. The stones in each hand

222

glowed ever so slightly from within. As she breathed, the soft sound of it resonated with the stones in her hands and on her chest. The Great Singing Stones, in turn, chimed life into the lesser Singing Stones of the dome. As her breath quickened, the vibration bouncing within the arched ceiling built upon itself, becoming louder.

Her breath came faster still as the thrill of the sound under the dome coursed through her body. She felt numb and heightened at the same time. She could no longer feel the pressure of the floor below her feet, or see the glisten of the marble around her. The world had gone dark except for the glowing pinpoints of colored light that were the lesser Singing Stones, scattered across the dome like stars in the shell of the night sky.

From the pit of her stomach it came, building slowly. She felt like she was going to scream, but that which was rising within her wasn't so coarse as that. It felt elegant, smooth and polished as it rose, but wildly powerful and truly unstoppable. She stopped breathing. Her lips parted, and the shape of every sound that had ever been made in every place in the universe escaped her lips all at once.

The sound swirled Chenda in the darkness, and the intense ringing glow of the lesser Singing Stones swirled as well, leaving streaks of color across her vision. The colors melted together, flying faster and faster until it all blended into a white glow around her. She saw faces in the glow, hundreds of thousands of faces. They looked at her, and started to speak in angelic tones that filled the whole world. Somehow, Chenda knew she was the only one who could hear them.

"With you we are pleased. You have come a long way, following Our call. You are brave. We saw you from across the ages and knew you. We are thankful that you have come to accept Our gift. In return, We ask that you remember only this: Bring Our message to all the people. We are many gods, and we are One. Any who have faith in One of Us, have faith in Us all. We are all things to all people of faith. Those who crush One of Us, crush Us all. One god is all gods. All gods are one. Do you understand, child?"

"I do," Chenda said. The message was unexpected. The

concept intrigued her. "Faith lifts all men. Faith is the key. No man should crush the faith of another."

"Yes," the voices replied. "Now, Pramuc, our gift..."

Chenda felt the Fire first. It started in her fingertips and palms, and raced through her body. The Fire burned her completely. Her body fell away and only ashes remained over her soul, dripping to the nothingness below her. She felt the burn dissolve her earthly form, but she felt no pain. The Fire was now hers.

The next to pass through her spirit, as her body was gone, was the Air. Her ashes whipped away in a swirling wind, and Chenda could feel the weight of clouds, and the sensation of lift under a bird's wing. She juggled snowflakes and smelled fresh hail. The Air was now hers.

Water invaded next. Chenda could taste a thousand types of water: bitter, brackish, ice, sweet, sparkling, rain, fog, steam and snow. She could see it hidden in rocks and plants. It called to her like waves call back to the pull of the moon. The Water was now hers.

And then the Earth made its claim, sharing its deepest secrets with Chenda. Dust, minerals, raw metals, complex organic compounds, stone, sand, soil and grit, all paraded through her, bowing to her authority. She knew them all like her own children. The Earth was now hers.

The emptiness inside her, the place that once grieved, was now filled. Chenda felt the draw of her companions around her again, anchoring her to reality, holding her in the marble room. She felt her body return, complete and undamaged, exactly as she had been before, but wholly new. She sank back to them, her companions, steadfast as ever.

As her toes began to feel the floor below her once again, the gods, separate but still One, breathed forth a benediction upon her, "Take with you always the blessings of the gods, We are always with you," and They enrobed themselves in the spaces between the darkness and the light.

Chenda opened her eyes. She stood with her hands above her head, arms spread wide, just as before. Her body was unmarked by her transformation. Her companions were there,

224

arms locked around her, but somehow they now faced her. She smiled at each one of them. They glanced at one another, slightly confused.

She relaxed her arms and realized that her Singing Stones were no longer in her hands, and the gold necklace that held the stone to her chest was empty. She glanced at the floor to see if they had fallen there, but there was no trace of them. Her instinct took over, letting her know that it didn't matter. She need not search for the stones, as they, too, were gone now forever. Their purpose had been fulfilled.

Her companions looked at her, their eyes asking one question: what now?

Chenda said, "It's done."

At her words, a massive earthquake started.

Chenda and the Airship Brofman

Chapter 18
RUN

Pranav Erato ran from the shadows to the group under the dome, his arms flailing wildly. He shouted to them as soon as his hand made contact with Verdu.

RUN! Back the way we came in! The Dia Orella is about to collapse.

He ran back to the hole in the floor and dove head first into the tunnel. The shaking intensified as Verdu shoved Candice through the rough opening in the floor. He paused long enough to be sure he wouldn't be jumping directly on top of her and then dropped through as well. Sections of the sparkling dome were crashing down now and the carved columns around Chenda were buckling. Chenda pulled Fenimore toward their escape, and watched in horror as Fenimore paused, pushing her to go down the hole first. She thought about arguing, but there was no time. She fell through without letting go of Fenimore's hand. It had the desired effect of pulling him through the hole immediately after her, but they ended up in the tunnel below heaped like rag dolls.

The others, already running up the passageway, took the light with them, leaving Chenda and Fenimore to untangle themselves in the near darkness. Fenimore staggered upward and leaned one palm against the rough wall of the narrow tunnel. With his other hand, he reached out to pull Chenda to her feet, but he kept his body over hers, deflecting the shards of marble bouncing through from the collapsing level above.

After what felt like an eternity, they were both running after the others, following the dim light. The running went slowly as the earth bucked and shuddered under them. The light ahead stopped and Fenimore and Chenda were able to catch up to Verdu, who now held the lantern high, and the others.

"Why are we stopping?" Fenimore asked.

Verdu pressed himself against the wall of the passage so Pranav Erato could squeeze by him. "He needs to talk with the Pramuc."

"Chenda," Fenimore said through clenched teeth. "Her name is still Chenda."

Verdu nodded, but rolled his eyes. Pranav Erato danced over to Chenda, who opened her mouth to speak. A willowy hand covered her lips.

Heavens no, child, don't talk. Not yet. You might just bring the cavern down on our heads. Look at me and will your thought to be heard in my head. You can do this. In fact, from time to time, you already have.

Chenda screwed up her face in concentration. *LIKE THIS?*

Pranav Erato flinched, but his eye shone in pleased annoyance. *Not so loud, child. Shush.* He smiled at her. *You've got the theory. I guess you understand now why I don't speak aloud very often. Too dangerous. You will be able to, however, once you get your emotions under control. It also helps to not be in an enclosed space. You will see.*

He looked at Chenda approvingly. *Nice earthquake. Do you think you can turn it off now?*

Um, how? she asked.

Hey, you let it out, you just need to pull it back in. He leaned back against the wall of the tunnel, his stick-like arms folded across his chest.

Chenda placed one hand on each side of the narrow tunnel, feeling the vibration in her hands. It tingled there across her body, from palm to palm. She felt the various textures moving in the rock around her, the different types of rocks and sand, pockets of water and air. All of it was in motion. She tentatively sent out a thought toward the shaking earth.

Stop?

Nothing happened. She tried again.

STOP!

Still nothing, she looked at Pranav Erato and shrugged. He

gestured like he was pulling something toward himself with a rope.

Pull it back in. I guess he said that. Here goes nothing.

Chenda felt for the vibration again and began to draw it toward her. Little by little she could feel the power leave the rock and move into her body, where it crammed into the little spaces between her cells, filling any available void. Finally the earthquake stopped, and she dropped her hands from the tunnel walls.

She could feel the power twitching inside her. It yearned to leap out again. Chenda struggled to keep it under control, and she could not concentrate on much else. She was frightened and a bit distracted by what was circling in and through her. She hardly noticed when Pranav Erato placed a single finger on her elbow.

Well done. We need to go. He clapped his hands and looked at Ahy-Me. She spoke aloud, "Ve run now. Up. Out. Not safe now. Dees soldiers come soon. Follow." She turned on her heel and started to run and everyone followed.

Several tunnels were littered with fallen stone; others had collapsed completely. More then once, Pranav Erato waved for them to backtrack to a fork in the passage, and they would proceed in a new direction.

The group came to the surface in time to catch the last bright rays of the setting sun. The Pranav turned Chenda bodily to look back at the city of Kotal. Chenda gasped – the Dia Orella was gone.

Did I do that?

Yes! Pranav Erato danced where he stood. *Neat trick, huh?*

Chenda started to shake and tears ran down her cheeks. *How many died? How many did I crush to death?*

Some. He replied. *Don't worry about it. Nothing can be done about that. Not now.*

Chenda gripped Pranav Erato so tightly that her nails bit into his papery skin. *Don't worry about it? I hate this. Get it out. GET IT OUT OF ME!*

I'm sorry, he said, *I don't think I think that's possible. You are going to have to cope.*

She sobbed, and as she did the wind kicked up around her.

229

"Whoa, hey! The wind! Chenda! Stop!" Fenimore was covering his eyes, trying to keep the blowing dust from blinding him.

Chenda sucked back in her emotions and the wind settled. She placed her hand in Fenimore's.

I'm sorry, it just got away from me.

"Yikes, you too? Is anybody going to talk out loud anymore? I mean, the gods gave me ears, people, let's not let them fall into disuse." He wiggled his ears.

Chenda laughed inwardly, and Fenimore seemed to like hearing her laughter, even if it only sounded inside his head.

"Now what do we do?" he asked her.

Chenda turned to Pranav Erato, who said, "We find someplace open and we talk." His real, outward voice sounded so different coming through Chenda's ears. It sounded frail, almost feathery, and very dry.

"You can TALK!?" Fenimore shouted. "He's not talking, then he is, and she was but now she's not. I give up!"

"We've been talking for two days, Fenimore, or haven't you been listening?"

Fenimore spluttered, "With your mouth now, not squishing your voice right into my brain! You know what I mean."

Pranav Erato bubbled with his usual joy. "Come. We are exposed here. The city is crawling with soldiers who know that SHE is here now, and the hierarchy of the Dia Orella, what's left of them, will be whipping them into a frenzy to find you and take your head, my dear. We've got to get to some help. Then, we need to see how your new gifts work. Does that seem reasonable to you, Pramuc?"

Everyone was looking at Chenda now. "Fine," she said, and a geyser shot out of the ground beside her. *Great,* she thought, looking at her soaked friends. *This is going to take some getting used to.*

The group walked into the night, down the hillside and away from Kotal. They could see torches in the distance leading parties of soldiers on the hunt for the newly invested Pramuc. Fenimore and

230

Ahy-Me led them through the darkness, she showing the way and he scanning the horizon for danger.

As they walked, Chenda kept to herself. The power within her itched, or at least it felt something like that. It annoyed her. It constantly searched for a way to get out of her, and she resented the constant struggle. Chenda felt like perhaps she had made a big mistake coming here, following Edison's letter. She simmered in a petulant rage, her arms tightly crossed over her chest. The small group walked for several hours under the cover of night. Chenda gave little thought to where she was headed.

Toward dawn, Verdu matched strides next to her. Chenda didn't look up at him.

"You are unhappy." His words weren't a question. "I'm sorry about that." He slipped his hand into the crook of her elbow, gently pried her arms from her chest and placed his hand in hers.

"Talk to me, please. Are you in pain? You look a little bit like you might be in pain."

No, I'm fine. It's just the power they gave me, it's trying to fly out of me in every direction, and I'm just flailing around trying to keep it from spilling out and hurting anyone else. Chenda sighed deeply, and thunder rumbled in the clear sky. She frowned, knowing it came from her. *I also think it's getting worse. Building up somehow, like static electricity. This is too much for me. I think I hate this.*

"I see," Verdu said thoughtfully, stroking the back of her hand with his thumb. "I can't begin to imagine what happened to you in the temple, but I would like to try to understand. Could you tell me?"

I'm not sure I have the words to say what it was like. What do you want to know, specifically?

"Well, why you? That's my biggest question. This is such a burden. Who would do this to you?"

Chenda snorted. *I guess I hadn't actually thought that to myself until just now. I think I will be asking 'why me?' a lot now. You were right there beside me. Could you hear the gods as they spoke to me?*

"Wow, the gods? No, we were standing there for a few seconds and couldn't hear anything but the humming of the

231

stones, and for half a second the whole world went black, and in the darkness, somehow we got turned around. We had been facing out, then we were all facing in, toward you. I'm still confused about that one, but now that you say some of the gods were there, I have to imagine that's the type of trick that would amuse them. Which gods were there?" Verdu asked, his voice filled with awe.

All of them. That's the whole point, I am sure. That's what they wanted me to understand. They said, 'all gods are one god,' and that any who suppress any particular god, suppress all of them. I got the sense that it is more important to the gods for people to have faith in some part of them, rather than to reject any part of their continuum. Chenda bit her lip, deep in thought. *The Tugrulians say there is One True God, but they reject the gods of other people. I think the gods are angry about that. All gods ARE one god. To accept one god, you must accept them all.*

"An interesting message," Verdu offered, "but what are you supposed to do with it?"

The gods did not say. In fact, they asked me if I understood, and I said I did, then they gave me the Power. I have to say, I wish I could give it back. There's just no keeping it inside me.

"Maybe you aren't supposed to." Verdu brightened. "Wait, just a second. Let me check where we are. I'll be right back."

He dropped Chenda's hand and ran ahead to consult with Pranav Erato, then with Ahy-Me. Suddenly the whole procession came to a halt under the weight of Verdu's conversation. Chenda strolled up to the circle of her friends, who were deep in heated discussion.

"No. I get it, Verdu," Fenimore spoke. "But the only thing her setting off fireworks will accomplish is bringing all the soldiers in a ten-mile radius right to us."

"Depends on what she does, she just needs to keep it subtle," Verdu answered.

"I think it's worth a try," Pranav Erato whispered. "If she doesn't try to do a few things, she'll never learn to use her gifts. That power surely must take some getting used to. Mine is nothing like hers, and it took years for me to control it. And it itches a little."

"Chenda will have plenty of time to practice when she's someplace safe," Candice chimed in. "But for right now, she's much better off if she keeps this all under wraps."

"I'm not so sure. She says the pressure of it is getting worse. I think the gods have rigged it so she will have to use the power on a regular basis. They gave her the gift so she can deliver the message I told you about. So, something wild and miraculous is going to be happening around her every so often – perhaps every few hours, I suspect. I think it's better that she give it a try out here first, relatively out of harm's way, before we encounter any large populations of people." Verdu pleaded to his companions, his hands in a position of surrender. He saw Fenimore start to object again and he added, "There's no way we can get her off this continent if she doesn't learn some level of competence over her power. Do you think we can put her on a boat if she's unwittingly attracting lighting or boiling the sea? I know you plan on meeting the *Brofman* soon. Are you willing to put Chenda aboard? Tell me you haven't thought about her bringing the airship down-"

"Fine!" Fenimore said, cutting Verdu off. "You're right. I have thought of that and a hundred other things that could happen, but I also promised her that I would get her out of here." He glanced at Chenda and spoke softly, "Maybe you do need to try out what your power can do, but if you attract a lot of attention... Well, we'll just have to try to keep you safe as best we can." He threw a half smile.

Chenda touched Pranav Erato with one hand and Verdu with the other. *What do you propose I do?*

"Let off some steam," Pranav Erato said, thrilling at his own wit. He sent several thoughts at Chenda all at once. *You control the fire and water. Seek the water in the air around you...* He paused for a moment, and went on. *OK, not DIRECTLY around you, and certainly not around me or the rest of us, and once you've got it firmly in your grasp, set it on fire. Boil it. That should use up a good bit of your pent up energy. Ready to try it?*

Chenda nodded. *At this point, I'll try anything. If I don't, it's going to try itself.*

"Stand back," Pranav Erato said with a weak giggle.

233

"She's gonna blow!"

Chenda turned her back on her companions and took several steps away from them. Ahead of her she could see acres of barren rock in the predawn glow. The air was always pretty dry in this part of the world, but at that moment, just before dawn in the cool air, there was a good amount of moisture near the ground.

She realized she could easily find the element she wanted just by thinking of it. She thought to herself *Water*, and all liquid in the immediate area called out to her: the dew on the rocks, the scant wetness in the few scrubby plants, even the water in the blood of her companions behind her. That intrigued her. There was a shape, for lack of a better term, to the water element that resided within people. It was distinct. She called for water to reveal itself across the next mile or so ahead of her. She could see birds and lizards of several varieties, but no other people.

She focused on the air, swirling it through the moisture. She played with those two elements for a while, pushing the water with the air and then back again. She knew if she wanted to, she could separate them completely. She could wring the water out of the air! She really started to wish she had a bucket handy. And... it felt good. Using the power was like the relief of a long sigh after holding your breath.

Pranav Erato softly cleared his throat. "Play later. Get on with it so we can keep moving."

Chenda nodded. *OK, boil the water in the air. I guess I need some fire. Hmm. I just need a spark to get me started, I think.* She searched around for the most elusive of elements, and came up short. No fire. She spread her search farther out. Nothing. Not a single spark. She could feel the deep fire of the earth far, far below her, but she couldn't see how she could get a grip on it and bring it to the surface without causing another major earthquake – or worse: a volcano.

How can I make fire?I don't have any matches. Could I rub the air together make some lightning? That's less than subtle and would cause some attention to be drawn here. Hmm....

And then she remembered her chemistry tutor and the concept of pyrophorics: substances that ignite at around room temperature. The simplest was iron. She had been fascinated the day her aged teacher struck flint to steel, making sparks. He explained that the flint had very little to do with making the sparks, but had everything to do with exposing the iron, the real, unoxidized iron, to air. She reached up under her bejeweled Tugrulian gown to her pouchbelt and felt around for the knife she had taken from Daniel Frent. A strong steel knife. She held it at arm's length and turned her power and concentration toward thoughts of the element earth. All she had to do was separate the invisible layer of rust that clung to all things iron, and the steel would ignite on its own – creating a spark.

Here goes nothing...

She focused on the double point of the Tugrulian knife, and she ripped the atoms of iron oxide away. Hot sparks jumped. Chenda, in a moment of agonizing release, let go of the pent up power within her. It caught the spark she created and shot away into the air before her. It raced from her like a hooked fish, thrashing and jerking away. She pushed it toward the water. The water absorbed the energy, sizzling and hissing as it expanded.

Chenda laughed out loud. This felt great. Better than great. Relief. As the power dissipated, and the heat and sparks blew away on the gentle breeze, Chenda turned to face her companions.

"I did it!" She shouted, and she was relieved all over again when she realized she spoke out loud and hadn't caused a natural disaster. "Oh, and I released most of the power. Ahh..."

"Great," said Fenimore, lying face down on the ground with the rest of Chenda's friends. "Try not to steam us like shrimp the next time."

Chenda hadn't noticed the moist heat all around her until that moment. "Oh!" she said. "Sorry."

Verdu stood up quickly and walked over to her. He put a reassuring arm around her shoulder. "You did very well, all things considered, but you are just a little dangerous. Now you know that you can at least do that little procedure to release some of the pressure you have building up inside you, assuming that you have several hundred feet of clear space around you when you do it. The flaming dagger, now, that's a way to say 'messenger of the gods' if ever there was one. That we need to show the local villagers."

Chenda snorted.

"Not to mention that both of those things can be considerable weapons." Fenimore added, satisfied. "You may just be able to steam clean any spots that darken your path."

Chenda's face turned white. "I could never...."

"What a horrible thing to say, Fenimore!" Candice chided. "What kind of brutal monster are you?"

"I'm just looking at this from a practical perspective. I think Pranav Erato is right. The Tugrulian hierarchy will not allow this kind of power to exist, not when they can't control it. When we cut back toward the coast to get out of here, we're going to have to fight our way out. We're going to need every weapon we can get."

"Wait," Chenda said. "I'm not here to be a weapon. Just because I can kill with a few thoughts, doesn't mean I will or I should. That's not the purpose of the Pramuc, is it Pranav?"

All traces of humor left his wizened face. "Yes and no, my dear." He thought for a moment. "You say that the gods gave you a message. Well, if they waited so long and brought you so far to receive it, can we say that *hearing* that message was your primary purpose? What good is a message meant just for you? Not much. I believe the message was given to you to share. In sharing it with us, you have fulfilled some small slice of that duty. The telling has no need for power. So what is it for? It must be there to protect the messenger, and to prove the message, as it were. Do you see?"

"No, not exactly." Chenda said as she looked to the wise eyes of the mystic.

Pranav Erato continued, "You've been given power equal to that of a god. You have that power so you can demonstrate it. So everyone who meets you will know that your message is true, from the gods, or the one god made of many gods. That concept makes my head go all funny if I think about it too long." Pranav Erato scratched his head in confusion, then shrugged. "Beyond that, what good is a message from the gods if someone kills the messenger? There are those in this world who will refuse to hear your message, or will fear it. They will come at you with the zealot's passion, and will be willing to kill themselves if it means that they can silence you."

He paused to let the thought sink in. "So, think of it this way. You may need to defend yourself, because without you, Candice, Verdu and Fenimore won't get out of this land alive. Of that I am sure."

Fenimore looked at the brightening sky. "There's no stopping the dawn. We're exposed. What shall we do now? Walk or hide out for the day?"

"I vote for taking a rest," Candice said. "I'm exhausted, and these pretty slippers are just not made for walking in the desert. I wish I still had my aeronaut boots." Candice grumbled some more, then said, "There should be a place we can find some shade up ahead. There seem to be the right formations that would indicate caverns there. We could get lucky."

As the small group headed toward the taller rocks ahead, Pranav Erato turned to Ahy-Me and asked, "Do you think you can make it to the Village of Hoe-Lend and back by nightfall?"

"Of course," she said. "Vhat vould you like me to do?"

"You know the Resistance there. Get some of their leaders and slip out. Bring them here. We need to have Chenda visit with them for a time. She needs to deliver her message and keep moving. Also, we will need to find out just how organized the hierarchy is in their search for us. I won't be surprised if the Emperor himself is out looking. We'll stay here until nightfall, then we will be heading due west overnight."

"As you wish," Ahy-Me said as she placed her hands on the sides of Pranav Erato's face. He blessed her in return. She turned to Chenda and did the same.

Chenda released the young woman at the end of her blessing, and, for the first time, really felt that it meant something. "Please be careful, Ahy-Me," Chenda said as the girl trotted away to the north.

The remaining members of Chenda's group quickly found a sheltered outcropping amongst the rocks and crawled into the cool shade. They settled in amongst the rocks to rest.

Candice pulled off her slippers and rubbed her own feet.

237

"Life is too short for walking in the wrong shoes," she complained. Chenda sat down next to her. She put a hand on Candice's knee.

I am thinking that I need to shunt off some more power, and I think I can help you at the same time. Let's see...

Chenda leaned over and put her hands on the rock near Candice's feet. She thought hard about the stone under her hands and looked for cracks within it. She selected several fissures that roughly made a bowl shape. Chenda released some of her energy and squeezed all the molecules within those fissure borders. With a loud pop, the rock crumbled to sand. Chenda scooped the loose bits of stone out and then concentrated on the air in their cool shelter. She thought about water, and she could feel every droplet in the air around them. She drew the moisture together over the newly created basin and, as the drops pushed together to form bigger drops, a fog appeared, and then splashed down like rain into the basin, slopping out over the sides.

"Soak those feet, Candice," Chenda said with a smile.

"Well, well." Candice said touching the water with one toe, then submerging them all. "Aren't you handy to have around?"

Verdu leaned over Chenda and stared at the foot bath. He spoke in mock piety, "And so it came to pass, that the Pramuc went out into the desert and issued forth the power from her hand. And, lo, the miracle of the pedicure was poured out onto the people." He sighed. "Where's the dignity?" Verdu walked off to sit next to Fenimore on the far side of the stone overhang, grumbling as he went.

"You just leave her be when she's helping her fellow man, or in my case woman," Candice called after him, patting Chenda on the back. "She just needed to release some more power, and I for one am pleased at the progress she is making." She turned to Chenda again, "Very nice control, dear. How does it feel for you now?"

"It's okay. I feel so much better when I *use* the power, rather than just hold it in. It builds up inside me over time. It didn't take too long for me to build up enough energy to make this little bowl and fill it. But if I tried to do it again right now, I think

238

I would fail. I don't feel like I've... charged my batteries enough, especially after that 'air boiling' thing. Does that make sense?"

"You say it and I believe you," Candice said splashing her feet. "Thanks, by the way, this is very nice."

"You are most welcome," Chenda said, biting her lip. "It was sort of a bribe. I had a few ideas that I want to pick your brain about. I think there's a lot you can teach me about using my gift."

"I'm a geologist, not a theologian. What on earth can I do to help you with about a gift from the gods?"

"Well," Chenda started out slowly, "the prophecies about the Pramuc spoke of the companions, right? You and Fenimore and Verdu, you were all foretold as part of my story. Fenimore is the soldier, and all he sees in my power are potential weapons. Verdu may not seem like a saint, but he talks as if my power is best used when I spread the faith, the message from the gods. I don't think that either of them is right."

She took Candice by the hand. "But you, you are the scholar, and together, I think we can really do some good. With a little practice and a little know-how, I'm going to be able to make the earth dance and the wind blow, and make sparks write messages in the sky. But only if I know which elements I need. The only reason I could make the air boil is because someone taught me about Fire Steel. You know all about the earth, about chemistry, about how stuff works on the most basic level. I can see the elements around me; you can tell me with ones will help us do what we want."

"So," Candice said shaking her head, "you want me to teach you chemistry?" She laughed. "You best be careful, girl, because once I get teaching, getting me to shut up is the trick!"

They both laughed, and Candice added. "I think you might have a plan already started. What are you thinking?"

"At this point, my plan is all about what I don't want to do. I think we, and the gods, too, for that matter, aren't going to be well served by using my power to cut down vast swaths of people. That's foremost in my mind: not killing people.

"The other thought I have is that Verdu, to some extent, is right. We need to help these people. The Tugrulians have no faith in themselves or their land to sustain them. They need to see signs of hope. They need to learn a new way. I almost don't care about who's right, the Emperor and his One God rule, or the pantheon of gods who have their own messages. None of that is useful to the people who are starving. It's better to be useful than right, don't you think?"

"I think you are on to something with that," Candice replied. "So, let me see if I understand your priorities: You want us to get out of here, but don't want to mow a bloody hole through the Tugrulians as you go, right?"

"Correct."

Candice continued."And you also want to help the oppressed people on this continent to be free of the lie that their soil is a poisoned wasteland."

"It's the least I can do," Chenda said, "and it can be showy, you know, something that would really make the people remember the truth. That they can do for themselves. It would be good that way, too. Right?"

"Yes," Candice said, rubbing one finger on her temple. "A tall order, but at least we have a goal we can all work toward. I have a few ideas, but I think we will need to talk it through with Pranav Erato and the mimic twins. We are going to need more information to plan this right. Let me have a think while I soak, and then we'll weed through the ideas. You look like you could use some rest, by the way."

Chenda yawned, "You may be right about that." She stood up and walked over to where Verdu and Fenimore were leaning shoulder to shoulder, resting.

"I have something to share. I can see people at a distance now, even if they are hiding," she told them. "People are mostly giant water bags with bones. Very distinctive. If you want me to, I can scan the immediate area, up to a few miles, anytime."

The men gave her matching smiles of pleasant surprise. "Useful," Fenimore said. "So, anybody close?"

Chenda concentrated for a moment. "Yes," she said, "Ahy-Me is heading due north, or at least I think it's her. And there is another person due west of here. About three miles away. Not moving at all."

240

Fenimore looked at Verdu. "Perhaps a lookout?"

"Could be." Verdu thought for a moment. "I'll keep watch for a few hours and you all get some sleep."

Verdu put a hand out to Chenda and he pulled her down as he pulled himself up. He walked to the edge of the shade made by the overhang and focused his attention outward, scanning the horizon.

Fenimore slapped his side, inviting Chenda to lean back into him, which she did. "Well, Pramuc, what do you think?"

"As if you ever considered me the Pramuc," Chenda replied.

"Nope, you are just plain old Martha to me," Fenimore replied. "I mean Chenda!" he corrected quickly as she elbowed him in the ribs, and they both laughed.

"Who knows, I may just decide to be a Martha soon, because being Chenda isn't what it used to be. I'm somewhere between overwhelmed and estranged. There's just way too much and we're collectively alone in it, if that makes any sense."

"Not really, no. But I am a simple creature. I know that what I am here to do right now is help and protect you as best I can, until you don't need me anymore. I'm hoping, in the end, I get back to my ship. So, that's what I will do."

"Oh, good. That is pretty simple." Chenda yawned again.

"Sleep now," Fenimore said, "and we'll just keep tackling what comes."

Chenda fell asleep under the protective arm of Fenimore. As she slept, she could feel the power trickling into her, storing itself in the deep recesses of her body. When she awoke several hours later, she felt like she was vibrating under the pressure of it. She pushed on the heavy arm around her shoulder.

Fenimore, get off, I'm gonna spark or something. Scoot!

"Fen's not here, actually," Verdu said as he listlessly raised his arm, freeing her.

Honestly, how do you two keep switching places on me?

Verdu chuckled and went back to sleep, muttering "I'll never tell."

Chenda had an idea to expend a good bit of her accumulated power. She made her way over to Candice's now

241

abandoned foot bath, and ran her toes through the sand beside the water. She concentrated on the water for a moment, and began it swirling. It swirled faster and faster until Chenda drew it into a thin tendril. Chenda concentrated a minute more, then plunged the finger of water through the sand and shot it toward the smooth rock wall on one side of the enclosure. She started to draw. The picture was infantile at first, barely identifiable as the outline of a hand grasping a knife. As she persisted, the picture became clearer, more defined. After a few minutes, she had discharged most of her accumulated power, and looked over her sand blasted creation.

"Nice." Fenimore said, "Your hand holding the sparking knife. Why carve that in the rock?"

"It just came to me," she said. "I guess I wanted to mark our passing here. That, and it burned off a lot of my power relatively quickly. But controlling it slowly, in a stream rather than a burst, that's difficult, and not very satisfying."

"Well, it's not very quiet, either," Verdu added, looking disturbed at having been drawn away from his slumber.

"Sorry," Chenda said. "I'll keep looking for another discharge method."

"I say whatever keeps you from exploding is okay with me," Fenimore said. "Can you see any people around?"

Chenda turned her thoughts toward water and the surrounding miles of stone. "Yes, she said. About a dozen people are coming from the north. It could be Ahy-Me and the others from the Resistance. They are coming back along the same route she took."

Fenimore made a quick double hiss at Verdu, who was up and at his side in an instant. "A dozen coming from the north," Fenimore whispered. "Can you scout them out? Come at them from the east?" Verdu nodded and left the outcrop at a loping run. "Our lone person to the west?" Fenimore asked Chenda.

"Gone," she said. "Nowhere around."

"Hmm," Fenimore considered it for a minute and then shrugged. "Well, if it is Ahy-Me, I guess we should be ready to meet our guests. If it's not, then it's a fight. Candice! Pranav Erato! People are coming this way!"

242

"It's just Ahy-Me," Pranav Erato said. "I can hear her thoughts coming from miles off."

Chenda turned to the willowy man, "I've been meaning to ask you about that. Why is it that you can talk to her over a great distance, but the rest of us need to touch you to hear your thoughts?"

Pranav danced happily. "I don't know," he said. "I just know I can, so I do."

"You are a very accepting creature," Fenimore noted. "Well, how do we want to do this?"

"I say we just accept what comes," Pranav Erato said. "They will have questions. We will answer them. OK, mostly Chenda will answer their most pertinent concerns. Then, we will see what information they have for us. Simple." Pranav Erato took Chenda by the arm and moved her to a low rock in front of Chenda's stone carving. "Nice work, dear," he said gesturing to the wall as he pushed her down onto a rock. He settled next to her, collecting up his various bouncing, gangly limbs. "I would ask the companions to join us, but I know they will just position themselves defensively with their guard up. So predictable."

"They just care about me," Chenda said. "You can't fault them for their loyalty."

Pranav Erato turned his sparkling eyes to her and placed a finger on her hand. *No, dear. Not loyalty. They love you, and that's a whole different matter.*

Chenda turned that thought around in her head, trying to understand what he meant by it, when she heard Ahy-Me arrive. One look proved that it had been a long hard day for her. She wobbled toward Pranav Erato and proceeded with the usual holy greeting. Then she slumped at his side.

"I bring ten. Six are leaders from Hoe-Lend. De six know de others." The men warily assembled themselves in the shade, eying Chenda and the other Kiters with distrust. All were quiet.

"Wonderful, darling," Pranav Erato said, "You must be exhausted. Here, drink from my canteen," he said gesturing to the small flask on the rock beside him. She picked it up, and shook it.

"Empty," she said, her voice aching with disappointment. She turned her sweaty face to Chenda. Dust had collected in the crevices around her eyes and neck, making her look older than she was.

"Oh, no," Chenda said. She was sure she had built up just enough power to fill the canteen with water from the air. She picked up the empty vessel and concentrated, squeezing the air. A cloud formed, and then a trickle flowed into the flask in Chenda's hand. "There, drink up." Chenda handed the water to Ahy-Me, who drank deeply.

"And now the gentlemen have all seen the great Pramuc perform a miracle," Pranav Erato said. Chenda looked up. She hadn't noticed the people who had followed Ahy-Me into the shaded overhang. She was so distracted by the girl's suffering that she paid the others no mind. Now, they all stared at her with awe on their faces.

Pranav Erato spoke to the assembled men in Tugrulian. Chenda could just hear Verdu translating for Fenimore and Candice, "You have seen. Now, will you listen?"

Chenda placed a finger on Pranav's hand. *Did you just set me up?* she asked.

He-he. I'm good, aren't I? Now they are ready to hear you. Thank me later and start talking.

Chenda looked at the dark Tugrulian men before her, and fell back on her well learned manners.

"Welcome. I thank you for coming to speak with me. I am... Chenda. Some would call me the Pramuc. I leave that for you to decide. Something happened to me, and I want to tell you about it."

As she spoke, Verdu translated her words to the small crowd. She spoke of her time in the West, of Edison's murder and the Singing Stones. She spoke about the elements and how they came to settle inside her. She spoke of her transformation in the Dia Orella under the Dome of Lesser Stones. Finally she told them the message from the gods, and of the collapse of the temple in Kotal.

When Chenda finished speaking, the silence around her was deafening.

Chapter 19
DEPARTURES

Chenda's voice shattered the trance that seemed to cover the Tugrulian guests. "Any... questions?"

A man stood, and stiffly bowed several times. He turned to Verdu and spoke. Verdu smiled and answered him, evidently in the positive. The man quickly sat down again and turned eager eyes to Chenda.

With a chuckle in his voice, Verdu said, "They believe you, every word, but they are men, and you did make such a convincing picture on the wall." He laughed again. "They want you to show them the sparklers."

Chenda suppressed a laugh. "I see." She pulled her knife from under her dress and released a thin stream of her power that separated the iron oxide from the blade in a slow stroke from bottom to top. Sparks sizzled and hissed, and each man before her sat agog. She set the knife aside and held what Chenda hoped was a dignified pose.

One by one, the ten men approached Chenda, and placed their hands on the side of her face. One by one, Chenda blessed them. They started to mill about talking excitedly, and other than the occasional glance back toward Chenda, she and Pranav Erato were mostly ignored.

What do we do now?

The men are discussing what they are going to do. Eventually they will figure out that they don't know enough to decide what it is that they can or should do. Then they will turn to us and ask what it is that they should be doing, and THAT is when

we will start asking questions and decide what to do.
You have got to be kidding.

Pranav Erato giggled inside his own head. *Nope, that's how matters of faith usually play out. We could just tell them what to do, but they would never do it. They will need to ask for guidance. Watch.*

Several of the men had laid out bundles of food on the rocks and were sharing it amongst themselves. Chenda's mouth watered. She couldn't recall the last time she ate. Thinking about how hungry she was, Chenda could feel the corners of her mouth pull down into a pout.

Finally, they all turned to Chenda and Pranav Erato. The bold man who asked to see the flaming dagger had evidently been proclaimed spokesman for the group. As he spoke, Chenda could hear his words through the thoughts of Pranav Erato, neatly translated.

Great Lady, wondrous messenger of the gods, divine worshipful - Good grief! He's going to go on like this all day, I think... Ah, now he's getting to it... The tone of Pranav Erato's thoughts returned to that of translator. *...Angel of heaven amongst us, we find ourselves at odds as to how we may serve you best. Pray tell, what do you require of us?* Pranav Erato's bubbly tone chimed in- *Good - Ask about the soldiers, and the fallout from the destruction of the Dia Orella.*

"Thank you, most gracious and humble of men," Chenda began, and Verdu translated in turn. "First, I would be pleased to hear news of the people. What news do you have of the Emperor's soldiers? We know they seek us. What retaliation do they seek across the land for the destruction of the Dia Orella?"

Oh, well said, Chenda. Well said. You are a natural at this, Pranav Erato thought at her. The leader spoke again, and the mystic translated. *The soldiers sweep the land, scouring the cave villages and barren rock for you, Great Lady. They say that anyone claiming the Pramuc lives, that the savior of us all has come, will be relieved of his head. Many examples have been made already. Rumors fly that the ports at Wha-Rhen and Trum-Bhal have been closed. It seems that the Emperor is willing to grind all the land into a fine powder so he can sift you out.*

246

Chenda looked to Pranav Erato, who spoke aloud to the men and Chenda heard the Pranav shape his words into her head. *That is helpful to know, my brothers, even when it causes great sadness to me. The Pramuc's companions and I seek to spread the message, and we are grateful to you, our first witnesses. All we ask for now is that you remember. Remember what you have seen here and let the faithful know that the gods have not abandoned us. The Pramuc lives. Do not hide this glorious news.*

Pranav Erato stood and pulled Chenda to standing as well. *We will leave now from this place, and you all must return to your own places. Word will reach you soon of what will come, and what the faithful will be asked to do. I bid you all go in peace.*

Pranav Erato walked with Chenda out of the outcrop and into the setting sun. He turned west and started walking at a stately pace into the setting sun. Soon, Candice, Verdu and Fenimore fell into step next to them.

"Where are we going?" Chenda asked.

"West," the mystic replied in a bubbly tone. "We've got to get up and do this again in the morning, don't you know."

The same scene repeated itself over and over again throughout the next several days. Ahy-Me, and occasionally Pranav Erato himself, would arrange for leaders and sympathizers of the Tugrulian Resistance to assemble, and Chenda would talk to them. They were eager to hear her message, and in the end, all wanted to serve the Pramuc. Always, she would bid them to spread the message, and wait. A time to act was close at hand.

With each passing day, Chenda focused more intently on one thing: leaving this land of horrors. On several occasions, imperial soldiers left less subtle warnings for those spreading word of the Pramuc. Rows of heads on pikes met them as they entered small villages. Chenda recognized a few of the faces. Once, she released her powers and cracked the dry earth behind the severed heads, calling forth a wind to neatly bury the lonely heads.

Despite the efforts of the Empire to suppress information about the Pramuc, word spread quickly. Sometimes hundreds of people would come to see Chenda. As the crowds got larger, Fenimore and Verdu became more concerned for Chenda's safety.

247

Fenimore was on constant guard, vigilant against an attack, and Verdu mingled in the crowd talking with people. He listened for any hint of false sincerity amongst the people of the crowd, hoping to stop any spies before they could report back to the hierarchy. Luck seemed to be with Chenda's companions, as there was never any trouble among the congregants.

In their spare moments while traveling from place to place, Chenda and Candice planned a way to be most useful to the Tugrulian people. The problem with most of their ideas was that the two of them were fairly sure attempts at assistance wouldn't survive the ever-prowling Tugrulian soldiers. Chenda and her companions gathered a good bit of information as they traveled. Most of it they sifted through, looking for a way to escape westward without being trapped by patrols. The Empire controlled its people chiefly by restricting the flow of food. The Tugrulians had long believed that a hundred years of civil war had poisoned the land, and that it would not sustain farming. Ostensibly passed as a rule to protect the people, there was now a law that forbade planting crops on the land. All the food that the Tugrulians produced for themselves came from underground caverns and ponds - mostly mushrooms, mosses and algae. Not the best sources for human nutrition. Malnutrition ran rampant in some areas, especially places out of favor with the Emperor.

Chenda and Candice knew they could show the Tugrulians how to farm again, but the problems of avoiding vengeful soldiers seemed formidable. Anything the people planted would be destroyed almost immediately. The women were stumped.

Seven days after the collapse of the Dia Orella, Chenda and her companions were waiting out the daylight in the underground village of Lhil-Bhan. Chenda had finished up her meeting with the area's resistance leaders and had retreated to a cool cave deep within the hillside. The villagers had been hit hard already by soldiers looking to suppress her supporters. Chenda laid her head on Candice's lap and wept as they sat on the floor of the small chamber.

"They are getting more brutal," she cried, thinking of the heads of the small children mixed amongst the pikes leading into the town. "How can they do that to the little ones?"

"I don't know," was all Candice could say as brushed her fingers through Chenda's feathery hair. The pace of the journey and the stress of constantly being hunted was starting to wear on all of them. They needed to be done.

"We have to do something." Chenda sobbed. "Maybe there is no alternative. Maybe a bloodbath is the only way to set things to right and get out of this broke-down, hellish continent. Am I just wasting time trying to be peaceful? Should I just kill them all and let the gods sort them out?"

"Stop that," Candice snapped at her. "You know that isn't what is in your heart. We will think of something." Candice held Chenda as her sobs slowly gave way to the slow, rhythmic breath of sleep." Candice shifted Chenda's body onto the floor, and scooted away from her.

She approached Verdu, Fenimore and Pranav Erato, who were already gathered in the corner of the cave.

"Ah, Candice, how is she doing?" Fenimore asked.

"Not well. We've got to get her out of here. If the soldiers don't find us and kill us, this pace will. How is our plan coming?"

"Same problems as always," Fenimore said. "Even if we can get on a boat and get it sailing out into the Kohlian Sea, we will never be able to evade or outrun the Tugrulian patrols. The *Brofman* dropped us onto the *Tjalk* inside the patrol line, which is why it was so easy getting in. I can't see a way to get us up into the air from within the borders of the Empire. Our only hope is meeting up with the *Brofman* at Crider Island. But we still have to find a way to get past the patrols.

"We could use Chenda's power to blow the ships right out of the water, but then the Resistance will know that the Pramuc has left them, and all of the support that has been laid here will be lost. Pranav Erato can lead the people in the name of the Pramuc, so she doesn't really need to be here physically. People just need to think she is near. Chenda needs to get someplace safe, without anyone knowing that the Pramuc is gone."

"So, the escape plan is still a non starter," Verdu said. "Where are you and Chenda on the serve-the-people plan?

Candice sighed. "We have figured out everything we need to do to get these people planting farms above ground again, except for a way to prevent soldiers from destroying anything we do the minute we finish sowing the fields." She sighed again, "We've got a way to acquire seeds, and Chenda can carve out several irrigation systems in a hot minute, and with just a few amendments to the soil, anywhere around here could hold flourishing farms in no time. But how do we stop the spiteful destruction that is starving these people into submission?"

They all sat there stewing in their own misery until Ahy-Me returned to the cave carrying a large crock and a stack of bowls. "Des folks starve, but to us are very generous. Dey give too much."

Pranav Erato smiled looking into the crock of murky soup. "It's hard to eat when you know the people who gave you the food are hungry, but eat we must. We cannot help these people if we are weak."

"Says the man who never eats," Candice chided. The Pranav waved a bony hand at her dismissively. They all watched as Ahy-Me ladled the soup into the wide but shallow bowls. Candice had given up on reasoning out why most of the Tugrulian food they had seen was an olive-gray color. She decided days ago that she would eat whatever came and be grateful for it. This day would be no exception.

Candice realized that Chenda's transformation into the Pramuc had changed her as well. As a scientist, residing in the live-and-let-live atmosphere of the West, she had never given much thought to the gods. They had always been there, just down the street from her apartment in the University district in an area the students lovingly referred to as Holy Corners, but she hadn't paid then much mind. The gods were there for another day, and her work, her science, begged for her attention first.

Now that Candice had been there, in the presence of the gods, or at least in the presence of a woman in the presence of the gods, they had become much more real to her. Suddenly, she believed. What she was going to do with that belief, she had no clue, but there it was.

She trailed her spoon through her gray soup, saying a silent prayer to whatever god could hear her. From what she could gather from Chenda, the gods weren't too picky about how they were worshiped, they just seemed to want to be remembered, and thanked for being there. That suited Candice just fine. She found that a prayer of gratitude every now and again helped her to remember how blessed and lucky she was. But today, she slipped in a tiny request for inspiration. That wasn't too much to ask for, she thought.

In the moment her spoon dropped into her soup, the handle sliding below the surface of the warm puree, she knew her prayers had been answered.

"Look!" Candice shouted, and everyone around her jumped. "Did you see?!?! I dropped my spoon!"

"Good gods, she's cracked," Fenimore whispered to Verdu, and they both nodded in perfect agreement.

"Candice, I believe you have had a soup epiphany of some kind. How wonderful." Pranav Erato's limbs started to quiver, just begging for a reason to dance. "We may be a bit slow, but if you lead, I think we will get there with you eventually. Can you please explain?"

Candice fluttered her hands over her soup. "Oh! Well, yes. I think I have the solution to both our current problems! Invisibility!"

Pranav Erato's limbs fell still and his ever constant grin faded slightly.

"Bonkers," Verdu and Fenimore said at the same time.

Candice looked at the disapproving faces around her and calmly collected her thoughts. "You just listen! I dropped the spoon in the soup after I said a prayer."

"You pray?" Verdu said, quite surprised.

"Shut it!" Candice snapped. She gave Verdu her best teacher stare and the large man backed down. "Anyway," she continued, "once the spoon slid in, it disappeared. That's what we need to do with the crops *and* ourselves. I can't believe that I didn't think of this before. If we can get into the sea, perhaps with a small enough vessel, and hoping that Chenda can store up enough power to do it, I think we might just be able to go UNDER the Tugrulian patrols!"

"Gods with a thousand faces! That's brilliant." Pranav Erato said, his legs already in full bounce. "Now, tell me quickly

251

my child, how we make the crops invisible!"

With great excitement, Candice said, "No clue, but that's what we have to do!"

"Well, whoopie! It's a start," the mystic replied. "I feel confident that this is the path to our solution. Now, a much more pertinent question," he said, the sparkle firmly back in his eyes, "How are you going to eat that soup without a spoon?"

When Chenda awoke, Candice could hardly contain herself. "I've got it!"

Chenda grabbed her hand quickly. *Will it keep for two minutes?*

"Oh, sure. Do that thing you do. Sand blasting again?"

I think I want to try something a bit more direct. Stand back.

Chenda put her hand onto the rock face and concentrated. With a soft pop an avalanche of sand fell, revealing another image of a sparking dagger. She was getting better at that particular image.

"That worked. Great." She sighed and turned to Candice. "You are excited. Tell me all about it."

"We go under the Tugrulian patrols!"

"Say, that is different thinking. Why didn't we think of that before? Hmm...." Chenda started running several scenarios though her head. "I'm stuck on bubble, and that is going to take too much power. I don't think I could hold us ALL in a bubble under the water for very long, not more than a few minutes, what did you have in mind?"

"What if we get a vessel that would keep the water out, could you move us along under the water, and refresh the air?" Candice asked.

"Probably. Pushing us along, I could do for a little while. Cleaning the air, I don't know if I could do that at the same time. How fast would I have to move us, and for how long?"

"Good question, I think we should come at this scientifically. Once we get the proper vessel, we will have to experiment to see how much of your power it takes get going, maybe we could chart it, and then we-"

"Forget that." Fenimore interrupted from where he sat across the cave. "We've only got three days to get out of here, I think."

"What do you mean?" Chenda asked.

"IF we can get by the patrols in this... *swim under*, and that's a very big IF, what are we going to do? Float our way across the Kohlian? I think not. Remember, our best shot is getting airborne with friends, and that means meeting the *Brofman*. We've missed the first date to meet up with Captain Endicott at Crider Island. He agreed to attempt to meet us a second time ten days later. That's three days from now. I'm not saying we couldn't find another way, but this opportunity is waiting for us. However, wasting time, dickering with charts and experiments, is out of the question."

He elbowed Verdu. "The question is, how realistic is it? Can we get to the coast, find a boat, or boat-ish type thing, and drift to Crider in three days?"

"If we leave from here in the morning, we might make it. But that just leaves us with about 14 hours to find a way to make fields invisible." Verdu said.

Candice said, "What's the next best thing to invisible?"

"Translucent?" Fenimore hazarded.

"Obscured." Verdu said.

"Repulsive!" Pranav Erato said with glee. "Why don't we fix it so nobody will *want* to go looking too closely for these fields?"

"I bet we can do more than one thing to hide a few fields," Chenda said. "Imagine a plateau, one inconvenient to get to in the first place. If I sink the center of the plateau about four feet, then no one could see it from the ground to begin with. If we laced the area with something really stinky, I think it could be a strong deterrent for moderately curious soldiers. What's the stinkiest compound in nature you can think of, Candice?"

"Oh, there are several that really will knock your socks off. Most of the ones that smell like vomit or skunk or decomposing bodies would be very difficult for us to come up with on short notice. Chenda, you might be able to find the right molecules and mush them together the right way, but I'm not in favor of wildly experimenting with stuff that rank, or if we do it wrong, that deadly. But sulfur, that's simple *and* effective. Chenda could get the earth to cough that up easily enough, don't you think?"

"I think I could," Chenda said. "Pranav Erato, do you think that we can set this in motion tonight? We have all these people who have visited with me this week. They want to take some action. Can they help us find the right location, and any seeds they have been hiding?"

He sprang to his feet. "We're going to try! Ahy-Me! You stay here and see if we need anything else. I'll be listening for you. We've got work to do." Pranav Erato danced toward the mouth of cave, and called over his shoulder, "I'll get this started and will be right back!" A second later, the willowy man was gone.

Chenda and Candice clutched each other's hands and danced around. "This really could work!" Chenda said.

"It's only a start." Candice said. "But if we can prove the land is fertile, that's all we need. One really successful crop growing hidden within the Empire. When word gets out, there will be no stopping the people. Once they know they can feed their children, the Law of the Emperor will mean nothing. This will show them the way."

Candice looked thoughtful for a moment. "Verdu! I think I need to write some instructions for the people who will be tending these fields. I'm going to need you to translate for me. I'd hate to grow a bunch of plants, and then not have anyone know what to do with the beans once they are grown, assuming that's what we are growing."

Verdu and Candice huddled together in a corner and started to translate instructions for basic gardening. Fenimore looked around the room, unsure what to do while the others were busily making plans, and said to no one in particular, "If I didn't know us, I'd think we had all gone mad. But this may just be crazy enough to work."

As the sun set over the dry Tugrulian landscape, Chenda and her companions followed a guide upwards to a small plateau several miles outside of Lhil-Bhan. Chenda had been storing her power for several hours, and was ready to let it go to work. She probed ahead and felt the presence of 15 vertical water bags - people - waiting for them above. She also sensed pockets of water flowing below her. She was sure there was sufficient water she could draw to the surface for irrigation. Chenda had faith in her plan.

She reached backwards to Candice. *This place is going to work. This place has everything we could want.*

"Oh, good," she replied. "I don't think that we've got time to select another."

Tell Verdu that there are 15 men ahead. I'm sure one of them is Pranav Erato, the skinniest waterbag of a person ever.

Candice dropped Chenda's hand and trotted ahead to pass her message to Verdu.

Chenda turned her thoughts from water to earth. The plateau was fairly rocky and very uneven with many dips and bumps. She let her mind feel its way through all of the textures: pockets of sand and clay, layers of soil and dust. As she thought about the surface of the plateau and how she was going to go about rearranging it, her pace slowed slightly. Fenimore, who had been bringing up the rear of the little party, suddenly stood beside Chenda. He put a hand on her shoulder.

"Something wrong?" he asked.

Oh, nothing, I'm just thinking about what I need to do up there. I guess I got a little distracted. Thanks for asking, though.

"You think you can do this?"

Yes. I really think I can, and it costs me nothing to try, I'm just estimating how much power I need to hold back so I can stinkify the bottom of this plateau. But if I have to, I can just wait an hour or so and try again.

"That's my little human battery," Fenimore said, grinning. "Can I tell you something?"

Sure, always.

"I'm not crazy about you being able to put your voice in my head."

Then stop touching me, and my voice won't make it that far. Chenda found she could not keep the hurt tone out of her thoughts any more than she could keep it out of her voice.

"OH! I'm such a cad. I didn't mean it to come out that way. What I want to say is that I really like the sound of your voice, in my ears, that's all. I know you aren't speaking the old fashioned way because something, um, bad, might happen if you do. At best, this power is an inconvenience to you, and at worst, I imagine it causes you some pain." Fenimore grimaced. "I'm just sorry, that's all."

Aww, Fen. That's sweet, really. But don't worry about it. Give me a minute to work, and I'll be just plain old chatty me again. AND there will be something really great here to show for it. Have a little patience.

"OK, I will." Fenimore gave a very meaningful look to Chenda.

What?

"I was just testing you," he said. "I just wanted to see if you could hear me talk to you without me moving my lips."

Chenda laughed inside. *No, Fen. Your thoughts are a mystery to me until you voice them. Sorry.*

"It's just as well. I was thinking about the punchline to the dirtiest joke I've ever heard, so I am kind of glad you didn't hear it."

Come on! Now I really want to hear it! Tell me the joke.

Fenimore and Chenda were still giggling about the dirtiest joke ever, when they caught up with the others at the top of the plateau.

I'm going to try to go do something divine now, which may be impossible with that ribaldry amongst my thoughts. She smiled and pulled away from his hand. She placed one finger on Pranav Erato's elbow.

Seeds?

Pranav Erato danced with excitement. *Oh, yes! I'm shocked at the variety! I've got them sorted by type atop that rock over there if you would like to take a look.*

I will. Have everyone stand well back behind the seeds. I'm itching to get this started.

Chenda looked at the assortment of vegetable and fruit seeds laid out into 25 little piles on the rock. Candice stepped up beside her.

"Once you get the ground ready, I'll help you with the spacing for the seeds. I recognize most of them, and it will be no problem."

Perfect. The women grasped each other's hands for a moment more.

Let's do this!

"Yes!" Candice said as she stepped back.

The top of the plateau was perhaps five acres. Chenda walked to the center of it and spread her hands, palms down, over the rocky area. She started feeling for fissure lines about ten yards in from the edge of the shear face. It was tedious, but after several minutes she had marked her boundaries. She pulled most of her pent up power to the front of her mind and slowly let it wash over the rocky earth. It was like a billion miniature earthquakes being released one after the next in a wave across the mesa, each stone grinding the clod next to it to sandy pieces. The vibration shimmied through the loosened earth, shifting the soil back and forth across the plateau, mixing it. After several minutes of scooting the fresh dirt around, Chenda was satisfied.

"Candice!" she called. "The first batch of seeds. Name them as you throw them into the air."

"Beans!" Candice shouted from a few hundred yards behind her. "Plant them 12 inches apart, one inch deep, rows two-and-a-half feet apart!" She threw the beans into the air and Chenda caught then with a column of wind. A few seconds later, all the beans were planted.

"Next." Chenda demanded.

"Pumpkins!" Candice replied. "Three seeds to a hill..."

For the next hour, Chenda followed Candice's instructions, and the entire plateau was planted. With the last of her power, Chenda created a borehole into a deep pocket of water that rose and bubbled through the neat rows of the field.

"Tilled, planted and irrigated in less than two hours. Very impressive." Candice said.

Chenda sat down hard on a rock. "I'm spent!"

"You take a well deserved rest, dear. I'm just going to pop over to those gentlemen and see if they understand what needs to happen to these plants once we leave here." Candice shuffled off to stand next to Verdu and Pranav Erato.

Fenimore sat down next to Chenda in the darkness. "That was amazing. My dirtiest joke couldn't stop you from being divine."

"Thanks, Fen," she said with a small giggle. "It felt very right. This may sound a little ironic now that I've pulled 30-thousand gallons of water out of the ground, but I really could use something to drink. You got anything?"

He laughed and handed over his canteen. "Feel free to drink it all. I know this really neat girl who can fill it for me later."

Chenda snorted. "Stop. The water's going to come out my nose and that will cause some catastrophe where a peninsula falls off the continent or something."

She leaned her head on his shoulder, and closed her eyes. When she started to snore lightly, Fenimore gently laid her across his lap and then sat very still.

"That's it, baby," he said, looking down at her lips, smiling faintly in the moonlight. "You just rest a minute. You've earned it."

Verdu stood among the Tugrulian men who witnessed what they were already calling the Miracle of the Sunken Garden. To the assembled there, if any would have cared to take notice of him, they would only have seen the slightly pleased yet unmoving smile pasted on his face. Those around him, so ebullient over the work of the Pramuc, took no notice that the smile never touched his eyes.

Verdu had many reasons to be happy. Through Chenda, change was not only coming for his homeland, it had begun. He held every confidence in her, and also in the Resistance who would now take over the tending of this field. Once the crops took hold, there would be no stopping the Resistance. People know the Empire's lies, and reject them. The cruel leaders would fall. He was sure of it.

But at this very moment, he couldn't enjoy his seed of victory.

Verdu's eyes kept drifting over to Chenda, exhausted from

her night's work. She lay cradled across Fenimore's lap, limp as a rag doll. He could see her breathing, slow and even in the moonlight. It annoyed him. At first he thought his peevish feeling came from the indignity of it, the Pramuc napping there like some worn out child at a picnic. She looked ridiculous. But as his eyes drifted to her yet again, just to watch the pale moonlight shine on her cheek, her lips, her chin, he realized that her dignity had nothing to do with his inner turmoil. In an instant, his annoyance shifted to anger and then to self loathing. He was *jealous*. He was jealous of *Fenimore*. He was jealous of Fenimore because of *her*. Worse yet, Verdu felt shame for thinking of Chenda that way. She was the Pramuc after all, a holy person, touched by the gods. He chastised himself for thinking of her soft skin instead of her miracles. He should strive to be worthy of *sitting* at her right hand, not wishing he were holding it.

Pranav Erato danced to a halt next to Verdu. "My, my," he said. "Such a parade of emotions just crossed your face."

"So what?" Verdu replied in a whisper. "It's nothing. And I don't need or want to talk about it."

"Fair enough," Pranav Erato said, "but allow me one observation. In becoming the Pramuc, Chenda changed, but not so much as your expectation of her did. She is who she is, a whole person. You can't love her in slices."

"That's three observations, and none are relevant." Verdu protested. "And I'm not in love with her."

"Sure you aren't," Pranav Erato said as he walked away.

Chapter 20
DUE WEST

Chenda dreamed about pumpkins, which, to her, always felt pretty good. Throughout her childhood, pumpkins had intrigued her. The broad, slightly prickly leaves, the earthy smell, the way their wrinkly orange skin soaked up the sun throughout the hot sunny days and released it back slowly in the evenings, it all felt magical to Chenda. The nuns grew pumpkins in the orphanage garden. In her dream, she saw the devout ladies in their broad straw hats, bending over the rambling vines, hoeing the weeds and watering the soil.

Chenda enjoyed the aesthetics of pumpkins, but the nuns valued the practicality of them: easy to grow, generous of yield and hearty for storage. A field of pumpkins would feed a dozen poor families through a winter. The pumpkins, as far as the nuns were concerned, were a gift to be shared with those most in need.

In her dream, Chenda sat on the warm ground and she clutched a pumpkin to her. She drummed her fingers on its warm flesh, listening to the hollow thump echoing inside it. Lately, she herself had been feeling a warm hollowness within. She sat there rocking the pumpkin like a baby, dreamy and calm in the sunlight, until the rocking was all around her.

A chorus of voices spoke to her, "Well done, Pramuc. Very clever. You and your companions please us."

Chenda recognized it as the voices of the gods. *Thank you. It gives the people a fighting chance, I think.*

"We will bless these fields, and they will grow strong. It will succeed."

Chenda made a pleased sigh, but couldn't think of

anything she wanted to say. She held her warm pumpkin closer, resting a cheek against its smooth skin.

"Pramuc," the voices chided, "melancholy does not suit you. If you are lonely, it is because you choose to be so. The world is full; seek your joys in all things around you. We would not burden you with so much if we could not give you great gifts as well." She heard a few solitary giggles from among the gods.

As the last voice of the gods faded, Chenda heard another voice call to her. "Chenda, you need to wake up and raise a stink."

"Narf?" she replied, feeling herself gently rocking from side to side. Fenimore was carrying her down the narrow path that zigzagged down the cliff face from the plateau. By the looks of it, they were about halfway down already.

"Come on, Chenda, I know you are exhausted, but Candice says you have to. Just a little woeful odor, and I promise I'll carry you all the way to the sea. Cross my heart."

"Deal," she said. "Am I standing yet?"

"Um, no. Do you need to be?" Fenimore asked.

"Let's find out." Chenda reached out with her mind and located some sulfur pockets deep below the plateau. She released her power and burrowed several narrow tunnels into each pocket, releasing various gasses. Suddenly the air around her was markedly more offensive.

"Bleck!" Candice shouted somewhere up ahead of Chenda. "Yup. Dat will do!" Candice said while pinching her nose.

"Ugh. Maybe we could have waited a little longer before we pulled that particular cork out of the bottle," Verdu said. "Remind me to be upwind next time."

Chenda retorted sleepily, her eyes still closed, "Do not mock the great miracles of the Pramuc, or I will turn you into a pumpkin, crush you utterly and plant your seeds in my sunken garden."

Verdu made a nervous laugh, and said no more. Fenimore leaned closer to Chenda's ear, "Can you really do that? Turn someone into a pumpkin?"

Chenda, too tired to move her lips, pushed her thoughts

toward Fenimore. *What do I look like? A fairy godmother? Now, boil his liver, that I could do, but that's no way to treat my saint, is it?*

It hardly surprised Chenda, when she woke up several hours later, that she was in Verdu's arms and not Fenimore's. Just about every time she fell asleep next to one of them, she woke up beside the other. By now, she simply chalked it up to one of the many little pranks that kept the gods amused.

She stretched and looked up at Verdu, his dark features highlighted by the first bright orange rays of dawn. *Good morning. I must be heavy to lug around so. You could put me down.*

"Do you want me to put you down?" he asked.

Well, she thought to him with a bit of giggle in her voice, *It was only a silly promise that Fen made to carry me all the way to the sea. I know you guys are best buds, but you don't have to carry me just because he said.*

Verdu stopped and dropped Chenda's legs to the ground. "Well, if you would rather have Fen, go find him." He stalked ahead sourly.

Chenda ran a few steps and caught Verdu's hand. *Hey! What is that supposed to mean?*

Verdu pulled his hand free from Chenda, turning his body to walk away again, but then he stopped, struggling within himself. His feet decided to stay, and the rest of his body gave in. He put his hands on each of Chenda's shoulders, and let his left thumb stroke her neck a moment before he said softly, "When I carry you, it's no burden. I held you in my arms because you needed it; I've watched you push yourself to the limit. I also carried you... because it pleased me. When you are close to me, when I can hold you and touch you, I imagine no heaven more divine. I know you think of us as a set, but when I think about you, angel, Fenimore never enters my mind."

His hands slid down her soft arms as he looked into her surprised face. He squeezed her hands and then let them drop as he took one step backward. Then another. Verdu turned his back to the rising sun and kept walking.

She stood there a moment, thinking to herself. *Oh.... OH!* She bit her lip trying to sort out her feelings about what just happened, and had no success. She looked to the east and the beautiful sunrise, and saw Candice and Fenimore approaching, evidently bringing up the rear of the small party. They were deep in conversation, but as Fenimore glanced at Chenda, she knew he had witnessed her moment with Verdu, and he wasn't thrilled about it. In fact, if Chenda were pressed to name the emotion rolling across his face, she would have said jealousy.

She turned west and started walking again, neither slowing to join step with Candice and Fenimore, or hurrying to catch up to Verdu. She thought it best to just keep to herself for a while, letting the two men whom she now found herself between settle themselves.

She rolled her eyes at the heavens as she walked, sending her thoughts upward. *You all think this is pretty funny, don't you?* Deep in her mind she heard a chorus of snickers from the gods.

Two hours later, the sun began to feel like punishment. Up ahead, Chenda could see Pranav Erato, but she wasn't sure if the bounce of his limbs was an optical illusion caused by the waves of rising heat, or if he was just really excited. Either way, he came to a halt in the shade of a large rock formation. The mystic waited there for the others to catch up to him and Ahy-Me, who seemed to have just returned from scouting ahead. The air, despite being baking hot, moved briskly past them carrying a salty hint of the sea. They were approaching the Kohlian Coast.

As the group gathered together once again, Chenda scanned the area for other people. She found two, almost a mile away, and they were moving fairly quickly. She decided to keep tabs on them as Ahy-Me started to speak.

"I find dees dings you ask for. De Resistance near de port - very helpful. I know some! Old friends. Ve go now to de house of Ma-Took, pickle merchant. Ve stay der today. He give us de tub. It work great to go under dees patrols. Tonight you go. No problem. Come, we have short way to go."

Ahy-Me handed veils to Chenda and Candice, and wrapped herself as well, and they all stepped out into the sunshine. As they walked, Pranav Erato and Verdu took the lead, and discussed the plan for when they reached the coast.

"What town is this?" Verdu asked.

"Nivarta. It's the smallest port from which one can quickly reach Crider Island. On a fast boat you could be there in a matter of hours. In a pickle tub..." Pranav Erato ended with a shrug.

"We'll be lucky to get there at all," Verdu sighed. That's going to take a lot of effort for Chenda to push the four of us under water for such a long time. Do you think she is up to it?"

"It hardly matters what I think. It only matters if *she* thinks she can. If she believes it, I know she can do it. She is preparing herself as if she is going to try her best, storing up her power and so on. I would say your chances are fairly good."

"But not great?" Verdu said.

"No, not great."

"Did Ahy-Me see many soldiers in Nivarta?"

"Yes, and we may have a spot of luck there; the soldiers seem to be congregated around the perimeter of the city and along the docks. So, at least we have some of their patterns mapped out already, and if we can get into the town, we should have little trouble until we try to get out again."

Chenda interrupted them by shouldering between them and grabbing each by the hand.

There are two men to the south of us, almost a mile away. They were heading away from us, but now they are moving parallel to us and heading the same way we are. I can't see them with my eyes, but I know they are there. I get the sense that they don't want to be seen, at least not yet. They are taking a rocky path – a secluded path that can't be seen from the road. There is a considerable amount of steel about them as well. What do we do?

Verdu made the double hiss to call Fenimore. "Just two you say? One of us should check it out." Fenimore trotted up and Verdu explained what Chenda had seen.

"Sounds like scouts. I'll go pay them a visit. Let's see if they take a swipe at me," Fenimore said as he turned away. Chenda grabbed his arm.

I'll keep my eye on you, but don't do anything stupid, please?

265

"Don't worry, angel. This is what *I'm* good at."

Fenimore jogged ahead, due west, for about a mile, and then darted south. Chenda watched in her mind as the two men came closer to where Fenimore waited. Finally, the path of the two strangers intersected with Fenimore, where they stopped. Chenda held her breath. The three were close together for several minutes, then one came back along Fenimore's path. She prayed it was him. She focused on that single, moving column of human water, as the other two did not move, their water seeping into the earth.

To her relief, Fenimore appeared on the horizon, waiting for his companions to catch up. Although he seemed uninjured, he didn't look very happy.

Verdu looked equally stern when he finally spoke to Fenimore. "Well?"

"Scouts," he said. "I think they had already spotted us, but they won't be reporting in now. We're going to have to be very cautious; they know what we look like. Well, at least they know Chenda."

He pulled a small bundle of papers from his pocket. Most of it was bits of Tugrulian writing, which he handed to Verdu, but one was a sketch of Chenda. He held it up for them all to see.

She grabbed Fenimore's hand. *I know that picture of me! It was in the papers the morning I left Coal City.*

"It surely was brought here by the spies that followed us from the west. They have been dogging most of our steps for this whole journey," Fenimore said. "They got to Taboda and must have someone, or probably several, inside the Resistance. We've been very lucky. The only place I know you are safe from spies is on the *Brofman*. I know I can trust everyone there."

Chenda could see groupings of people up ahead. *Are we getting close to the town?*

"Yes. Another mile or so. Are you starting to see lots of people?" Verdu asked. She nodded. Verdu took the lead and said, "Fen, it's time to take up your spot in the back of the line. And it's time for you ladies to act like fine Tugrulian women."

Chenda brimmed with stored power now, and she felt ready for anything. She focused on the people in and around the

266

town ahead. Nivarta was surprisingly small. Most of the people she saw there were either patrolling the top of the city wall or were standing guard at the small harbor. There were only 100 or so people actually within the small town. There were more empty stone houses there than people. This troubled Chenda. Did the Tugrulian soldiers evacuate the town? Was this a trap? Were the Tugrulians the sort to get their citizens out of harm's way if it were?

Chenda realized she was out of time to express her doubts; the small party approached the gates. A bored looking Tugrulian sentry approached Verdu, and began what sounded like a stock speech. Undoubtedly, the squat little man rattled it off to every visitor at the gates. The guard's mouth fell open when Verdu interrupted him. Verdu kept on talking and made a big show of rummaging through his pockets. He pulled out the wad of papers that Fenimore had taken from the scouts and pulled Chenda's picture out of the pile. He waved back in the direction from which he had come, and then started to point to the northeast vaguely.

The guard's eyes bulged with suppressed interest. He waved Verdu and his party through the gate and then ran into the guardhouse shouting excitedly. Verdu casually led his party through the gates. A few minutes later, well inside the city of Nivarta, Pranav Erato knocked on the door of Ma-Took the Pickler, who opened his entryway personally. Chenda realized this was her first visit into a real Tugrulian house. As she filed in with the rest of her group, Chenda's eyes looked everywhere at once. The entrance hall was broad but sparsely furnished. The few chairs and lone narrow table looked more like props than well used possessions. The room was a formal place used to transact business. No real living was done here.

Ma-Took said nothing, but led the group through the formal front room to an opening in the back wall. He turned sharply and led on, down a long flight of stairs cut directly into the stone floor. He opened a door at the bottom landing and gestured the line of people to go inside. The chamber within welcomed, cool and dim. Narrow skylights let slivers of day light bounce off a selection of soft looking cushions and rich, red Tugrulian carpets scattered around the room. The space was

267

informal and welcoming. After Fenimore entered, Ma-Took firmly closed the door behind him. He turned to the assembled and smiled broadly, the first sign of emotion on his broad face.

He spoke pleasantly to Verdu as Ahy-Me pulled off her headscarf. He waved at the others to do the same; his gestures said *Make yourself at home.* Ahy-Me took Chenda and Candice by the elbow and guided them to a small circle of cushions on the floor in one corner of the room. They all sat.

"Dat Verdu - he is clever," Ahy-Me said. "He tells dat guard, 'I meet your soldier friend and he say, I dink I see dis girl. He say me bring vord to da gate of Nivarta, den you pay me, yes?' Dat Verdu is so da trickster! Dat dumb guard take de bait."

Ahy-Me looked longingly at Verdu. "You dink he need wife?" she asked casually.

Candice snorted and gave a sidelong glance at Chenda "Oh, I'd guess he IS interested in a wife, Ahy-Me. You should get right on that."

"Vell, you ladies stay here. I go see about some arrangements. I come soon." She sprang to her feet and shuffled over to where the men were talking, or in Fenimore's case, standing and listening, but not comprehending.

Chenda turned her attention to Candice. "That was mean, Professor."

"What? What did I do but encourage the girl? Doesn't she deserve happiness as much as the next fellow? I saw that little exchange between you and Verdu today. It was clear, even from where I stood, what he was saying to you. Fenimore didn't like it much, I can tell you that."

Candice tisked at the ongoing romantic shenanigans. "What are you thinking about all this?"

Candice pressed her finger to Chenda's elbow waiting for a reply, but the girl just looked at her friend with eyes wide, her thoughts frozen in confusion. Then her thoughts tumbled out in an angry rush.

The only thing I can think is that in about six hours, I have to do the impossible. The second worst that can happen is we all die. The worst is getting caught, which would be a killing blow to the all the groundwork we've laid here, and the Tugrulian people will continue to live lives of starvation and oppression. I'm splitting at the seams with pent up power already, so if you're asking me which of those two I want to pass love-notes to in study hall, I haven't had the time to give the matter any proper thought. And, by the way, to add to the distraction of it all, the gods think this little love triangle is HILARIOUS! So, please, cut me a little slack, and let's just keep focused on NOT dying!

Candice patted her irate friend soothingly on the arm. "Well," Candice said, "take comfort in the notion that I now have something in common with the gods. I think it's hilarious, too."

Ma-Took took great delight in formally meeting Chenda, and was a flamboyant host. He brought a fine selection of his pickled goods, and, while the group ate, he answered Chenda's many questions.

So, why are so many of the houses empty?

Verdu translated the answer, "When the port was closed, the local sailors, mostly fisherman and seaweed harvesters, couldn't work. Some were then conscripted, but others had to find another way to feed their families. No fishing, no food. So, they followed the fish they could go after. They went to stay with relatives who have access to some of the underground lakes. This latest action may just have killed this town. I have no one left to buy my pickles!"

That would be a shame, Ma-Took, you make wonderful pickled... what is this? It's delicious.

Verdu translated again for Ma-Took, "Pickled squid. Thank you for your compliment, Pramuc."

Well, thank you for your hospitality. Without you, I would never have known how much I enjoy pickled squid. Chenda smiled warmly, and Ma-Took was charmed. He didn't seem to mind that Chenda's thoughts came pre-translated into his head.

Ahy-Me said you had a pickling tub you might be willing to part with. May we see it?

"Of course, Pramuc. Whatever you need."

Ma-Took led Chenda and the others out a small door behind a curtain on the back wall of the comfortable room. They entered what could only be called the pickling factory. The center of the space held rows of broad cutting tables, where various fish and fungi were cleaned, sorted and chopped. Giant wheeled buckets sat waiting to be filled at the tables and dumped into the monstrous pickling tubs that stood like soldiers around the perimeter of the huge room.

Candice spoke first. "You, sir, must make a LOT of pickles."

Verdu replied for Ma-Took, "Yes, but none today. No fishermen, no fish to pickle. The Empire's ways are bad for business." Ma-Took spit in disgust. His eyes lingered over his idle factory. It was obvious to the assembled that this man had a pickle calling, and it pained him to refrain from his life's work.

Chenda examined the pickling tubs closely. Each one was basically a large metal tube, about four feet wide and 12 feet tall, with a broad funnel at the bottom, and a large flat lid on the top held firmly in place by clamps. She looked over at Candice with a satisfied smile.

"This is perfect!" Candice exclaimed. "But how will we sneak this through town and into the water?"

Verdu, who had been translating for Ma-Took, conveyed the man's reply, "Not a problem. I have several that are already in my warehouse down on the dock. Any or all of them are at your disposal."

"Well then," Verdu said, "What are we waiting for?"

Pranav Erato instructed Ahy-Me to stay with Ma-Took while he escorted Chenda and her companions to the warehouse. Even though she had known for a while that Pranav Erato and Ahy-Me would be staying behind in Tugrulia, it still surprised her when the moment of separation arrived. She'd grown accustomed to the thickly accented banter of Ahy-Me, and her simple dependability. She loved this Tugrulian woman.

Chenda sobbed and embraced the round faced woman. *I miss you already.*

*"*Also, I miss you," she replied placing her hands on the sides of Chenda's face in the traditional way.

For Chenda, letting go of Ahy-Me at the end of the blessing hurt. She feared that she may never see her friend again.

270

Chenda sniffed and followed Verdu out the narrow door and into the darkness.

Chenda composed herself in the cool evening air, and adjusted her veil, hoping it would be for the last time. The pain of leaving Ahy-Me shifted Chenda's focus. Finally, she started to feel like she was heading toward home.

Verdu led Chenda through the shadows. It was just the two of them; Fenimore suggested they split up in order to attract less attention. Verdu went first on the theory that if Chenda didn't make it to the warehouse, there was no point in risking it with the others. Chenda keenly felt the pressure of the plan as they approached the immense gate to the warehouse piers. Twilight still lingered over the water as Chenda placed her hand against the gate locks and released a tiny stream of her power, turning the inner workings of the brass lock into powder and grit. Verdu pushed open the gate just enough to slip through.

Chenda pressed her back against a dark wall and used her power to search for soldiers. It was a bit more of a challenge on the pier to seek out the human shaped bags of water that indicated people, as the water below called out to her most loudly, but she found several. Six soldiers were patrolling through the warehouses and around the piers. Several dozen more lounged in a make-shift mess hall and barracks at the far end of the last pier.

Chenda pressed these thoughts to Verdu.

"Will there be a gap long enough for us to run down the pier into Ma-Took's building without being seen?" Verdu asked in a whisper.

Yes, very soon. The next soldier on patrol is really taking his time, so when the one we can see there turns the corner, we should make a break for it.

"Good. I hate waiting."

After what seemed like an eternity, the guard turned the final corner and moved out of sight. Verdu and Chenda ran to Ma-Took's warehouse. Chenda broke the lock and pulled Verdu inside, just seconds before the next soldier on patrol turned to walk down the pier. There had been no time to spare. She took Verdu by the hand.

The others are going to need a whole lot of luck to find a

271

gap in the patrol. Maybe we should go back for them?

"No. You are one pickle tub away from getting off this gods-forsaken rock. I know Fenimore, he'll be quick and careful. What we need to do now is get that vessel ready to drop into the water as soon as they get in here. Come on."

He pulled Chenda down the dusty planks of the dark warehouse to where several of Ma-Took's pickling tubs lay on their sides. Verdu kicked the chocks away from the first one and started to roll it toward the opening in the floor over the water. Once he had the tub positioned, he set one brace to keep it from rolling into the loading slip and started to unclasp the lid. Chenda walked around the tub as Verdu worked, touching the metal and checking for any leaks or weak points. She checked the valve in the funnel and made sure it was closed securely. By the time Verdu had the lid off, Chenda was satisfied that the tub they had selected was shipshape.

"We are ready. All we need is our last two passengers and the one who will send us off."

Then they waited.

Minutes passed in dark silence. Chenda felt for Verdu beside her. *Where ARE they?*

"I don't know," Verdu whispered, worry evident in his tone. "Where are the guards?"

Drat! I've been so worried where the others were I forgot to look. Chenda concentrated for several seconds. *Six guards are still on patrol, but slowpoke has picked up the pace now. I THINK that our three are still on the far side of the pier's main gate, but I'm not sure. There's too much water around for me to sense people clearly.*

"All we can do is wait," Verdu reassured her.

Chenda turned her attention to the sea. *What are most Tugrulian patrol boats made of? Wood or metal hulls?*

"Metal. Wood we just don't have much of," Verdu replied.

Chenda searched the sea for metal, and found several ships slowly patrolling a dozen miles from shore. She mentally followed them for a few more seconds, until her concentration was suddenly broken by the sound of the door to the warehouse opening and closing quietly.

IS IT THEM?

Chenda was almost in a panic. She could feel herself losing a grip on her pent up power. Water splashed in the loading slip. She started to breathe heavily and too fast. She barely heard a double hiss sound from a space next to the door.

Fenimore.

Verdu hissed in response and two pairs of footsteps approached.

"Fen, over here!" Verdu shouted in a whisper.

Fenimore pulled Candice along, and Chenda could hear her muttering, "...gotta go back... maybe we can help... gotta go back..." Fenimore put a single finger on Candice's lips.

"No," Fenimore said in a hushing tone. "He knew what he was doing. It's too late anyway."

"Fen, where's Pranav Erato?" Verdu asked.

"We were waiting in the shadows by the gate, and we couldn't find a break in the pattern of the guards. There was no time to run here without being seen. Then Pranav Erato said 'Well, if we can't do this without getting caught, let's get caught' and he ran out onto the pier, waggling those rubbery arms of his, and the next soldier in the watch charged after him and around the corner...."

"We can go get him," Candice said adamantly.

"No! The only place he could have ended up was running into the back of the next guard on patrol. He sacrificed himself so we can get out of here. Now, we need to go before this place is crawling with soldiers who want to cut our heads off."

Verdu grabbed the quaking Candice and pushed her into the pickle tub. "Help her pull it together, Fen."

Fenimore glanced at Chenda, who was trembling and near the edge of losing control. She struggled every moment to keep the power of the elements from flying out of her. She was in no shape to bear anymore.

"She can't handle this. She's gone too long without discharging any of that power!" he said to Verdu.

"Not now." Verdu replied, matching Fenimore's angry face perfectly. "Get in there and get Candice ready."

"Hurry!" Fenimore growled, but he ducked his head went

inside the small tub.

Verdu pulled Chenda to the side of the tub and spoke quickly to her. "You've done enough for my people, our people, do you understand? I've seen you, witnessed what you can do. I know you and, more than that, I love you. So, you need to let Fenimore take you someplace safe. Someplace where you can learn the extent your power, and how to live with it. You're going to be fantastic, and when you've had a chance to fully understand that power, you'll make it dance. You are going to help people, a lot of people, all around the world, and it's going to be so easy for you. Don't worry about us here – you've given the Resistance hope. You've done the hard part. So, I'm going to take that hope and set a lot more things in motion."

He pulled Chenda's shaking body closer to him. "Shh," he whispered in her ear. "Peace, my dear. Fenimore is going to do what he promised. And I am sorry I can't go with you. Without Pranav Erato, the people here need me."

Chenda, afraid to speak, bit her lip and stared into Verdu's eyes. Despite the shock of losing Pranav Erato and the itch of the power within her trying to claw its way out, she could see the longing in Verdu. She couldn't ignore his eyes as they begged for answers about her loneliness, perhaps even her love. She already knew that time apart from him would pain her, but curiosity, and the memory of Edison's promise about the love of her life being out there, gave her courage. She touched his skin and thought, *Try*.

Verdu's breath stuck in his throat. He could feel the double meaning of her single word, and understood.

He lifted his hands to her face as he brought her closer. His eyes never left hers as their foreheads touched. He turned his head to the side slightly, and his lips pressed against hers. He closed his eyes then, concentrating on wrapping himself around her. His arms pulled her up, his hands clutched at her back. His lips parted and enveloped hers. He tasted her. With every move she responded. Trying.

Just as quickly as it started, the kiss broke. Verdu and Chenda rested with their eyes locked together, their foreheads touching. Verdu's hands eased her feet back onto the ground and

274

made their way back to the sides of her face. She moved her hands to the back of his head, and slowly stroked down his neck, shoulders and arms until her hands reached his elbow. She gently pushed him away, completing the Pramuc's Blessing.

"At least we tried," Verdu whispered.

Chenda made a sorrowful half smile and a curt nod. *I'll always love you, and pray the gods bless you and keep you until I see you again.*

Fenimore, who had poked his head out of the tub to see what the delay was, stared at the two of them, horrified. He turned on Verdu. "What the holy hell do you think you're doing?"

"I'm saying good bye," Verdu said. "Take care of her. She's all yours now." He backed Chenda into Fenimore's chest. "I love you, brother."

With a mighty shove he pushed Fenimore and Chenda into the tub, repositioned the lid and quickly started clamping it in place. He could hear Fenimore's protest from within, but once the first clamp caught firmly, there was no escaping. A few seconds more and Verdu finished sealing his companions inside. He kicked the chock away and pushed the make shift sailing vessel into the water below, where it bobbed for several seconds, and then slowly sank, leaving no trace of it on the dark surface of the sea.

Emilie P. Bush

Chapter 21
CRIDER ISLAND

Chenda fell down hard inside the pickle tub. Verdu's heavy blow had knocked the wind out of her. What little moonlight had filtered into the darkened warehouse disappeared the moment Verdu slammed the lid down tight. Neither the lack of light nor Chenda's gasping body knocked atop his slowed Fenimore much. He pushed Chenda aside and banged on the lid.

"Hey!" Fenimore scrambled to his feet. "Verdu! NO! We're not leaving you behind. STOP!"

Fenimore started to slam his shoulder into the tub trying to break out, but it did no good. Suddenly, the tub rolled, throwing the three bodies within sideways and to the floor. They slid around in the darkened tube as it fell through the warehouse floor into the sea. The impact slapped them all to the floor again.

Chenda could feel the water right under her, and she was ready. Without lifting her head from where she lay, she reached out to the water with a thread of her power, demanding it take the buoyant pickle tub down below the surface. It was harder than she thought it would be, holding the air-filled tube under the water. The fact that she couldn't see was a bit of a challenge, too. Candice's whimpering and Fenimore's angry snorts distracted her.

She bit her lip, concentrating. *OK,* she thought to herself, *one bit at a time. I'll get us out of sight of the coast and then take a break.* Chenda repositioned herself. She sat up and crossed her legs. She found that pressing her palms flat on either side of her helped to connect with the water elements around her. Once she persuaded the water to push the tub clear of all the pier pilings, she had the water draw them due west. After 20 minutes, beads of

277

sweat rolled down her face. She started to feel weak, even though she still brimmed with elemental power. She felt lightheaded. She needed to take a break. She pulled back her power and the pickle tub bobbed to the surface of the Kohlian Sea.

Chenda despaired for a little light. She pulled up her dress and rummaged around in several pockets in her pouchbelt until she finally found that for which she was looking: Edison's pocket watch. She wound it several times and opened it. The dim light within, just barely enough to illuminate the face of the watch, shattered the oppressive darkness around her.

"Ah..." she sighed.

"Why are we stopping?" Candice asked.

"I'm getting dizzy," Chenda said, risking a few words out loud. She was much relieved that it didn't cause a tidal wave or other disaster.

"Me, too," said Fenimore. "What's happening?"

"We're breathing up all the air. We need some more oxygen," Candice said. "I've got the stuff we talked about if you have the spark."

"Sure, I'm free." Chenda giggled.

Candice pulled a bowl and a narrow metal tube out of a bag tied to her waist. She set the tube into the bowl and handed a steel knife to Chenda.

"One spark should do it; after that, the reaction should be able to keep itself going," Candice said weakly.

Chenda held the knife point over the white crystals in the bowl and let off a single spark. The tube ignited, and sparkled faintly.

"Wait a second, how is burning something going to create more oxygen in here?" Fenimore asked. "Doesn't fire consume oxygen?"

"Usually, but this is granulated sodium chlorate. Ahy-Me did a fine job finding all of the things I needed to mix up this batch. There's a bit of iron and a few other chemicals mixed in. Anyway, when sodium chlorate decomposes, it actually releases more oxygen that it takes to combust, which is good for us, sealed in this wee tube."

"Interesting. Why didn't we just light that up when we got

278

started and save ourselves the dizzy spell?" Fenimore asked.

"Well..." Candice said, looking sheepish. "I'm not entirely sure it won't kill us. One of the minor byproducts of it is chlorine, and I did see about adding some barium peroxide to absorb the chlorine, but who knows if I got the mixture right and then there could be other impurities in the-"

"Fine," Fenimore interrupted. "Working without a net. I get it. I guess we just need to hurry on to our destination and get out of this stinking tube. Chenda? How are you doing? Can you get a fix on where the patrols are?"

Chenda shook her head to clear it. "Sure. I think the oxygen generator is working fine, Candice. My head is starting to clear. You're brilliant." She focused her thoughts outward, combing the water around her for anything large and metallic. "Mu-huh," she said. "There are three patrol boats within five miles of here."

"Are they coming closer?" Fenimore asked tensely.

"Who cares?" said Candice. "Submerge us and let's be gone. The bigger question is can you find Crider Island without seeing it?"

"I think so. If I am focused on the element of water, I think an island would look like a big hole in the sea to me. If I get within about ten miles of it, I could see it."

Chenda sighed. "This is really hard, trickling the power out slowly enough to pull us there. I can't say that I like it much. I'll get us started again, and you tell me about the island. If there is something specific about it I can focus on, it might help me home in on it."

Chenda closed her eyes and concentrated, releasing her power to make the water below the surface pull them along. Once she got the tub moving, she settled in to the excruciating task of keeping the power flowing from her in a steady stream. The power always wanted to burst forth from her in a rush. For the most part, she preferred to just chuck it out that way, but control was the necessity of the moment. She was happy to hear Fenimore start talking. She knew his voice would soothe her as she struggled through this tedious task.

"From Nivarta, Crider Island is west by west-northwest.

So tack in that general direction," he said.

Chenda clenched her teeth to reply. "Do I look like sailor to you? Speak plainly!"

Fenimore chuckled and said, "You say you have had us heading due west, right? Focus your attention mostly to the right as we go along. That's where the hole in the sea will appear. Relatively speaking, Crider Island is very close to the Tugrulian coast - only about 65 miles or so."

"Speaking of points of the compass," he said, "How do you know which direction we are heading?"

"Oh, I have a compass in my pocket." Chenda said.

"Have you been looking at it in the dark?" Fenimore pursued.

"Well no, I can just hear it pointing north. Don't ask."

"I find that strangely intimidating," he said.

"Get over it," Candice said. "Now, more on Crider Island. What's it like?"

"Oh, it's nice. It's got beautiful sienna beaches and smugglers love it, since it's practically inside the Empire, and it's the kind of place where lots of deals go down. Like Atoll Belles, it's neither Tugrulian nor Republic, and both nations know that the other would start a war if one pushed to control it. It's got several airship piers, but they are high up the mountain. They've got an interesting incline system to transport cargo to and from the airslips and boat docks. I've been there several times, and I know a few people there who can help us if we are too late to meet the *Brofman....*"

Fenimore sat distracted then, thinking of all the details to attend to once they reached Crider Island and praying to any god that could hear that Captain Endicott's airship would still be there. His worries piled up. Where should they try to come ashore? When? How should he contact the *Brofman* without drawing attention? How many Tugrulian spies would be on the lookout for them on the island? If they miss the *Brofman*, what should they sell to secure accommodations? If the gods smile, and they reach the airship, what would he tell the captain and crew about Verdu? Verdu. What about Verdu? What was that ridiculous scene he made with Chenda back at the warehouse?

"How could he do that?" Fenimore said mostly to himself.

"Are you fretting over Verdu staying behind?" Candice asked.

"Um, yes," Fenimore lied.

"I think he knows what he is doing but-" Candice said.

Chenda interrupted, "This is a topic that is rather distracting, and I would much rather focus on the matter at hand, especially as I feel my abilities are highly taxed at the moment. Please, I beg you, let us discuss this at another time."

"Of course," Fenimore agreed too quickly. He intended to never bring up the topic again.

"So," Candice asked, searching for any topic to break the tension, "How fast are we moving?"

"It's hard to say," Chenda replied. "I know we are moving faster than if we were just drifting along, but not nearly as fast as the patrol boat that just passed over us."

"That would put us in the range of six-eight miles an hour," Fenimore said, sounding impressed. "Do you think that you can keep pushing us along for eight or ten hours?"

Chenda bit her lip. "Probably. Do I have a choice?"

"Will we have enough air?" Fenimore asked Candice.

"Maybe," she replied. "How close will the Tugrulian patrols get to Crider Island?"

"Close, and possibly on," Fenimore said.

"Probably, maybe, possibly, close. I love a little certainty in life." Candice quipped. She rested her back against one side of the pickle tub and stretched her legs out on the other side, reclining as much as the diameter of the tube would allow. "Well, it looks as if we have several more hours to kill, and much oxygen to conserve. I think I will take a nap if no one has any objections."

"Go right ahead," Chenda replied.

Candice threw an arm over her eyes and, in moments, was breathing softly and evenly, sound asleep.

Chenda sighed. "Fen, if you want to drop off as well, I can handle the ship." She chuckled slightly.

Fenimore, who had been resting with his back against the pickle tub's lid, slowly slid forward on his knees to where Chenda sat in the middle of the metal tube, her back to him and legs crossed.

"I'd rather talk, if it's not too distracting," he said.

"Sure," she said. "Can we sit back to back? I'd like to lean up against something. I'm starting to ache." Fenimore turned, and Chenda leaned into him. "Better?" he asked.

Much, she thought at him.

Minutes passed in silence, neither of them moving.

For a man who wants to talk, you aren't saying much.

"I noticed that myself," Fenimore whispered. "I have things I want to say. But I know that when I do, it will sound comprehensively wrong. I think, on those matters, I may just prefer to keep silent."

I think I understand. How about I do some of the talking for you, and you can just agree if I get close to the right words?

"We can try that, I guess."

Verdu is on your mind, yes?

"In many ways."

Don't be angry with him. Once Pranav Erato was gone, someone had to close us in here. He felt strongly that he had more he wanted to give back in Tugrulia. It was like a calling to him. Don't hold it against him.

"I'm not angry about that," Fenimore said softly.

You're upset that he kissed me.

Fenimore moaned. "Yes."

Fen, don't be. I'm not.

"Do you love him?" Fenimore nearly choked on the question.

How do I answer that? What kind of person would I be not to love someone who has sacrificed for me the way he has? You all have? You, Verdu and Candice. The gods themselves tied you three to me, and I to you. I love you all, deeply and forever. But...

"But?"

Verdu, like you, I suspect, fell IN love with me.

Chenda let the thought hang in silence, and then she asked. *Did I guess that right? Are you in love with me?*

The quietest word in the history of forever escaped Fenimore's lips, "Yes."

The words bubbled out of him in a quiet panic, as if he could negate the truth of his most recent word by quickly adding a hundred more. "Ah, see, here's the part that I worried about coming out all wrong. I really hate not being able to explain, you see, because, crap, Verdu, my best friend, my brother? How can I be jealous of how he feels when I'm right there with him, and he - "

STOP! Chenda shouted into Fenimore's head. He pulled his lips together tightly and covered his face with his hands. He radiated embarrassment. If Fenimore hadn't been in a dark metal tube 20 feet under water, he would have been running as fast as his feet would carry him.

Just... listen for a minute. Remember when I nearly drowned, and I had my vision, you know, with Edison? I told you then everything relevant to you, but there was more, and I think it will help you understand. He told me something else that day; well, he showed me, really. He said that I was the love of his life, but he was not the love of mine. I needed to look for it. He showed me the feeling that would let me know I had found the passion – the true love the gods had set aside for me...

"Oh," Fenimore said in sudden realization. "The yummy noises?"

Yes. Chenda blushed. She was grateful he could not see her face, too.

I think the gods clued Edison in to my destiny, that it was going to have costs and rewards. He wanted to make sure I didn't get lost in the loneliness and the pain of being the Pramuc. We've seen so much suffering. But the promise of finding the love of my life, it's kept me going through the really hard parts, the responsibility, the heads on the pikes, finding my mother and then losing her again, even the plain, bone weariness. I need something to live for.

"So," Fenimore asked sheepishly, "it's Verdu, then?"

Chenda laughed sorrowfully inside. *Are you sure you want to hear about this?*

"I have to know..."

Well, kissing Verdu was nice, very enjoyable. He's rather good at it, I think. But no, he's not the one. I'm grateful we tried, but knowing that my counterpart is out there, I can't in good conscience mark time with Verdu. So, no, he is not the one I am looking for.

Fenimore didn't realize he had been holding his breath until Chenda delivered her verdict, then he let it all out in a rush, muttering, "Oh, thank the gods."

You were set to be monstrously jealous, weren't you? Chenda said in a teasing tone.

"Who, me? No," Fenimore lied with a slight chuckle. "What now?"

I think I am going to have to wait until you summon up the courage to kiss me yourself, then I will know if you are the man I'm searching for.

Fenimore slid sideways, pulling his back slowly away from Chenda's and twisting his torso to bring his face closer to her ear. "Kiss you...," he whispered, his breath tickling her. "Hmm. Not just yet. But I'm going to take your words as an invitation."

He slowly and gently stroked his finger down the nape of her neck, sending a shiver down her spine. "If I only get one shot at convincing you that I could be the right one, I want to be sure there are no distractions, and perhaps someplace a little less... pickle tub."

"Fair enough," she said aloud. "But the way the gods laugh about these things, I doubt it really matters."

Fenimore settled his back against hers again. "Well, it matters to me. I'm a traditionalist: mood, moment, whatnot."

Chenda sighed and pushed the little tube along in silence for a moment.

Fen?

"Yes, Chenda."

I don't want you to take this the wrong way, but I love it when you touch me.

"How could one possibly take that the wrong way?"

I don't want it to sound like a promise or something. I don't want to set you up to get hurt or confuse anything. Sitting here with you, I don't know really what the connection is or if it means anything. But I believe I'm safe when I feel you there

284

beside me.

"Maybe that's why I'm your soldier, and not your saint."

Let's not talk about Verdu for now, okay? It's just too painful. I miss him already.

"I couldn't agree more." Fenimore turned around, and sat on his heels. He scooted forward until he had a knee to each side of Chenda's hips. He rested his hands on her waist; she shivered again. "Is this too distracting?"

No, not yet.

He slid his hands forward until they passed over her midsection, pulling her back against his chest. He rested his cheek against her hair. "Feeling safer?"

Uh-huh.

"All right then, I won't let go," he said, brushing his lips against her ear and across the back of her neck.

Ahhh...

He held her there in the quiet darkness for hours, never moving. Chenda found that with Fenimore's arms around her, concentrating on the slow release of her power into the water surrounding them was less tedious. The touch of his skin grounded her body, while her mind worked endlessly to measure out a precise and steady stream that pushed the little makeshift submarine along. That, and he smelled so nice.

Candice eventually awoke and looked to her companions on the other side of the sparking make-shift oxygen generator.

"Awkward," Candice said. "I have the sudden feeling I should be someplace else, but can't seem to find an exit."

Fenimore laughed, but didn't let go of Chenda. "He's anchoring me," she said aloud.

"Oh, so THAT's what the kids are calling it these days," Candice said under her breath. "Are we there yet?"

"Almost," Chenda said. "I think I see the hole in the sea that I have been looking for. Does Crider Island have a bit of peninsula that points to the southeast?"

"Yes, that's it!" Fenimore gave Chenda a squeeze. "You are brilliant!"

"I'm just glad it's the island we are looking for, because we are going to have to stop there no matter what. I'm almost

completely tapped out - of the gods-given power and my own."
Chenda said.

Don't let go of me, she thought to Fenimore. *If you do, I
may collapse.*

"I got you, baby," he whispered in her ear.

"Where do you want me to beach us?" Chenda asked out
loud again.

"I think it's best if we get ourselves out of the water the
same way we got in: let's aim for the pier on the eastern side of
the island. It's busy, and hopefully, no one will notice us. We can
blend in and disappear."

Chenda started to scan the water for boats above them,
and she found several. She followed one that had the basic shape
of a cargo ship, and it led her toward the pier. She slowly
squeezed the pickle tub between two pilings under the center pier
and pulled in her control of her power. She slumped back against
Fenimore.

Oh, gods, I feel ill. That was so difficult.

"I bet. I can't imagine pushing us underwater all this way.
You are impressive!"

Candice, ever practical, looked around and said, "OK,
who packed the can opener?"

Everyone laughed. Chenda lay as limp as a rag-doll
against Fenimore. "I'll open our little tub in a second, let me catch
my breath. Fenimore, tell us what the plan is."

"Even though the island is neutral, it's still crawling with
Tugrulians. We can assume that most of them are going to be on
the lookout for Chenda. Keeping you out of sight would be my
preference. We've got to get over to the airslip tower, but I am
sure that there will be folks looking for us there. We need to be
pretty sure that the *Brofman* will be there when we go, or we're
going to get noticed. Besides, we will need to buy tickets for the
incline to get us up to the airship tower. There is a cafe in town
where a lot of Republic expatriates like to hobnob. I know the
owner, and I think he still owes me a favor. If Captain Endicott
has been through, this guy will know it, and I trust him. That will
be our first stop."

Fenimore looked down at Chenda's exhausted face.

"Ready?"

I need you to help me. I'm just so tired, I can't lift my arms. I need a knife, too.

He pulled his knife out of his boot and pressed it into Chenda's hand. He lifted her up, cradled in one of his arms, and helped her press the knife to the top of the pickle tub. "On three," she said weakly, "We make a quick circle."

"One, Two, THREE!" Chenda sparked the dagger and released what little power she had left as Fenimore swirled her arm in a smooth circle. The metal of the tub melted where the knife point touched it, and a circle of hot metal fell into the tub with a soft clang. The makeshift vessel was flooded with bright sunshine and the sounds of commerce from the pier above.

"Ha HA! We did it!" Fenimore cheered, gently shaking the girl in his arms. Chenda didn't move. "Chenda?" He put a finger under her chin and tipped her head back. She was unconscious.

"No, no, no - NO!" Fenimore rubbed his hand on her cheek. He looked to Candice with desperate eyes.

"What happened?" Candice asked.

"I can't get her to wake up!" Fenimore wailed.

"Calm down and let's see what we can do," Candice ordered. "Put her down."

He laid her on the floor of the tub and took a closer look at Chenda in the daylight. She was pale, and her closed eyes rested in dark circles, but she was breathing.

"She's exhausted, but I don't know if there is anything much we can do for her. We need to get her some food and water, that's for sure, and I think fresh air," Candice assessed. "How much attention is it going to draw for us to carry an unconscious woman across the pier?"

"Here? Some, but not enough to make us particularly memorable. I think we need to keep moving," Fenimore said.

"No time like the present. You get up there and I'll push."

A few minutes later, Fenimore had dragged Chenda to a secluded spot between two market stalls on the smooth, sun bleached boards of the pier. He leaned her against a pile of fishing nets and Candice arranged a veil over Chenda's face. She turned

287

to Fenimore. "Let's go."

He picked up Chenda as Candice gathered the last of her things into her shoulder bag, and the three of them stepped out onto the bustling boardwalk. He looked down through the slit in the veil over Chenda's eyes, and he worried that this could be more than exhaustion. Had they asked Chenda to do too much? Was Chenda permanently damaged from the strain of this undersea voyage?

A few people gave sidelong glances at Fenimore, but no one seemed to find the trio exceptionally noteworthy. They walked off the pier and into the small, rough looking waterfront area at the base of a tall mountain.

"Are there no taxis?" Candice asked. "Like the ones back at Atoll Belles?"

"A few, but I don't see any. Besides I don't have any money. I'm going to have to see what we've got to sell or trade so we can get some water. Don't worry, Laura's Folly isn't too far. We can walk it."

They made their way deeper into the small town. The farther they got from the bustling wharf, the more pleasant the neighborhoods became. After ten minutes, they turned a corner into a beautiful square with russet colored cobblestone sidewalks. A fountain bubbled in the center, and several little shops and cafes lined the plaza. Fenimore made a bee-line to the closest one.

The colorful sign out front read *Laura's Folly: A bit of Kite's Republic Far from Home*. Two steps inside the door, Candice believed it. Every smell, every picture, every accent and face screamed *Republic*! Candice's mouth watered as she passed a table of westerners eating platters of beer battered fish and chips, hamburgers and finger sandwiches.

Fenimore walked past the bar and trust his chin out in greeting as he walked by. "Hey, Ryan. Can you help a fellow out?"

The barkeep, hearing his name, looked up from the taps and gave a surprised look at Fenimore's retreating back. He wiped his silver spectacles with a bar towel, then followed Fenimore to an empty booth at the back of the cafe. "Fenimore Dulal. Well, I'll be. Look what the cat dragged in!"

Fenimore sat down on the narrow bench and cradled Chenda in his arms. "Yep. Seems like business is good for you. How's the wife?"

"Great! Never better. We have a beautiful daughter now, that's new since the last time you visited. And you're lookin' so tan. So, yeah, we gonna keep up the small talk, or do you want to tell me about the unconscious Tugrulian girl you're cuddlin' in my cafe, and exactly what you want me to do about it?"

"Ah, Ryan, you always did like to get straight to the point. The Tugrulian behind you is Professor Candice Mortimer, of the Geology Department at Kite's Republic University. I believe she would be most grateful for some food and drink, and perhaps a new set of clothes. The exhausted one in my arms is my wife, and she could use some of the same as well."

"Are you calling in your last favor to me?" Ryan asked tapping a finger on his pointy chin expectantly.

"Yes."

"Done!" the thin man said with giggling glee. "Get those stupid veils off them right away. Tugrulians are bad for business." He hustled off behind the bar and disappeared into a back room.

"This place," Candice marveled, stuffing her veil into her bag, "is a little slice of HEAVEN! I didn't realize how much I missed the Republic till I stepped in here. The people look so varied! They are eating things that don't come out of a cave, and favors are currency!" Candice gushed, "and I smell beer!"

Fenimore, only half listening to Candice, made a weak half smile. He pulled Chenda's veil off and tossed it to Candice. He brushed his fingers through Chenda's short, dirty hair, trying to make some improvement in her appearance. Mostly, he finally admitted, he just wanted to keep touching her. He rocked her back and forth as Candice babbled on joyfully about the Republic.

For as much as the professor had relaxed, Fenimore didn't dare. He knew he was nowhere near the Republic. Laura's Folly was a reminder of the homeland, but carried none of the rights or security. He tried to keep that tension from his fingers as he cupped his hand behind Chenda's neck.

Ryan appeared with an armload of varied bits of clothing. "Lost and Found," he said, handing the bundle to Candice.

289

"Washroom's through there," he said, pointing though a narrow doorway. "What can I have the cook prepare for you while you get westernized, professor?"

"Fish. Chips. Burger with cheese. Beer. Supply that and my ETERNAL devotion is yours, my good man." Candice trotted with the clothes toward the washroom.

"Same for me, please," Fenimore said, "And thanks."

"I'll put that order in and be back in a minute. You look like you need to talk." Ryan turned and walked into the kitchen.

Alone with Chenda, Fenimore continued to rock her slowly. He rested his cheek on her forehead. "Come on, baby, open your eyes, just for a second."

No, Chenda thought at him petulantly, and snuggled into his chest, snoring softly. A wave of relief washed over him. "OK," he said. "I'll let you rest now that I know you are not in a coma."

When Ryan returned, settling on the bench on the far side of the table, Fenimore had relaxed considerably, and thought about what Ryan had said to him. "Wow. A daughter, congratulations. I'm an uncle now! Where is my sister, by the way?"

"Upstairs in the apartment. I sent one of the girls up to tell her you were here. She'll be down in a second. Laura's in the middle of feeding the baby. We named her Gretta, by the way."

"Gretta, how wonderful." Fenimore frowned slightly. "I hate to change the subject, but have you seen or heard from Captain Endicott?"

"Yes, he was here, oh, nine days ago, maybe. I was surprised to hear that you weren't with him anymore, and Verdu, too?" He glanced at Chenda. "Does she have something to do with that?"

"Everything, my friend," he said. "We parted company with Verdu very early this morning in Nivarta."

"Nivarta? What were you doing inside the Empire? Trying to get yourself killed? I hear all kinds of rumors coming out of there. Is it true civil war is brewing?"

"That's a good term for it. Verdu stayed behind to feed the fires for that particular war. Listen. Other than Endicott, if anyone comes asking about me or the ladies, you've not seen us. OK?"

290

"Whatever you say. He did say he planned on visiting again soon, if that helps."

He looked at Chenda. "Your sister is going to kill you for not sending word that you married."

"Well, I actually spoke too soon. It's hard to explain. Wishful thinking perhaps, but she's the one for me. I just need to convince her."

"Fenimore Dulal in love. Good luck with that," Ryan said.

Candice appeared at the table's edge, looking fresh and western.

"Ta-da!" she beamed. "The old me!" She frowned a little, laying the extra clothes on the table. "I was hoping for beer by now."

Ryan laughed, and left the bench. "Keep your pants on, I'm going."

Candice took Ryan's place on the bench. "Any change?"

"Um, yes. She got annoyed with me and now she's snoring."

"Oh, progress," Candice said with a smile.

Ryan returned with a tray heavy with food and two tall glasses of rich brown beer.

"Thank the gods and Kite's Republic," Candice exclaimed as she popped a few chips in her mouth. "Mmmm... fabulous."

"I brought some juice for the half-dead looking object of your desires," Ryan said, placing a frosty glass on the table near Chenda. "You know, for whenever she comes to."

The smell of hot, comforting food tugged at Chenda's sleepy brain. She stirred in Fenimore's arms, and opened one eye. "Fen?"

"Yeah, honey?" he said in a soothing tone. "I'm right here. Bet you are starving." He helped her to sit up and pressed the juice into her hands. She took a sip, then drank deeply, looking around. Her eyes settle on Fenimore.

"Did I wake up in Coal City?" she asked.

"No, just the next best thing," Fenimore said.

"I fell asleep in your arms, and I woke up there too. That's a first," she said as she eyed the hamburger.

"Eat," Candice ordered, a slice of onion half hanging from

291

the corner of her mouth.

Chenda dove in, still tired, but becoming more alive with each bite. "Oh! Gods in heaven," she said, her mouth full. "When did I eat last? I have no idea..."

Chenda, Candice and Fenimore ate happily. By the time they finished, Fenimore's sister joined them at the table, and introductions were made all around. Chenda could see the resemblance between the two, especially in the sandy hair and light eyes. Laura was several years younger, but still looked at her brother discerningly.

"So, will you be visiting long?" she said.

"No, we are about to go. We need to get back on the *Brofman* and head west. You might want to think about moving a little farther from the Tugrulian Empire yourself. If civil war breaks out, you might not be safe here."

"I'll think about it," she said with a sniff. "Why don't you come upstairs and see the baby?"

"I'm sorry," he said, his voice dripping with regret. "We have to go now. Kiss my niece for me." He stood and wrapped his arms around his sister. "Take care. I will come back when I can."

Chenda pulled a tattered western gown over her Tugrulian dress and scooted to the end of the bench where Fenimore's hand waited to pull her to standing. "Ready?" he asked.

"Have to be," she answered and she pulled herself to standing. Everything hurt. She started walking on her wobbly legs. Fenimore wrapped an arm around her waist to steady her.

Chenda thought to Fenimore *Do we need to leave some money for the clothes and the dinner?*

"I don't think we have any." Fenimore said.

I've got about ten thousand in Republic currency in my pouchbelt.

"Mostly, that's just colored paper here," he replied with a smile. "Ryan does a good bit of trade with merchants from the West, but they all still do business in local currency. Maybe we can get a few coins for it. We're better off to pawn some things and buy ourselves some tickets for the Crider Incline."

They walked down the street toward the mountain. Fenimore guided them to a jewelry store on the way, where he ducked in with several of the trinkets from Chenda's pouchbelt. He returned a few minutes later.

"Well," Candice asked. "How did you do?"

"We got enough," he said, and he pulled Chenda along the street toward the Crider Island Incline Station, where they bought tickets and waited for the next car. Fenimore kept looking up at the sky, and the thin outline of the airslips above.

"Is she there?" Chenda asked. "Can you see the *Brofman*?"

Fenimore pressed his lips into a thin line. "No. Not yet."

Finally, the incline car arrived, and they piled on with the other passengers. Chenda leaned against the glass window and looked out at the mountain as giant cables pulled the small car upward. As they rose higher and higher, she could see the beautiful sandy beaches to the east. She held Fenimore's hand.

This place is lovely. I see why your sister likes it here.

"I thought my sister was insane to leave the Republic, but I think she is happy here. Who am I to judge? I just worry about what's coming to this island if Verdu succeeds."

I'm worried about what will happen if he fails.

The incline jerked to a halt at the end of its track, and everyone filed off. Fenimore led Chenda and Candice to the passenger elevators leading up to the Airship Terminal. When they reached the top, Fenimore made his way to the information counter, and put on his most charming smile.

"Excuse me," he said sweetly to the pretty girl behind the counter. "Do you have a reservation today for an airship named *Brofman*?"

The girl looked down at her ledger. "Yes," she said. "Today at 2:00 p.m. Renting a slip for one night. Slip 23."

"Thank you," Fenimore said, turning and looking at a large clock on the wall. It was ten minutes of two. Fenimore smiled and walked toward slip 23.

"I think we are going to make it," he said excitedly.

Candice sighed with relief. "That's great, because I am ready to go."

Fenimore's smile started to fade as he looked around the assembly areas near several of the slips they passed. He pulled

293

Chenda closer to him, using his hand to pull her face into his chest. To the casual observer, they looked like a cuddling couple, but the tension in Fenimore's hands put Chenda on alert.

What's wrong?

"There are far too many Tugrulians lingering up here," he said, "Keep walking right past number 23." He hissed to catch Candice's eye, and shot her a warning look. She nodded, and followed her companions more closely. They slowed their pace slightly, as they made a complete circuit of the terminal. As they approached number 23 for the second time, Fenimore saw the *Brofman* closing in on the airslip. He leaned close to Chenda's ear and quickly started whispering instructions.

"You're going to have to run for it, I think. So, here is how we are going to do this. I'm going to let you go ahead of me, and I want you to take Candice by the hand. Run out the door to slip 23 – all the way to the end. With your free hand, put one finger in the air and wave it in a circle. That's the signal for Endicott to get the *Brofman* turned around and get out of here. Run straight to the end of the pier, understand? He'll get you. I'll be right behind you, I just need to be sure that no one comes out that door after us." Fenimore's voice was commanding. "Take Candice and run. NOW!"

Chenda reached back and grabbed Candice by the hand and ran to the door to slip 23. As she stepped out, the cold wind hit her like a slap. Chenda could see Lincoln in the bow of the *Brofman*, preparing to hop over with a mooring line. Chenda waved wildly at him, then made the signal to turn the ship. Lincoln looked puzzled for a moment, then dropped the rope and turned to signal to the wheelhouse. As Chenda and Candice ran to the end of the pier, the *Brofman* quickly turned. It was now perpendicular to the end of the pier, and sinking slightly. Germer appeared at the mid-ship rail.

"Jump, my girls! JUMP!" he called.

Chenda could feel Candice start to shy away, so she planted her feet at the last second and pulled Candice forward, flinging her off the end of the pier at Germer's waiting arms. Candice landed with little grace, but she was aboard. Chenda backed up a few steps, ran forward and leaped. She sprawled

294

across the deck, and Stanley was there, helping her to her feet.

"Fenimore," she pleaded. "Where's Fen?" She looked over the railing of the *Brofman* as the airship slowly passed the end of slip 23. She saw Fenimore running at full speed toward the end of the pier, pain etched on his face and a bright bloodstain on the front of his shirt.

"NO!" Chenda yelled, watching as Fenimore threw himself off the end of the pier. His eyes locked on hers as he sailed through the air, his hand reaching for the rail of the *Brofman* and not quite reaching it. Chenda screamed as Fenimore disappeared below the airship.

Chapter 22
THE WELCOMING REPUBLIC

The *Brofman* accelerated and began to gain altitude. Chenda scrambled to her feet and ran to the railing. She had one leg over when Stanley tackled her and wrestled her to the deck.

"STOP!" he yelled. "Germer is coming with a bitter-end for you. Be still!"

Chenda thrashed and sobbed. "Fenimore!" she screamed. Her head was spinning with panic. She couldn't imagine the *Brofman* without Fenimore. In her mind's eye, all she could see was his broken body smashed on the mountain below. Chenda fought against Stanley's grip, screaming "FENIMORE!"

"What?" Fenimore answered as he pulled himself over the side of the ship's railing, the bloodied aft mooring line in his hands. He collapsed next to Chenda, who kicked Stanley in the shins until he let her go. She grabbed Fenimore around the neck as he lay on the deck, panting and still clutching the rope that saved his life. She buried her face in his chest, sobbing.

"I thought you fell!" she cried. "I was so scared! You're bleeding."

"Yep," Fenimore said. "That's what happens when one of the three Tugrulian thugs you're fighting stabs you with your own boot knife." Despite pain and the breathlessness of exertion, Fenimore managed to sound a little embarrassed.

He reached an arm around Chenda's waist and tied the mooring line tightly around her. "Non-negotiable," he said. "You set foot on the deck of the *Brofman*, you wear a safety line."

Chenda laughed through her tears. *You're always looking out for me.*

"Always," he said placing a single finger on her cheek. "OK. I need a doctor."

Chenda looked down at Fenimore's shirt. Blood was flowing out of a deep wound in his side.

"Kingston! Somebody get Kingston!" she called.

Candice appeared by her side, pulling Chenda back so that Stanley and Germer could haul Fenimore to his feet and help him make his way below decks. Chenda wanted to follow, but she couldn't untie the knot in the mooring line fastened around her. Her fingers were shaking too much.

"Chenda, calm down," Candice said reaching for the rope. Her fingers quickly loosened the knot.

Captain Endicott opened the wheelhouse door and called out to them, "Hold on, I'll come help." He jumped down and grasped each lady firmly by the arm. At the top of the steps, he released Chenda and she flew down the stairs. Candice however, he wouldn't let go of.

"Welcome back," he said, relief evident in his every feature. "I was worried about you."

Candice threw her hands around his neck and squeezed. "I missed you, too."

"Come on up to the wheelhouse and tell me all about it," he offered. "And I'm really hoping you don't throw up this time."

"Your lips to the gods' ears," Candice replied.

"How about my lips to yours?" the captain said, his eyes smiling.

"That," Candice said, "is something we can negotiate."

Chenda flew to the end of the end of the passageway and into the galley. Fenimore was stretched out on the table with Kingston already at work suturing his patient. Germer, Lincoln and Stanley all stood back, not wanting to look at the bloody wound, but all unwilling to be the first to leave.

Chenda quickly assessed the situation, and said, "Thank you all so much for helping us aboard. I'm so sorry we've made a mess of deck, the rope and so on. I'll be happy to go up there and take care of the mess just as soon as I check on Fenimore here."

They all started speaking at once, "Oh, we can do that."

"Wouldn't hear of you cleaning up." "We'll get right on that." Germer, Lincoln and Stanley fell over themselves to trying to be helpful and productive elsewhere.

Chenda settled into a chair across from where Kingston stood working, and she held Fenimore's hand. His eyes met hers.

"You're a mess," he said.

"You're the one who's trailed blood all over the ship." She smiled and pressed the back of Fenimore's hand against her chin. They stared at each other for a moment, until Kingston cleared his throat.

"Hello, Kingston," Chenda said without taking her eyes off of Fenimore's face.

"Oh, well hello, Chenda. So glad you could bring Fenimore back in such fine shape. I was thinking that all I needed to make my day complete would be a stab wound after lunch. Thrilled you could oblige."

"He's making jokes," Fenimore said. "That means it's not too serious."

"Good," Chenda replied as a tear of relief rolled down her cheek. "Shame on you for scaring me like that. I thought you'd fallen to your death."

"I would have, but the aft mooring line was dangling behind the ship for some reason. I caught the end of it. It was truly lucky." He ran a finger across the dark circles under her eyes. "How are you hanging in there? You still look exhausted. Here. Lay your head down." He patted his shoulder.

Chenda rested her cheek on his warm skin and closed her eyes. For a minute she listened to his heart and the sounds of Kingston stitching the wound in Fenimore's side, then she slipped into a deep and dreamless sleep.

When she awoke, she realized she was alone, and it was freezing. Lying on her side in the familiar, boxy, cramped bottom bunk, she pulled her knees up to her chest, shaking. It didn't help. *Clothes*, she thought, *I need more clothes*. She scrambled out of bed and over to the nameless cupboard that had been hers just 20 days ago. There was nothing much in there to keep her warm. She looked up and saw Verdu's name on the door. She hesitated, but a spasm of chill racked her again.

She opened the cupboard and pulled on two of Verdu's heavier shirts. She cinched them around her with a bitter-end belt. She turned back to look at the bunks. Kingston, Stanley and Germer were fast asleep, but Spencer, Lincoln and Fenimore's beds were empty. And, of course, Verdu's.

She missed Verdu a lot. She could smell him on the shirts she had liberated, and that made her feel his loss more keenly. She worried about how he was managing as she walked across the passageway to the galley, looking for Fenimore. He wasn't there. She went back to the passageway and up the stairs to the main deck. She attached a bitter-end tether to her belt and stepped out onto the ice cold boards. She longed for her aeronaut boots and flight coat. She saw Fenimore standing in his usual spot in the bow, and she tip-toed up beside him.

"Hey, sleepyhead." He reached an arm out to wrap around her shoulders, and winced slightly as the stitches in his side made themselves known.

Careful, she thought to him. *We don't want to have to go wake Kingston to fix what he has already fixed.*

Fenimore, not wanting to be treated like an invalid, let the remark go by. "You've been asleep for almost 14 hours. Are you going to cause an earthquake or something? Shouldn't you go boil some air?"

Yes, I thought I would go make the wind blow behind us, see if we can drift a little closer to the Republic before the sun comes up. Do you feel well enough for a walk to the rear of the ship?

"I'll follow you anywhere," he said, lacing his fingers with hers.

They ambled to the stern, where Fenimore stepped aside, giving Chenda room to work. She focused her power, and released it. Giant gusts rolled toward the ship and pushed it westward.

"Feel better?" Fenimore asked.

"I do." Chenda replied. "It usually feels pretty good to dump out that pent up power. I always feel it trying to escape me. Now that I've let it all go, I feel most like myself."

The *Brofman* drifted along in the predawn blush, a speck

floating in a gentle purple sky. Soon, the ship would spring to life again when the sun cleared the horizon. But for now, as far as Chenda cared, the whole world slumbered and was at peace. She turned her attention to Fenimore, whose gaze was already locked on her.

He took a step closer to her and he reached one hand out. She took his hand in both of hers, lightly tracing a finger over his bruised and scratched knuckles. "You gave those Tugrulians all you had yesterday, didn't you?" She met his eyes as she gently kissed each knuckle."

"I just put hands on them before they could lay a hand on you. I regret that one of them noticed the knife in my boot before I remembered to use it. I was far too fist-oriented in that fight." Fenimore recognized he had started to babble, so he pulled her close to his chest and stroked her hair. He took in a deep breath.

"I'm having a little trouble stirring up that courage you've been waiting for," Fenimore said, his chin resting on the top of her head.

"Why is that, do you suppose?" she asked. "After all, I'm right here, without distraction. Beautiful setting. I could stretch the truth and say I'm even well rested. But I can't imagine I could ever be more willing to give us a try than I am right now."

"Yes, I can tell," he said, "And I think I rather like the way things have been between us of late. But if I kiss you, I mean really kiss you, the way I have been wanting to... Well, then it's all over. One way or the other, you'll decide if I'm the one you've been promised. I'm afraid of failing. It's a lot of pressure for a fellow like myself, someone profoundly in love with you. If you tell me afterward I am not meant for you, I don't think I will be able to let you go. Not with any grace, that is."

"Hmm. Perhaps we shouldn't try then," Chenda said as she lifted her chin and looked up into his smoky gray eyes.

"Trying could just ruin everything," he breathed, his lips touching the end of her nose. He held her there a few seconds more, then moaned, "I think I'm really going to enjoy screwing this up."

He brought his lips to Chenda's, freeing his desire for her, a fervor she welcomed and absorbed. As his arms wrapped

301

around her, lifting her feet off the floor, waves of tingling energy prickled through her skin, and danced down her spine. She shivered and laced her fingers together behind his neck. He lifted her up further and plopped her on a large crate. His lips traced over her chin and jaw. Willingly, she moved with him as he arranged her limbs around his body, one arm around his neck, the other around his back. She wrapped a leg around his waist. She wanted to embrace every part of him, and never let go. With every kiss, she wanted two more. Each caress demanded another. She kissed his neck, wrapping her other leg around his middle, and he flinched, pulling back from her slightly. She gasped and released him.

Fenimore hunched over slightly and swayed a little. "Stitches," he said in a strangled pant.

"OH, my!" Chenda said, "Fen, I'm so sorry!"

He straightened up and leaned into the crate on which Chenda sat. As each tried to catch their breath, Fenimore put a hand on each of her thighs, and walked his fingers up to her hips. He pressed closer to her, kissing her chin, keeping his calm. Using his lips to tilt her head back, he breathed softly on her exposed neck, slowly dragging the tip of his nose up the line of her jaw until he reached her ear.

"Forget the stitches," he whispered. "I'd rather bleed to death than give this up right now."

She kissed him in agreement, unable to speak or even think in that moment, and she knew what she wanted to do with the rest of her life.

"Yummy," she whispered.

"Really?" Fenimore looked deeply into Chenda's eyes.

She brought her lips back to his, more slowly this time. She realized that there was no need to rush. She was certain.

Really, she answered him. *You didn't screw that up at all.*

Sunrise brought Chenda and Fenimore to a dramatic halt before they could get too much further in their joy. The first rays of the sun brought deckhands up from below. Chenda sighed, untangled herself from Fenimore and slid down from her crate-top perch. She pulled him out of the way of Stanley, Spencer and Lincoln, who hustled about their morning duties of shining and repositioning the photovoltaic tubes.

"Let me take a look at your stitches and see what damage we've done," Chenda ordered.

Fenimore loosened his flight coat. Even before he pulled his shirt up, Chenda could see blood seeping through the bandages and onto his shirt.

"Oh, drat," Chenda said. "Let's have Kingston take a look."

Hand in hand, they headed down to the galley. Kingston took one look at Fenimore's bloody shirt and fussed, "I'll go get some more tape and bandages." He also took the opportunity to lightly dope-slap Fenimore on the back of the head as he passed.

"My love," Fenimore said, enjoying the phrase immensely, "we need to talk about what has to happen next."

"Were you thinking marriage, or sex?" Chenda asked.

Fenimore blushed for a moment. "Um, I was thinking about when the *Brofman* docks in the Republic. But we can talk about the other options, too. I'm open to both."

Chenda giggled with embarrassment. "What's left for me in the Republic, really? Everything I want is right here. I love the *Brofman* almost as much as I love you."

"Really?" Fenimore asked.

"The *Brofman* is a great airship and the crew is-"

"NO!" Fenimore cut her off. "I mean, you love me? Really?"

Chenda kissed the end of his nose. "Yes, I do. I think I knew that a while ago, but up on the deck there, you sealed the deal. Does that make you happy?"

"I just like hearing you say it." Fenimore sighed, hating to get back to the topic at hand. "First of all, Candice has to go home. She *does* have a life to go back to there. But" he paused, thinking things through, "I also have some things I need to attend to as well."

"Of course," Chenda replied. "Just so long as we have some time to talk about those other matters."

"Oh, we will – repeatedly and often."

The *Brofman* crossed the Kohlian Sea in record time, thanks to Chenda's thrice daily bursts of tail wind. They even made a quick stop at Atoll Belles, where Captain Endicott paid his respects to Jason Belles at the card table at McNees's Opera House. Out of respect for Captain Taboda, Captain Endicott lost a considerable amount of money to Jason Belles. At the atoll, Fenimore acquired some fresh clothes, flight coats and aeronaut boots for Chenda, which made the remainder of the trip considerably more comfortable.

Just three days after leaping aboard the *Brofman* high above the paradise of Crider Island, Fenimore, Chenda and Candice stepped onto the airship pier at Terminal Station. They took the fancy elevator down to the bottom and walked onto the streets of Coal City. Fenimore looked at the Terminal Tearoom as they walked by and he slowed.

"What's the rush?" he said. "Let's have a little something to eat before we take Candice home, what do you say?"

The women looked at each other, nodding in agreement. Neither really cared about dinner, but they knew their time together was coming to an end. They were greedy to spend just a few more minutes together. The tearoom seemed a perfect place to end their adventure together.

"You ladies go find us a table, and I'm going to freshen up." Fenimore gave Chenda's hand a quick squeeze and he disappeared down a hallway that was labeled *Gentleman's Lounge*.

The Tearoom hummed with activity. Chenda and Candice made their way to the nearest empty table with three seats. Chenda marveled at the thought that it had only been a month since she had last been there, meeting Candice for the first time. The bustling waiters and brightly polished brass fixtures were just the same. So was the smell of exotic teas and sugary pastries. And yet, the whole world was different. She was different.

"So," Candice said. "Here we are again."

"Yes. You know I used to come here all the time. They have lovely spice cake."

"We should get some, then," Candice replied politely. "We've been halfway around the world together and run through miles of underground tunnels – some of which were collapsing. We've planted fields in the desert, and I still feel a bit closed in within this teashop. It's like the whole trip evaporates. Sad, really. The lawlessness of it. I wish I could publish it in some scholarly journal. Hmm."

"Candice, don't feel awkward. I'll remember our journey, and Fenimore will, too. It was grand," Chenda whispered. "Thank you for coming with me. I'd have never survived without you. You helped me to change my whole world. I'll never be able to thank you enough."

"Well, don't make a fool of yourself trying," Candice said, lightening the mood. "Just keep in mind you owe me a favor, a big one, I mean you will *always* owe me. Forever. Since I think you and Mr. Handsome will be trotting off into the great unknown in a bit, I'll expect you to check in with me from time to time so I can call in that perpetual favor we have between us. In fact, consider that my first cashing in -- you come back and see me regularly. Say 'yes'."

"Yes, Candice." Chenda said like a schoolgirl reciting lines.

"Fine. Now! Spice cake all around?" Candice asked.

By the time Fenimore had returned to the table, the air of seriousness between the women had melted into their usual witty banter. The three had all but finished tea when Candice looked up at the approaching form of her friend Henrietta.

"Man *alive!*" Candice shouted. "Professor Hoppingood! As I live and breathe, you are a sight for sore eyes."

"Candice!" The plump woman hustled across the crowded aisle and embraced her friend. "I despaired of ever seeing you again. But here you are! Oh, and Chenda! I'm so sorry to hear about your passing, I read about it in all the papers." She bobbed her head in the universal gesture of sympathy. "My condolences, and what a wonderful new haircut." Henrietta turned her attention to Fenimore, who hadstood politely when Henrietta approached the table. "Well, hello, Mr. ...?"

"Dulal." Fenimore said. "Pleased to meet you, Professor."

Candice recognized the salacious look in her best friend's eye, and pinched her on the elbow. "That one belongs to her," she warned, "And after her, he belongs to Captain Endicott, so don't bother getting in line."

Henrietta harrumphed and her lips sagged into a childish pout, which lasted for all of a second. She suddenly flapped her hands at Candice. "SO! What did you bring me?"

Candice turned to her companions at the table. "If you will excuse me," she said, "I see here an opportunity to gracefully take my leave of your company. No need for long tearful goodbyes at my apartment door. I love you both. Ta-ta!"

She picked up her small case, and stepped to Henrietta's side. "Funny you should ask what I brought you, Hen. Have you ever heard of *Chalk of Contentment*?"

"Ooh. That's sounds intriguing..."

The two professors, happily chatting away, walked arm in arm toward the exit of the Terminal Tearoom, and then vanished into the crowded streets of Coal City.

Chenda sighed as Fenimore signaled a waiter to bring the bill.

"It's just us then," she said.

"I'm okay with that," Fenimore said. He threw some cash on the table and took Chenda's hand. "Shall we?"

They leisurely walked out of the tearoom, and Fenimore stepped to the edge of the sidewalk to signal for a taxi.

"Where are we going?" Chenda asked.

"Jail," said a voice from behind them. "Fenimore Dulal, you're under arrest."

Chapter 23
AMENDS

Within a few heartbeats, both Chenda and Fenimore were in handcuffs and pushed into the back of a police van. Fenimore, who looked neither surprised nor upset, glanced meaningfully at Chenda. "Don't say anything or do anything. It will all be okay."

As the police vehicle bounced along, Chenda pressed her elbow against Fenimore, and began a game of twenty questions.

Blink once for 'yes' and tap your foot for 'no'. Can you do that?

Fenimore blinked.

You don't seem very upset. Did you know this was going to happen?

Blink.

Did you do something wrong?

Blink. Tap.

Which is it? Yes or No?

Fenimore rolled his eyes.

I'm asking the wrong questions.

Blink.

Should I bust us out of here?

Tap. Tap. Tap. Tap.

Before Chenda could ask any more questions, the van shuddered to a stop and Fenimore and Chenda were ushered out. They were in a secluded alleyway. A heavy steel door in the brown stone building nearest them stood open, and the policemen guided them in. They went down several flights of stairs and were placed in a small, dark paneled office. All of the officers, except one, left the pair. The last man unshackled Chenda, and then

Fenimore. "Wait here," the officer said, and then he left.

Chenda, frightened and confused, grabbed Fenimore's hand. *What's going on? Why are we here?*

Fenimore pulled Chenda close and whispered into her ear. "I'm here because I am an exceptionally good liar and manipulator. This is the part of my life that I am not particularly proud of, but is required of me. This, in part, is how I must make amends for the things I've done."

A door on the far side of the room opened and a tall, lean man with a silver mustache strode into the room. He was reading a document, and didn't look up until he was standing directly behind the desk.

"Agent Dulal, please have a seat." He gestured to one of the pair of leather seats facing the desk. "And you as well, Mrs. Frost."

Chenda sat, confused. She stared at Fenimore. *Agent Dulal?*

"Thank you for having us bring you in, Agent. What do you have to report?"

Chenda interrupted. "YOU are a SPY?"

Fenimore looked apologetically at Chenda. "For about 15 more minutes, yes." He turned his attention back to the man behind the desk.

"Verdu is in the Tugrulian Empire working with the Resistance toward the liberation of the people though a combination of theological grass roots networking and an exposure of the agricultural suppression conspiracy. I can confirm any rumors you may have heard about the destruction of the Dia Orella, and the mass executions of supporters of the Resistance."

The man with the silver mustache probed further. "What about this savior figure, I get reports about? Some Praw – mook?"

"It's real. A powerful figure. The Pramuc is nonpolitical -- not interested in the Republic, only the starving people of the Empire. The Resistance has rallied around the Pramuc, and Resistance will be keeping the heirarchy busy for awhile."

"Can you give us any description?"

"No," Fenimore said. "Look. Verdu is there. The groundwork is laid. At best, the Tugrulian leadership will be kept busy for the next ten years weeding out the Resistance and trying to neutralize this Pramuc character. At worst, the society collapses over there, and the tribes of the East go back to fighting among one another again over resources they just doesn't have. Either way, the best thing you can do is send seeds. Fuel the reemergence of surface agriculture there, and it will help the Republic." Fenimore paused, taking a long look at the man across the desk. "Now, I've done what we agreed to. So, I'm finished."

"And I'll let you think that for now, but Mrs. Frost here has a few actions to answer for. Let's start with some things about your husband's death."

Chenda tightened her lips. "Who's Mrs. Frost? I hear she died in a fire."

"Please, let's not play games...."

Chenda stood. "Oh, I'm not playing any games. And I'm done with answering questions. I'm done being bullied into owing people favors. I'm done with people telling me where to go and what to do." She picked up a paperclip from the edge of the desk in front of her, and she flipped it over and over in her fingers. Chenda's voice turned angry. "Spies, lies and riddles. Is that what this Republic has devolved to? Who are you anyway?" She thought about it for a moment and said, "Never mind, I don't care."

"Fen!" Her anger towards Fenimore crackled in her voice as she called him. "You are walking out of here with me."

Fenimore stood and walked to the door with Chenda. The man with the silver mustache yelled, "Hey, we're not finished here! Someone has to explain the dead body in the Frost mansion!"

Chenda whirled around, raising her hand. Sparks flew from the paperclip between her fingers. "The MAN whose body burned there was Daniel Frent. He died trying to kill Chenda Frost. I suggest you leave her alone, or you might just end up the same way." Chenda drizzled her power into a thin, flaming line that slowly circled around the room. "Now, do you want to challenge me?"

The man froze, watching the tongue of flame stop just inches from the end of his nose.

"We won't be seeing you again," Chenda said as she pulled her power back in. "Not me, not him. And don't even think of approaching anyone from the *Brofman*." Fenimore opened the office door and they walked out the way they had come in.

When they got to the street, Chenda grabbed Fenimore's elbow and started screaming her thoughts at him.

HOW COULD YOU BE A SPY! GODS! I FEEL LIKE YOU LIED TO ME! Chenda turned, made a fist, and punched Fenimore in the chest.

"OW!" Fenimore said. "That hurt a little."

"I am so tempted to set you on FIRE right now, Fenimore, don't tease me."

"Can I explain?" Fear crept into his eyes. Chenda fumed, but her resolve was crumbling. The way she felt about Fenimore, there was little chance she could shut him out.

"You can try," she said in a very warning tone.

"Remember the story I told you about how I came to the *Brofman*? About the pub fight I got into that put my school chum in a coma? Robert was his name, by the way. Like I said, I was sent to jail for that."

"A year, you said." Chenda glared at him. "Go on."

"Well, I was sentenced to 15 years. When that guy with the mustache came to me, and said he could fix it that I could get out after only a year, I made a deal. I became a watcher for the Republic. A spy. I thought I was a patriot. I wanted to make my amends to Robert by serving."

"Is that what Verdu meant about a deal with the devil?" she asked.

"Yes, Verdu knew all about my deal with the Republic. For a time, he helped me find information to pass on. He believed, as I did, the Republic was looking to help ease the suffering of the Tugrulian people. But the more I gave, the more they wanted. And the more I realized that the great Republic was really pretty shallow.

"My primary purpose, in the end, was to make sure the Empire was in *no* position to change. The balance between East and West, as far as the Republic is concerned, needs to stay frozen. For all we claim to be -- the moral and cultural leaders of the world -- we're still rather weak and petty."

He sighed. "That may be the most important fact that I uncovered as a Kiter spy. I guess that makes me just as shallow. I was willing to keep a nation of people oppressed and in starvation rather than go back to prison."

He looked at Chenda, "I'm sorry. I wish I could have told you. I never wanted to lie."

Chenda tucked her chin to her chest and bit her lip. "It's like a disease, this spying. It's infected so many around me. Edison was a spy, and so was my father."

Without looking, she held her hand out to Fenimore. He clasped it like a life preserver.

This isn't right. What the Republic is doing, we can't let it go on. You want to make amends? You want to get this situation back to right? We're going to go make that happen. You and me.

"How?" Fenimore asked, hopeful now for the first time.

"We'll just have to figure that out as we go," she said, her voice full of forgiveness.

"I'm sorry. I'm never going to keep anything from you again. I am such a fool to annoy the woman I love, especially when she can boil my liver from across the room."

"I love you too much," she said.

"I don't want to put you in any more danger," Fenimore said.

Chenda turned to him with a genuine smile. Her face had lost every trace of doubt, and, to Fenimore, she seemed somehow older. "Don't worry," she said. "I know who I am, and I can take care of myself."

Epilogue

Sitting in the rich mahogany study of the Law Offices of Abugado, Odvjetnik and Rechtsanwalt, Chenda relaxed. Lyle Abugado, on the other hand, was nearing panic. The old man was continually wringing his small, papery hands and tottering thoughtfully as he paced behind his desk, racking his brains for a solution.

He looked at Chenda sheepishly through his gold rimmed reading glasses. "Things get messy when people die," he said. "We at A,O & R have had many cases where members of the *family* have contested a will, but" he waved a hand at Chenda, "never the *deceased*, however. The cash money has already been dispersed, and the property, it's already under contract to be sold. This is a mess that will take some time to work out."

"I'm not worried about the money," she said. "Really, I want the nuns of St Elgin to have it. And the land, I don't have any need for that, either."

"What would you like me to do?" Lyle asked, rubbing the white fuzz on the top of his head.

"I would like you to act as my representative here in the Republic. I am going to be gone for some time, and I would like you to manage a few... transactions for me."

She stood up and laid a small bag on the table. When she tipped it over, the glittering gemstones Chenda had clipped off her Tugrulian gown spilled out onto the table. "Please arrange for these to be sold. Open an account with that money for a Mr. and Mrs. Fenimore Dulal at my bank. Please make one Dr. Candice Mortimer a signatory on the account, as well as yourself."

She handed several numbered letters to Lyle. "Keep these

for me. I will contact you from time to time with instructions."

"Lastly," she said, "I just need you to keep my life a secret. I am happy to stay legally dead."

"You can count on me," he said. "I'll do all I can to help you. You Frosts have been faithful clients now for, well, more than a dozen years. I still feel bad about executing your last will and testament when you were actually still alive. That may be the worst transgression of my lengthy career."

Chuckling, Chenda turned away from the desk and Lyle walked her to the door. "Do you usually check the corpses of your clients personally? Or is the professional standard still a signed death certificate?"

"I usually believe the coroner," he confessed. "In your case, I'll be more thorough from now on." He smiled as he shook her hand.

In the reception area, Fenimore was waiting for Chenda. He held a large paper bundle under one arm. Chenda eyed the package questioningly.

"Oh, a wedding present," he said. "Darling, we need to get going, or we will miss our own wedding. The *Brofman* has a schedule to keep, you know."

"What are we waiting for?" Chenda said, pulling Fenimore out of the law office and onto the street. The couple raced through town, dodging trolleys and pedestrians. Out of breath, they rode the elegant elevators to the airship piers at the top of Terminal Station.

Chenda wasn't sure if she was more excited about marrying Fenimore, or becoming a part of the crew of the *Brofman*. In some respects, she felt like she was marrying the airship.

Captain Endicott met them at the railing. "Cutting it pretty fine, Dulal." He wagged a finger at his first officer. He kissed Chenda lightly on the cheek in greeting. "What was I thinking, allowing a woman on my crew?" he teased. "Well, welcome home."

"Thank you!" Chenda replied. "We're just going to take our things below, and we'll be right back."

Chenda flitted down the stairs to the crew quarters and

found Fenimore unwrapping the paper package. He pulled out a new creamy white flight coat, and a matching pair of aeronaut boots. "From Lillianthal's," he said.

"What a lovely wedding gift!" she crooned as she pulled on the soft lambswool flight coat. Fenimore helped her with the buckles and straps. "This is like the day we first met," he whispered, his hands lingering on her body. "Well, with less bruising and more kissing, but you know what I mean."

She put on the new boots, and stepped back so he could take a better look. "The most beautiful bride in the history of forever," he said. "But wait! There's more!" With a great flourish, he pulled out a stubby pencil. "Ta-da!"

"Oh," Chenda said, not knowing what to make of it.

Fenimore smiled and pulled Chenda over to the row of cupboards, stopping in front of the only door without a name.

"What do you think?" he asked, handing her the pencil. "Should we write 'Mrs. Dulal', or 'Pramuc'?"

She snorted as she grabbed the pencil and quickly wrote CHENDA on the door in small, solid letters.

"No matter where I go, or who I marry, or what gifts the gods give me, I am always going to be Chenda." She kissed Fenimore and said, "Let's not keep the captain waiting."

They ran up the stairs and into the bright sunshine where Captain Endicott waited in the bow of the airship. "Finally," he said with a barking laugh. He whistled loudly and the members of the crew of the *Brofman*, ragged misfits all, gathered around Chenda and Fenimore.

The happy couple laced their fingers together as they turned their attention to the ceremony. "Dearly Beloved," the captain began as the airship gently floated away from Terminal Station toward the east.

THE END (for now)

Acknowledgments

I would be a complete fool if I didn't thank some folks for helping me. I find it to be true in life that nothing can be done alone.

First, I am eternally grateful to Patricia Early for inventing Henrietta Hoppingood, and then giving me this orphan character to play with. I didn't make her the star of my book, but like Patricia, she is the very best friend a middle aged armchair academic could have. Love you, BFF.

My husband is a trooper to put up with the kids while I locked myself in the basement to write. All. Night. Long. For weeks. Never has there been a better man than you, baby. Thanks for giving me Elly and Sara.

My friends who were the inspiration for my characters, thanks for being such great dorks. When I thought of you all as characters, the book just wrote itself. Perhaps I'm just that much of a controlling egomaniac. Laura and Ryan Riviere, Jason McNees, Amy Cauble, Bambi Maxwell, Tony Bush, Charles Salley, John Jones, Patricia Early, Orlando Calvalcanti, Christine Seelye-King and Sir Martin Brofman for inspiring me.

Every character has a theme song, at least in my head, so I want to thank Justin Taylor, Colin Hay, Kirsty MacColl, Eddie Vedder, Abney Park and Coldplay for letting me borrow their poetry to write my own.

A special note of thanks goes out to my friend P.R. who literally came back from the dead to cheer me on through the re-writes. I love you and missed you every day you were gone. I am glad I could share this book with you.

Bambi Maxwell – you are a saint. Thanks for your help with my book and with my life. Next breakfast is on me..

Visit me at CoalCitySteam.com for podcasts
and so much more.
Thanks for reading my book.

Made in the USA
Lexington, KY
17 March 2011